FROM SCRATCH

A Memoir *of* Love, Sicily, *and* Finding Home

TEMBI LOCKE

SIMON & SCHUSTER

New York London Toronto Sydney New Delhi

Simon & Schuster
1230 Avenue of the Americas
New York, NY 10020

First Simon & Schuster hardcover edition April 2019

SIMON & SCHUSTER and colophon are registered trademarks of Simon & Schuster, Inc.

For information about special discounts for bulk purchases,
please contact Simon & Schuster Special Sales
at 1-866-506-1949 or business@simonandschuster.com.

The Simon & Schuster Speakers Bureau can bring authors to your live event.
For more information or to book an event, contact the
Simon & Schuster Speakers Bureau at 1-866-248-3049 or
visit our website at www.simonspeakers.com.

Interior design by Ruth Lee-Mui

Manufactured in the United States of America

1   3   5   7   9   10   8   6   4   2

ISBN 978-1-5011-8765-0
ISBN 978-1-5011-8767-4 (ebook)

For Saro, who lit the fire of love

For our daughter, Zoela, the eternal flame

Think not you can direct the course of love, for love, if it finds you worthy, directs your course.

—KAHLIL GIBRAN

Contents

PROLOGUE

In Sicily, every story begins with a marriage or a death. In my case, it's both. And so it was that I found myself driving a rusted Fiat through a winding country road on the outskirts of Aliminusa, a small Sicilian village, with my husband's ashes in a small wooden box tucked between my legs. I was about to break into an olive grove in the rural foothills of the Madonie Mountains on the island's northern coast; it was Saro's family's sloping land, dotted with old-growth apricot and pear trees.

Along this road, he had once plucked ripe berries from the mulberry tree; he had twisted the stems of plump grape clusters from the vine; he had unearthed soil with his hands to show me exactly how the bulb beneath wild fennel grows. I had watched him pull back layers of the bulb's outer skin. Then he made me close my eyes. He brought its heart close to my nose, bidding me inhale the earthy licorice scent, awakening me to the mysteries of this place. He was intent on showing me the strength and delicacy of this natural world—his birthplace. Last summer, we stood surveying the hills where he had played as a child.

"Do what you will, but bring some of my ashes to Sicily," Saro said to me last summer, as we stood on this very spot. His cancer had recently returned, but his death still felt like an abstract thing. I thought we had a few more summers ahead, maybe five. Still he was preparing, and he was preparing me. This was the place he wanted part of himself to remain forever, so here I was, having flown nearly seven thousand miles from our house in Los Angeles in order to keep my promise that I would do so.

The sounds of late-summer crickets and cicadas and the scurrying of lizards taking refuge from the setting Sicilian sun surrounded me. The air was thick with the intoxicating scents of eucalyptus, burning wood, and ripening tomatoes. In the distance, the town church bells struck, calling people to afternoon Mass. For a moment, I imagined my seven-year-old daughter running barefoot on the cobblestoned street. She was the other reason I had cast myself on Sicilian shores, the only way I knew to keep her dad alive in her memory.

I pulled the car over at the top of a steep hill, put it into neutral, and double-checked the brake. Then I pried the box containing my husband's remains from between my thighs, sticky with sweat. The little wooden ring box where he had once kept his guitar picks now contained a portion of him I had saved for myself. It left a design of vertical lines on his favorite spot in my flesh. The time had come. Yet I couldn't bring myself to get out of the car.

Saro, a chef, had always said he married an American, an African American woman, who had the culinary soul of an Italian. In his mind, I was Italian the way all people should be Italian: at the table. Which to him meant appreciating fresh food, forging memories and traditions while passing the bread and imbibing local wine. It was a life I had stumbled into by chance when we literally collided underneath the awning of the best gelateria in all of Italy. Luck, fate. One look and I could see he had the kind of deep brown eyes that carried stories and that would entice me to tell mine. His profile could have been lifted from an ancient Roman coin, and his configuration of features—olive skin, firm jawline, and head of wavy, charcoal black hair—conjured a vision of me entangling myself with his body that came to me like a crack of lightning on a clear day. I said, "*Mi scusi*" in my best college Italian. He said, "Hello" back without a moment's hesitation. Right then, the fire met the pan.

I could see now that Saro had appeared in my life and almost instantly created form where there had only been space. He soothed the places I hadn't known needed soothing, seemed perfectly willing to embrace the parts of me that were wanton, unsettled, unfinished, and contradictory. Together we had engaged life as two forks eating off one plate. Ready to listen, to love, to look into the darkness and still see a thin filament of moon.

Finally I cracked the car door and cooler air flooded in, along with more memories. I thought about Saro and the last earthly pleasure we had shared together, a rocket-shaped ice pop. The specificity of the memory overwhelmed me. It took me right back to our last day. When the expanse of our life and everything in it had been reduced to the tiny intimate gestures death necessitates: feeding my dying husband an ice pop. How I had put it to his lips, having troubled the hospice nurse to take one out of the freezer at the top of every hour, just in case he awakened and was able to eat one. It was delicate, steady care I wanted to offer, my final acts as his caregiver and lover. I wanted the last sensations on his palate to be soothing, soft, and even pleasurable. He deserved that. During years of standing beside him in the kitchen, he had taught me that details are everything. The impact of the first taste happens only once. If ice pops were required, I decided, they would be the most inspired ice pops: freshly squeezed lemonade with a touch of agave.

In those final days, there were both compression and elongation of time. And although I did my best to prepare our daughter, Zoela, who had just turned seven, for a life without her dad, to keep her close, to include her in the event that would change her life forever, I worried that I had not done enough.

On the final day, I closed the pocket doors to our study and sat beside him on the hospital bed. I rubbed the melting treat against the flesh of his lips. A lifetime of kisses had been mine for the taking from those lips. Then I kissed his forehead, and when I pulled back I could see that a bit of the juice had met his tongue. He never took his eyes off me. I licked from the iced juice, too. He smiled. We had exchanged a moment of pleasure, just as we had in the beginning when he'd whispered in my ear after we made love, "I have an endless thirst of love, the love of your body and soul." And then he was gone.

His death put pan to flame once again. All the strength I had gathered as a woman, mother, and lover wilted, instantly and completely. It was like being flung onto jagged rocks at low tide, belly up at high noon on the longest, hottest day of the longest year of your life. There seemed no bottom to my grief, no way out, just through. Through darkness, isolation, and the deprivation of his touch. But it was my final promise to him that had brought me, months later, to this orchard in the heart of the Mediterranean, desperate for a sliver of light.

The last church bell rang, and I held the ring box of ashes in my hand. *Amore, l'ho fatto*—I did it. I have brought us this far. I got out of the car.

The setting sun reminded me of our first road trip together through Sicily, when we had driven the remote interior. There had been nothing to see but mountains, wheat fields, cows, men on donkeys, and untold olive groves. We couldn't get radio reception, so we ended up talking for hours along the winding roads, with interludes of silence and the endless downshifting and upshifting of the tiny Fiat. I remember that the afternoon light was another passenger in the car, witnessing two lives in motion. Now the sun was again my witness, as I finally stood free of the car and fully erect. The earth felt slightly loose beneath my feet.

Before me stood a large iron gate and colonnade of country stones, compacted earth and clay, stacked on top of one another to flank the gate. It created an impressive but simple rustic entrance. Along either side of the main entrance ran a barbed-wire fence atop a stone retaining wall. It separated the family land from the road. I looked at the fence and walked a tiny bit of the perimeter in the hopes of finding an easy opening. There was none.

Suddenly exhausted, I sat down on a haphazard pile of rocks that formed an impromptu retaining wall and stared at the town below. I could see the church cupola and beyond that fields that dropped precipitously into a valley that led to the sea. Then I heard a tractor approaching in the distance.

I didn't want to be seen in that moment, I didn't want to explain to a passing farmer moving along the road, returning home with the day's harvest, why I was standing outside the all but abandoned orchard. Worse yet, I didn't want word of it to get back to the small town that the black American wife had been spotted in a place no one else ever went. So I stood up and quickened my pace. I desperately searched for an area of loose stones, the result of shifting earth and rains, so I could force my way under and push my way in. I'd try to find the exact spot where we'd picked pears off the tree and Saro had held our daughter up to get the fruit closest to the sun the previous summer.

In Sicily, love, truth, and grief are neither simple nor straight-forward. Each runs as deep as the roots of the olive trees that have dotted the island for centuries. Secrets often run deeper. What I was about to do not only was secret, but technically it was probably illegal. In rural Sicily, cremation is rare to nonexistent. We had already had the official interment in the town cemetery weeks earlier. Putting ashes, even a portion of them, anywhere but in a cemetery probably violated religious and civic law. But my life was well outside convention as I scrambled along the earth looking for a way in.

Had I thought a bit in advance, had I planned this better, had I not had to lie about my whereabouts to everyone close to me back in town, I could simply have procured a key for the gate. I felt particularly unsettled about my mother-in-law not knowing. She was, after all, a woman with whom I had not always been on the best of terms. Saro's parents had declined an invitation to our wedding, less than thrilled that their beloved son was marrying an American, a black woman. Yet here now, my daughter and I were guests in her home, together, a bereaved family. Maybe I could have avoided the dirt and scrapes I was surely about to endure. I could have walked into this place in the open truth and then sat peacefully under the setting sun, falcons flying high above, the bray of a mule in the distance. But my grief and love didn't work that way—and I had made a promise to the love of my life. So I got onto my knees, let the dirt coat my skin, and rolled under a barbed-wire fence. I was determined to follow my chef's last instructions from scratch, in the hope that they might somehow lead me to take my first steps in reimagining my life without him.

Part One

BEFORE

Tutto sta nel cuminciare.

Everything depends on the beginning.

—*Sicilian proverb*

FIRST TASTES

I exited the plane in Rome, jet-lagged with a gaggle of fellow college coeds headed for customs and immigration, my passport in hand. I was twenty years old, and it was my very first time abroad. My exchange program from Wesleyan University to Syracuse University in Florence had begun.

In the terminal, I got my first sounds and smell of an Italian bar. It was teeming with morning patrons downing espresso and eating *cornetti*. I went up to the pastry case, put my hand on the warm glass, and then pointed like a preverbal child when the barista asked what I wanted. I held up three fingers. Three different *cornetti* in a bag for the road. One plain, one with cream filling, and one filled with marmalade. I didn't know yet that a version of this bar existed on every street corner in Italy. That what I had in the bag was as common as ketchup in America or, more to the point, a doughnut. I was just happy in anticipation of the first bite.

Italy had never been in my grand plan. The only grand plan I had at the time was becoming a professional actor after college. I had wanted to be an actor since I remember being conscious. It was the big-picture plan of my life as I could see it, even if I had, as

9

yet, no specific road map as to how to achieve it. It would be a leap. Nor had I planned to leave Wesleyan and its sleepy college town along the Connecticut River, except that I had stumbled into an Art History 101 class at the end of a difficult freshman year. The class was taught by Dr. John Paoletti, a world-renowned Italian Renaissance scholar. On that first day of class, when the lights dimmed in the auditorium and the first slide came up, a Greek frieze from Corinth circa 300 BC, I found myself spellbound. Two semesters of college finally came into focus. Within three weeks, I became an art history major. The next semester I was studying Italian, a requirement to complete my major. By the end of my sophomore year, I had taken up a tepid but steady affair with my Italian TA, Connor.

Connor was a senior and New England blueblood who had family in Italy. After one late-night romp in his bedroom on the top floor of his frat house, I helped him clean up beer cups while he helped me decide to take a semester abroad in Italy.

He assured me it was the only way I could achieve fluency, and I could also take a much-needed break from the confines of small-town Connecticut and still graduate on time. He suggested Florence. He had a sister there, Sloane, who had cast off the idea of an undergraduate degree from Vassar College in favor of life in Italy as an expat. She was a few years older than I was and had a long-term Italian beau, Giovanni, with whom she had gone into business, opening a bar called No Entry. Connor assured me that she would take me under her wing. His instructions were simple: "Find the nearest pay phone when you arrive in Florence and call Sloane—she'll introduce you around." Her number was tucked inside my passport when I boarded the Alitalia flight from New York.

• • •

The reward of jet lag is a new set of coordinates, a new language, and local delicacies. Italy did not disappoint. Eating my pastries as I looked out the window, on the bus ride from the Rome airport to Florence, I watched the passing cypress trees, hills, and farmhouses. It was like seeing a place for the first time that you felt you had known your whole life. When we finally made it to Florence under the midday summer sun, we stumbled out of the bus near the church of San Lorenzo. By then I realized I couldn't wait to get away from the bulk of the girls on the exchange program. One transatlantic flight and then a two-hour bus ride was enough.

Unlike them, I wasn't in Italy to shop and hang out with my sorority sisters. I didn't have my parents' credit card in my wallet, and I wasn't looking for a tryst with an Italian boy and trips to Paris once a month. I had a semester's worth of modest spending money, and I actually wanted to study art history. There was more I wanted, too, from my three-month stay. It was a yearning I couldn't put into words yet.

After I gathered my duffel bag from the luggage compartment of the bus, our large group was divided and shuttled off to a series of *pensioni* near the train station for the first night or two until we would all be assigned and delivered to our Italian host families. The first thing I did after walking up three flights of a narrow stone staircase to my three-person room was put my duffel down and get into line to use the telephone in the main entrance. I did what every other girl did: I called home. Or two homes, actually—first my mom's and then my dad's—and assured both of them I had arrived safely. Then I called Sloane.

"Ciao, Tembi!" Her voice rang out as if we had just seen each other a couple of nights before over an *aperitivo*. "Connor told me about you. I knew you'd call. Where are you?"

"I'm near the station at a hotel." I didn't say *pensione* because I wasn't sure I'd pronounce the Italian correctly.

"I'm coming to get you," she said in a smoky New England lilt overlaid with an Italian cadence. I knew in an instant that she was more European than I'd ever be. "Let's have dinner. I have to be in the city center tonight anyway for work. Pick you up at eight."

It was sometime after lunch when I hung up the phone, as best as my jet lag could tell. Time enough to nap and then shower and be ready for my first real Italian dinner. When all the other girls began joining up and making plans to explore the area around the hotel, perhaps window-shop and get something to eat, I declined their offers to join them.

"I have a friend who is picking me up later," I explained. It was the kind of understated brag that didn't win me any friends.

Sloane whizzed up to the *pensione* at 8:45 p.m. in an old bluish white Fiat Cinquecento. It was a car I had seen only in *I Vitelloni*, a movie I had watched in my Italian Neorealism film class. She pulled it up onto the sidewalk, hopped out of the driver's seat, and came around to throw her arms around me. Apparently, we were long-lost friends who had been dying to get reacquainted. She had curly auburn locks that fell at her tan cleavage, which she managed to somehow have even though she was braless. Her smile was as bold and bright as her pastel Betsey Johnson floral minidress. But it was her infinitely long legs that I couldn't take my eyes off of. Connor had mentioned that she had been a theater major, and that made perfect sense as she carried herself as though she were stepping onto or off of a stage. Standing next to her I felt like a troll in Gap jeans, V-neck T-shirt, and lace boots, a look that had seemed so cool while walking across the lawn back at Wesleyan.

"Hop in!" she said when she finished hugging me. She opened

the door on the passenger side and crawled over the gearshift to take her place behind the wheel. In the process, she threw her fringed leather purse into the back seat, then, on second thought, reached back, put it onto her lap, and pulled out a joint.

"Want some?"

"No, thanks." It looked as though she had already had a few drags. There were lipstick stains on it.

"Later then, there's time." She turned the motor. "We're going to meet my friends near San Casciano first. Dinner at their house. He's a painter, she does the window dressings for Luisa. Then we'll all head to the bar." She took a long drag, then extinguished the joint on the floorboard of the car.

"Put this in back," she said, handing me her bag. "And yours, too," she added, lifting my maroon canvas backpack from my lap.

I did as I was told and we set off, summer city wind blowing through the open windows of the car. She drove us through a labyrinth of timeless passageways and narrow cobblestoned streets lit by amber streetlights. I stuck my hand out the window, and Florence moved through my fingers.

When we finally arrived at Massimo's house, a Tuscan villa somewhere near Niccolò Machiavelli's childhood home, I was fighting carsickness and nerves.

"Does anyone here speak English?"

"A bit, but I'll translate. Come on."

With that she turned the knob of the unlocked front door and immediately charged through the house like a tornado that had just touched the ground, following the sound of jazz and chatter that seemed to originate from some far corner of the first floor.

I trailed behind, timid and awestruck by the sights around me. I was convinced that I was walking through what was surely a

Merchant Ivory film set. Stone floors, exquisite tapestries, mahogany bookcases. Sloane looked back to grab my hand just before we entered the outdoor terrace, where I could see at least ten to twelve Italians gathered in a smattering of duos and trios. Every conversation seemed intimate and theatrical, all happening behind a scrim of cigarette smoke.

Sloane squeezed my hand and leaned in for a whisper. "I'll make Massimo show you his art collection before we leave."

I anxiously tugged at the back of my T-shirt, pulling it over the backside of my jeans. Self-conscious, I was unable to conjure up a response.

"He has a Picasso in his bedroom." With that she thrust me onto the center of the terrace.

"*Eccola, Tembi! Un'amica americana.*" Then she gave me a dramatic kiss on the cheek, pivoted, and left me. Were people doing tiny lines of coke off a farmhouse coffee table?

I turned to join the impossibly cosmopolitan and bohemian group clustered in conversation. I knew enough to decline the coke. I never did ask to see the Picasso. Frankly, I didn't know how, and I wasn't ready to ask a man I had just met to take me to his bedroom. Still, even through my jet-lagged haze, a self I had never known was beginning to come into focus. The energetic pulse of the evening took over me, and I vowed then and there to welcome the unexpected. This new me would embrace every part of the adventure. I was open, for better or for worse, to whatever might come. Like an egg with it yolk exposed, I was vulnerable but jolly. Sloane would point the way, and I would follow—within reason. I already liked the feel of this new country on my skin, its language taking root in my mouth. And over the course of the night, as I fumbled through my kindergarten Italian, I stopped blushing, growing more and more confident with each conversation. In one day, Italy was already making me easy with myself. My expectations were few. After all, I told myself, I would be here for only a few months. When I looked around the terrace, I couldn't imagine that any of the people would ever be lifelong friends. Italy was just a quick adventure, a time apart from time. A perfect interlude.

By morning I was back in my three-person room at the *pensione*, staring at the ceiling and seriously considering pinching myself. The smell of coffee from the breakfast room below rose up through the stone floors. The clatter of cups hitting saucers, spoons clinking against porcelain, plates being stacked, the aroma of coffee and fresh pastries, seduced me. Full of delight, I couldn't wait to take on another day.

Two months later, Sloane found me scrubbing the toilet in her bar, No Entry. It was in the heart of Florence's historic center, near Piazza Santa Croce and a stone's throw from the Arno. As was typical, she had dropped by in the afternoon and found me, scrub brush in hand, Billie Holiday mix tape on the boom box. My friend had by then become my boss, so I was cleaning the place. Despite my early promises of discipline, in six weeks I had blown through a semester's worth of spending cash. It had disappeared in the form of belts, purses, dinners, and weekend trips to Rome and Stromboli. I was broke but refused to ask my parents for more. As a result, I cleaned toilets at No Entry off the books, before or after my classes.

"We need vodka!" Sloane pronounced, dumping out a bowl of day-old maraschino cherries. Her bar was almost out. In a flash, she decided we should drop everything and head to another bar, MI6, immediately. She was friends with the owner, and they borrowed stock from each other when liquor was running low. It was just a few blocks away and presumably fully stocked with vodka, plus her sure-thing joint connection would be there. The promise of an afternoon hit made her already fast pace that much more brisk. I trailed behind, struggling to keep up with her long-legged stride and drug-induced urgency. I had never liked drugs, but in Florence I was trying to be open to the light stuff. *A puff here and there can't hurt, Tembi. Come on, don't be such a dork.* I imagined Sloane had tried everything, which was exactly what I was thinking about when we rounded the corner of Via dell'Acqua and I collided with a man. "*Mi scusi,*" I mumbled.

As fate would have it, Sloane knew him. Of course. She knew everyone. She introduced him: Saro.

"*Ciao, mi chiamo Tembi. Sì, Tem-BEE,*" I said in my best classroom Italian. I sounded stilted, as if I weren't sure that the words were coming out right. My saving grace was an accent that wasn't totally embarrassing and the fact that I could say my own name with relative ease.

"*Sono Saro. Tu sei americana?*" he asked, smiling. He wore a black leather bomber jacket and white pants. *In October.* His jacket was open, and underneath I could see a white T-shirt with the word DESTINY written in big orange bubble letters across the center of his chest. Its design was a mélange of graffiti complete with random illustrations including a rocket, a slice of pizza, an amoeba, a guitar, a constellation, and the number 8 floating randomly and all topsy-turvy in hues of blue and yellow. It struck me as a cartoon of someone's unconscious. I hoped not his. *And why do Italians wear shirts with random English words emblazoned across them?* I turned away, but not before I saw his shoes. They were ankle-high black boots. Instantly I thought of elves.

I looked at him and smiled. "*Sì, sto studiando la storia dell'arte.*" Bam! I had run out of all of my Italian. So I let Sloane carry on the conversation without me. We were standing in front of Vivoli, which, I had been told, made the best gelato in all of Tuscany. I turned away from Sloane and Saro to get a better look at the crowd spilling in and out. When I turned back, I really took in Saro, all of him. A blind person could see he was handsome. But the way he had kept his eyes on me made me suddenly aware that I wished I had worn a better bra. His gaze was sultry and focused. It made me conscious of my own breath. It made me take note of his brow line and the length of his eyelashes. I had to focus to listen to them talk. I began to gather from the exchange he and Sloane were having that he was leaving work at Acqua al 2, a well-known restaurant popular with locals and tourists less than a block away. He was a chef. He was a sexy black-haired, brown-eyed guy with a beautiful olive complexion in a country full of handsome, black-haired, brown-eyed, olive-skinned men. But this one put my body into a tumult.

For the next few weeks, he made it a point to be at No Entry each evening after he finished work, and we would chat for twenty minutes. Each time he reintroduced himself, which I found endearing. I learned that he had been born in Sicily to farmers and had lived briefly in Buffalo, New York, when his family had relocated there during his teen years. The United States hadn't agreed with them. They had returned to Sicily and he left home within a year to study translation at the University of Florence and in so doing had broken a bloodline of farmers going back centuries. After two years of studies, he had dropped out and found his way as an apprentice chef. We talked enough for me to know he was attentive, kind, engaged. Often, when we finished our conversations, he said, "Let me take you for dinner."

Each time I gave him a noncommittal "Sure, maybe, sometime, of course."

Saro, in all his ease, openness, and attractiveness, was not the kind of guy I went for—stateside or in Italy. He seemed way too available, way too nice. My kind of attractive was aloof, noncommittal, and definitely hard to catch. After having had multiple on-campus affairs that had gone nowhere fast, I wasn't looking for anything serious. I needed to focus on school, not men. But that was easier said than done.

In fact, my first hookup in Italy had been with a guy on the island of Stromboli off the coast of Sicily. How could I have been so stupid as to have a one-night stand on a tiny island during the off-season, where the only departing ferry left once every five days? Not my finest hour. I had spent four days hiding from the locals and my new *amico*, Rocco, who wanted to show me the island's *vulcano* just one more time. They had names for girls like me back home in Texas. And stupid wasn't one of them. The next tryst had been with a person I had nicknamed "Il Diavolo." He was a rapturous combination of every stereotype of Italian men—sexy, attentive, allergic to monogamy. He worked construction, restoring fifteenth-century palazzi in Florence's historic center. He was arrogant, aloof, a master of mixed messages, and he didn't speak a word of English. But again, I wasn't in it for the conversation. The whole thing had lasted a few weeks, tops. But when he had finished with me I looked like I had seen seven miles of bad road, barefoot in a windstorm. The whole thing was doomed and I knew it, but every time I saw him, somehow I found my way back to his place. He was kryptonite sprinkled on a pizza, my personal weakness.

I had no intention of going out with this chef in the bomber jacket. Despite the fact that every time I saw him, something sparked inside me. I tried to keep him in the friend column—no sex—until one night I couldn't.

David Bowie was singing "Rebel Rebel" as I had made my way from the bar through the crowd of Florentine bohemians, European PhD students, and recent North African immigrants that had descended on No Entry that night. Secondhand hash and reefer smoke clogged the air, making me feel as though I were starring in a remake of *Scared Straight*. My eyes burned, and my clothes reeked. When I made it back to my seat, I nursed my third whiskey sour alone and sang, "Rebel rebel, you've torn your dress. Rebel rebel, your face is a mess" to no one in particular. Then I felt a tap on my shoulder.

"Come outside, I have something for you." I turned from my cocktail to see Saro standing there. The neon light blaring the bar's name gave his tufts of jet black hair a crimson halo. *Wow, maybe I should have stopped at two drinks.*

"What time is it?" I asked.

"One a.m.," he said. His skin glistened. I wanted to reach out and touch it. Instead I looked down. He still had on checkered chef's pants and again those curious boots.

"I actually need to get going. I have a morning class at the Uffizi." I downed the last of my drink and stood up. This time my legs wobbled. It occurred to me that I must seem like the textbook cliché of the American girl in Florence—compulsively shopping, lit up on Chianti, and floating from one Italian beau to the next, all under the guise of studying the Renaissance. Somewhere inside me I admitted that I was missing the point. I had not come to Florence to be a frequent barfly by night and a hungover student by day. I was lucky to be experiencing a veritable European dream of culture, art, and ideas, but I was doing it through a haze of cheap Tennessee whiskey. I felt a headache coming on. Then I took a step toward the exit, tipped forward, and had to brace myself against Saro's shoulders. That's when I noticed that his cheeks were flushed and he was slightly out of breath.

"Here, you have a seat. I'm leaving. Take mine." I am nothing if not polite when buzzed.

"I'm fine," he said, beginning to unzip his jacket. His neck was flushed. It was the first time I had seen a cluster of hair at his neckline. I wondered what his chest looked like. "I just ran here in the hope that you would not have left." Did he just say "in the hope"? English never sounded so lyrical. Without a second thought, I reached in for two kisses on his cheeks, my Italian hello and goodbye. But I teetered, and in the process, I propped myself against his shoulder just a moment too long. He smelled of charcoal, olive oil, and garlic. I inhaled deeply. The combination was salty and beguiling. It took me a moment to recover.

"Just come outside, one moment. I want to make you a surprise." *English should always sound like this.* I let him take my hand.

He led the way, and the gust of wintry air that greeted me on the other side of the door sobered me instantly. I batted my eyes to buffer against the wind. Suddenly everything seemed harsh and in sharp focus. Shadows were elongated by the amber streetlight above. And there, just outside the door, leaning against the massive stone wall, was a bicycle. It was candy apple red with a basket and bell.

"For you. You said you needed a bike to get around in the city. Better than the bus, no?" With that he handed me the key to the oversized padlock. "It is all I could find in such a short time."

My mouth fell slightly agape. "No, I can't take this." Yet I wanted it so badly that I had to stop from screaming right there on the sidewalk and waking the residents above. No man had ever heard a need of mine in passing and manifested it days later. But then another thought crept in: *Nothing comes for free.* "Let me pay you for this." I reached for my purse, a double-stitched tote purchased for a small fortune my first week in Florence. I loved carrying it around town even if it was big enough to contain only a hairbrush, a copy of my passport, one lipstick, and a crinkled Baci Perugina chocolate wrapper with the Oscar Wilde quote "To love oneself is the beginning of a love affair that will last a lifetime."

"I would take offense to be paid. The bicycle is a gift. Here, take it home."

If you don't pay him now, you'll be paying him later. Shit. "Please let me pay you something. It would be the American thing to do. How about we go Dutch?" The reference was lost on him. "How about I give you thirty thousand lire?" Which was all I had in my wallet. Even drunk, I knew that was only about $18, with the best exchange rate. The offer was paltry and insulting, but I didn't care. For $18, I figured I could have my peace of mind *and* a brand-new bike. Then, as if overcome with some sudden attack of high-minded principles, the kind my grandmother in East Texas had taught me to have, I added for emphasis, "I won't have it any other way."

"*Va bene.*" He said it in the casual way Italians concede and dismiss an argument in the same breath. "But at least let me accompany you home. It is late. I have my Vespa, I can ride alongside you to be sure you are safe."

I felt gushy inside, flush with liquor and excitement. My pant leg caught the pedal as I tried to mount the bike. I was in no position to refuse. The rush of adrenaline and liquor in equal measure told me so.

"You are living with a family near the stadium, no?" This guy had really been paying attention during our chats.

We rode through the streets of Florence that night in silent unison. We passed Michelangelo's *David* and Donatello's *Judith Slaying Holofernes*, and the play of shadows danced across his face. A nocturnal bike ride through the center of Florence on a foggy morning with an Italian chef at my side. I had not expected as much as this from my semester abroad. But maybe somewhere deep down inside I had hoped for it. I wanted to pinch myself. But I didn't need to. This was too good to be real. Saro was too good to be true. This puff of Italian romance would implode in a moment. I knew it would. I didn't trust what came easy. I certainly didn't trust love or me at love.

As we turned onto Viale Alessandro Volta, the boulevard that would take me to my host family's home, I got scared. I was falling for him.

"I can take it on my own from here. Thanks for the bike. See you around." With that I rode off as fast as my flushed legs would pedal, without so much as waving good-bye. I dared not look behind me to take one last look at Saro. I could fuck up a good thing even in the most romantic city on Earth.

For the next month I left No Entry long before his restaurant closed and thereby avoided reliving the awkwardness I had created between us the night of the bike. I also dropped the curtain on the third and final act of my operatic drama with the stonemason Il Diavolo. He had dumped me for another American girl, with long black hair and her father's credit card. I wrote term papers on the Medicis' artistic rift with Pope Leo X and moved into my own apartment with two other women—one American, one Canadian, and one very impish Italian DJ who slept with the Canadian. All the while, I felt exhilarated, lost, charmed, but somewhat vexed by my new life in Florence.

One week into the new year, on a bright winter day, I bumped into Saro on the street again. When I saw his face, a light went on inside me. I had finally surrendered to the fact that I couldn't come at love from a defensive position—what I wouldn't do, what rules I would have to follow. None of that had worked for me. I suspected I had to be open, as spontaneous and brave and intuitive as the woman who had chosen to come to Italy in the first place. Something inside me said, *You're in the most romantic place on Earth, if not now, when? Go for love.* Without a moment's hesitation, I threw my arms around him, American style, and asked, "Do you want to go out?" His face was warm and open. I noticed the slight curl of his lips for the first time. He had been hiding in plain sight.

"*Sì*, of course, I am off tomorrow." It was effortless with him. "My friend is editing a film at a studio near the duomo. You like film and acting, no? Do you want to stop by the editing room and then have lunch?"

Had I also mentioned that I dreamed of one day becoming an actress?

"Yes, I do. Acting is also a part of my studies back in the States."

"I will meet you at Piazza del Duomo tomorrow morning. Eleven o'clock?" With that he released the brake on his Vespa, and I stood in perfect stillness as I watched his figure recede into the crowd as he headed across the Ponte Vecchio.

The next day, snow fell in Florence for the first time in more than a decade. I parked my spit-polished crimson bicycle at the edge of Piazza del Duomo, retrieved my backpack from its wicker basket, and made my way to the cathedral steps. That morning Florence was in a state of wonderment and scurry. Children, enchanted with the large sloppy flakes, stuck out their tongues to the sky as their parents drifted into and out of coffee bars, murmuring in disbelief at the snow. Florentines donned helmets to shelter them from the gentle flurries as their mopeds left tracks on cobblestoned streets. Even the buses took extra time to load and unload passengers, and the street vendors had all taken cover.

On the steps of the duomo, I positioned myself in front of Ghiberti's voluminous bronze cathedral doors and waited for Saro. Behind me the cast relief figures from the Old Testament appeared all the more stoic and timeless as the snow grazed their frozen forms. Then I watched as the snow fell further and melted away as it landed on my scuffed boots, the chill of the marble steps beneath me penetrating the soles of my feet. I felt barefoot. The clock struck 11:00 a.m. My date was late.

By 11:15 a.m., my hat and coat were soaking wet. Of course I had taken our meeting time as an exact thing. Had Italy taught me nothing? Punctuality was only relatively important, time was always approximate. I reached into my bag to see if I had anything to eat. I looked across the piazza to the people seated inside sipping cappuccino and pounding back espresso. I began to wonder if this date would end like the less than perfect romances I had had since arriving in Italy months earlier. Just the thought made me want to get onto my bike and head back to my tiny new apartment in Piazza del Carmine.

Twenty minutes was more than even I could bear in the cold—picture postcard or not. I didn't have classes that day, but I did have a shred of common sense. The last thing I needed was to catch pneumonia while waiting for someone who clearly wasn't coming. So I pulled my coat tighter and tried desperately to remember where I had misplaced the gloves my grandmother in East Texas had sent. I brought my fingertips to my mouth and gave a hearty blow to warm them up. Then I took the duomo steps, two at a time, back toward my bicycle. *What kind of guy gives you a bike and then stands you up for a first date?*

Blinking snow from my eyes, wondering what on earth could have happened, I pedaled my way back across the Arno to my apartment.

An hour later, I looked out the window of the penthouse apartment in Piazza del Carmine. It was too late for breakfast, the only type of food we kept in the house, and I was too worried to go out for lunch. I wanted to wait for Saro's call. I knew it would come. I would have bet my life on it. I felt as though I knew him. Well, I didn't really *know* him, but I knew his heart. Surely something serious must have happened for him to have stood me up.

Then I heard a ringing. I slid across the marble floor at breakneck speed to be the first to grab the communal phone that hung on a pillar in the center of the living room.

"*Mi dispiace.* Sorry. I am sorry." Saro's voice was sped up, urgent.

"What happened?"

Silence.

"I overslept." Then, in rapid fire, "Robert Plant came to the restaurant last night. I made dinner for him and the band after his show. They didn't leave until two in the morning. I got home at three. I am sorry. Would you care to meet me again in the center? We can still have lunch, no?"

"I have a class in an hour and a half. I don't think so," I lied. I wasn't exactly sure why, except that the idea of going back out into the cold didn't appeal. Maybe I wanted him to come to me.

"I will take you to your class, and then I will wait for you."

"That's not necessary." I now regretted my earlier lie. Hadn't I played hard to get enough with this guy?

"Then come to the restaurant tonight. I will make you dinner." Before I could respond, his voice broke with sincerity. "Please, come. Invite a friend, if you please. It would be my pleasure." Then he paused. "I think we could be something great."

No one had ever said anything like that to me. Those two words, "something great," jolted through me like a lightning bolt. He conjured a vision of an *us* and greatness so effortlessly that it suddenly seemed as right as butter on bread. I was taken aback by his boldness, his certainty. He was inviting me into a vision for my own future that until that moment, I didn't even know I wanted. But as the words registered, I understood that there was no going back. Of course, yes, I wanted something great, and maybe, with him, I could have it.

"*Va bene*," I said, quietly exhilarated that my destiny with greatness might just begin with a good meal.

Acqua al 2 was packed that night, people milling outside the front door, braving the cold and hoping for a table. I waited at the crowd's edge, looking for my two exchange student friends Caroline and Lindsey. I had followed Saro's suggestion and invited them, partly because I didn't want to dine alone and partly because I was curious to see what Caroline and Lindsey thought of Saro.

Lindsey, a lanky lacrosse jock from Mount Holyoke with a coif of red kinky curls that she called her "Irish 'fro," was the first to arrive. "*Que pasa, chica?*" Her Italian was choppy and spoken with a nagging stutter, so she had a habit of using her other default foreign language, Spanish, to get by. It sounded equally distorted and hopelessly Anglo, but she seemed comforted that at least she was speaking a foreign language. "Caroline will probably be late—she's walking from the other side of Boboli Gardens. You know she's afraid to take the bus at night."

Of course, how could I forget? Caroline was a devout Southern Methodist who prayed every time she crossed the threshold of Italian public transportation. She had nearly been speaking in tongues on the three-hour speed boat ride we had had to take to get from the mainland to Stromboli. Of course she would be late.

"Let's go!" I said, turning toward the glow that came from inside the restaurant.

Once in the narrow entrance, I made my way up to the hostess. Saro had told me to ask for her, Lucia. "*Mi scusi.*" She looked up, took one glance at me, and sprang from behind her station at the end of the dessert bar. The smile on her face resembled that of a cat, after eating the canary.

"*Sei la Tembi, no? Vieni.* Come." Then she cupped my face in her hands and kissed me twice on the cheeks. Apparently I needed no introduction. In a flash she grabbed me by one hand and led me into the heart of the dining room. Lindsey bounced along behind me.

Lucia went before me in skintight Levi's 501s, a tanned bottle blonde with Roman features, a smoky voice, and an infectious laugh. As owner and hostess, she orchestrated the front house of Acqua al 2 the way an opera singer commands center stage. With her firmly gripping my hand, we arrived in the heart of the dining room and she announced boldly, "*È lei!*—It's her!" Then she pivoted on a dime, grabbed my face again, and said, "Saro make a table for you. You understand my English, no? I go get wine from the cellar, *la cantina*." She pointed to a narrow set of cobblestoned stairs at the end of the dining room and promptly gave me another kiss. In a flash she was gone, leaving me in the center of the restaurant. It was like being back at the villa that first night in Florence. I had been put center stage with no idea as to what exactly to do next.

Standing there in the main room, I could see why foreigners flocked to Acqua al 2. Its sampling menu and undeniable Italian hospitality were just the beginning. Booths wrapped the circumference of the intimate candlelit dining room filled with communal butcher-block tables. It was the kind of place where upcoming Italian movie stars, indie musicians, leftist politicians, and veterans of the stage dined alongside tourists. Diners conversed over mouthwatering platters while bottles of wine—Montepulciano and Chianti Classico, lush Tignanello, and slender bottles of pale, fizzy Moscato—flew by at lightning speed. The scene was at once convivial, bibulous, and pure theater. Acqua al 2's trademark paper placemats on each table had been designed by a well-known cartoonist. On them was an illustration of a waiter serving a steaming plate of pasta to lovers seated on a baroque proscenium stage. Above the curtain, the caption read, *Love born in the theater will always continue.* The place was 1,200 square feet of Florentine charm packed into frescoed walls, vaulted ceilings, and fifteenth-century arches.

From my place at center stage, I could see Saro moving like a wizard behind a scrim of sizzling heat, orchestrating the clamorous clanging of pots; setting the pace and unfurling magic onto plates from Acqua al 2's narrow, searingly hot kitchen. At first glance, the kitchen looked like Aladdin's cave. There was Saro in a white T-shirt, floor-length apron, white clogs, and red bandanna with James Brown hollering out, "This is a man's world" from a boom box in the background. Saro caught my eye, smiled, and signaled that he would be out later to say hello.

"I think she has slept with him." Caroline had finally arrived, and Lindsey was getting her up to speed moments later while we settled into our corner table downstairs in the cantina.

"It's none of our business." But I knew Caroline thought Saro was every bit her business. She was a southern belle from SMU who wrote daily love letters to her high school sweetheart and donned gingham just for the hell of it. All indications were that she thought I was a man-hungry trollop who had yet to find Christ. I was sure she had been praying for my salvation from the moment we had landed on Stromboli and Rocco had laid me down on volcanic sand. But I also suspected she was the kind of girl who could spot the "boyfriend type" from a mile away. Given my track record in Florence, her opinion was worth putting up with evocations of Our Lord and Savior in even the most mundane conversations.

"No, I haven't," I insisted. They seemed dubious.

"Do we get a menu?" Lindsey asked as she saw a waiter bring an armful of platters to a nearby table.

Before I could answer, Lucia was tableside, opening a bottle of white wine. "*Cominciate col vino bianco.*" As quickly as she poured, she was gone again. When she reappeared, she was carrying a single platter of what looked to be green risotto. The aroma reached my senses before my eyes could process what I was looking at. It smelled earthy, creamy, and woodsy with a hint of mint.

"*Risotto con sugo verde* is first. Saro will to make you samples of the menu. *Tutto menu.* All of it." I loved the way Lucia doubled down on verbs to make a point. The platter hit the table with a gentle bounce. "This is the first. *Buon appetito.*" With that she disappeared like a hostessing Merlin into the stone walls. The spell was cast, and I hadn't even taken the first bite.

I brought my fork up to my mouth and dived into what can only be described as epicurean heaven on a plate. Nothing in my repetoire of rice had prepared me for this. Each grain was soft yet firm at its core, melting delicately like textured velvet in my mouth.

"Okay, this is way good," Lindsey spoke first through a mouthful. "How do you know this guy again?"

"He's my bicycle thief, remember?" It was the nickname I had given Saro as homage to my favorite film of Italian Neorealism. It was also a reference to Florence's black-market bike trade. I had come to learn that my shiny red bike with a basket and a bell—the gift that had turned the page in my friendship with Saro—was, in fact, probably stolen goods. Saro had bought it on the cheap the way everyone bought bikes in Florence. He had warned me to be sure to lock it. He also told me if it turned up missing he would search the city to find it. Then he would buy it back again.

"I think you should really consider spending time with this man, even if he did steal a bike," Caroline said, staring into the platter before scooping up the last remaining grains of risotto.

"He didn't steal a bike! He *bought* the bike."

"How do you know?" Lindsey asked with a wink. She was forever suggesting that Italian men had a predilection for danger. The idea of it thrilled her.

"Because he told me so." My irritation was thinly veiled because now I was focused on Caroline eating the last creamy cluster of risotto. When she finished, she licked her lips in a way that was self-satisfying and, dare I say, sexual. Her blue eyes closed slightly, and she uttered a full-bodied *Uummm*. She looked like a sinner at a tent revival who had just been saved by the laying on of hands. It was clear that Saro's risotto was her culinary come-to-Jesus moment. After eating it, she had the glow of a new convert. I half expected a *hallelujah* to follow.

"Is it wrong to ask for more?" she asked sheepishly.

"Maybe you could ask Lucia to make you your very own plate?" For me, last bites are cardinal. Sharing Saro's risotto with her was suddenly making me possessive. She was devouring that last morsel of my possibly soon-to-be chef boyfriend's exquisite creation without the slightest act of contrition.

Lucia returned again and again, with heaping plates of *strozzapreti* with braised red radicchio in a mascarpone sauce; fusilli in a fire-roasted bell pepper sauce; gnocchi with gorgonzola in a white martini reduction with shaved aged parmigiano. I began to see that Saro was speaking directly to me, each dish an edible love letter: succulent, bold. By the third and fourth courses, I accepted that this chef who wore elf boots was making love to me, and we hadn't even so much as kissed.

By the end of the dinner, I was in rapture, satiated, giddy, lightheaded with the possibility that Saro was boyfriend material. I briefly considered a cigarette, though I had never smoked in my life.

Caroline and Lindsey got up to leave sometime around 11:00 p.m. Lucia called them a cab because Caroline was in no position to walk all the way back home and Lindsey, well, Lindsey was ripped from three shots of dessert wine. As she left Acqua al 2, she made it a point to say good-bye to everyone in the restaurant, waving enthusiastically. "*Adiós, muchachas.* I love tiramisù," she added as she nearly tripped at the base of the stairs. "I'll be back, amigos." With that she and Caroline fled into the night, leaving me alone in the cantina.

Within moments, Lucia plopped herself next to me with another bottle of *vin santo* and that feline smile. I knew something was up. "*Sei americana, no?*" Florentines always suspected I might be Brazilian or Ethiopian. It sometimes seemed a little bit of a letdown when I said I was just a suburban black girl from Texas. Not this time.

"Texas! Cowboys! Dallas!" Lucia said. Quickly I realized she didn't mean the city, she meant the 1980s TV show, with JR. It was still in syndication in Italy. "I love JR and *Beautiful*." *Beautiful*, I had learned, was the soap opera *The Bold and the Beautiful*. I had never seen it, but apparently most Italians had and often asked who was dating whom on the show. So for a moment I thought I had been cornered for a primer on American pop culture. But then Lucia inched ever so close to me and asked, "You like Saro, no?" It was more a statement than a question.

"*Sì, mi piace Saro*," I said in my best formal Italian. She wasn't buying it.

She leaned in closer. I could see the liner on her lips and smell a pack of Marlboros. "*Sul serio, no?*" *Serio* means "serious." Even after a bottle of Chianti and sips of *vin santo* I knew that. She wanted answers. But before I could utter a word, she charged at me.

"*È bello, no?* Beautiful. Saro is beautiful." She cupped my face and made her final plea. "*È un amico del cuore. Trattalo bene. È unico.*— He's my close friend. Treat him well. He's one of a kind." Then she was gone, the sashaying back pockets of her Levi's the lasting image.

I stood up, tingling with a kind of excitement I hadn't ever felt, and began to make my way upstairs to the main dining room. The crowd had thinned some. It was now mostly Florentine locals dining in duos, but it was still lively. The grainy but wispy jazz vocals of Paolo Conte came through the speakers, the dessert case was nearly empty save a single portion of tiramisù. I blushed when I passed the kitchen to say good night.

Saro smiled. "Did you enjoy it? I wanted to make you something that pleased."

"Yes." He made me feel as though I could walk barefoot on hot coals.

"Tonight has been busy, I could not come down to say hello." He was unguarded, his ease alluring. "I'll come by your school tomorrow."

"Sì." Monosyllabic responses were all I could summon up. Then Saro reached out and gave me a kiss on the cheek. His skin was dewy, sheened with olive oil and perspiration. Our cheeks made a little suction sound when he pulled away, an audible marker that we had indeed touched. I was hoping we could leave it at that. One kiss was delightful. Two kisses just might do me in. He had already filled me with his food, his creativity. Now having to take him in the flesh—his eyes, nose, mouth, and gentle brow—made me rock back slightly on my heels. But no. He wasn't done with me yet. He reached for the second cheek and whispered in my ear, "I am happy to do this again and again. Just tell me when."

I tumbled out onto Via dell'Acqua just after midnight, hypnotized by his skin, his food, how his hand had met the small of my back when we had said good-bye. I took the long route home, riding alongside the Arno River, always my favorite place to ride at night when the city was asleep. I rode across the Ponte Vecchio and stopped to look into the still waters of the river below. The bridge was lit in amber, and the waters reflected the night hues that shone from streetlamps and a smattering of windows.

As I left the Ponte Vecchio toward home, I rode past the corner of Borgo San Frediano and Piazza del Carmine, and I looked up at the church across from my apartment. It boasts a fresco believed to be the first known work of the teenage Michelangelo. Firsts are no small things, firsts hold the beginning of something great. I suspected I had just fallen for a bicycle thief chef: and as clichéd as it might sound, it was love at first bite.

•   •   •

Love, as a lasting thing, was a concept that was elusive to me. My parents separated when I was seven, divorced by the time I was eight. My mother remarried when I was nine, my father when I was twelve. While I was in Florence, my mother was divorcing again after nearly twelve years with my stepfather. Throughout my childhood, I had lived in five different houses over the course of ten years. This parent's house versus that parent's house. Mom's second house, Dad's place as a new divorcé or the one he had as a newly remarried man with a child on the way. When my college friends talked about "going home," they often referred to a specific place with a bedroom in which they had lost their first tooth or first sneaked a boy inside. That version of home was foreign to me. I didn't have a fixed place to which I could attach memories. Sure, there had been houses, homes even, but they came with emotional caveats. I had had a kind of bifurcated childhood, trying to fit into whatever configuration of my parents' life was presently in formation. It was common to my generation of baby boomers' children. My parents, Sherra and Gene, were no different.

They had met as young university students thrust headlong into the cultural revolution of the late 1960s and '70s and the Pan-African Liberation Movement, which we had grown up calling "The Movement." My parents were desperate to reshape the United States into a more just and equal place. They married at the ages of twenty and twenty-two. They didn't know themselves, and it's safe to say they didn't deeply know each other. I assume they liked the promise of each other. He was a student activist; she was the dean's-list beauty who stood front row when he spoke on campus. They were idealists remaking the world.

As a result of their countercultural endeavors, my parents both had files with the FBI. My father had been jailed for inciting a riot.

My mother had organized labor from within at a factory job while holding her position on the dean's list at the University of Houston. I spent late nights with them at the African Liberation Support Committee, the former nuns' residences of St. Mary's Catholic Church in Houston's Third Ward. They typed leaflets while smoking cigarettes. The Staples Singers played on an LP in the background. My dad traveled with Stokely Carmichael, the former Black Panther, to Tanzania and Zaire to try to teach revolutionists on the Mother Continent the same resistance techniques they were using to take down the Man in America. It was a heady time, one that could easily subvert a marriage. And it did.

My name, Tembekile, was given to me by none other than Miriam Makeba, who at the time was married to Stokely. Makeba was the exiled South African folk singer known as Mamma Africa. She was also public enemy number one for the South African government. She sang about freedom, advancing an anti-apartheid agenda from Paris to Japan to New York City. By the time I was old enough to understand who she was, I began to spend hours wondering about this woman, this hero, this person who had chosen a name for me before I had even taken my first breath.

But it was learning about her in the fourth grade that made me first understand what it meant to be exiled. To be cast out of home. To have no home. I was not exiled, for sure, but as a kid I didn't always feel rooted. At times I even fantasized about making a home with Miriam Makeba. I saw her as the godmother my atheist parents hadn't given me. In my childish fantasy, she and I could be two exiled people, flung around the globe.

By the time my parents had turned thirty, the Movement was dissolving, and the Reagan Era was on the horizon. They, along with many of their generation, took a step back from the picket lines and began to figure out how to make a living in a United States that wasn't all that willing to change. By now Sherra and Gene had two children—my sister Attica was born three years after me—whom they took along with them as they each, in their own way, began to reconfigure their own idea of family. They were already redoing adulthood in their formative years, already parents, already having experienced lost dreams.

Now in Italy, barely twenty years old, I was trying to decipher what made people come together and stay together forever. The idea that Saro had suggested, that a pairing could yield something great and lasting, was beautiful but untested. Still, when he said it, it felt real and possible. Even though I had extended my stay and I was set to return to America in a few months, Saro floated the idea that we could spend the summer together, that he'd come visit me at Wesleyan. One occasion after we had made love, he told me, "People eat all over the world. I can be a chef anywhere. You can only act in Los Angeles or New York. I will be at your side."

I was willing to take a risk with him. There was something so utterly confident in his vision of our future. He was unwavering. He saw what he saw, and his every action inducted me into that vision. And I felt safe. Safe to open my heart, to be vulnerable. Safe enough to take a risk on something no one in my family had seen coming— a potential long-distance relationship with an Italian man twelve years older, without a college degree, who was banking on "cooking" as the means of supporting our future together. It was improbable, romantic, idealistic, unprecedented. The journey I was willing to take had no guidelines or examples I could look to in either my own life or the lives of my parents. His parents, from the little he had told me, had been married his whole life and lived in the town where they were born. Saro and I would be making our own way.

There was no one with whom we could compare ourselves, no one to whom we could turn to for the ins and outs of long-distance, bicultural, bilingual, biracial love. That was scary, but it was also freeing. As though for the first time in my life, I was making a brave, bold decision of the heart that felt expansive, intuitive, a wish from my soul.

My family, on the other hand, had reservations. When I told my father during one of our weekly Sunday conversations from Florence that I was seeing a man, the mere mention of it when I was so far away from home, so young, set off his parenting alarm. To make matters worse, I was talking about staying in Italy even longer than the stay I had already extended. I told him I might not come home for the summer. Or if I did, I would work briefly at his law firm to make just enough money to buy a plane ticket back to Italy. That was all he needed to hear. He and my stepmother, Aubrey, booked the first ticket they could get to Europe. They left my three young brothers at home with Aubrey's mom, the youngest of whom was barely a year old and whom I had met only twice. They boarded a plane to Switzerland, the cheapest my dad could find. Then they rented a car and drove across the Italian border, then south into Tuscany, and finally to Florence. He told me he wanted to see how I was doing, visit his daughter in Italy, and treat Aubrey to a brief vacation. What he didn't tell me, but what I sensed, was that he had every intention of looking a certain Italian man in the eye. He had every intention of telling him to step the hell back, if needed.

Dad arrived in Florence in full Texas regalia, complete with cowboy hat, denim pants, and alligator boots. His jacket was suede, and I'll be damned if there wasn't some fringe on it. The sight of him coming down Via Calzaiuoli and filling Piazza della Signoria with his presence was enough to make me adore him just a bit more and also wonder what the hell I had set into motion. That he was going to meet Saro was nonnegotiable. In fact, he had casually suggested that Saro and I join him and Aubrey for a drink in "downtown Florence." So Saro was set to meet us shortly after I linked up with my family. I was quite nervous, afraid that Saro would be so intimidated by my father that he wouldn't say a word or, worse yet, would try too hard.

Instead he arrived on time and at ease.

"Nice to meet you both." Saro shook my father's hand and gave Aubrey a hug. "I was thinking we should have dinner together tonight. I've made arrangements at my restaurant."

He was setting the tone for hospitality and transparency, things I knew my dad greatly respected.

But it was Aubrey who could see Saro's love on view in plain sight. Later, after a walk through Florence, an afternoon of window browsing, and then dinner, she told my dad, "And don't even think about objecting to their age difference. You and I are also twelve years apart. It's plain as day how he feels, you do not have to worry about this." She shot down any lingering doubt, assuaging my father's concerns. Aubrey was Saro's ambassador into my clan.

My mother would be a tougher sell. She was coming off her second divorce and had bounced herself into a new relationship with a man whom, ironically, she had met while visiting me in Florence. He was Senegalese, a diplomat's son, Muslim, educated at the Sorbonne. He was the antithesis of my stepfather, the Mexican American, self-claimed entrepreneur, Armani suit–loving man with whom she had spent the last twelve years of her life. That marriage had gone up in a bonfire of lies, questionable business decisions, suspicions of infidelity, and other accusations I caught wind of. By the time I had left for Florence, the marriage had been coming off the wheels. My mother hadn't talked much about it, or maybe I hadn't let her talk much about it. Their separation was exhausting. My stepfather had been hard to feel attached to despite the fact that I had spent half of my childhood under the same roof. He was dodgy by nature, and it didn't help that he liked to tease me for sport.

As soon as her divorce was complete, my mother had been more than happy to hop onto a plane and come visit. It was Christmas break, and I had never spent a Christmas away from home. As much as I loved Florence, I hadn't yet started dating Saro, and I was terribly homesick.

As she and I sipped cappuccinos and sampled pastries in a café across from the Boboli gardens, out of nowhere she began a quiet but very determined inquiry into why I was studying in Italy at all. To her way of thinking, I was the child of activists, people who had instilled in me a sense of cultural pride and political awareness. I had been raised to sympathize with the challenges facing people of color across the African diaspora. Why, then, had I come to Italy, the heart of European culture, to study abroad? Why was I not in Kenya, like the daughter of her friend Mary from her former Movement days? Mary's daughter was on a Fulbright and teaching Kenyan children English as part of her studies at Wellesley. Why was I not more like Mary's daughter? And why in God's name was I continuing to hook up with "white boys"? She wanted something more for me. And she took her time telling me so as we sat eating and drinking.

"But, Mom, I'm an art history major. My graduation requirement includes being proficient in either French, German, or Italian. Studying in Kenya—"

She jumped in before I could continue. "It's about the bigger-picture life choices you are making. By being here you are virtually excluding yourself from the possibility of being with someone who is nonwhite." Her Afrocentrism came with conditions, and at that moment those conditions included black first, second, and always.

"I don't know what to say. I like being here, and I am not excluding anyone or anything."

"Yes, you are. By virtue of where you are, you are excluding."

It was a conversation from which there was no out. I would never win. I was the daughter of a black activist who was suggesting I had sold out. Pass me another slice of pizza, please. I knew she was having her say.

Once I began dating Saro, if my parents talked about it with each other, they spared me the details. Ultimately, when it came to affairs of the heart, each of them was wise and intuitive enough to keep a distance. They were willing to say their piece and then let their children either sink or fly when it came to love. No matter what opinions they might have had, at the end of the day, I believe they wanted me to be happy. And if it was a chef from Italy who made me happy, they were willing to support that. If nothing else, they had raised a daughter who knew how to follow her convictions and was also learning how to follow her heart. Somewhere, deep down inside, they might have even celebrated my bravery. The odds against our love were so improbable, so steep, but they had taught me to fight for what mattered.

By March, I was still renting a room in the penthouse apartment in Piazza del Carmine. One night I was waiting for Saro to get off work, and I sat up most of the night talking to a new American roommate, Cristina, from San Francisco who had filled me with stories like a tumbler of whiskey. By the time we adjourned, it was after midnight. My plan was to lie down just for a few minutes, rest, and wait for Saro to arrive in the piazza below sometime just after 1:00 a.m. It had been four months since he had bought me the bike and we had shared the ride across the Arno. We had a routine at this point that when he finished work at Acqua al 2, he left Florence's center and rode across the river to Piazza del Carmine to wait outside my apartment. He would stand across the street from my building and wait for me to come to the front window. Upon seeing him, I would buzz him in. He couldn't ring the bell because of one of my roommates, whom Cristina and I jokingly called "The Den Madame" but who was, in fact, a Canadian trust fund transplant whose name was on the lease on the rooms we sublet. She was famous for discontinuing the tenancy of any girl who took up with bothersome boyfriends. Ringing the bell after 10:00 p.m. qualified as bothersome.

When I awoke three hours later in a Chianti-induced sweat and full of panic, it was 3:30 a.m. I had gone so far and deep into sleep after my roomie's tales of woe that I had lost sense of time and place. I sat upright in my tiny twin bed and immediately realized that something was desperately wrong. I sprang from my bed and nearly broke my neck running along the marble floor through the corridor to the front windows of the apartment, thinking *I know he won't be there. I've missed him.*

When I got to the window, flushed with anxious nerves, the first thing I saw was that it was pouring rain. *Shit! Really?* Could this be any worse? As I peered out into the night and looked down, there he was. My Saro. His coat was drawn tight, his hair was a wet, soaking mess. He was looking up at the window of our apartment.

One look at Saro, and something new about him came into crystalline focus. This man, this chef, was showing me who he was deep down, the persistence of his character, his unflinching willingness. He had declared his love, he had laid out his vision, but now he was making that love an action. Standing in the rain, it was as if he were drawing a line in the sand. On one side of it, he showed me the kind of love I could have in my life with a man who was undeterred in his commitment, unafraid, clear about what he wanted—someone determined above all else to stand for love no matter what, no matter how. No matter.

On the other side of that line was another life. It was the one I had been leading before taking up with Saro, one rife with middling commitments and ambivalent relationships. The line was as clear and as black and white as any frame out of Neorealism. There was my new lover, a man kept waiting, standing in the rain past the point where it would have been understandable to leave. He was a man in love with me down to the bone. To wait for someone in this way, in this circumstance, was an extraordinary act of faith and love. But more still, it was the act of a man who was persistent, whose character was unshakable.

When I went downstairs to let him in, the first thing he did was wet me with kisses. As I helped him take off his jacket, the first thing he said was "I'm glad you woke up."

Before coming to Italy, my father and I had gone jogging one day in his Houston neighborhood and he had given me a piece of sage advice. I might have shared my suspicion that my mother's marriage was moving toward a swift and decisive end. I had just spent the summer working in his law office, where I often fell asleep during lunch. I was bored in the way that a college student is who returns home and hasn't a clue as to what she should do next.

He sensed I needed to know something about relationships that had, until that moment, been unclear to me. "Tembi, there are many people in this world that you can love," he said between breaths.

"Okay, Dad, c'mon." I was uncomfortable with the sudden intimacy.

"Now, let me finish."

I didn't want to show it, but he had my attention.

"There are many people, maybe even *thousands*, that you can love. But there are *few* people," he continued, his words measured, "maybe only one or two on the planet, that you can love *and* live with in peace. The peace part is the key."

He stopped short in his 1987 Bar Association T-shirt and looked me square in the eye. I hoped like hell he wasn't going to ask me specifics about my love life. My dad was telling me something—the kind of stuff I usually overheard him say only when he shot the breeze with his friends over a glass of bourbon and local barbecue. It felt true. In relationships, real partnerships, the love is only as good as the friendship.

What I didn't know was that loving someone long term, in that "peace" that I so desperately longed for, would also mean loving parts of them that remained unseen. As much as Saro's heart was an open book, there was a mystery in him. My familial love was given, steady, open, even when out of sight. When he spoke of his origins, his family (which was rarely), there was a trace of pain, something unsettled, an air of disappointment I couldn't quite identify. It was a part of his life that hadn't yet been fully revealed to me. It would be soon enough.

AFTERTASTES

Sicilian sea salt boils faster than Morton's. Add fresh basil near the finish, not the beginning, when simmering tomato sauce. Laurel will bring out bitterness. Soak garbanzo beans overnight, a pinch of salt in the water. That was the extent of what I knew. Years spent with a chef, and how salt boils and when to add basil were the centerpieces of my culinary education. I had never planned for this day, the day I would stand at the stove and cook my first meal alone.

Early-April light filtered through the windows of our Silver Lake home and into the kitchen Saro had designed—galley style with a four-burner stove, deep industrial sink, and granite countertops the color aptly called "coastal green." Those features lined up along a wall with a picture window onto our back-yard garden. The window was framed with an Italian marble backsplash of hexagonal tiles that reached the ceiling. I thought about all the cooks in whose kitchens I had stood before meeting Saro. None of those cooks had left much of an impression. With the exception of my father, Gene, and my grandmother in rural East Texas, I essentially hailed from a long line of pot watchers, people content to have someone else cook and feed them food. I had enjoyed the complacency of knowing hunger satiated by a ready-made plate.

Sure, I knew some things, perhaps more than many home cooks. I had been lazy, but I hadn't been blind. I could approximate. But that is not the same as intuiting. Could I cook with his essence? Would I ever taste his alchemy at the end of a spoon again? Or was my empty palate evidence of a grief that would never leave?

I looked out the window at the hundred-year-old fig tree that stood just outside the kitchen door. Then I reached for his knife.

The first thing that took my breath away was its weight. Instinctively, I had selected the largest knife in his collection. It was on top of the other knives resting in the block and the one knife in the kitchen he handled most. It was seamlessly crafted steel, and each nick in the handle told the story of a meal, an emotion. It had divided, sliced, and julienned a thousand raw ingredients. The weight of it in my palm forced me to sit down; a wave of dizziness and nausea bore down on me. *My husband is dead. He is gone. Saro is gone.* It was something I had had to process over and over again in the seven days since he had taken his last breath.

Hours before, I had taken Zoela, our daughter, to school for the first time since her dad died. Returning to her first-grade classroom after a week at home was a first big step into a new but strangely familiar world. She needed to climb trees, hang upside down over a sandbox with her friends. She needed time away from a home life that had lost its tether.

I wasn't ready to return to my career as an actor. I couldn't imagine breaking down a script, trying to push my grief aside to burrow inside the life of someone else. I couldn't see myself walking across a studio lot, I couldn't imagine standing before a camera and showing up for an audition in any cogent capacity. Acting had always been my creative salvation. I was proud of the career I had built as a working actress with worthy film and television credits and a well-earned pension, but now I feared that maybe my career had died with Saro. He had been my soft-landing spot, my constant in the steady stream of rejections the industry doles out. My agents and managers knew I was in the undertow of grief, barely able to leave the house. "Tell us when you're ready, and we'll send you material," they'd said. That had about a snowball's chance in hell of happening at that moment.

I was in the land of the newly widowed, which felt like floating in the outer rings of Mars while my body was tied to Earth. All morning it had been like having one language in my head while the world spoke another that pierced my ears like hurried gibberish through a scratchy loudspeaker. My senses were jumbled. Sound was a bitter taste stuck to the roof of my mouth, and sight was a rough touch grazed against my eyelids. At ground zero of grief, up was down and down was sideways. I didn't remember where we kept the salt; holding a knife took effort. I looked down at my feet because I didn't trust the earth underneath me to be there. Nothing, absolutely nothing, made sense in the known and unknown world. Except being at home, near my bed, in Saro's kitchen and in the room where we had said our last good-byes.

From the kitchen I could see my former office turned hospice room, which now held an altar, the soul center of the house. That night, Zoela and I would do what we had done for the last six nights: gather in the room, read poems by Rumi, play Saro's favorite music—bluesman Albert King and jazzman Paolo Conte, burn sage, and say prayers for the newly dead from a book of candlelight rituals. Those rituals were our desperate attempts to find a way out of the darkness.

• • •

Our undoing was cancer. Saro had first been diagnosed ten years before with leiomyosarcoma, a rare soft-tissue malignancy that had initially appeared in the smooth muscle of his left knee and metastasized into his femur.

Because we had weathered so much over the last decade—so many ups and downs, clinical trials, remissions—I had no way of knowing that a series of hospital stays in a single month would be a sign of the end. A kind of medical chaos had begun to ensue after he had had an adverse reaction to a new drug. Suddenly we had descended into a medical landscape of dueling specialists, expert professionals each of whom saw one piece of the puzzle that was Saro's body. I was the only one looking at the whole of his life, his body, his heartfelt desires. I tried to humanize the patient behind the chart. His name is Saro. Call him Saro, not Rosario, his given name. Not Spanish, Italian. A chef, a father. Married twenty years. As the heads of hepatology, endocrinology, immunology, gastroenterology, and orthopedic surgery made their rounds, I succumbed to writing my name on the hospital room whiteboard: "CARING FAMILY: Tembi, wife. Black woman sitting in the corner." It was my response after two nurses had asked me if I was "the help."

I employed everything I had learned as a caregiver in the face of escalating symptoms, conflicting diagnoses, and the longing of a daughter whose father was away from home more and more. I put books of poetry in each hospital room. I brought him an eye mask, a sound machine, a flameless candle. I sprayed aromatherapy in each room to balance the scent of disinfectant and rubbed Bach Flower Remedies on his temples at night and on his abdomen while he slept. I brought meals from home, from our own stove top, because hospital food is both nutritionally vacuous and psychologically oppressive.

Especially for a chef. He was put first on a salt-restricted diet, then another diet high in protein. I purchased high-protein organic shakes in three flavors and kept them in an ice bucket at his bed.

Each night, I kissed his heart chakra before I left the hospital. Then I watched Beverly Hills fall away behind me so that I could be home for Zoela when she awoke in the morning. In the mornings I'd rise early and call the charge nurse for an update, I'd feed Zoela breakfast, assure her that Babbo (Daddy) was okay, and take her to school eastward, only to turn around and drive westward back across the city to Saro. I would spend the days trying to understand what was happening in his body, trying to ease his way.

Somehow in all the chaos that month I managed to put myself on tape to audition for the producers of two TV pilots because it was the network hiring season and we needed the money. Then I called my agents to say I was "booking out" until further notice. I had never, in twenty years, done that. I was taking a leave of absence from jobs I didn't yet have and might never get. I was pulling myself away from possibilities. Because I had to make space for another possibility—that Saro would be leaving me.

When Saro had almost died of congestive heart failure on the operating table, it had been a turning point. I couldn't look away from a growing awareness that this was likely the beginning of the end of our cancer fight. He had woken up in the ICU after surgery, taken one look at me, and said, "*Vittoria*—Victory." It was the victory of a dying man.

I smothered him with kisses. I wanted to crawl into the bed with him, to feel his skin next to mine. I wanted to soothe his body with my touch. If it had been possible to make love to him, I might have done it then and there. But I couldn't let down the guardrail. He was hooked up to an IV and monitors. The best we could do was hold hands. The best I could do was lean in and make him a promise.

"I will get you out of here. I will get you home. My love, I promise you our story will not end here."

As he drifted off, I made other promises, too, the kind of promises the living make to the dying when we have the sudden realization that we are all, in fact, "the dying." That life is fleeting, capable of bending the other way at any moment. We reach hard for life.

I promised him a road trip to the Grand Canyon and another up the Alaskan coast. If he could just get out of the hospital, maybe those things would be possible. I would have promised him the moon and stars, if I thought I could deliver. In the short term I focused on two things I knew I could make happen right away: "I will make sure your sister comes to visit, and I will bring Zoela to see you."

After two days in the ICU, Saro was in a regular room. Everything inside had the stench of institution, including me. The trench coat I hadn't taken off in weeks reeked of it all. I stank. I carried the worry of a woman who felt the love of her life slipping away. I walked the halls while Saro rested. The sound of the heels of my winter boots clomping on the floor rose up and pierced my ears. A new father passed me in the hallway, he had an IT'S A GIRL balloon in one hand and takeout from The Ivy in the other hand. In my hand, I had two hospital-issued ice pops for Saro that I had retrieved from the tiny box of a kitchen galley on the fifth floor of the hospital's pediatric ward—one lemon, one cherry. In my other hand, I cradled my cell phone.

I was talking with his mother, my mother-in-law, Croce. She was a widow, having lost her own husband to cancer three years earlier, choosing to wear black and leave her house only to go to church. Saro called her "Mamma," but since the birth of our daughter, I had called her "Nonna."

Nonna's voice was loud and frantic; it billowed in the space between my ear and my shoulder. I tried to picture her some six thousand miles away in her living room, one small room in the wildness and foothills of a mountain in Sicily.

"How is he?" she asked me in Italian, our only common language.

"I am taking him something to eat." I stopped to lean against the wall.

It was an answer without being a real answer. But I knew the power of visuals. So I gave her one I knew would let her picture me feeding her son. It meant he was still well enough to eat.

She had told him she was having dreams in which the Blessed Mother visited her to tell her that her son was being called home.

"What do the doctors say?"

"They are watching. They want to see how his liver stabilizes." I pulled myself off the wall and continued the walk to Saro's room. "Please tell me Franca is coming." Franca was Saro's sister and only sibling. She had never in all our years of marriage come to the United States to visit.

"She is."

When I got to his room, *Goodfellas* was playing on the TV above his bed. A red-framed school picture of Zoela sat next to him. The hospital had a policy that children younger than twelve years old couldn't go past the lobby. It was infuriating, disheartening. One time in those days, I had been able to bring Saro down to her in a wheelchair. They had had to embrace in a public lobby to the sound of a whirring Starbucks coffee grinder and the lobby piano playing "Rocket Man" on a baby grand. The first thing she asked him was why he was wearing a dress, then if she could sit on his lap. The first comment made me laugh, the second question made me cry. When they parted fifteen minutes later, I knew he might never see her again if I didn't find a way to bring her to him.

As the days turned to a week, I learned how to sneak my daughter into the hospital to see her dying father. When she got there, she kicked off her ballet slippers and crawled into bed with him.

"Babbo, let me tell you about a story I wrote about a wolf who likes ice cream."

I had watched them in bed, each lit up by the presence of the other, and I wanted to take us away. I wanted to hold on to the tenderness of that moment for all eternity. But things continued to speed up. The end of life goes slowly and then fast and then slowly again. We were in a hospital waiting game.

Then a chief of staff came to visit Saro. I had stepped away for a moment and returned to find them in midconversation.

"The only option left would be a liver transplant," she said.

Saro looked away, then back at her. "I don't think so. Save it for someone who can use it," he said, his skin sickly yellow with jaundice.

I felt the earth give underneath me and had to lean on his hospital bed to stay erect. The only option left wasn't really an option at all. Before I could fully process that, she was leaving the room, going on to her next round. It took me a few seconds, minutes, to fully register her absence, take in what had just happened.

I left Saro's bedside and chased her down the hall, quickening my pace to catch up with the doctor and a resident who had been with her. My boot heels clicked rapidly on the marble floor as I caught up with her in the hallway.

"What exactly are you saying?" When I saw her eyes avoid mine, any lingering hope I had had that he might bounce back or even stabilize disappeared. She had said it all without saying a word. Still I needed to hear it. The sound of my own voice scared me as I asked, "Is he dying?"

She looked up, then down again. She nodded.

Then. Slowly. Finally.

"Yes, he is dying."

You are never prepared for those words, no matter how long the illness has been. Part of me splintered in that moment.

"And if there is nothing left to do . . . then how much time?" I needed to know.

"Two weeks, perhaps, two or three. At best."

"What will it look like? Will he be in pain?" With each question that formed in my mouth, I was moving myself closer to a world without Saro, closer to widowhood.

"Liver failure is a relatively pain-free way to die. He won't have pain, he'll just get really tired until he is gone."

That was the first time it was actually said out loud: Saro was dying. I heard it there on the marble floors of a top hospital, expensive art adorning the walls, a meal cart wheeling by.

I went back to his room, where he was falling asleep. I leaned over him as he slept, kissed his forehead, and, filled with determination, made a new, fervent promise: "Our story will not end in this hospital. I'm gonna get you out of here."

I went out into the hallway and up to the nurse's station. "What do I do? I have to get him home. Please tell the attending we want palliative care," I said to the charge nurse. She could see my desperation.

"I'll let him know the family is requesting hospice. He'll have to write an order for it." The way she said it gave me no sense of assurance.

Sometime between the ICU and the conversation about a transplant, Franca had arrived with her husband, Cosimo, from Sicily. Saro could not wait to see his sister. When she showed up, it was clear that she was not prepared to see her brother so frail, his breathing labored. My stoic sister-in-law cried openly at the first sight of him. She spoke to him in his native tongue, and I knew it was a salve to his soul. She knew she was bringing him comfort. He would get to say a personal good-bye, hold her hand, see her face.

When Franca kept Saro company at the hospital, she made him smile with childhood reminisces about Sicily. She brought him lentils she made in our kitchen and transported to him in a glass jar. She pushed aside the hospital food and spooned a serving onto his lunch tray. From morning to evening, they tried to cheer each other up. But each night, she wept silently when I drove her back to our house and he remained there. When I returned to the hospital later in the night, he'd tell me he was worried about her.

"When will they release him?" she asked as her stay was ending. I tried to explain the procedural steps in a medical system that was more complicated and bureaucratic than any with which she was familiar in Sicily. "Saro needs platelets so he can be stable enough to leave the hospital. Getting him home requires a precisely timed transfusion, immediate discharge instructions, and EMTs waiting on standby."

She was crestfallen. "Do you think it will happen?"

"I'm doing my best."

Two days later, the moment came. We exited through the ER off the back elevators. The EMTs guided the gurney through corridors and secondary hallways. After years of seeing the flurry of hospital activity in one direction, seeing the same hallways in reverse felt as though I were moving in slow motion. I held on to Saro's gurney, as if it might roll away if I didn't hold on. He had never *left* the hospital on a gurney.

When the glass doors slid open, the air felt crisp, a harsh assault on my lungs. I could not breathe the air of normal life. Under the overhead lights of the parking garage, Saro looked more ashen and jaundiced than he had just a second before. I took off my coat and put it over him. As the paramedics took great care to hoist him into the back of the ambulance, they warned me that it would be a slow drive. No sirens.

The doors closed behind us with a heavy thud, as though they were vacuum sealed. I held his hand. The vehicle began to move. Soon I watched the lights of Beverly Boulevard shimmer past. People emptied out of late-night restaurants, others walked in duos and trios laughing along the sidewalk. We had once been the couple who tumbled out of restaurants laughing; we had ridden bikes across the Arno in Italy. Now holding his hand was the only thing that mattered. He didn't have the energy to speak. Not even a word. When we crossed Vermont Avenue, I realized that we were almost home. Hospice would be waiting. Zoela would be asleep upstairs. I was bringing Saro home to die.

In Silver Lake, that March was cold and wet. Still, the fava beans in our front garden were going strong. Fava beans are sacrosanct in Sicily. They are eaten around Easter. The bean is associated with resurrection, renewal, sustenance. Saro had taught me that favas are the only plants that actually give back to the soil, they don't deplete it. They enrich it with nitrogen, spreading generosity and determination with every sprout. The fava beans that spring stood tall in the garden, the last connection to Saro's culinary life, his culture, the garden of his construction. Years earlier, while he had followed his doctor's instruction to rest and let his body recoup from the chemotherapy until his immune system was strong enough for his next surgery, he had made it his mission to design a front-yard garden. He had spent two weeks rendering its landscape in a sketchbook—raised-bed planters in diamond formation around a central fountain with a gravel pathway to move between each planter. Within a month he had transformed our front yard, with the beans as a centerpiece. And here they stood now, verdant and swaying in the wind, impervious to my husband dying in the next room.

Inside, the house had swelled with the necessities and unfamiliarity of hospice. A nurse passed me, people came and went. I stepped over a game of Twister while I talked to Margaret, a social worker, on the phone. It was Tuesday midmorning.

Margaret worked exclusively with kids who had lost parents to cancer, AIDS, ALS, and other illnesses. After asking a series of questions about how old our daughter was, how long Saro had been sick, and what our funeral plans were, she sped to the heart of her counsel.

"Children, especially those your daughter's age, are prone to magical thinking. You will need to help her understand what is happening because her brain will want to forget. Her brain and heart will not be able to hold it." Her voice came to me slow and steady.

I had to sit on the floor, moving Twister out of the way.

She continued, "You must let her be part of this process. When her father dies, bring her to him. And do not let them take his body away without her seeing it. Let her have a moment with him. Let her touch him. Ask her how it feels. This is important. She'll need to remember how his skin felt."

"I don't know if I can do this." My voice echoed in my head.

"You can, you will," she said. She struck me as the kind of

woman who could perform field surgery in the trenches of war under a starless sky. "Do you have someone to help you? Family?"

"Yes, sister, dad, stepmother. They're here," I said.

"Then you can." But she wasn't done; she had more. "And I know this sounds morbid. But you need to take a picture of your husband after he has died. Not with your daughter and him. But of him. Take the picture of him." Her repetition was deliberate and direct.

"I don't understand." I hunched over, unsure if I still had bones in my body.

"Then I want you to put that picture away." She said it as though it would be as easy as pulling a pie from the oven. "And here's the good news. You may never have to see it again. But one day you might need it. And you'll be glad you have it. One day when she's sixteen and all her grief is new and fresh, triggered by all the ways he is not in her life, she will be angry and hurt and confused. And mad at you, mad at life. She may say, 'And you never let me say good-bye to my dad' or 'I never got to go to his memorial service.' And she won't be making it up. It will be real to her. Children can bury what is too big to bear. *That* is why you will have the picture."

Margaret was flashing forward ten years into a future without Saro. To Zoela as a teenage girl who was angry and hurt. To me as a single parent. She was describing a world I had not yet even dared to consider.

It was only days earlier, before we had brought Saro home, that I had told Zoela that her father was dying. A friend had gone to get her from school while I had rehearsed the words in my head the way I did while learning lines of dialogue for an audition. I tried saying "Babbo is dying" three different ways. With three different intentions. With three different approaches. Comfort her. Be clear with her. Empathize with her. But this was no acting exercise. Each time I choked on the words in my mouth. No amount of rehearsal could prepare me.

When she got home, I invited her into my room. She played on my bed, and I told her she could sleep with me that night. I asked her to tell me about a recent school trip to the California desert. She spoke of coyotes, desert squirrels, and six-foot cacti. They all sounded like words from another planet. The planet of the living. Not the world I had been inhabiting in hospital corridors. I tried to focus on her eyes as she spoke. I took in the fall of her pigtails. I wanted to cup her face, kiss her. Then I said, "Sweetheart, I need to tell you something. It's about Babbo."

"I know," she said, her voice registering neither surprise nor distress. Prescience.

Seven years old, and she said, "I know."

"I know he is dying, and it's breaking my heart," she continued. Her eyes didn't leave me, as if there were a possibility that this wasn't happening. A possibility that I could pull her close and say "Oh, no, baby, not that." Instead, I said this.

"Yes, mine is breaking too."

"When?"

"I don't know, but soon."

She looked away then, lost in thought, in irreconcilable thoughts. She stared, unseeing, at the drawn curtain behind my bed. The look on her face, her composure, gnawed at my heart. It was too much for seven years old. "Your heart is breaking, and so is mine," I said as I reached to take her. "Come here, sit with me."

She curled up in my lap and began to cry. I caressed her head. We let ourselves fall back onto the bed in an embrace. We lay there for a long, sacred moment, tethered to what we still had. Each other.

I was shaking as I hung up the phone with the social worker. All

I wanted was to be near Saro. I picked myself up from the floor and went to him. I pulled back the pocket doors of the room that, just a few days earlier, had been our study. Friends who had learned of the latest news had been dropping by with flowers. Buds and blooms filled the room. On the table next to the hospital bed was a candle, his favorite book of poetry by Rumi, a prayer card from Nonna in Sicily, and a crystal. Where my desk would normally have been there was now the oxygen machine, humming low and steady. Our study was now a hospice womb.

Saro's head was turned away. He was lost in thought.

"*Ciao, tesoro*," I said, coming around the foot of the bed to face him. Zoela's stuffed animals were on top of the coverlet at his feet. She had lined them up in formation to face him. Tied to the bed's side rail was a WELCOME HOME balloon from the supermarket, a silver Mylar heart that Zoela had picked out and then decorated with her first-grader print: "*TI AMO.*"

When I settled on the edge of the bed, he met my eyes, paused, and then looked past me.

"Just me," I said. "Nurse Cathy is outside."

A smile came across his face.

"Apple juice?" I offered the plastic cup with a rainbow straw that Zoela had left at his bedside before going to school that morning. We had all agreed a normal day for her was best. But she had wanted to have breakfast with him. The apple juice had been her parting gift.

He nodded, and I bent the straw and held it to his lips. When I did, he shifted and motioned for me to draw closer. His skin was warm, I could still smell his signature earthy mix of salt and spice over the scents of medicine, iodine, and baby wipes. I kissed him long and hard on his forehead.

"Where is Zoela?" he asked. He had forgotten.

"School." I smoothed his coverlet, then walked over to turn up the volume on his iPod at the other end of the room. Then I returned to sit at his side. Over the years, I had given thought to the eventuality of this moment. It was one way I wrestled with the anticipatory grief. I'd be driving on the freeway stuck in traffic on the overpass of the 405 near the Getty Center en route to an audition, and instead of going over my lines in my head, I would think of what music I might play for Saro in his dying hour. I knew that sound is the first sensory connection humans have in utero, and I had seen a documentary on the Tibetan Book of the Dead that explained that sound is also the last sensory connection we have when dying. Saro would be able to hear me, hear everything around him, even if he couldn't eat, see, or speak.

The theme song from *Cinema Paradiso* played in the background. I could sense him drifting toward the infinite.

"*Sto passando una primavera critica, la più critica della mia vita*—I'm passing the most critical spring of my life," he said to me as the music played.

For a flash I could smell the eucalyptus and spring grass. I saw Zoela running around laurel bushes, her honey brown skin glowing in the spring Sicilian sun. *Spring*. He had called this moment his "spring."

"I want you to know love someday. Another love. Your love is too beautiful not to share." He said it with ease, not a trace of distress or ambivalence. As if it were the most natural thing for a husband to say to a wife. "I want you to live your life."

"Don't. Please. Don't," I said. But I knew he was saying what he needed to say. He was strangely lucid. Clear as a bell. Then he became less so.

I felt the shift of energy as I lay there next to him. From the moment we met, his body had anchored me. Now I could feel it transforming, searching for a new axis.

"Where am I going?" he asked, looking at me but through me.

"I don't know, but I think it is beautiful. It is full, you will be peaceful." I caressed the back of his hand, let my fingers massage his.

"Wake me when Zoela comes home." He closed his eyes.

"Of course."

I left the room to let him rest.

Two doors down I heard the church bells strike 11:00 a.m. Sometimes I hated that we shared our street with a church. The bells punctuated moments that needed no punctuation.

In the dining room, my dad, my stepmother, Aubrey, and my sister, Attica, were gathered at the table. They were heading up what can only be described as a hospice command center—receiving all the phone calls, notifying family, coordinating visitors. Between the Friday night when we had brought Saro home in an ambulance and that morning, a world of change had happened. My mother had left L.A. to return to Houston for work. My dad and Aubrey had arrived to take over the family support role in her place. My sister shuttled between her own home and mine, picking up food, running hospice errands, offering care, and making sure that Franca and Cosimo had food and anything else they might need. One of Saro's cousins had flown in from Buffalo, New York, to share a final good-bye. Franca and Cosimo had gathered around Saro's bed for their own final good-bye before they boarded a return flight to Sicily, petrified with grief. The comings and goings of family and friends were dizzying.

When Zoela came home from school that day, she went straight to her dad's room. She called him "sleepyhead" and asked if she, too, could have an ice pop.

Later we ate dinner at his bedside while he rested. Then Zoela watched *Puss in Boots* and painted her grandfather's fingernails because it was what she wanted and no one wanted to take more away from her. She said good night to Saro, she told him she loved him. Then I put her to sleep.

She had been asleep about two hours when Saro's breathing changed. I called Nurse Cathy in immediately.

"Is this what I think it is?" I asked. The hospice nurse had given me a pamphlet about what to expect in the final stages of dying.

"Yes." She was calm, solid, a lighthouse in my darkness.

The oxygen tank whirred.

"How long?"

"Depends. Everyone is different. Could go on like this for a while, even a day or two days."

I leaned forward onto the bed rails. The chrome was cold despite the heat that rushed to my head. *I can't do days.*

I took Saro's hand in mine. He didn't reach back. But his touch still contained his presence. His *aliveness.* I massaged his index finger and looked toward Cathy. She knew us well enough to know to leave the room. The pocket door rolled to a squeaky close behind her, and I turned to him.

This was the moment. It had arrived.

"Saro, go easy on me. Please, honey, make this easy for me."

Over the next six hours, as night pushed into morning, I sat at his bedside. I held his hand, kissed him incessantly, kisses not unlike ones I had given him for nearly twenty-one years, quotidian but rich. And I talked to him.

"You have been an extraordinary partner and an incredible father. You have honored my life. I will love you for all eternity. It is okay to go, my love."

I spoke softly into his ear. I felt the warmth of my breath come back to me.

"This body has served you well, but now you will leave it. *Amore*, I will always welcome you in my dreams and look forward to our next time together.

"*Ti amo, amore mio bello.*"

I repeated this like a poem. A mantra. A refrain of my love. Over and over. When I tired of my own words, I read Rumi out loud. I caressed his feet. I stroked his hair. I climbed into the bed. I got out of the bed. I adjusted the covers each time he kicked them loose. And when his body seemed in distress, I called the nurse. Then I whispered, "I love you" as she dropped liquid morphine from a baby dropper into his mouth to ease his breathing and relax his muscles. With each drop, I felt the shiny sting of betrayal. Morphine. He hated drugs.

I knew he wanted to stay clear and unburdened by the fog of sedatives for as long as he could.

"Is it too much, do we have to do it?" I asked Cathy. My voice was low but full of new fear. *Am I doing this wrong?* I knew that morphine was necessary to ease dying. All the hospice pamphlets said so. Yet nothing about dying was easy. Not for him nor for me. It was labor, as much labor as coming into this world.

"Yes, it is for the best, and I'm giving him a small amount," Nurse Cathy assured me. I watched her crush half a white tablet. It dissolved quickly in water before she put it into the dropper. "It will ease the respiratory distress." And it did. His tongue released the swell at the back of his throat.

By 3:00 a.m. I was exhausted. I asked my sister to stay with Saro. I went upstairs to lie down next to Zoela.

In my room, Zoela's body felt warm and small. She was peaceful, emitting a gentle snore. She seemed to me in that moment both angelic and strong. I thought for the first time that it was us in the world, just the two of us. Then I allowed myself to close my eyes. To savor the respite. Just for a moment, I told myself. I'll sleep just for a minute.

The next thing I knew, my sister was standing in the glow of twilight at my bedside.

"His breathing has changed a lot. I think you need to come now," she said.

I took the forty steps from my bedroom to the hospice room.

When I pulled back the pocket door, his face was looking toward the door. He was staring straight at me. I could hear what I knew were his final shallow breaths.

Oh, my love.

I crawled into bed with him. A single tear had formed in his eye.

"I am sorry I made you wait. I fell asleep. But I am here now. I am here."

He had waited for me to be at his side. I kissed his tear away. Then there were only a few more breaths. They were shallow, faint, then faded into nothing as I lay beside him. I was breathing in new air, air in which he was gone.

He had waited for me, the same way he had waited for me in Florence, standing by the lamppost in the winter rain. He had left this world characteristically tenacious in his love, and I couldn't help but feel he was telling me he'd also be waiting for me in the next.

I lay there in silence for a long time. The air was pregnant with an energetic pulse. I kissed him again. Maybe I needed to be sure of his physical goneness. Twenty minutes passed. No breath. Finally I felt oriented enough to stand up. I was willing to brave my first step into a new life. I had to go tell my daughter her babbo was gone.

I turned the knob of my bedroom. It was just after 7:00 a.m., and sunlight filtered softly into the room. The day was carrying on.

"Sweetheart." I rubbed her back. I didn't want to wake her, because when I did, her life was going to be completely changed. My words stuck like glue in my mouth. Saro's tear was still on my lips. But I willed myself forward because what happened next, how I handled everything from this moment, would stay with her for the rest of her life.

"Zoela, *amore.*" I pulled her close. I kissed her cheek. "Zoela." She turned over. I kissed her again. I wanted to bring her from the sleep state to reality as gracefully as I could. That morning was one she would remember forever.

When her eyes were sufficiently open and she was folded into my body as we had done so many mornings since she was born, I said, "Babbo has died, sweetheart."

"When?" Her eyes were barely open.

"While you were sleeping." She stared at me expressionless, flat of understanding. "I think we should go down and see him. He wants us to say good-bye." She didn't protest. I hoisted her onto my hip, and we walked out.

When we got downstairs, I did all the things the social worker had told me to do. Zoela read a poem. She put a flower on him. We told him we loved him. Twice I reassured her that he was not just sleeping. As hard as it was for me, I didn't rush her. The whole process lasted fifteen, maybe twenty, minutes. Then I told her that her grandparents were in the other room. Her grandfather would take her out for breakfast. She would get to pick the place.

I sat with Saro for another hour. Then I called Nonna.

"*È andato via*—He is gone," I said.

Her voice wailed before I could form more words. Then it went silent. I could hear her on the other end of the line as she cried. Silence conjoined us, and we stayed like that for a while until she asked how Zoela was doing.

"*Così così*," I said, and we let silence shroud us again.

Then I heard her rise and push her chair over the ceramic floor of her kitchen. "I am going to church to pray. Everything now is in the hands of the saints."

The logistics of death took over. I called and spoke to my mother-in-law in Sicily every day. She told me about a dream in which Saro had appeared to her, and she reported who in her Sicilian town had stopped by to offer condolences. They were hard, brief three-minute conversations in which every day she would ask about funeral arrangements. In rural Sicily, the dead are buried within twenty-four hours. From the moment of Saro's death, Nonna had been asking where he was. "*Ma dov'è il suo corpo?*—But where is his body?" She couldn't imagine her son suspended in limbo between death and final rest in a foreign country. She couldn't picture his body being attended to by strangers, his American wife not even sure where he was. I could only tell her what I knew. That his ashes would be ready in ten days for pickup or delivery and that there would be no funeral but rather a memorial service a week later. I tried to explain the concept of a memorial in Italian to a woman for whom no such ritual existed. Still she kept asking about his body.

I hadn't yet told her I'd be bringing some of his ashes to Italy, a final promise I had made him. I hadn't told her because I wasn't sure about the details. I needed time to process everything. Moreover, I wasn't sure when I wouldn't be riddled with anxiety about just leaving the house, let alone leaving the country with my daughter in tow.

I couldn't even imagine making lunch.

• • •

I turned on the gas and lit a tiny flame in all that darkness. I wanted to set fire to my grief, I wanted to bring him back. Maybe water boiling in a pot would bring him back to me, even for a second.

As I stood in Saro's kitchen, I caught a glance of my family as they gathered around the dining room table. They were navigating burial arrangements, hospice wrap-up, and memorial details. They did it with vigor while I was struggling just to drink a full glass of water.

Earlier that morning, my stepmom had knocked on my bedroom door after Zoela had left for school.

"Yes, come in."

Aubrey appeared in the doorway, all five feet of her, with a cup of chamomile tea.

"I'm doing a final proof of Saro's bio for the memorial program. Would you like to reread it once more before I send it?"

I had forgotten that I had somehow written out his life story the second day after he died. Flashes of manic productivity followed by hours of total incapacity seemed to be part of how the initial impact of losing my husband was playing out. She handed me a typed piece of paper, his life in six paragraphs, single-spaced in Corinthian font.

I had never imagined writing what amounted to my lover's obituary. But I had. I had in fact pulled quotes from his journal, his letters, and the backs of postcards. Things he had jotted down piecemeal in the final year of his illness. Things he wanted to be known to himself and others, things he wanted our daughter to know.

My eyes fell on words in the second sentence, Saro's own words about his origins: "from a lineage of peasant farmers that reached back to Byzantium. They labored for olives, lemons, garlic, and artichokes from an impervious soil, hillside and rocky." Farther down, he called himself "an accidental chef." Even farther down, in a paragraph about his fatherhood, I had added an excerpt from a poem he had written on the occasion of Zoela's birth. He had described the arrival of her love in his life as a "seasoned vessel" steady enough "to cross tormented waters" and "bring a seaman to his native home."

An invisible trapdoor opened up beneath me, and I felt a part of me fall in as I handed the paper back to Aubrey.

"It's fine," I said.

She showed me two pictures of Saro and asked which one I wanted to use. I didn't want either; I wanted him. But I chose the one I had taken of him on our tenth anniversary—the one in which his smoldering eyes seemed to promise a lifetime.

She asked me about white flowers and whether I wanted a soloist to sing. I rallied all my focus. I tried to summon answers through the gray fog in my brain that made it difficult to finish thoughts, and then I collapsed back into bed. I wept into his pillow until my eyes were nearly swollen shut.

An hour later, I had come downstairs and found my family seated at the table. "I don't think I can go to Saro's memorial. I don't think I can. I'll stay home. You go," I declared.

My family gently convinced me otherwise. They promised to shore me up. Friends stopped by daily in small groups and alone. They hugged me, then we'd sit on the couch and stare at the walls in disbelief. Death is like that. The specter of its possibility was grand and had been on full display for years of Saro's illness. Then, when it happened, there was only disbelief. And for me, there was fatigue and its companion, disabling anxiety. I felt as new in the world as I had been the day I was born. And just as vulnerable.

Aubrey, in a gesture of grace, had decided to move in with us temporarily. She had been with me three days earlier when a grief counselor had advised that we not be left alone for at least the next three months. I don't think the woman meant it literally, given that Aubrey lived four states away in Texas. But Aubrey had heard the call. And being who she is, what she could see before her eyes, she knew I was in no way capable of caring for myself, let alone a child. We were raw, and simple tasks took mammoth effort. The mere sound of running water hurt my ears, Zoela cried from 8:00 p.m. until nearly midnight each night, asking for her father back. When I attempted to get behind a wheel, it took me upward of ten minutes to back the car out of the driveway. Space and time disoriented me and flooded my memory. Panic rose in my chest before I even attempted to get out of bed. Eating was perfunctory. So Aubrey was there to make sure I took a bath, to prepare Zoela's lunch, and to turn the sheets down for me to crawl back into once I dropped her off for her first day at school.

Zoela's school and former preschool community had circled around us and organized meals during hospice and in the immediate wake of Saro's passing. It was a steady stream of southern California fusion, mostly vegetarian cuisine. High-quality food from serious home cooks surrounded us. Yet when Zoela and I sat down to eat it, the texture and taste of it on our plates were unfamiliar and difficult to digest.

Grits were the fallback Texas comfort food. Hominy was in the ancestral lineage. In times of need, keep a pot of it on the stove. Aubrey's grits with butter were the only thing I could stomach. Every time I went to spoon some onto a plate, I thought of it as Saro's polenta—but leached of its natural color and flavor. Yet under generous pats of butter and seasoned with salt, the grits went down smoothly. Though I deeply appreciated all the food gifted to us in those weeks and often wept at the bottomless generosity of our close circle of friends, in all honesty, it was emotionally indigestible. Much like my new life. Quinoa, in particular, had become my personal grief aggressor. Whereas I had loved it before, in grief it took work to eat, work to digest, work to make it into something that soothed. Take-out wasn't any better. I would sign for it, take the bag, open it, and look down at lukewarm food whose aesthetic and texture has been undone by moisture trapped in plastic and tin. I'd move it around my plate because everyone around me kept telling me to eat. The thought of a lifetime of this hung at the back of my mind, a different kind of loss not easily explained to anyone who had never been loved by a chef.

It was that aspect of my grief that took me to the kitchen. It was both an instinct and a desire. There was also fear. I wanted to be near my husband. My family intuitively knew that and left me alone in there for the first time in a week. I understood that in this first attempt to cook on my own, my grief demanded that I take it slow. Feel my way through. Trust that I would be led in the right direction.

"Begin with the *soffritto*," he'd say.

So that's what I did. I chopped my first tiny pile of garlic. I brushed it into a narrow white line with the palm of my hand, as I had seen Saro do at the beginning of thousands of meals. The palm of his hand had guided the garlic toward what was to come next.

He had told me, "It's a humble herb, but it adds a dose of courage to every dish. A little goes a long way."

Il soffritto is an act of submission, submitting onion and garlic to oil.

Cooking is about surrender. He had always demonstrated that.

So I diced the onion next, rendering it into rough cubes.

I had watched Saro bring raw ingredients to a state of surrender, releasing their form and flavor to create something new. He was my master alchemist. I felt like the onion I had just placed in the pan, translucent and vulnerable.

I wanted to get back to the first tastes—the *risotto con sugo verde* I had tasted at Acqua al 2. I understood that everything that happened to me next, at this stove, in my house, in the world, would from here on be a life of second firsts.

Fai una salsa semplice—Make a simple sauce, I imagined he'd say.

I reached for a bottle of tomato sauce, the last one from our previous summer in Sicily that sat in my cupboard. I opened the bottle and poured a liquid Sicilian summer into the pan, on top of the *soffritto*.

"Use basil, not laurel. Add a bit of sugar to balance the acid."

I mimicked the movements and gestures Saro had shown me, and I stirred.

Un piatto di pasta ti farebbe bene, amore—A plate of pasta will do you good. That was always his advice.

Like water, doubt is fluid. A week after Saro's death, I doubted I could do much, either in the kitchen or in life. But I knew how to put a pot of water onto the stove. I watched the water fill the pot, aware of its fluidity, its pliability. Was my life like that now, a thing that flowed according to the capriciousness of life's situations?

I turned off the water, put the pot onto the stove. I added salt and waited for it to boil.

"A fistful is a single serving. Always do two fistfuls, six if friends are coming over."

Six fistfuls of pasta seemed unimaginable. For now, preparing a single-serve *pasta col sugo di pomodoro* was all I could manage.

Twelve minutes later, I drained the water from the pasta and let the vapor warm my face. I poured the sauce over the fistful of spaghetti I had made, finishing the pasta in the pan the Italian way. I had made my first meal for one in Saro's kitchen.

I took a bite. It wasn't great, it wasn't bad. I could taste doubt and love, maybe a pinch of faith, a dollop of determination. After a few bites, I pushed the plate way. As I looked out onto our back yard, the fig tree with the promise of summer fruit had fully formed bulbs facing the sun, I made a decision: I would take Saro's ashes to Sicily this summer. I would keep a promise to my lover, and I would, maybe, in the process discover a new promise for myself and for a future that at the moment felt incomprehensible.

A VILLA. A BROOM.

Saro took the lead in nurturing our long-distance relationship. When I returned to the United States after my extended stay in Florence, he devised a plan: I would come back to Italy during the summer and read books by the beach while he did a summer stint as a chef on the island of Elba. He visited Wesleyan in the fall of my senior year, then came again for my graduation in spring. After I graduated, he searched for apartments for us in Florence while I did summer stock theater in the Berkshires until we could figure out next steps. We were making it work across time zones, an ocean, two languages, and being at different stages in our lives. And even though I still hadn't met his parents, we were following the dream of our relationship, and sooner than we thought I would follow another big dream: a career as an actress.

While doing summer stock theater, a New York talent manager agreed to represent me. It took all of about half a second to decide that my future was in New York, not Italy as Saro and I had thought. And I couldn't wait to tell him the news. When I called him, I was standing at a roadside pay phone in Great Barrington, Massachusetts, between rehearsals. "Luckily, people eat all over the world," he said with excitement in his voice. "I can be a chef anywhere." A month later, he decided to sell his interest in a successful new bar he had opened with friends. Two months later, he gave notice at Acqua al 2 and was ready to move to New York.

"Are you sure?" I asked him. By then I was living in New York and sleeping on my aunt's couch on the Upper East Side to save money while taking acting classes during the day and waiting tables at night.

"Of course. I don't see a future without you," he declared. I couldn't wait for him to join me in the States, but I knew it would take a few months for him to wrap up his life in Florence, and it would be hard for him to say good-bye to all his friends.

But I knew he welcomed the idea of moving to America. I hoped he'd see it as a sort of reclaiming. He had, after all, spent his teen years in Buffalo, New York, when his parents had emigrated there briefly. His father had taken a job in a pasta factory, and his mother had gotten shift work on a jacket assembly line. His father hated the snow; his mother had been assigned the mind-numbing work of attaching the same lapel to the same style men's sports jacket for three years. Saro had told me about their disillusionment with their American dream. His family had ultimately returned to Sicily when he was seventeen and had just graduated from an American high school. He hadn't wanted to leave.

At that time, this story of his parents going from farmers to factory workers, then back to farmers again was the cornerstone of what I knew. Also that neither had more than a fifth-grade educa-tion. I felt empathy for the dreariness I imagined in those Buffalo years. And I was curious about people who could pack up their kids, move them to the land of opportunity, and then deliver them back to the place, Sicily, where Saro said they had less opportunity. His parents struck me as determined, hardworking, and committed, if not terribly imaginative—things I could say about certain people in my own family. What I didn't yet feel was their resistance; what I didn't yet understand was the depths of the complexity and strife that ran through their relationship. That reality came crashing down on me just two nights before Saro was set to finally depart Florence to come join me in New York City.

"What do you mean, you haven't told them yet?" I was pacing in the sparsely furnished apartment I had secured us on the Upper West Side, winded by the five-story walk-up. I had chosen it because I had an idea about the kind of first apartment a couple like us should have: indoor/outdoor space, brick walls, a tiny but serviceable kitchen, and a closet large enough to hold mostly my clothes and some of his. I had just come back from waiting tables at Jekyll and Hyde, a theme bar in the West Village, and I was pissed and incredulous at what I was hearing.

"Telling them is a big deal," he said. His voice was tight and slightly rushed. I could hear the Italian street sounds behind him— Vespas and an ambulance siren in the distance.

It was late November. For a second, I imagined chestnuts roasting in steel drums and people sipping hot chocolate in Piazza della Signoria. Then I was pulled back to the gravity of what he was saying.

"Of course it's a big deal. We're going to be living together. In America! I think you need to give them a heads-up." I was trying my best to be supportive, but I was impatient with his handling of it.

"I will. I will," he said.

"Saro, you leave in two days!"

"I know that. I just need to figure out how to break the news. They are going to be devastated. They'll think that they'll never see me again."

"What? Why would they think that?"

"Because for them when people leave Sicily, they don't come back. Life in America means forgetting home." I could hear the distress in his voice.

"That doesn't make sense. You can fly to Sicily anytime you want." By now I had taken off my black work T-shirt and was standing in my bra looking out the back window onto the terraces of the apartment on 91st Street, not caring if anyone saw me. "You have an uncle in Buffalo, and you're telling me he *never* goes back to Sicily?"

"Maybe once every few years. But his life is in America, his family. Sicily is his *past*. It's a place you visit, not a place you stay."

We had different understandings of mobility. I had been getting onto planes since I was ten years old. However, Saro had taken his first big trip when he had traveled to the United States on a ship—an actual transatlantic ocean liner named SS *Michelangelo*. It had taken three weeks of nights spent in a third-class cabin. He had taken his first flight when his family returned to Sicily. And although he had come to visit me in the States several times, he seemed to be suggesting now that traveling back to Sicily was somehow different, if not physically, then emotionally.

I pressed on. "Fine, then. Just promise them that you will visit. Done."

"It's not that easy. I'm not going to go there until I can take you. And that's a long way off. Who knows when that will be?"

"Wait, what do you mean?" This was the first time he was saying what had until then remained unspoken. In the two years we'd been together, we had never talked about my visiting his parents. We had been so busy just trying to keep a long-distance relationship going—buying tickets to and from the United States and Italy—that the thought of going to Sicily had never fully entered my mind.

"I mean, I keep my personal life separate from my parents. I learned that with Valentina."

Valentina was his ex-girlfriend. They'd dated for five years before she had become a Buddhist and moved her things out while he was at work. Valentina was code for "failed relationship."

"What exactly did you 'learn' with Valentina?"

"That my parents don't approve of mixed-cultural relationships. Can we talk about this later, like when I'm there?" He was ready to be done.

"Wait! What are you talking about?" By now I had taken off my work jeans, put on sweats, and was sitting on the couch about to open a bottle of wine. "Valentina was Italian!"

"No, she was from Sardinia."

"Sardinia is a part of Italy."

"A part *from* Italy. An island *away from* Italy. Being Sardinian is different from being Italian and definitely different from being Sicilian. My parents didn't approve and didn't get along with her. When I took her there for a visit, she hated it and my father told my mother that our relationship would never work. Tembi, this isn't important." He had gone too far into a conversation that should never have happened on the phone with an ocean between us. "I need to go, really."

"Okay, so that was then. What does that have to do with you telling them you are moving here?" I knew what it meant, but I wanted him to say it.

"They will think they have failed me as parents. I'm abandoning them, not marrying an Italian or a Sicilian. But I love you. That's all that matters. And right now, I need to swing by Acqua al 2 before I leave."

"You *need* to handle this, Saro. That's what you need to do. And I love you, too."

The whole situation left me feeling a little more aware of the deep fractures that must have existed in their relationship. And the whole Valentina thing felt insane. Like saying someone from Louisiana couldn't have a successful relationship with someone from New Jersey. I was getting hot under the collar trying to process all this. I left the couch and poured myself another hefty glass of the kind of wine that can be found in a corner liquor store for under ten dollars. Despite trying to push Saro's parents to the margins of my mind, inside I felt a weird mixture of confusion, frustration, and anger at the mountain people I had never met. Furthermore, they seemed to paralyze my perfectly capable man with indecision about whether to even talk to them about the most important aspects of his life. And if what he said was true about his parents' reaction to a girlfriend from a different island in the Mediterranean, what the hell would they think of an American black girl from Texas?

On a crisp afternoon in late November, Saro arrived at our front door after tackling five flights of stairs with all of his luggage from Italy. I had spent the whole day in an excited mania—cleaning, stocking the fridge, rearranging new throw pillows from Pottery Barn on the white shabby chic couch I had purchased with my cash tips from the bar. I had even bought his Italian newspaper and placed it on the kitchen counter. I wanted the place to be perfect and for him to feel at home as soon as he walked through the door. I imagined that we'd make love and make our way across Broadway for a late-night snack, then walk back home via West End Avenue.

The first thing he said when he crossed the threshold was "We did it. I'm here."

I jumped on him, tying my legs around his waist, refusing to let go. I couldn't believe the reality of the moment. He held me for a while, and then I gave him a tour of all five hundred square feet of our new home. He loved the exposed brick wall best of all.

"After we settle in, I'll make us some pasta and let my parents know I made it."

"What did they say when you told them?" I asked, trying to be casual and nonjudgmental.

"Not much. They aren't very talkative. My father said nothing. My mother sighed and said, 'Take care of yourself.'"

"That's it?" I tried not to betray my feelings about their less-than-supportive response as I began to help him unpack a few of his clothes. Still, I was unable to push back even as I felt a growing apprehension and distrust for people who could wall off parts of themselves. People like that seemed destined to inflict a world of hurt on themselves or others.

It didn't take long to finish unpacking. Saro's wardrobe was minimalist compared to mine of many colors, shoes of every heel height known to womankind. When we were done and he had put his last T-shirt away, I handed him the phone to call his parents. His younger sister, Franca, who was recently married and pregnant with her second child, answered.

"Tell them I arrived," I heard Saro say in Italian. Then they talked for a few more minutes in Sicilian. Unsure if what I was hearing was a dialect of Italian or a language unto itself, either way I didn't know or understand a word of it. Hearing just one side of the conversation, it was hard to tell if Saro's parents were home or not, harder still to gauge how the call home was settling with him. When he hung up, he just smiled and headed into the kitchen. As much as I wanted to launch into a full inquiry, I chose to let it be.

He was visibly tired. It was our first night in a new city, starting our new lives. All I wanted was to make love, eat, and perhaps take an evening stroll along the Hudson. In that precise moment, I was more than willing to let his parents remain at the margins of the dream life that was just coming into fruition.

Saro mixed fresh pasta dough delicately by hand in that postage stamp–sized kitchen. I came up behind him, looked over his shoulder, and said, "I think we should get married." In the three days since he had arrived, that was all I could think about. We had talked about it generally for months, but now that we were living together the desire had new urgency.

He didn't look up. "Sure, of course."

My asking him to marry me while he was making pasta just seemed the most natural and logical thing to do.

"We need it for the INS. You need to have permanent resident status so you can work. We can go down to City Hall."

He laid the dough out on a cutting board and sliced into it, making ten-inch-long strips and then rolling them over into long thin tubes.

"Of course, let's do it, *amore*." And he reached over and kissed me. It was the kind of kiss that was both simple and affirmative. Half an hour later, we ate while looking out onto the terrace and back sides of the brownstones of 91st Street. We agreed we'd tell no one of our marriage plan. A wedding would come later. For now, this moment was just about us. We chose my close college friend Susan to be our witness. Susan was good with discretion and anything romantic. She worked at the World Trade Center, near City Hall in lower Manhattan. A quick call, and she agreed to meet us on her lunch break and be our witness.

We applied for a license and bought rings in the West Village. They were simple silver bands—two for twenty dollars from a vendor who sold incenses, roach clips, and I LOVE THE BIG APPLE T-shirts. We put the rings on and then walked around the corner to get a cappuccino at Caffè dell' Artista on Greenwich Avenue. I loved that café, with its mismatched antique tables, bohemian lamps, and deep couches throughout. But my favorite thing about the café was the custom of patrons leaving an aspirational message, confession, desire, or literary quotes in the drawers of the desktops and tables throughout the café. Sometimes there were whole love letters written years earlier. That day I left my own message: "I want to spend my life in love and companionship."

When we finally stood in the small government office with the justice of the peace at a podium and a sliver of a view of the East River through a small window, I was giddy in a white floral blouse and black pleated pants. Saro had his Italian newspaper in hand. Susan, always one to wear her emotions on her sleeve, stood behind us in tears. I held Saro's hand and couldn't believe the clipped speed at which the county clerk married folks. In less than five minutes, we were husband and wife, and neither of our families knew. It was just what we wanted.

The sun was bright as we left the dark recesses of City Hall. We figured the best way to celebrate was with a slice of pizza and a slow walk back uptown. Traversing Manhattan as newly married people would happen only once. We took the scenic route, stopping in Chelsea, crossing Times Square, and then passing Lincoln Center before making our way back to the apartment on 92nd Street. We stopped and bought cheese at Zabar's. That night we had pecorino grated over more of Saro's homemade pasta. I poured wine, and we toasted each other. My life felt rich with possibility. I had the man of my dreams at my side and the sense the career I had always dreamed of was within arm's reach. I was in the pulse of magic.

"You've got to tell them," I said to Saro as we went for a late-morning jog around the Hollywood Reservoir, a glorified municipal pond perched on a swanky hill among celebrity compounds and eucalyptus trees. Our time together in New York had turned out to be short lived. After I landed a minor recurring role on a soap opera, my first real TV credit, I had immediately gotten an agent, who told me I needed to come to Los Angeles as soon as possible. We had no furniture or jobs but plenty of aspiration. I booked my first audition and immediately I told Saro, "I think I could get used to this."

The years since we'd been in L.A. had flown by in a clipped pace of auditions, scripts, rejections, and figuring out where to get the best Italian coffee. We didn't know many people yet, and the sheer expanse of the city was mind-numbing. But we had the distraction of planning our official wedding, which would take us back to Florence to exchange nuptials in front of friends and family.

In the nearly five years that Saro and I had been together, I had barely even so much as exchanged hellos with his parents over the phone. Still, it was a surprise for me when I learned that Saro had yet to tell his parents that we were getting married (again), this time in Italy.

The invitations had been ordered in English and Italian. "We request the honor of your presence at the marriage of . . ." Saro had scored a rather grande dame of a sapphire ring with facets so blue it was audacious enough to make the Mediterranean go green with envy. It was a five-carat Ceylon royal blue oval flanked by six round-cut diamonds in an antique setting of 18-karat white and yellow gold. I knew that ring would take me a lifetime to grow into. Everything was coming together.

"I know, I know," he continued the conversation. He struggled for breath, him the tortoise to my hare. "Slow down!"

"So when?" I picked up the conversation in the confines of our tiny Toyota as I coasted down the winding Hollywood Hills and Saro searched the floorboards for a stray bottle of water. Any mention of his parents reminded him of their relationship, fraught with disappointment, worry, and fear. Those had been fracture points long before he had fallen in love with me.

"Not on the phone. I have to do this *my* way," he said, flushed with growing anger by the time he turned the key to our apartment on Kenmore Avenue in Los Feliz.

"Saro, you are not leaving this apartment until you sit down and write the letter," I said, angling past him to be the first to get into the shower and putting in my final two cents' worth.

Exactly five drafts, three days, and two nights of painful insomnia later, he had a letter ready to send. It read (in Italian):

Dearest Mamma and Papa,

I had hoped to not have to share this news with you in a letter, but there is no way I can say this in person. I am getting married. I love Tembi, and we will spend the rest of our lives together. Our wedding will be in Florence this summer on July 26. I hope you will choose to come. I welcome your presence.

Your son,
Saro

I mailed the letter, and then we waited.

When the response came from Sicily two weeks later, it was decisive and delivered in a three-minute crackly phone call. His father, Giuseppe, said, "*Non ho più figlio*—I have no son." Saro was devastated. Watching him retreat inward was painful, like wanting to soothe a wounded animal but having no means to do so. I tried to cheer him up, but I was crushed under the weight of my own free-floating disappointment and disillusionment. I had never seen this coming.

If mistrust had a minion, Saro's father was its most loyal one. That much I had gathered from the bits and pieces Saro had reluctantly offered up over the years. I knew, for example, that Giuseppe hadn't spoken to his own brother-in-law for nearly twenty years because of a joke—he hadn't liked the punch line. I also knew he raised garlic and fermented his own wine; he had flat feet and knobby knees; he played cards, not dominoes, but never for money. Money he kept in a tight wad, swaddled in plastic and stuffed between the slats under his mattress. Rarely in the bank. He trusted the post office more than the bank because the postman lived in his town; he knew where to find him. The banker was from one town over. Basically, Giuseppe trusted no one born outside the entrance and exit of his nearly forgotten mountain town. That included me.

I didn't think their estrangement could get any worse, but now he was cutting Saro out of his life and using me as the scalpel. A potential no-show at the wedding I could handle, but casting a son out of his life was beyond my wildest imaginings. I suspected the first time I would meet my in-laws would be at someone's funeral.

"But what about your sister? Will she come?" His silence told me everything. Not waiting to court any more disappointment, I said, "Well, I'm sending them an invitation anyway." I had had fifty shimmering, ocher-embossed invitations specially printed in Italian for friends in Florence and in the hope that, even though we weren't exactly close, someone from his family would come. I'd be damned if I wasn't going to send them.

"Tembi, I told you. They will not come. My father is the head of the family. He conditions everyone to his wishes. My sister won't come out of respect for him."

"Saro, please with the 'respect.' Enough, already. What am I in, a *Godfather* movie?"

His mouth curled into a smile as he squeezed lemon juice onto a plate of fennel, sliced paper thin atop a bed of parmigiano and arugula. He was trying to feed me out of a fight.

"Look, my father thinks he will be gossiped about, even mocked. He thinks all Americans divorce. And in his mind, I am marrying 'down.' "

"Marrying down? Please! I've got news for him. Growing garlic isn't exactly highbrow." I broke a baguette in two with my bare hands.

"I know. I know." With that he handed me the plate and gave me a kiss, which was intended to remind me I was marrying *him*, after all, not his family.

"Well, they are getting an invitation. Let them deal with the consequences of their actions," I said as I hoisted a forkful of aromatic, citrus-sweetened fennel into my mouth and turned my attention to how I was going to break the news about Saro's parents to my family.

I come from a long line of progressive, barrier-breaking Texas black folks. At the top of the list is my great-great-grandfather Roebuck Mark, who was brazen enough to start his own post office/feed store for newly freed slaves in the backwoods of rural East Texas. He fended off robbery and threats of lynching and is said to have trained his horse to travel alone, in the dark of night, back to his homestead so that he could return undetected on foot through the backwoods, avoiding Klansmen and small-time robbers. After Roebuck, there were a president of a historically black college, a mayor, one of the first black colonels in the US Army, an uncle with a university library named after him, and my great-aunt Altha of Coldspring, Texas (population 649). Among her claims to greatness were not only the prizewinning tomatoes she grew every summer but the fact that she had had the balls-out audacity to marry the town's only (and very Irish) doctor, "Doc," in 1962. Altha and Doc defied Jim Crow by setting up shop in a one-story redbrick ranch house across the street from the Coldspring jailhouse and hanging rafters. Their presence is said to have ensured that not another Negro was hung outside the jail, because "Doc" was revered in town.

Then there are my mother and father, activists. Those are the people I come from.

So when I made the call to my parents, long divorced but still friendly, to say that Saro's family would not be attending the wedding for reasons they could probably imagine, I hoped they wouldn't turn their backs on a long family history of rising above less-than-ideal circumstances. And I hoped that whatever opinions they had about what I was about to say, they would have the good sense to keep them to themselves. My dad had loved Saro since they had met in Florence. My mother had sat next to him at my college graduation. He'd made pasta alongside my dad's barbecue at my graduation after-party. He and my mother shared an appreciation of *Siddhartha*. They adored his sense of humor, his generosity, and, undoubtedly, the way he loved me. Still, I dialed their numbers with a pit in my stomach. I couldn't take any more drama. It was my dad who finally said, "Well, his family will be missed, but we are going to have a damn good time in Italy."

They did not disappoint. It was exactly the response I needed.

Saro had come to understand that our wedding was about celebrating with my family, if not with his. Having the wedding in Italy left the door open in the event that his father changed his mind. Where, exactly, Saro put his feeling of loss during those days, I don't know. It was off limits; he wouldn't talk about it. It pained me, but I respected his process. I chose to love him through what I didn't understand. He kept saying "You don't know them." And he was right. I had, in fact, seen only one picture of them. They were standing outside their house in Sicily. In the photo, Saro's father appears to have just come back from working the land, standing in a window opening in the front door. He is wearing a *coppola* (the traditional Sicilian cap), and his hands are still dirty from the day's work. Saro's mother is standing just in front of him on the sidewalk in the foreground. She is wearing an apron and stands bent as the sun shines down on them. The wind is blowing. It must be just before lunch. She looks just like Saro, and I kind of love her for that. In her hands is a broom, and she is frozen midmotion in the act of sweeping. The tableau is striking and full of the intimacy of domestic life, marriage. When I looked at that picture and thought of the in-laws I might never know, it hurt.

When we were planning our wedding, I worked for months disabusing Saro of the fear that our celebration would be like something out of *The Godfather*. He imagined ill-fitting suits, a priest, and a hot church, a gaunt Christ hanging crucified above the whole ordeal. In short, he imagined every Italian church wedding he had ever seen. It was an image of a marriage ceremony that I knew nothing about.

I had to tell him that what he was dreading was an impossible scene, one in which I would never cast myself. I had to remind him that I was not Catholic and that my formerly atheist, onetime Communist parents had made sure I was never baptized. So a church wedding in Italy was conveniently out of the question.

Still, his reticence about the whole affair bordered on near-corrosive fear. If he got past his images of his walk down the aisle—the prayers and the spectacle—his mind wandered to the reception. Friends and my family crowded into some hotel restaurant and dining on average food, that, if his family actually did come, guests would talk about for years to come. What they liked, what they didn't like, the portion sizes, who had gotten indigestion, who had drunk too much. He didn't want a wedding that, at the end of the day, was associated with gossip, sweaty armpits, and family who clung together at one table, fearful of the people on the other side of the room. Somewhere inside he hoped he'd be able to escape the whole affair or at least make it as low key as possible.

Except that I was a girl from Texas who had dreamed of being an actress and had fallen in love with an Italian chef she had met on a street corner. Having a summer wedding on my birthday in an Italian villa that stood next door to the one owned by the Ferragamo family seemed the most logical thing in the world. I was in magic-making mode. When I made up my mind about anything in this state, there was no stopping me.

"It could be fun. Trust me."

I found our wedding venue, Villa di Maiano, in the back of a magazine. A palatial fifteenth-century villa with colossal Tuscan columns and sprawling groves of lemon and olive trees in the hills above Florence. It was a thing of Italian Renaissance fairy tales. The main house had in fact been used in a scene from the film *A Room with a View*. It was owned by a woman whom we called "The Duchess," the title she inserted when introducing herself. Saro was the first to speak to her by phone. It was for the best. Even with some fluency, I still got nervous speaking Italian on the phone, in the absence of eye contact and gestures. Plus it was expensive to call overseas and I didn't want to risk running up unnecessary minutes repeating myself for clarity, searching for some elusive verb that refused to leave the tip of my tongue. So it fell on Saro to make the first round of calls and set up our appointment with The Duchess on our upcoming trip to Florence.

His only resistance to our plan was the very real reality of his slight Sicilian accent. It could thwart all our plans. At the time, the social hierarchy in Italy relegated Sicilians to second-class status when compared to the perceived cultural superiority of their northern countrymen. When dealing with Florentines, Sicilians were looked at as barely a rung above "North Africans," which was cultural code, a way of dismissing them as both non-Italian and non-European. It was intracultural discrimination on display, something with which Saro and I were familiar. Saro had, in fact, been discriminated against so often trying to find housing when he had arrived in Florence as a university student a decade earlier that he had paid all cash up front for a year just to be able to lay his head on a pillow at night in the city of the David and the Medici. He hated the Florentine bourgeoisie.

In April, we flew to Florence to finalize our plans, and we met The Duchess, *La Duchessa*, in person. She suffered the unique, and very European, plight of having the trappings of nobility (name, villa, and perhaps a chest of jewels somewhere) without the cash. She was forty-five, slim, very textbook Florentine in a cashmere twin set and Gucci loafers, auburn dye job, and tanned skin. She looked like she had just come from a weekend getaway on the island of Elba. Her bone structure was strong, chiseled. She resembled the tennis star Martina Navratilova but walked like Sophia Loren.

At the first sight of the upper garden with its groves of lemon and olive trees and its breathtaking view of Florence's duomo in the valley below, I was close to tears. Its two-story stone-walled Tapestry Room with wraparound interior balcony made me gasp. Thank goodness we had negotiated the price beforehand, or else she could have taken me to the cleaners.

Saro, on the other hand, saw it differently. He could talk himself into a stupor about the petit bourgeois class and recount his university days as a strident Leninist. He said his friends would deride his choice for the capitalistic spectacle of it all. That always made me laugh. I reminded him that one of his best men, Antonio number two, drove a Lotus and also had a Maserati. So much for anticapitalistic ideals. Sometimes it struck me that I was marrying some younger, artistic Italian version of my father, who had spent his youthful days as an activist. The contradictions between our points of view had me in stitches, and I was quick to remind Saro that my life's aspirations were decidedly bourgeois when seen through his eyes. I wanted kids, a second house, if possible, a career in the arts, and great vacations with a view of the sea. I was a suburban black girl from Texas whose parents had picked cotton for their grandparents, who had scratched against systemic oppression to become educated and generous citizens along the dirt roads lining miles of pine thicket. I was now in Italy. This was a moment my ancestors could not have imagined. It was my "look how far we've come" moment. I was going to enjoy it.

However, the second reason Saro drifted off to the periphery of the garden as I talked details with *La Duchessa* was more subtle and reflective of our internal differences. Saro was fundamentally understated to the exact degree that I liked to stand out. He was comfortable under the radar in direct opposition to my need to be out front, often while I was wearing a sundress and heels. He was the ground to my flight. The contrast suited us well as a couple. But it also made him nervous. No one among his family or friends had ever attempted to pay an aristocrat to throw a party in her house. He had no template for what I was attempting to pull off.

On that fragrant April day, perched above the valley in which sat one of Europe's most revered and storied cities, he quietly and politely deferred to me. We would have a wedding in The Duchess's home. He calmed his nerves by telling himself we were already married. The idea that our marriage was already done allowed him to distance himself from the stark reality that his wedding was happening in Italy and his parents wouldn't be there.

My boisterous black American clan descended on Florence with a sugar high of excitement, as if they were tasting homemade buttercream icing melting on an oven-warm cake on my grandmother's back porch back in East Texas. The combination of Italy, food, nuptials, and fashion thrilled them. They were prepared to shop Ferragamo and Gucci with frightening determination. It was the late nineties, after all. The dollar went far against the then Italian lira.

As I was dressing myself in my wedding gown in a room just off the *gran salotto* of Villa di Maiano in Fiesole, my sister kept coming back to report on the goings-on in the other side of the villa. Saro and the best men were readying themselves. He had been on edge as our trip to Italy approached and the festivities were coming into focus. Once we got to Florence, his anxiety had really taken flight.

To make matters worse, he had a persistent and nagging tooth-ache that, just two days prior to the ceremony, had landed him in the hospital. He had an abscessed molar and required immediate emergency oral surgery. As a result, on the morning of our wedding he was on painkillers and sporting a swollen left jaw.

Light filtered through the six-foot-high windows that looked out onto the garden, and I was full of anticipation and delight that it was all really happening. I could see the chairs that had been set up. A single bouquet of flowers sat on the end of each aisle. There were going to be about fifty guests in total: twenty Italians, all friends from Florence, and thirty or so Americans. My sister alternated between giving me the blow-by-blow of events just outside the room where I was getting ready and taking pictures of me and my mom, who was responsible for helping get me into my dress. All I could think of was how Saro and I were pulling off something magical and unprecedented for both of us. Nothing in either of our personal histories would have lead us to believe that we should or even could be here, in Fiesole, among breathtaking stone and marble. Yet there we were, in a living film set, about to get married.

That it was also my twenty-fifth birthday made the day somehow more transcendent. My sister had gone to great pains to get me a white gardenia to wear above my left ear, à la Billie Holiday. It was a nod to the voice that had kept me company as a new exchange student cleaning toilets in the bar where I would first get to know the man I was about to marry. My grandmother had gifted me delicate antique rhinestone shoe clips, a throwback to her time in East Texas attending education and holiday banquets. She had used them for years as a way to dress up her regular shoes and make them seem "new and sparkly" for a special occasion. She had never had money for luxury. Wearing her shoe clips as "something borrowed" was the most special part of everything I wore that day. And I had my sapphire blue engagement ring (something blue) and my discounted dress by an Ethiopian designer, Amsale Aberra, that I had found for a third of the price when a swanky Beverly Hills department store was going out of business (something new).

My dad appeared in the anteroom of the villa's dressing room. He stood beaming in an earth-tone linen suit and cowboy boots. Dad had only two kinds of shoes: cowboy boots and running shoes.

"You ready to do this? Ain't no time like the present to start your life," he said. My father was full of self-coined truisms, folksy East Texas speak that he was constantly refining. "I'm ready to walk my daughter down the aisle in Italy, twenty-five years to the day that I first laid eyes on you, girl." He offered me a big smile that radiated love and pride.

"Dad, please. You gonna talk the whole time we walk down the aisle?"

"I might."

"Okay, then, let's get started." I took him by the arm and held on tight. In pictures from that moment, my eye still travels to the center of the frame, where the folds of linen in the crook of his arm tell the tale of my nerves. I am practically squeezing with all my might.

Aubrey sang the soul classic "Flesh of My Flesh," a capella as I walked down the aisle.

After we said "I do" and kissed, we turned to jump the broom, an African American wedding ritual dating back to slavery. Jumping in unison signals the leap into matrimony. I hoisted my dress with one hand and held Saro's hand with the other. When we landed, I noticed four faces on my walk back down the aisle that I had not seen earlier. It took a second for it all to register. The woman had a face that was almost a replica of Saro's mother's face. There was a man seated next to her. I glanced at Saro and saw a tender look of recognition on his face. They were his aunt Rosa, his mother's sister, and her husband, Uncle Peppe. They had come from Switzerland with their two kids. I grabbed Saro's hand even tighter.

Unbeknown to us, they had driven down using the address on the invitation I had sent them. They had told no one they were coming, not Saro's mother, not Saro's father. To do so would have been a family betrayal. Still, there they were. Saro was speechless, moved to tears by their gesture. And for the first time, I sensed what we had missed in not having his parents there. My heart opened wide.

After a round of pictures was taken, including a group photo in the center of the garden with our small eclectic tribe of family and friends, the aging yet stunning villa our backdrop, we went inside to have a five-course dinner among centuries-old tapestries.

Canopied under the moonlight of a summer Tuscan sky, my family had one hell of a good time. They danced the Harlem Shuffle on the garden terrace and cast laughter out into the valley of Florence's mesmerizing night lights. Back at the hotel, telegrams from Sicily waited for us from various relatives to whom I had sent invitations. Instead of dancing the night away with his sister, uncles, aunts, and cousins, we had received messages on telefax paper that said: "*Rammaricati per non poter essere presenti alla ceremonia. Vi auguriamo una serena e lunga vita matrimoniale.*—We regret we can't be present at the ceremony. We wish you a serene and long married life." There was nothing from his parents.

I read those telegrams privately the next morning, feeling freshly wronged and quietly angry. His family had forsaken him. In the afterglow of the magic of the night before, I felt so many mixed emotions. It was all achingly bittersweet. I began to wonder if I would ever meet the people who had missed one of the most important moments in their son's life because of me—and if I could ever forgive them for breaking not my heart but Saro's.

I put the telegrams on top of the hotel dresser in plain view, in case Saro wanted to read them later, alone. Then I looked out the window of our hotel room onto the Ponte Vecchio and the Arno River flowing gently beneath its arches. I wrestled with the truth of the moment: in creating one family, Saro had lost another.

Part Two

FIRST
SUMMER

Nun si po' aviri la carni senz' ossu.
You can't have meat without the bone.
—*Sicilian proverb*

ISLAND OF STONE

"*Allacciarsi la cintura di sicurezza.*" At first I didn't understand the flight attendant's words over the loudspeaker. They were disparate pieces of a jigsaw puzzle I couldn't quite put together. Then a flight attendant in the aisle next to me said it in English: "Fasten your seat belt," pointing to my seat belt. As we prepared to land in Sicily, everything needed translation, even a language I had spoken for twenty years.

From the airplane window, I was confronted with two contrasting visions: a lush, sapphire blue sea below me and a mountain of barren stone straight ahead. Water and stone. Fluidity and impenetrability. Nothing in between but me, being flown through the air, descending into a piece of stone confetti in the middle of the Mediterranean, the island of Saro's incarnation.

All I could think about was his ashes in a duffel bag in the overhead bin and how I had promised his mom, a week after his death, that I would bring his ashes to her. But now I had a sinking feeling in my stomach. *How the hell am I going to get through the next month?* It wasn't enough to be a widow in my own home, in my own language, sleeping each night in the bed I had shared with Saro. Instead, I had taken my grief on the road because I had promised to do so. I was hurling myself through space in the general direction of a mountain of more unknowns, more tenuousness, more feelings that had no end. Grief, Sicilian style. I was taking up residence for the next month in a home where *il lutto*—mourning—hung on the front door like a shroud.

Suddenly my decision seemed like a bad choice. How was I going to keep it together in a place where everything, including the arc of the sun, was different? There was no part of me that could have chosen to leave well enough alone. I could not have chosen the easier way, the way that didn't lead to concentric circles of grief. I feared I was asking so much of myself, testing my mettle too soon. Saro had been dead just four months.

Zoela was deep in sleep on my lap, her favorite stuffed panda under her arm. Her eyelids fluttered as I caressed her hair. We had crossed nine time zones, and she had closed her eyes for only this last leg of the trip.

In a matter of minutes, we would deplane and travel an hour and a half's drive east—past the mountain of stone that lay ahead—to a woman, a mother, and a town waiting for my return. His return. Saro was coming back to rest alongside his father, Giuseppe—the man who had once rejected his own son because of me. I was returning with Saro's daughter, the only person left carrying his name.

The plane touched ground with three gentle bumps, and I held Zoela closer, careful not to wake her just yet. She was the little girl with eyes like chestnuts and a face Saro adored. She was the one who had brought us all even deeper reconciliation and love. She was the reason Saro had been willing to struggle each year, against what was medically convenient, to return to Sicily. Being with his daughter in his homeland healed his heart as much as, if not more than, the chemotherapy healed his body. Seeing his daughter sitting at his mother's table brought color back to his face; laughter spilled from him effortlessly. He had carved out timeless experiences in the face of the little time that was left him. He had given her memories of him dancing with her at the edge of the Mediterranean. Part of me hoped like hell I could keep giving her Sicilian summers, beautiful memories of time with his family. But I questioned the physical and emotional toll it might take at a time when I was still trying to find my bearings and help her find hers.

I was acutely aware that I was traveling with a seven-year-old child who still grieved so hard that her body shook at night until she fell asleep. A child who pushed dinner away because she wanted to wait for her dad. A child who refused even to speak to her Italian grandmother on the phone because the sound of her voice reminded her of her dad. My choice to come here meant that I'd have to parent her and her mercurial grief almost seven thousand miles away from home. My grief and love demanded all the strength I had and then asked for more.

My parents had questioned the wisdom of my going to Italy, especially alone with Zoela. I knew we had to do this, just the two of us. Despite my father and stepmother's offer to come with us, I knew we had to do this without the distraction and pressure of my family trying to take care of me. Without my trying to translate among Sicilian, Italian, and English. And I didn't want to have to take care of them in a foreign place. They'd never been there, and this trip was not the time for that kind of first. Plus I didn't want my mother-in-law having the burden of additional guests. Nonna and I needed alone time to grieve together and get to know each other. We had to begin at an ending and make a new beginning.

Still, my parents worried. In the four months since Saro had died, I was still raw with grief. My dad, ever the lawyer and a practitioner of Texas-sized common sense, cross-examined me with basic questions: Can you change your ticket if you want to come home early? My stepmother took a different tactic: What can you take to bring you comfort? Be sure you just rest. Don't do anything you don't feel like doing. My mother offered to create a care package for Saro's mom. Underneath it all, I wondered if my family of origin also held the tiniest traces of resentment about the way the Sicilians had once rejected their daughter.

Everyone could see the physical toll grief had taken on me. Along with his spirit and the comfort of Saro's body, gone were his pastas and soups. I had dropped fifteen pounds while Saro was hospitalized. Those closest to me reminded me to hydrate, eat, sleep. I assured them I was fine, but the truth was that I needed Ativan to get through the car pool lane at Zoela's school.

I still woke up each morning in tears. Saro's absence in the bed beside me gutted me before my feet touched the ground. I pushed through the days by sheer will, the primal pull of motherhood, and a sense that if I collapsed completely I might never stand up again. At night, I prayed that Saro would come to me in dreams. I wanted to make love to him. I wanted to see him. I longed for his voice, his smile. I craved his smell. When my grief became manic, I focused on the practical, such as doing feverish calculations on scraps of paper of how long Saro's modest insurance policy could last with private school, two therapists, medical debt, and the inherent uncertainty of my work.

I also started writing letters to him, one-sided conversations: *Saro, my sweet, what will we do with all this loss? Help me put one foot in front of the other. Show me how to be a family of two, a solo parent, now that you are gone.*

But I had also felt a sense of urgency take hold in the months since I had called Nonna to say I'd be coming to Sicily. I had a restless, inarticulate desire that Zoela know home and family as something even greater than death. After all we had gone through to finally become family, life would seem unbearably cruel if it just snatched that away. As much as I wanted this for Zoela, I needed to know it for myself, too. I wanted to test its permanence, the idea that family is about whom you choose and how you love. I needed to prove it to myself and Zoela. I wondered if the connections for which I had struggled so hard, the family I had struggled to make, had the durability of love.

Still, as we taxied to the jetway, for a brief moment I seriously contemplated collecting my bags and boarding a plane back to L.A. Because to continue moving ahead with Saro's wishes—to both inter and scatter his ashes—would really mean that he was dead. Not just dead in L.A. but dead in Sicily, dead at his mother's house, dead in the room where we had always slept, dead having morning coffee, dead at his mother's table. It felt impossible to bear. Yet I pushed forward in the name of love.

The dry, salt-laden midday July heat confirmed that we were in Sicily. Zoela fell back asleep on my lap, in the back seat of the un-air-conditioned Fiat as Cosimo drove and Franca sat in the passenger seat. Zoela had awakened long enough to run her finger along the baggage carousel, hug her aunt and uncle, and walk to the car. I envied her sleep. I wanted nothing more than to close my eyes and have whatever came next be only a dream.

"*Passami un fazzoletto*—Pass me a tissue," Franca said to Cosimo as he drove. She was otherwise silent and wrestling with carsickness as we headed to Aliminusa, Saro's hometown. We passed the coastal towns that line up eastward from Palermo. We passed the long-ago-shuttered Fiat factory and the new Auchan supermarket. Then we turned off the highway and began our ascent into the foothills, passing a landscape I knew as well as my own back yard.

We curved past the dilapidated Targo Florio car-racing stand, erected in the 1950s for European mountain racing. I watched the smatterings of stone farmhouses that sprang up in wheat fields and small family vineyards. I took in the amber hills that seemed to stitch earth to sky, searching for the familiar sight of sheep grazing at their base. But it was too hot; even the sheep knew when to retreat.

Cosimo passed the time changing radio stations. We tried to catch up on what had transpired since we all had last seen one another in the spring—their first and only visit to L.A., just as Saro was going into hospice. They had left three days before he died, having said their good-byes in that particularly wrought-up way people who live halfway around the world carry the additional suffering of knowing that they will not be there for the final moment of transition, left forever wondering if their good-bye was enough.

"*Come vanno i maiali?*—How are your pigs?" I asked Cosimo. His chickens, pigs, and olive trees were always subjects that urged him toward conversation.

"I killed them for meat this winter," he said with an elongated shrug.

"And work? How is work for you?" I asked, hoping to cover the ride with more small talk, despite the fact that I felt shaky with fatigue and free-floating anxiety. Talking was a strategy to not fall apart, to hold it together for Zoela when she woke, and for whatever was to come when we reached town.

"I lost my spot when I came to Los Angeles in the spring. I am waiting to see if they will need me this summer with all the tourists.

But the city just declared bankruptcy." He always dropped Italian and reverted to Sicilian when it came to discussing politics and its companion, corruption.

I knew he'd had a rough time between working as a traffic cop in Cefalù and farming. Like many Sicilians, he grabbed on to whatever fate threw his way. In his case, it was part-time seasonal work in a recently bankrupt town.

I looked at Zoela's flushed cheeks and cinnamon brown skin as Cosimo drove and talked. I wondered if, in the future, she'd remember any of this. Would she remember the time we had gone to see her grandmother with her father's ashes in a duffel bag at our feet?

La terra è vascia is the way local farmers describe this part of Sicily. Those words, "The earth is low," are both a statement and a parable. They tell a visitor that to work this land, to survive it, to turn seed into harvest, you have to bend low. Very low. You have to labor tirelessly and often without promise. The earth is uneasy in this part of Sicily. It is difficult to cultivate, rocky, and often impervious to the plow. Those who rely on the land to sustain them must submit to backbreaking labor in order to survive. *La terra è vascia* equates labor and love as twin experiences. As we pulled into Aliminusa, I steadied myself, grabbing hold of the handle above the rear passenger door. I knew now that everything that came next was going to be about both labor and love.

The first thing I saw when we turned left on Via Gramsci was a stoic brigade of aging women and widows lined up on a bench along the stone sidewalk. The widows, as is customary, were dressed in all black. Of varying heights and girths, they sat in front of Saro's childhood home waiting for us. They were prepared for mourning.

They had done this before, many times—for themselves, for family, for neighbors, perhaps since the dawn of time. Sicilians were accustomed to welcoming home the dead.

When we had passed the final pizzeria in the neighboring town of Cerda, Cosimo had phoned ahead, as he always did. It was an act of consideration so that my mother-in-law, Croce, a beloved woman whose given name means "cross," as in the cross on which Jesus was crucified, would not have to sit on the bench outside her home too long in the midday heat, waiting. Her name is weighty like her character, an unquestionably biblical name for a woman of uncommon reputation and affection in a town where betrayals and transgressions can follow you for generations.

The women of Via Gramsci—Saro's mother, her first cousin, another third cousin through marriage, and neighbors—always emerged from their homes to greet us when we arrived. They insisted on being there to witness Saro's homecoming.

As we made our way up the street, Cosimo deftly maneuvered his Fiat around a tractor parked partially on the sidewalk in the middle of the steep one-way street. He passed two more shuttered houses and brought the car to a halt in front of Nonna's narrow two-story house nestled halfway up the street before it dead-ends. We were there. And so were the women.

Before I could wake Zoela and lift her head from my lap, the door was flung open. My mother-in-law's arms reached in.

"*Sei arrivata*—You have arrived."

In a flash, her small but strong seventy-nine-year-old hands were on my shoulders. I was still emerging from the car when her cheeks came flesh-to-flesh with mine. At their plushness, I wilted into a deeper realm of loss. Again, time suspended. We each took a moment to linger, or an eternity. Time was again elastic. We stood there, disbelieving that this, the moment we had known for years might come, was happening.

Then she released me and reached past me back into the car for Zoela, her beloved grandchild from her only son.

"*Amore mio. Amore mio.*—My love. My love." Her voice trembled. She raised a tissue to her damp eyes. She helped Zoela from the car and took her in her bosom. Zoela was waking up exhausted, hot, disoriented. In her grandmother's embrace and so far from home, she began to cry and reach for me.

"*È stanchissima*—She's very tired," I said in Zoela's defense, worried that Nonna would be offended. Then the chorus of mothers, mourners, and grandmothers surrounding the car echoed in agreement. "*È stanchissima, certo.*"

I suspected that Saro's mom might have thought Zoela was crying because of her since they hadn't spoken in months. Nonna had never, in all her grief, forced me to bring Zoela to the phone. Instead, she just asked every day when we spoke, "*Come sta la bambina?*— How is the child?"

Now Nonna got to the reason we were all standing outside, encircling a car in the middle of the day: "*Dov'è?*—Where is he?"

She wanted the ashes. She wanted her son.

I reached into the car, lifted the bag from the floorboard, and gave it to her. Her face went from stoicism to the pallor of paper at the sight of my carry-on. The child she had birthed, reared, fed, and loved was inside.

Emanuela, her first cousin who lives across the street, held Nonna up. "*Entrate, entrate*—Enter, enter." She shuffled her toward her front door, away from the street scene, with the efficiency of a first responder. She moved to shelter her from the sun. Then the chorus of widows broke their circle around the car and in unison ushered Zoela and me inside, moving us all as one mournful herd.

As the widows of Via Gramsci ushered Zoela and me into Nonna's home, I suddenly felt as though I had made a big mistake. Surrounded by a cluster of aging widows, I felt overwhelmed and suffocated, as though there might suddenly not be enough oxygen for myself or Zoela. I reached for my purse. In it I had enough Ativan for one pill a day for thirty days. I worried that that would not be enough.

The entrance of Nonna's house was adorned with traditional hand-sewn lace curtains and shutters on a fading stone facade. You stepped through it and landed directly in the living room, straight from the street to the living quarters. Her home, like all the others on the street, had originally been an animal stall. It had been built more than a century ago to keep pigs, a mule, chickens, and barrels of olive oil. Families had slept on the wooden floorboards of a loft above their animals. By the time Nonna was married, electricity had arrived in town. By the time Saro was a child, there were running water, a semifinished bathroom, and ceramic floors to make it the home that I had come to know. The space had not been designed with transitions in mind. There is outside, and there is inside. The world of fields, sun, and wind and then, without fanfare, the world of home—a shelter without pretense, just function.

It was dark inside her home, not uncommon for a Sicilian house in summer. To push back against an antagonizing sun and elements of summer—winds that bring the sands of North Africa, a sun so intense it can dry clothes and make open-air tomato paste in an afternoon—the houses in town are shuttered closed during the day. The cooler air created by the combination of stone walls and low light was a relief. But also, the house seemed smaller, hollow, sad. It was emanating loss. The air was ripe with it.

A red candle with Saint Padre Pio painted on its glass burned on a lace centerpiece on the dining room table in the middle of the room. The dining table was now an altar.

Nonna placed the carry-on beside the table and instructed me to take the ashes from the bag. I did so. They were in a special travel box directly from the funeral home in Los Angeles. The box was adorned with a blue silk case that buttoned around it like an envelope. She put Saro's remains on the table next to the candle. The light in the room seemed to grow dimmer as more people arrived, crowding the room and blocking the light entering from the open door. For the first time, I noticed that the couch and chairs had been pushed to the perimeter of the room. They were assembled to encircle the table, which was also not in its usual place. Nonna took a seat closest to the table, closest to Saro. She told me to sit next to her. Zoela folded into my lap. I heard someone at the periphery of the room on a cell phone: "*Chiama il prete. È l'ora.*—Tell the priest it's time."

For the next thirty minutes, the room filled with more people, some staying briefly, others settling in. The most elderly sat in chairs, while the youngest stood on their feet. The doors remained open, with only the lace to protect us from the world beyond our collective grief. I had never witnessed a Sicilian wake. I had only heard about them from Saro. He explained how the dead were laid out in the living room of the home. Saro's cousin Giacchino is the town carpenter and also its coffin maker. The storage unit he uses to store some ten to twelve coffins at a time is next door to Nonna's house. She is often the first in town to know that someone local has died, which is anytime she hears Giacchino open the unit with a skeleton key. He retrieves a coffin and then takes it to the grieving family. The body is placed inside by relatives, and the mourning ritual begins. In the old days, it often lasted all night. At daybreak, the body is carried to the town church for a Mass and then borne through the streets to the cemetery at the edge of town. People emerge in their doorways to watch the funeral procession go by.

As I sat there, I began to realize that not only was I witnessing a Sicilian wake, I was very much in the center of it. Sure, I knew we'd be taking Saro's ashes to the cemetery the next day. But I'd had no way of knowing that so many neighbors and next of kin would descend on Nonna's living room to pay respects, say a prayer, offer condolences to Saro's child and me, his new widow, right away. I had assumed that after a day of international travel, I'd arrive at my mother-in-law's house and be able to rest. I'd sit alone with her. We'd eat, we cry, we'd talk as we had done before. But now a son and husband was dead. Nothing was normal.

Amid all of this, my mother-in-law sat saying the rosary, audible only to herself. And she rocked. Other women, old and young, did the same. They were in a chorus of prayer. More people came in and kissed her on both cheeks. They offered her condolences. She didn't rise. She didn't look up. She never stopped praying. None of them did. Not her cousins, not my sister-in-law, Franca, not the widows and wives of Via Gramsci.

Within a half hour the priest arrived. He, too, began to pray. His prayers meant that the official lament had begun. The wailing, the tears, it all formed a shrill and guttural song of loss that seemed to reach back to the ancient world. Zoela rocked on my lap, half asleep, half aware. My body shook gently. I cried new tears, tears I had never cried in L.A. Tears that could find me only in Sicily. And as the intensity of the lament became almost trancelike, a callout to all the losses of all time, I wanted to fall over. I wanted to lie on the floor. I wanted to howl at the top of my lungs. I wanted to run mad through the street. My husband was dead.

Instead I sat there jet-lagged, holding Zoela and unsure how this mourning ritual worked. Saro and I had never attended a funeral in Sicily. Weddings, yes. Funerals, no. I began to watch the box of ashes on the table closely, as if this had all been a mistake. He couldn't be dead in two places, two realities. My mind told me he might walk down the stairs of his mother's house at any moment, see the scene, and tell me how young Sicilian widows behave. He'd tell me the protocol. In another imagining, he'd come down and ask, "What's all this? Put up your tears. I'm right here." We'd smile and head out for a long walk in the countryside. He'd show me the mulberries in season. But none of that happened.

I pulled Zoela closer, and I grabbed the locket hanging from my neck. In it I had my own connection to Saro. Attica had given me a locket, and in it we had put some of his ashes for me to carry around my neck. It was a sisterly and sacred act.

My therapist had suggested that I take a bit of his ashes and scatter some privately while in Sicily. She knew the trip was causing me anxiety. She suggested that I do something just between Saro and me. After my session with her, I had had a dream about being in an orchard with Saro at my side. The next day, a friend had called to tell me that she, too, had dreamed of Saro. In the dream, they had been eating apricots. I took the confluence of my therapist's suggestion and the dreams and visions to mean that I should scatter some of Saro's ashes under an apricot tree in a place he had once shown me last year. For that reason, I'd had his ashes divided into three separate parcels: one for interment in L.A., one for his mother, and one for my own personal ceremony.

As I sat in my mother-in-law's house listening to Catholic prayers that were also tethered to the Arab and Jewish world, I knew this moment was for Saro's mother, his sister, his neighbors and cousins. This moment was for a town of Sicilians who had lost one of their own. We had had a memorial, a celebration of life, in Los Angeles. This was the funeral my mother-in-law had been waiting to give her son. I drew Zoela closer, feeling overcome as the sounds that emerged from the collection of voices around me spilled out, a heartbreaking chorus of lament that rose to the rafters above.

Just before the first sign of morning light, I awoke upstairs in Saro's parents' matrimonial bed. The faint first light of day filtered through the second-story shutters. I could hear sheep bells in the distance. The herder was moving his sheep to lower ground. Zoela slept at my side.

From downstairs came the sound of the soft, familiar choreography of Nonna in her kitchen. I knew she had been up for a while. She wanted to sit with her son alone in the room where she herself had been born. She needed to do so before burying a part of her own motherhood forever. And she had undoubtedly already made the pasta sauce for our midday meal.

The night before, she had told me we would rise early to head to Mass by 7:00 a.m. We would be at the cemetery by 8:00 a.m., in time to have a private ceremony before the cemetery was open to the townspeople. That last detail, "before it was open," was important, because interring ashes was uncommon here. She didn't want to draw attention. Franca had sought help at the town's city hall to handle all the Italian Consulate's paperwork. It had to be completed to Italy's exacting specifications in order for me to transport and inter his ashes. On my end, I had had numerous conversations and emails with her telling her that I needed an address and tomb number for the final resting place, neither of which she could provide because the cemetery in Aliminusa was situated on a street with no official name at the far edge of town. As is common in much of the rural interior of Sicily, cemeteries dating back to the Greeks and Arabs were placed just outside of a town, often on secondary roads downhill of winds, leading to a dead end. The people who lived there knew where it was, and that was all that mattered. Outsiders weren't buried there. Only an outsider would need a street name.

To make bureaucratic matters more complicated, at the time of Saro's death there had not been a tomb available in which to place his ashes. Construction had halted in the cemetery as a result of economic austerity or perhaps some indirect Mafia influence. The plots that were available were already taken, prebought by well-off families long ago for the generations of dead to come. Saro's family didn't have an empty tomb. They were not the only family in town to find themselves in this predicament. As a result, a de facto practice had arisen: people had begun "lending" a tomb to those families who needed it, the agreement being that, in the future, when a new space became available, the remains would be moved to a new crypt within the cemetery. At least that was how it had been explained to me back in L.A. as I had struggled to make sense of it and get all the travel documentation into order. It felt surreal, exactly the kind of Italian bureaucratic shenanigans that made Italy the punch line of many jokes.

I wanted to have no trouble transporting Saro's ashes into Italy. I was excessively meticulous about that. Perhaps my hypervigilance came from a childhood spent with parents who had taught me how to avoid confrontation with authorities. As an adult, I had faced the reality of being a woman of a certain color and age traveling into Rome. I had often been profiled. I had been pointed out by the carabineri and immigration police on more than one occasion. I fit the ever-changing face of European immigration. I could be a woman from Morocco or Cuba or Ethiopia or Brazil, depending on which stubble-faced official was looking at me and what the authorities had been told was a current threat. Over the years, I had learned to stay close to Saro through the corridors of the baggage claim and at immigration. I had learned to keep my American passport out and visible so that there would be no holdups or delays jeopardizing our connecting flights.

Carrying Saro's ashes with Zoela at my side was not the time to risk even a tiny margin of error. Before the trip, I had had nightmares about a search and seizure, of Saro's ashes being detained or, worse yet, taken from me in front of Zoela all because I had failed the bureaucratic task of crossing all my *T*'s. I would not, under any circumstances, travel with an undocumented box of dust. Besides, Italian law strictly forbade the clandestine transport of human remains. Ashes required their own travel documents.

The whole process had been an epic exercise in Italian clerical madness. Not to mention its costs, the equivalent of three months of private school tuition. I had to have two death certificates (English and Italian), a funeral home certification, travel documents, and birth certificates all translated into Italian and then certified with an *apostille* (a legal certification that makes a document issued in one country valid in another) and then stamped again by the Italian government. Every piece of paper and signature carried a fee and a tax. On more than one occasion, I told myself that if Saro had known how much it would cost me in money and stress to take his ashes to Italy, he would have told me to dump them into the Pacific and be done with it. But that was not what he had said. *Take part of me to Sicily.*

Had he never asked me to inter his ashes in Sicily, I don't know that I would have done it. I might have scattered them on our favorite stretch of beach in Santa Barbara, the exact spot where we had gone so often to lift his spirits during the years of treatment.

Zoela roused gently, stretching her lean frame against me.

"Sweetheart, Mommy's going to church soon and then to the cemetery this morning with Babbo's ashes." It struck me that I was speaking of myself in the third person.

In my heart, I was hoping she wouldn't want to go. I was exhausted from the hours of air travel and the winding car ride to Saro's family home. I didn't think I could handle being an attentive mother while sitting through a Mass. It was well within reason to imagine that I'd have to carry her along the cobblestoned streets through town to the cemetery. She would be tired and overwhelmed. Motherhood has its own demands. That morning bereaved wife and foreign daughter-in-law were the only roles I had in me.

"Can I see them?" she asked wiping sleep from her eyes.

"See what?"

"See the ashes."

That was not a question I had anticipated. I sat up in bed and let my feet touch the marble floor.

"Sweetheart, they are downstairs in the blue box on the table. You've seen them." I began to smell the scent of stove-top espresso emanating from the kitchen below. "Let's get you something to eat." I was punting, my classic parental redirect.

"But I want to see them. I want to see what's inside." She sat up in bed, clear-eyed and determined. The expression on her face told me that tears were waiting at the ready. "I want to see Babbo."

She had been asking to see her father for months. His death, his complete goneness, was inconceivable to her young mind. When I spoke of his death, it reminded her of when she had said good-bye to him, of his memorial service; when I tried to tell her about his body being gone but his spirit being with us forever, she balked. She hated this new world in which he was inaccessible to her physically but somehow still with her invisibly. At seven, she was fiercely literal. Invisible was equal to nonexistent. My child, who had not yet entered the second grade, was cutting her teeth on the great mystery humans have pondered since the dawn of time: Where the hell *do* we go when we die?

Ever intuitive and exacting in her wants, she was also the kid who, three days after her father died, had told me she was done with a house full of grieving adults.

"Everyone comes over here for you. He was my dad. Why don't they come for me?"

They had. In their adult way, family and friends had checked in on her, brought her toys and gifts, then marched out of her room and came and sat with me. Three days of that had been enough for her to see a pattern and call my attention to it. *I want to see my own friends.* Three days in, and she was teaching me what she would need.

The next day I invited five of her friends over. They played. They wrote messages to Saro at her urging. They created art in the room where he had died. They put flowers near the candle I kept burning. They sang, they danced. In short, my daughter had orchestrated her own elementary school–style wake.

"You can't see his ashes. They are sealed in the box. It can't be opened." I knew that wasn't true, but I needed to give a concrete reason for which her brain couldn't conjure up a workaround. The real reason, that I would rather eat nails than open the box on your grandmother's dining table, was too aggressive for a child of her temperament.

And as her tears were making their Sicilian debut, I added, "But I have some here in this locket. You can see those."

For the next few minutes, we sat on the bed and stared into the locket. On one side was a tiny picture of Saro I had cut from a photo, on the other side was a small sealed plastic bag that I had taped to the heart-shaped form. We stared at the locket until Nonna shouted from below, "*Tembi, sei sveglia? Caffè è pronto.*—Tembi, are you up? Coffee is ready."

An hour and a half later, I crossed the threshold from Nonna's kitchen into the street on our way to the church. Zoela had chosen to stay home with her teenage cousin Laura after all. She had in fact fallen back to sleep, and I hoped she'd stay asleep until I got back.

That morning the heat rose with determination. My mother-in-law and I walked arm in arm, striding in slow unison down her street and toward the main road that is the only entrance and exit to town. She held Saro's ashes and pulled me close as we passed the baker and cheese maker. We'd have bread and cheese made inside those shops when noon came. I wasn't sure what she had prepared, but we'd eat the food of mourners. Of that I was sure. It would be soothing, easy to digest. It would be the kind of food to give you the strength to go on.

We passed fresh laundry hung on lines and sheep dung–coated cobblestones. The postman zipped by on his Vespa, headed to the next town before he'd circle back to Aliminusa on his way back down the foothills to the coast. As we rounded the piazza, the only square in town, I could hear a fruit vendor in the distance hawking his wares in a raspy dialect over a loudspeaker atop the cab of his small truck: "*Pomodori e pesche, freschi, freschi, buoni, buoni!*" The tomatoes and peaches he promised were fresh and not to be missed.

I could see the pharmacy door being unlocked. The butcher was receiving his first customer, an old man wearing a *coppola* and snuffing out his cigarette before entering.

Nonna and I walked up the wide, smooth marble steps of the church and into the dark sacristy. We had been holding each other up during the whole ten-minute walk. Others were waiting inside. Now she broke away from me to give the priest the ashes and take her place in the pew nearest to the altar. I took the seat next to her. Looming above us all was a statue of Sant'Anna, the mother of Mary and patron saint of the town.

The priest said a brief Mass over the box of ashes. He sprinkled holy water over them, then he spoke of Nonna and her strength through his illness. He prayed for me and Zoela. I struggled through intense jet lag and fatigue to focus on his words. If I could only fix my attention on one thing, I could get through this moment. Instead, all I felt was an intense longing to have Saro next to me in that very pew. So I lowered my head and fixed my gaze on the table where the priest had put Saro's ashes. It was humble, small with an ornate cloth. I didn't take my eyes off of it until my mother-in-law grabbed my hand because it was time to go.

We walked back out the church, down the striated white steps to Cosimo's waiting car. Driving would help us avoid the steep descent on foot and ensure that we didn't risk encountering townspeople now that more people were surely out. The town's groundskeeper was waiting with a key to open the cemetery.

At the archway that led into the main corridor of mausoleums, there was a gentle breeze. We were a small cluster of mourners: Nonna, Franca, Cosimo, two cousins, two childhood friends, a painter friend from a town nearby who had known Saro in early adulthood, the priest, and the groundskeeper.

Throughout the ceremony, I leaned against a cypress. I needed to be held up by something with deep roots. Birds gathered in the tree above as if to oversee this human drama or merely to seek shelter in the alleys of the mausoleums. Either way, they were what I could focus on. I felt as though I were floating above my body, in the sky with them. To be present in my body would mean that I'd feel the weakness in my legs, the aches in my hips. I'd have to suffer the light-headedness that threatened to cast me down onto the cobblestones. My body was an awful, fearful, unstable place to be. So I floated above it. And I listened.

I listened to what was being said first by the priest: more words, more prayers. Then I listen to the words of Vincenzo, the painter friend who had also been a close friend to Saro's mentor Giuseppe "Pino" Battaglia, a well-known Sicilian poet. Vincenzo, the painter, began reading Pino's words as a call to prayer. It was a poem for the dead but as I listened, I imagined that the poem was really for me.

Il mio nome è aria,
il vento che soffia.
Ora io vivo ancora in campagna

My name is the air / the wind that blows . . . / Now I live again in the countryside

Poetry would save me. It was more real and stable to me than my own body. In that moment I realized why I had returned here to this island of stone: I needed a kind of salvation. I desperately wanted, even for a moment, to shake off the ever-present sadness and fill my spirit. The poem was the love, the poetry a thread connecting me to Saro, Sicily, and my home back in L.A. where Pino's books lined our shelves.

The groundskeeper gestured toward the ashes. That snapped me back into my body, as if a branch from the tree above had fallen and struck me on the head. I was almost crushed under the weight of a sudden crashing awareness. I understood for the first time that I was burying half my life in a tomb in Sicily. Every smile, every joy, every shared secret, a lifetime of aspirations. I was committing all of that and all of the me I had known with it to a marble tomb. The sounds of a distant mule, the scent of fresh-cut hay, salt from the sea in the air were my witnesses—the elements that would now watch over it all.

The groundskeeper climbed the handcrafted wooden ladder, fashioned from the wood of an olive tree and tied together with rope and what looked to be dried bamboo. The ladder, I imagined, had been made by the groundskeeper's father or grandfather as a way for them to reach the upper levels of the mausoleum wall. He ascended nimbly, holding a sledgehammer. Through my tears I noticed that he was wearing old but starched pants. His hammer hit the cement facade, the layer between the crypt and the marble front stone, and it shattered the cement, sending small pieces falling to the ground below. The sound caused the birds above to squawk and fly away in unison. Their departure forced an opening into the otherwise quiet, still air.

I closed my eyes. Someone leaned into me. It could have been Nonna or her cousin or simply the town mourner, who was a fixture in such moments. "*Tutto bene, forte stai*—It's okay, be strong." Someone asked my mother-in-law for the ashes. She handed them to the groundskeeper, who descended a few rungs to get them. When I opened my eyes, he was back up on the ladder, and I saw him place

Saro into the dark space behind the cement. I noticed that the cement facade had not completely shattered. He had deftly managed to create a small opening, just large enough to slip in the box. We all stood in silence as he reached for a pail of fresh cement and a trowel. In a matter of minutes, he had closed up the opening. Someone pulled at my arm to tell me it was over. It was time to go. I had done part of what I came to do. Saro was buried in Sicily. But I had yet to release him to Sicily.

As we drove home, exhausted and spent, I thought of Zoela there waiting for us. Everything that would pass between Nonna and me in the coming weeks would determine whether Sicily remained part of Zoela's past or could also be part of her future. Anyone could see that the three of us—mother, daughter-in-law, and granddaughter—formed a grief triad, that we were swimming on dry land. It was a dangerous place to start from. I hoped that spending a month together would forge a closeness, that the loss would not drive us apart from one another. Our future felt tenuous. But on the drive from the cemetery it was too soon to tell. Right then, all I wanted to do was put a kilometer of cobblestoned street between me and the cemetery and get back to my child. She was the person who gave me a reason to keep putting one foot in front of the other. Because even in grief, motherhood made me show up. It was my salvation then and had been from day one.

SOMETHING GREAT

I had always wanted to be a mother. Always. In elementary school, Attica and I had played together, dreaming up elaborate story lines wherein each of us had six kids—three boys and three girls. Their names all began with the same initials or had to rhyme. Our play was high in drama and full of sitcom plots we borrowed liberally from *Good Times* and *The Brady Bunch*.

I saw my role as "mother" as a series of clear-cut tasks: running the house; making elaborate meals; orchestrating frenzied trips to the pretend shopping market where Attica and I took turns playing cashier in my grandmother's living room using an upturned dining room chair as the checkout stand. We'd pull all the canned goods from the pantry and place them around the living room. I insisted that they be grouped according to food type: bread, crackers, and cookies together; canned peaches, canned meat, and canned string beans on the windowsill near the TV.

Saro and I had been married two years when I went off birth control and let fate roll the dice. One year later, I wasn't worried so much as I was curious. And I thought it was divine timing since trying to get my career off the ground would have been harder with pregnancy and a child.

By the fourth year, we were concerned enough that we decided to each get a fertility test. The results were neither definitive nor remarkable: my tilted pelvis and his low sperm motility, likely due to his work standing near searing heat eight-plus hours a day, made for challenges. We weren't excessively disappointed. We had plenty of time. I wasn't even thirty. We could also go the route of the turkey baster, if needed. But privately, I started learning more about adoption as well, an idea that had always been close to my heart.

With a little research, I found an adoption agency started by two moms in northern California that specialized in the placement of children of color, specifically transracial adoption. Every time I got one of their newsletters in the mail, my heart leapt at the family photos inside. I saw children of all backgrounds being parented by families of all backgrounds and configurations. I saw children being raised in a "forever home" with people who seemed brave enough to risk loving big and embracing the unknown. People like I imagined myself to be. They saw something more salient than blood when they saw family. The people on those pages also looked like the family I came from, a variety of shades and hues. They looked like the world I knew and the family I hoped to create.

My family had welcomed my cousin into our kin by way of international adoption just one year before Saro and I had walked down the aisle. I was watching her grow up from a distance, seeing her at holidays and family gatherings. I saw the joy in her parents' eyes. I saw the love. I saw the way adoption was deeply intentional and expanding. I saw another way a family could be formed, and I was hooked.

• • •

"Are we really doing this?" I asked Saro as I handed him a stack of forms. Two years after his diagnosis, he was in remission. The prospect of starting a family, the hope of life in the face of illness, was exhilarating and humbling.

"Of course we're doing this. This might be the best thing we ever do." He took the application, gave it the once-over, and then looked at me. "Do I have to type this?"

"No, write out your responses. Then I'll take care of it," I said.

"How are we handling the medical history?" he asked, peering up from the papers. A look crept across his face. I was just getting used to having his olive skin and flushed cheeks back again since he had stopped the harshest drugs. But the vulnerability on his face and the nature of the dangling question at the center of our lives were something I could never get used to. It struck fear in me.

"Truth. Always. We just tell the truth." I grabbed him and kissed his forehead.

If we were to become parents through adoption, everything would have to be predicated on truth. We hoped we might match with a birth mother who was equally willing to disclose her truths. We were taking a risk. A big risk. We wanted her to see us for who we were, illness notwithstanding. That we were people deeply in love, people who had seen pain, who had survived it, and who would parent from a place of knowing what really mattered.

"You have to answer the question 'Why will Tembi be a great mom?' What are you going to say?" I pressed him to get started as we sat at the dining room table with a stack of adoption information laid out before us.

"I'll say you're perfect." How he could be both flippant and charming, I still didn't get. I was always one thing or the other. His duality was still the sexiest thing in the room.

"That is the stupidest answer. It says nothing. Actually, it says more than nothing. It says you value 'perfect.' Whatever that is."

"Can you just let me do this? I love you. If I want to say you're perfect, I'll say perfect." He reached for a pen to start writing. "We'll be picked because the mother will see we are in love."

"Okay, yes, we're in love. But can you also be specific?" I liked that we could still fall into married banter. It was the marker of normalcy in the wake of illness, and I never wanted it to end.

"What have you said about me?" He put the pen down and reached for my application form.

"That you're one of the most intelligent people I know, that you write poetry, that you are generous, that your cooking brings people together, that you play blues on electric guitar, that you speak three languages, read five." I played footsie with him under the table. "However, I did not write that you used to confuse Kevin Bacon with Val Kilmer."

"You'll never let that go."

"Not as long as I have breath to talk."

"Are you sure you don't want to try to get pregnant? I don't want you to miss that, if you really want that." He momentarily put the papers aside, waiting to see what I would say.

It was possible; we had frozen sperm. The day he had been diagnosed, somehow this husband of mine had had the emotional and mental wherewithal required to leave an oncologist's office, drive two miles toward the Pacific Ocean, and walk through the doors of a sperm bank. Neither of us had said a word on the drive, nor had we considered turning back. Instead, we had arrived unannounced at the reception desk; he handed the woman the doctor's note and soon after he disappeared into the back rooms of the clinic. He was someone who was able to somehow keep an eye toward the future even in the face of a diagnosis, protecting what might be. When he emerged a half hour later, he said, "I don't know if what just happened gives us a future, but I did the best I could." And then we left. We had been paying a monthly fee on the possibility of conceiving biological offspring ever since.

"I don't really want to be pregnant. Trust me. The only thing I don't want to miss is being a mom."

I had no interest in retrieving the sperm. And neither of us was interested in returning to examination rooms and lab tests. I didn't want doctors in white coats to be the way we started a family. Plus Saro had gently confided to me one night that he wasn't thrilled about the idea of rolling the dice on his own genetics, given the unknown nature of his cancer.

For the next few weeks, we filled out what felt like reams of forms, we got fingerprinted, we did the FBI background check, got police clearances, got interviewed, turned over our financial records. We crafted a "Dear Birth Mother" letter, promising "It is our commitment to raise our child in an open-minded home with all the warmth, compassion and love that is his or her birthright to have."

We got letters of recommendations from friends. We wrote dossiers about each other, answering questions such as "Explain why you're so excited to become parents" and "Describe your home." We wrote about our dogs, our extended family, the local elementary school nearby. We acknowledged that this was a difficult decision for her to make, and we thanked the birth mother for giving us a chance to share who we were. And, most important, we got a letter from Saro's doctors stating that his illness was in remission.

When that was done, there was more. I finished working on *The*

Bernie Mac Show and went straight to the airport to travel to a workshop for preadoptive parents on caring for the needs of a newborn. In the class, I diapered and burped dolls with a focus on eye contact and the need for attachment. They told a room full of prospective parents that the beauty of adoption is that dads get to hold and feed the baby equally and that this increases the parent-child bond with the father. Then I got back onto a plane and returned to set to work on a show starring Andy Richter about a family with teenage quintuplets.

Saro and I even attended a workshop in L.A. on transracial adoption where we were given a certificate for challenging our thinking on "the issues of race," "white privilege," and "differences in the transracial experience for children of different races and ethnicities." Though neither of us had direct experience with knowing how those issues intertwined with adoption, we left the workshop confident that as an interracial, intercultural couple, we were cool on the potential of the cross-cultural aspects of parenting—despite the fact that we had parents in two different countries who couldn't even talk to each other.

We cleared out the small office at home in the hope that one day it would be filled with a crib, a rocker, and a changing table. Naturally, we tried out names for our future son or daughter. Boy, girl, it didn't matter. Race didn't matter. Combinations of races didn't matter. The only thing that mattered was that we asked not to be shown to birth mothers known to carry twins. That was our one stipulation. I knew we could handle a lot, but I knew we couldn't handle two kids at once. Then we waited.

I was in the middle of a pull-up on the Reformer in a Pilates class when I looked out the window of the studio near our house and saw Saro. His face was lit up and beaming with excitement.

"What the hell is that guy doing?" the instructor asked, releasing me from the rings on the machine as she watched Saro move hurriedly across the parking lot.

"That's my husband," I said locking eyes on him and trying to process why he was in a place he never came to. As the words were coming out of my mouth, the realization was settling into my brain. This was about the baby. I hopped off the Reformer and raced to the door to meet him. If I was right, this was happening fast. It had been only three months since we had started the process.

"She's been born. The baby has been born. We have a girl," he said. He handed me his keys. "We've got to go."

"Go where? Who called? Wait. Where—where is she?" There was a girl somewhere waiting for us. This was happening. And fast. I was mother to a girl. "Where is the baby?"

"San Francisco. The birth mother wants to talk to us. She picked us, but she wants to talk to us. You've got to come home. We have to call her in an hour. Here, you drive."

We left my car there in the parking lot. My first moment of my motherhood happened outside a Pilates studio in Silver Lake.

We went home. We called the agency, we got prepped on who our daughter's birth mother was, the health of the baby, and the circumstances that had led to the mother's choice. We were coached on how to talk to a woman who had just given birth: let her take the lead; what to ask: anything you want; how to reassure her: listen; how to say "thank you": just speak from the heart. We were told the conversation would last about thirty minutes, maybe less. In the end, our call lasted over an hour. She was wise, intuitive, grounded. I was moved that she had not made a decision about the adoptive family until she had held her daughter in her arms, if only for a few minutes. Before she chose parents for the child she was painfully and lovingly relinquishing, she stared into her eyes, knowing they needed that moment. When we spoke to her, I could hear love and hope in her voice. I suspected that the torrent of feelings and processing would emerge in the days and lifetime to come. I was learning firsthand how much loss is involved in adoption. She was letting go of the child she loved and cared for so that that child could have a life she couldn't give her. Saro and I kept looking at each other as we attempted to answer all her questions, even the one we were most worried about, his health. In the end she said, "When I saw you, I just knew."

We hung up the phone as new parents. Hurried, manic, excited, overjoyed parents throwing toothbrushes into a carry-on and heading to Hollywood Burbank Airport to catch the next available flight to Oakland.

When we arrived, we headed directly to the offices of the agency where we were to meet the young woman who had chosen us as the parents of her child. The facilitator, Karen, had encouraged us to meet in person as part of the tenets of open adoption. It was "open" insofar as it was not the "closed" adoption of yesteryear wherein neither party knew who the other was and records were sealed. We were adopting in an era when having the adults agree to sit together face-to-face was desirable. It would give us the opportunity to get to know each other and understand that each of us would be vital to the child's understanding of his or her own origin.

When Saro and I arrived, my body was aflutter with nerves and excitement. But this was unlike the nerves I had felt on my wedding day, unlike the nerves I felt when screen testing for some TV show or film. This was unfettered elation. I wanted to give myself utterly to the moment. I understood that my life was about to break in a new direction. And although I felt the anticipation in my body, there was also an internal calm that took hold because somehow I knew that everything in that moment was happening with a kind of divine rightness. Saro and I stood at the threshold of the office, grabbed each other's hands, and locked eyes, and he said, "*Andiamo!*"

The first thing I noticed about Zoela's birth mother was her incredible beauty. She was striking. The second thing I noticed was that she was also exhausted. She was doing the hardest thing she would ever do in her life.

The next thing I knew, we were hugging. I hugged her the way you hug someone you are thanking with your whole body. As though I'd known her my whole life. As though she knew all the secrets of caring for the child we both loved and by hugging she could pour those into me. We pulled back from each other's embrace crying and smiling.

Saro asked her how she was feeling. Karen sat with us and took pictures so that one day we would be able to tell our daughter that we had met, come together, and made a plan that originated in our shared love for her. We could share the pictures that captured it.

Then Karen explained who was caring for the baby while we sat in an office getting to know each other. We knew that this way of joining families was part of the agency's mission. Wherever possible, it tried to facilitate a moment for the birth parent(s) and adoptive parents to meet first, before the adoptive parents meet the child. The agency wanted us to come together as parents to truly under-stand that we were entering into a pact of love and commitment that should always be centered around the child's best interest. And in their twenty years of facilitating adoptions, they also knew that for a birth mother to relinquish and begin to heal, it helps to have met the family.

We told the birth mom what we planned to name the baby:

Zoela. Saro and I loved the name, an ancient Italian moniker meaning "piece of the earth." We thought it symbolic for the child who had brought strangers together. Her name reflected the diversity of her biology and cultures. She was African American, Filippina, Italian, and even, Saro added, Sicilian.

Then we offered to drive the birth mom home to give us more time together, away from the office. She accepted. We left the office in Oakland as three people in a new relationship and headed to her apartment in San Francisco. There was really little to say in the way of chitchat; there was only the heartfelt awareness that we had changed each other's lives and that we were changing the life of a child.

We passed a traffic circle and a park, and then we were at her apartment. The trees were still full in the fall. She got out of the car, and we walked her to her door and hugged again. We took one last picture. In the photo we are visibly raw with emotion; her eyes are red, and I have my arm around her shoulder as if I don't want to let go. The three of us, each from a different culture, each at a pivotal intersection in our lives, fundamentally changed. Then she headed upstairs and into a life that was hers, a life that would undoubtedly carry its own silent grief.

"I don't think I can do this," I said once Saro and I were back in the car. "I can't move, let alone drive."

I began to cry in a way that didn't make sense to me. I felt as though if we moved that car, if we left that moment, if we drove away, we would be doing something that would change all of us. We were taking custody of a bundle of love and leaving her birth mother in a world of hurt. I slumped over the steering wheel, paralyzed with conflicting emotions.

Saro grabbed my hand. "Our daughter is waiting for us."

"I know, I know." The thought of her, the baby we had yet to meet, the one with the beautiful eyes, a head of black hair, the baby who had come into this world waiting for us. That thought of her snapped me into an excitement as deep as my sadness.

"Let's call the agency. Let's tell them what is happening," Saro said.

I called Karen at the office and told her I was feeling conflicted in a way that I hadn't expected, that almost didn't make sense.

"This is very normal, very normal. It has been a big day," she said. Her voice was calm, cool, collected. "A lot has happened since yesterday. But I want you to know that this is the heart of adoption. Remember what you are feeling right now. Remember, because at the heart of adoption is this love and this loss, all at once. Your daughter will know this feeling one day. It is the realization that she had to say good-bye in order to say hello. That that is how your love as a family came to be. You have said good-bye, now you need to say hello to your daughter."

She was right. Her words, her voice, gave me clarity and purpose.

I hung up the phone and leaned in to Saro. "Let's go meet our daughter."

There was a handful of families in the Bay Area who volunteered their homes to infants who were discharged from the hospital but whose adoptive parents had not yet arrived in northern California to pick them up. When we pulled up to the house of the woman who had fostered Zoela for one night, again there was a rush of adrenaline, nerves, butterflies in my stomach, pounding in my chest.

"Welcome, come in. I know you can't wait to see her." The woman who answered the door looked like a combination of Joni Mitchell and a middle-aged women's studies professor from

Wesleyan. Her salt-and-pepper hair was parted down the middle, and she wore corduroys with clogs. Her house smelled of formula and sandalwood. She held the door open as though she did this every day, a kind of hippie doula fostering newborns in a rambling ranch house on a hill in Marin County.

Once inside, I could see she had two children, sons, one white and one black, about a year apart. The older, a three-year-old, had been standing just behind his mom the whole time. In the background, I could see her other son sitting in a high chair. She had stopped feeding him long enough to answer the door. She still had a spoon in her hand. She never put down the spoon as she scooped him from his high chair, hoisted him onto her hip, and told her other son to show us to the baby. In a matter of seconds, we were led down the hall of the midcentury home, stepping over toys, passing an aquarium. Then we arrived at a crib in the corner of the master bedroom.

Her son pointed inside. There, sleeping on her back in a blue onesie with a knitted cap on her head, was Zoela. Her presence and her spirit met in the space between us, and I knew I had found a new kind of love. Saro took one look at her and took a step back. Then he sat down on the woman's bed and let the emotion wash over him. He didn't move for minutes. The foster mother drew near and told us how often Zoela ate, when she got fussy, that she was easy to burp. When Saro finally held her in his arms, she grabbed his pinky finger and held on. He, too, had found new love. Nearly fourteen years earlier, back in Florence, Saro had promised me "something great." Here it was.

Motherhood made me into someone I was meant to become. Zoela forged a new person out of me, restructured me. When I held her in my arms during one late-night feeding and she was not yet four months old, I was scared. If what I knew of myself thus far were true, then I imagined the mother I was becoming would be equally flawed, fragile yet strong, and, on good days, blessed with moments of grace and wisdom. This child was along for the ride. "I will give you my best when and where I can," I whispered, my mouth close to the crown of her head, lingering above that tender spot on babies that reminds us of the fragility of new life.

With motherhood had come the blinding reminder that I couldn't fly from the anguish of what it means to be human. Life is tumultuous and complex. Illness had taught me that. Being a mother under the threat of Saro's illness drove the message home.

In just a few months, Zoela was expanding the scope of my vision in the world, my vision of myself, my capacities. She brought forth a well of determination and power within me. But I also felt incredibly vulnerable.

"I'll do anything to make sure you are okay in the world. I'll do my best to spare you unnecessary hurt," I told her as she slept. Yet I knew firsthand that mothers can disappoint, they can wound, they can make their love conditional. What mother hasn't done that in the smallest of ways or even more egregious ones? I thought specifically about the years Saro's mother had gone without seeing her child because he had chosen a love she didn't understand.

That night I made a promise to myself that if I did nothing else, I would be a mother who worked hard to set my own conditions and ideas aside and see this child I was blessed to parent for the person she might be. I'd be at her wedding, I'd be there for births and deaths.

As I rocked her to sleep, the expanse of L.A. city lights twinkling through the window above my chair, I thought about the various sadnesses she would undoubtedly feel someday. Pain is part of life. That much I knew. If I could just teach her how to be resilient, how to love big, how to fear less. How to weather hurt, either at the hands of others or even the hurts she might unknowingly inflict on herself. I wanted her to know that love can come in many forms. That sometimes it can look like letting go, but it can also look like never letting go. That one day she might have to love someone in ways the world wasn't ready for. That reaching for that kind of love would bring with it struggle, but in the end, it could be grander than her wildest imaginings.

BREAD AND BRINE

*S*even *years* later, Zoela was playing upstairs at her grandmother's house, watching *Pippi Longstocking* in Italian on a portable DVD player just a few hours after Nonna and I had left her father's ashes entombed in the local cemetery. Downstairs, I watched as Nonna moved about her kitchen like a sturdy, silent ship navigating turbulent waters. Her kitchen was the space where I imagined she unthreaded the tapestry of her life, inspecting each interrelated thread. I could hear the cacophony of midday street sounds as they rose and fell: a barking dog, the idling of a tractor engine, Emanuela calling Assunta from down the street to tell her that she had picked up her bread from the baker on the way back from the market. The sounds were familiar, comforting and discordant with the reality of my life in L.A., where my own kitchen had fallen silent since Saro's death. Just planting my feet in front of the stove conjured sorrow from deep within my bones. But here in Nonna's kitchen I could sit. I could observe. I could watch an expert hand dice fresh garlic, layer salt into the sauce with generous sprinkles as I once had done with Saro. I could be in company. Silent company. There was more to be said than either of us knew how to say.

I studied Nonna's kitchen. It was small, gallery style: utility sink, dish sink, stove lined up in marching order along a wall with laminate cabinets above. A backsplash of eight-by-eight-inch brown ceramic tiles and plain brown cabinets lined the space. There was a repeating motif of antique rural vignettes painted on three tiles: a man making wine, a woman serving a family dinner by oil lamp, and a mother and daughter washing clothes in the town square. At the end of the service line was an antique wood-burning wall oven, typical of the turn of the last century. It had been used throughout Nonna's childhood. Her mother had baked bread in there daily. It was where they had boiled water for pasta. These days Nonna threw her compost trash into its belly through a black forged-iron door with a latch.

At the other end of the kitchen was the house's single bathroom and next to it a closet that held the refrigerator. Form followed function here. Each of those spaces had become what they were as modernity had arrived in town during the twentieth century: electricity, running water, refrigeration. Appliances were placed where there was space and where there was access to water. Design was informed by access and necessity and often according to the timeline in which a family could afford appliances and upgrades. Refrigeration was the last technological change to arrive in the home, so when a family could afford a refrigerator, it was put into the only space that was left. People worked with what they had. It was an approach to the structural changes of life that I suddenly understood with new urgency.

A big loss has a way of magnetizing all the other losses in one's life. I was just beginning to realize that in the months after Saro's death. His passing had resurrected all kinds of feelings of loss, including the dissolution of my parents' marriage, which had happened when I was, as my therapist had pointed out, seven years old. The same age as my own daughter. It seemed that parts of me, both past and present, needed deep soothing, and grief commingled past and present. That Zoela and I had experienced a loss at the same age seemed to make the younger parts of me crave stability with searing intensity.

The comfort I got from Nonna was a strangely familiar feeling. It reminded me of being at my own grandmother's house in the summers after my parents' divorce. My maternal grandmother was the one who had cared for me and Attica each summer in the wake of my parents' divorce. Then I had been a child grieving the separation of family. My parents had divorced, having given up on the notion of forever, and had started down separate paths. Leaving us with my mother's mother for the first few summers postdivorce made the most sense as they went about the business of rebuilding their lives. Grandmother was retired, and as a former educator, she wanted to influence the lives of her only grandchildren. She wanted to give us something we couldn't get at home: stability.

As a child I often sat silent, watching my grandmother Odell cooking in her kitchen. Studying kitchens and the women who commanded them is something I have done since childhood. Hers was the place where I played as a toddler on the floor and ate seated on a step stool. It was a modest brick house painted white with black shutters. And, like Nonna's house in Sicily, you entered through the front door right into the kitchen. Built in the 1950s, it held all the promise of that American era: four-burner stove, laminate countertops, a Formica table, a refrigerator, and a deep freezer. An island with swiveling bar stools and a view into the living room that flanked her kitchen. A floor-to-ceiling pantry with a built-in lazy

Susan and spice rack. My grandmother had risen above her share-cropper roots; her kitchen was a testament to that.

Her mother, my great-grandmother Fannie, lived two blocks away, and her house was where I spent afternoons shelling peas or playing jacks. She owned a roadside café for "colored folks" travel-ing up and down Highway 59 and the secondary roads that led to the rural black settlements that eventually became East Texas towns. Fannie served fried pies, chicken biscuits, soda, collards—staples of the South and of the piney region between Houston, Dallas, and east Louisiana, places with sloping porches, shotgun shacks with newspaper fastened over the windows for insulation in the winter. A casual breeze would send little tears of flaking white paint from those porches into the wind like snow. The boards underneath were gray and ashen and gave off splinters without warning. People kept one chair at the porch's edge, a single pine rocker, maybe two for when someone stopped by to offer them a bushel of corn, sweet and fresh off the stalk. My family came from those sloping porches and various small backwoods points in between, including the town of Nigton, Texas, where generations of my family had been first slaves, then sharecroppers, and finally educators. From them I had learned about food as the physical and emotional sustenance that carried people across the terrain of hard-lived lives.

In Grandmother's kitchen, I took my first steps in cooking. I first learned to stir SpaghettiOs with a wooden spoon in a tin pot. I wanted to mimic her, her actions. In retrospect, I understand that she let me "cook" so that she could tend to bigger matters. She was caring for her aging mother, her mother-in-law, and her husband, my grandfather, who had Parkinson's disease. While she cooked, she sighed, leaking out her own pain, resentment, and loss. She put all that into her food, in combinations of sweet and savory, brine and butter. I could tell she cooked out of necessity, but she also cooked in a way that seemed to me a form of self-soothing. And I didn't bother her. Something told me, even as a child, to leave her alone or be quiet. Her kitchen taught me that flavor can bring forth love and set aside anger, and that something sweet can mend a fence and soothe a heart. "The love of a peaceful home" was her guiding principle.

Nonna stood at her stove, her back to me. That was how our meals had always begun. She put a metal pot on the gas flame. I noticed that the pot was smaller than the ones she had used in the past. The boiling pot was always the promise of pasta cooked in water flowing from the aqueduct that brought water from the Madonie Mountains. But there was less pasta to make that day. Saro could easily devour two bowls of anything his mother made. But that day it would be only Zoela and me.

I watched her salt the water with five-finger clusters full of sea salt likely extracted from the salt flats a two-hour drive from here. The salt was fine and damp, as if recently risen from the sea. She dusted what remained on her fingers over the water like a wistful prayer. I was still under the spell of the cemetery, the birds, the heat that commanded submission.

I couldn't quite tell if Nonna even wanted to make this meal. I couldn't distinguish need from obligation—the need to do something to feel alive in the face of loss or the obligation to feed guests who had come far. I suspected that neither of us was particularly hungry.

But that was what we did. It was what happened at midday, every day. The Sicilian lunch is sacrosanct. It was, as they say in Sicily, "*Nè tu letu, nè iu cunsulatu*—Neither you happy nor I consoled." Still we would eat.

I had changed into a tunic dress. Nonna had taken off her formal black shirt and skirt and exchanged them for the simpler, more comfortable widow's clothes she wore at home. The uniform was the same, a black shirt and tube skirt. The at-home version was less restrictive, made of cotton. She wore her wooden cross at her neck.

"May I help you?" I had asked that question in her kitchen for nearly fifteen years.

"No," she said, shaking her head. She liked her kitchen to herself.

She had never let me cook in her house. Never. Not even her chef son was allowed to. No matter how many nights I slept under her roof, no matter how many times she washed my bras and ironed my underwear, I was her guest. Even if I was also family. She preferred to work alone, at her own pace; she didn't want company while she cooked. In the past, I had just passed through, made small talk, but had never lingered from start to finish. She, like many women in town, saw their time at the stove as their domain. I was forbidden to even set the table.

So I stepped out on the street. I heard the loudspeaker of the latest roving street vendor: "*Susine, pere, pesche, uva!*" He was hawking fruit—plums, pears, peaches, grapes—varieties of which could only be found in Sicily and rarely in the supermarket. The vendor was fifty or so, narrow-faced, unshaven, tall with a subtle hunch in his back. He boasted a grin with teeth spread out in his mouth like missing dominoes. I'd seen him for years. For me his face was a collage of the island's cultures: dark olive skin, blue eyes, the Greek nose that appears on statues of Apollo, topped with a head of curly black hair. I was fascinated by Sicilians, a populace that over centuries had found themselves subject to first one, then another ruler from Greece, Spain, North Africa, and Normandy. Sicilians were a mixed culture of victors and vanquished, people who managed the often uneasy mix of different languages, religions, and ethnicities that had come to coexist. In the spectrum of Sicilian faces you can see a combination of African, Greek, Arabic, Jewish, Spanish, and Norman people. As a result of all that invading and accommodating, Sicilians are characterized by an openhearted skepticism that I find both vexing and endearing. Their food is an intoxicating mixture of cultures colliding on the plate.

The merchant stopped the Piaggio minitruck in front of Nonna's house, leaning his body out of the driver's-side window, microphone in hand. It's an old tradition in Sicily, the roving vendor calling out his goods in the form of song. Saro once told me that perhaps it dated back to the Arab rule in Sicily.

He stopped midway up the street, right in front of me. The location allowed the women who lived down the street to walk up to purchase and women from the houses at the top of the street to walk down. It was egalitarian, it was fair. Also, his speaker was cheap and didn't work well. From that point on the street the sound carried best. Even the women who had televisions blaring while they cooked could hear what he was offering. He continued singing out his wares: plums, pears, nectarines. I knew immediately that he wouldn't get much business. He was late in the day to be selling fruit. No one, I suspected, was going to step away from her stove to inspect, discuss, and then purchase fruit, especially since many of the varieties of fruit he was selling had already been gathered from nearby orchards by the husbands, sons, and sons-in-law who tended to the land. In Nonna's kitchen, I had noticed a small wooden crate of fresh pears on the counter. It must have been left while we were at the cemetery. Her house was always unlocked. The pears, I assumed, were from her cousin Cruciano's farm.

The man got out of the cab of the tiny truck and approached me. "*Buongiorno, signora.*" He extended his hand. I saw soil under his nails. When I grabbed hold, his hand was rough to the touch. "*Condoglianze per suo marito*—My condolences about your husband." And just like that I wanted to fall into his hairy forearms. Something inside me softened. This was what a small town could give me that L.A. never could. The guy at the grocery store in Silver Lake didn't know my husband was dead even though I have shopped there weekly for years. Here, a fruit vendor whose name I couldn't remember knew and remembered that my husband had died.

"*Grazie.*" My knees suddenly felt like noodles, and I was surprised by the sound of vulnerability in my voice.

He steadied his arm to brace my body, which was leaning on its axis.

"*Ma che si può far? La vita e così. Si deve combattere. Punto e basta.*— But what can one do? Life is like that. We have to fight. That's enough."

I nodded in agreement, and something more broke loose in me. My eyes formed pools of tears. He neither flinched nor looked away. Instead he nodded back. "*Sì, è così*—Yes, it's like that." Then he took a step back, turning to his fruit truck. He reached for a *susina*—a Sicilian plum, small, tender, and oval with a purple that boasts blues and reds. He put two fistfuls of plums into a bag and gave them to me.

"*Grazie, Salvatore*" I heard over my shoulder. My mother-in-law had been standing on the threshold unbeknown to me.

"*Signora, ha bisogna di qualcosa?*—Do you need anything?"

"*A posto*—I'm good," she said.

With that, Salvatore returned to his vehicle, grabbed his mic, and started once again calling out fruit as though it were a serenade.

Within seconds, he was backing down the street, hanging his torso out the window and lighting a cigarette all at the same time. His engine sputtered in reverse.

I turned back into the house with my bag of plums.

"*Banane e Patate viene più tardi*," Nonna told me. The vendor they all called "Bananas and Potatoes" would come by later. He was called that because those were the first words he called out as he rode up the street to sell his merchandise. I hoped to be asleep later in the day when he passed. Suddenly I needed to lay my head down. It would take everything I had to make it through lunch before stumbling upstairs to bed for a nap.

Back inside, I saw Nonna set the plates out on the kitchen table. Eating in the kitchen was always the case for breakfast. But for lunch and dinner we had always, for as long as I could remember, eaten at the dining table in the other room. The table sat under an oblong frame with a copy of a nineteenth-century romantic oil portrait of Joseph, Mary, and the baby Jesus. The baby Jesus sat full and upright like a man but with a teenager's face. He was extending to Joseph a cluster of lilies still on the stem. In the shallow background, there was a valley, then fields, then mountains. I knew from my art history studies that the lilies represented purity, chastity, and innocence. But lilies could also represent resurrection. The painting told me of innocence but foreshadowed the resurrection that would come after that innocence was lost. I had always liked it. I found its obvious pastoral romanticism the most optimistic piece of art in a house full of crucifixes and photographs of popes. But it was its handcrafted frame that I really loved. It had always reminded me of a similar frame my great-grandmother had in East Texas. Hers framed a trio of Martin Luther King, Jr., John F. Kennedy, and Robert Kennedy. That was a different kind of romantic optimism. A different kind of loss. Eating at the dining table in Nonna's had always been a private link to another life I had thousands of miles away. And I'd enjoyed that connection. But today that table was not set. Instead it served as the altar for a burning votive candle on a handmade lace trivet.

Back in the kitchen, Nonna moved a pot of lentils to the back burner. Prepared earlier that morning, before Zoela had awakened and asked to see the ashes, they were simmering again. I smelled garlic. I knew there was mint from the terra-cotta pot she kept under the bench on the sidewalk outside her house. We would have the lentils with the pasta, I suspected. They were grown here. I had never eaten lentils growing up. In fact, I don't think I knew what lentils were until I was past the age of twenty-five. It was Saro who had taught me how to enjoy them and later understand that in Sicily, they are more than a staple. They are fortune, and they are fate. From a culinary point of view, they are eaten for sustenance, especially in times of drought or scarcity. From a cultural point of view, they are known to bring luck to travelers, good fortune at the New Year. But they are also a mourning food. Lentils bring the full human experience to the table. *Lenticchie* were the food this family turned to for comfort and sustenance when life gave you something irreparable.

I sat there, thinking half thoughts in our shared silence. Fragments of memory rushed in and receded with equal speed. In Los Angeles, I had become obsessed with remembering everything. I had a deep-seated fear of losing more of Saro in the form of lost memory. I wrote everything down. I kept a notebook with me to remember images, like his knuckles when he held a knife. How he dried the lower half of his body first after a shower. The near-pathological commitment he had to driving miles for a printed copy of his Italian paper, *la Repubblica*, from a newspaper stand bordering

Beverly Hills because that guy held a last copy for him, rain or shine. The bridge of his nose the morning he had died. At Nonna's table, the memories were coming faster than I could grab hold of. I felt light-headed.

Nonna placed a shallow bowl of lentils with ditalini in front of me. On the table, there was water, no wine. Never wine. She didn't subscribe to the proverb *Mancia di sanu e vivi di malatu*—Eat with gusto, drink in moderation. Nonna didn't drink, never had in her entire life. Nor had she ever worn pants. I knew I'd have to find wine for the days to come.

She had cut the daily bread, *un filoncino*, a small loaf that, from the moment we sat down, she would consume silently, tugging one piece after another, pulling and twisting deftly the way one pulls ripe fruit from a branch. On the table she had also placed marinated olives, pickled artichoke hearts, and a salad of tomatoes with oregano, drizzled with family-pressed olive oil.

"*Chiama la picciridda*," she said in Sicilian. "Call the little one."

I lifted myself from the chair with its handwoven straw bottom and headed toward the narrow stone staircase that led upstairs. In a strange way, I felt comfort in maintaining the treasure of simple routine. I was climbing a rough mountain, smack in the middle of the unknowable, stranded in the heart of a wild grief. I could only hope that by following the bread crumbs of the familiar routines, I would eventually find my way out of the forest.

Upstairs, Zoela was on the bed. She had abandoned Pippi and the DVD. I couldn't tell if she was awake or asleep. There is a natural drama to Sicilian light at certain times of day. That light was casting itself across her small, narrow torso, strong and commanding. It's the kind of light that I have only ever experienced in Aliminusa. It came from the single window in Nonna's large but sparsely furnished bedroom. Zoela must have opened the shutters and pushed them back on their hinges. It was one of the details of Italian life that she loved. She had brought light into a room that rarely saw such a light, especially at that time of day. We both always found the dark of Nonna's house both disorienting and restorative. As I took in the sight of her back lying across the starched, sun-dried sheets, I imagined Saro there in the light. I imagined him holding her.

"*Vieni, amore. È ora di mangiare. La nonna ti ha fatto la pasta.*— Come, my love, it's time to eat. Your grandmother has made pasta," I said. I was slipping into Italian with her, as I always did within days of arrival. "Eating will do us good."

"Carry me," she said back to me as if she were scared or still sleepy. I knew that periodic emotional or development regressions were among the signs of grief in children. I'd seen it in myself, so I sympathized with it in her. I was willing to meet her where she was even if that meant carrying a seven-year-old. But I was secretly hoping that this was not what every day would be like. A fleeting but familiar flash of anger grazed me. For a split second, I wanted to kill Saro for dying. Those moments often caught me by surprise but also regularly appeared when I needed another adult to turn to for help. When she woke up in the night, when I needed an extra hand getting out the front door, when she wanted to be carried.

"Sure, but when we get downstairs, you will walk to the table."

She knew there were few things I would deny her while this far away from home. Giving in to her needs gave me purpose as a mother, as a grieving person, and as a former caregiver experiencing disorienting withdrawal from a decade I had spent tending to someone else.

A few minutes later, I pushed my chair in to the table and took in the meal before us, food that was both prayer and an oration of grief.

"*Ma che farai nelle prossime settimane?*—What are you going to do in the next weeks?" Nonna asked me as Zoela reached for a piece of bread.

I hadn't thought past getting there and interring the ashes. The rest was a blank slate.

"*Non lo so*—I don't know," I said.

"*Riposati, devi riposarti*—Rest, you must rest." She knew something about widowhood. So I listened.

We continued eating. When at the table, all else was suspended.

Her food went into me like mystical sustenance. I was like a child calmed by the comfort that lay in consistency and tradition—the comfort and consistency I craved. I had come to count on the woman stirring a pot. She showed up with steady grace and the understanding that the best she could give us was a full belly and lots of rest. It was a recipe to counteract the kind of brokenness the three of us—her, myself, and Zoela—now shared. There was a low hum of grief that undergirded everything; I heard it as constantly as the birds in the sky. It seemed as though everything going forward in my life depended on making peace with that hum.

We had four weeks ahead of us. That was a lot of time for three grieving people to be together, a lot of unpredictable emotional terrain to be surmounted. I didn't trust my own feelings. And I certainly didn't trust that any of us was up for the work of creating a new relationship when we were all so raw. As I ate the last bite of the earthy broth of lentils, they were like flattened pebbles of promise in my mouth. Then I looked over to Zoela, who seemed momentarily content, at ease eating at her grandmother's table.

SCHIAVELLI'S CAKE

"*Saro, this* is killing you." I was holding a picture of a cherubic baby wearing a pristine christening gown with an adult-sized gold necklace and cross dangling from her tiny body.

Since Saro had moved to America, his sister, Franca, had given birth to her second child. A child we had never met and, the way things were going, never would. Franca sent us pictures of her girls at holidays. But it was the baptism pictures of his second niece that showed me how dire the situation was.

"I'm fine. I'll see them one day," he said, glancing over my shoulder, then abruptly turning away as if he saw something in the picture that made him nauseous.

I had come to the realization that our marriage would suffer a silent loss if there weren't some attempt to change the narrative of his relationship with his parents. Though they hadn't exactly kept up the vow to never speak to him, the relationship was locked in a stalemate. They had exchanged hellos by phone only a few times in two years and mostly when Saro was sure his father was not home.

"One day when? When someone dies?" I was not above

employing a dramatic scenario to make my point. "You don't want the first time you see your parents again to be at a funeral."

"I won't go to anyone's funeral."

"Okay, that's extreme."

"No, I mean I can't go to their funeral. There won't be time. You can't get from Los Angeles to Aliminusa in twenty-four hours." He had screwed the top off a liter of San Pellegrino and was drinking it directly from the bottle.

"Wait, you mean you've calculated this? The hours, the flights?" I put the picture into the kitchen drawer. "I had no idea."

"Of course I have."

"Sweetheart, that means if something doesn't change, you could never see one of your parents again?"

"Yes and no. I guess so. Well, yes." He put the bottle into the fridge. "Let's not talk about it."

But talking about it had become the thing I liked to do. I had made peace with their absence at the wedding, sort of. But I had never expected this to go on for so long. Now I was seeing that he had resigned himself to play out this Sicilian family melodrama to its painful end. And the more that landed on me, the more I needed to meet these people. Ignorance was changeable. My love for him was not. If they wanted to hate me or dislike me, then at least they'd have to hate *me*, not an idea of me. But enough was enough. It was time for a good old-fashioned Sicilian sit-down.

I bought two tickets to Sicily for the next month. I added on a trip to Morocco, long on our wish list, in case our attempts at peace and reconciliation were met with indifference or, worse, overt hostility. I figured we could always make love on a tapestry in Fez and ride the train to Marrakesh drinking mint tea and devouring couscous and harissa at every turn. Morocco could be the palate cleanser if Sicily and family reconciliation proved too bitter a dish to digest.

"We are going to Sicily," I announced one night. Saro had just come home from his latest job at a five-star hotel in Beverly Hills. The smell of the grill and fryer filled the room as soon as he shut the front door. His clogs showed stains of soup or sauce, white with green flecks. Immediately I thought of herbed béchamel.

"What?"

"Sicily. We're going to Sicily." I took the phone off the kitchen wall and handed it to him. "Call your family now, tell them we are coming."

He hated an ambush. But ambushing had become the only way I knew to talk about the thing we didn't talk about.

"First of all, it's six in the morning there." He threw his bag and keys onto the counter with an emphatic thud.

"They are farmers, no? Up with the chickens?"

"Before the chickens."

"Even better."

"T., what are you doing? Hang up the phone. I just walked through the door."

I put the phone down. He took the stairs of our new home two at a time up to a hot shower and away from me.

I shouted after him, "If you won't call them, then write another letter. But soon. I already bought tickets."

He did call, and this time the response was an immediate, straightforward "*Non venite al paese*—Don't come to town."

I was beyond floored. There wasn't a word I knew in English or Italian to describe the pit in my stomach. Then, just as quickly, my spine straightened as though I were Oprah Winfrey's character, Sofia, walking down the road in the movie *The Color Purple*. Those four words, "Don't come to town," strengthened my resolve. His family was so dysfunctional, I would have to be the one to take the mountain to Mohammad. I loved Saro in a way that left no alternative. Their resistance was in direct proportion to my growing determination to try to make some kind of peace. I could ultimately take his family's rejection, if that's how it went down. However, I couldn't live with myself if I didn't throw one last Hail Mary pass in the direction of Sicily and try to end this.

Saro, on the other hand, was nervous about the possibility that this trip would in fact prove to be the final rejection. If it didn't go well, I imagined he'd quietly turn his back on them, push back his own history.

Uncertain but undeterred, six weeks later, we boarded a plane to that ancient island in the middle of the Mediterranean, with the hope of maybe visiting Aliminusa, a town built over a fifth-century Arab outpost in a part of the world I had seen only in movies such as *The Godfather* and *The Star Maker*.

What I knew about Sicily was snapshot details trickled down to me in the stories Saro had told me. He had played soccer at the edge of olive groves in shoes borrowed from an older cousin. His family could afford only one pair at a time, and his mother had forbidden him to ruin the shoes. He had eaten apricots off his grandfather's trees. The town, for many years, had boasted more heads of livestock than people. The kitchen in his family home had been a stall for the family mule until he was a teenager. And there had been but one television in town during his childhood. Although I hadn't seen childhood photos of him, I could clearly picture Saro as a boy, knobby-kneed with a head of thick black hair and piercing curious brown eyes. He had been too clever for a one-room classroom, terribly sensitive, and capable of harvesting a row of artichokes as fast as boys twice his age. He had kept a book of poetry under his bed at night. But there was so much I still didn't know.

Saro didn't have high hopes for the trip. But he said that even if the meeting with his parents didn't happen or, perhaps worse yet, if I met them and didn't like them, he promised I would *love* Sicily. Of that he was certain. I wanted to believe him, because I knew how much my loving Sicily would mean to him. So I said, "Of course" while secretly setting my sights on Sicily as little more than a pass-through to Morocco.

As soon as we landed, though, I was hooked. Sicily beckoned with her sapphire blue sea, her rocky arid terrain that, without warning, offered up verdant fields of poppies.

We handed over our passports and checked into a small family-owned hotel on the northeast coast near Cefalù that we would call home for the next ten days. Me, the black American wife. Saro, the Sicilian son who had married a foreigner who hadn't even bothered to take his name, legally or socially.

Hotel Baia del Capitano was our base to get over our jet lag and take our time building a line of communication to Saro's family in a town forty minutes away. The restaurant in the hotel became our second living room. We read the newspaper there, hung with the staff, ate with the chef. The foods I savored felt like the very origins of flavor; everything up to that moment now felt like approximations of tastes. I devoured tomatoes, fennel, asparagus, and oranges baked, cooked, sautéed, and cured into dishes that were pungent but delicate, complex but simple. The island was getting me even further into its clutches, one bite at a time.

And there was nothing like seeing a part of the world previously unknown to me through the eyes of a native. It was sublime to see it through the eyes and stories of someone I deeply loved.

Saro became my guide into the heart of his culture, his language, and his cuisine. I began to empathize with that part of him that was prone to reminisce after seeing *Cinema Paradiso* or *Il Postino*, each a cinematic portrait of Sicilian and island culture.

Now, in Sicily, we made love to the sounds of church bells in the early morning, then rose with an urgency driven by the desire for espresso and the pleasure of chatting with locals. We fell deeper in love as the man I had married crystalized into focus, like seeing a part of him that had been invisible to me until it was contextualized. Home was making him more himself. Whether I met the parents or not, this trip had hooked us into each other more fully. We had traveled together in the heart of the conflict as a team, risking rejection but willing and openhearted. I began to understand the hidden parts of him, which needed the light of the Sicilian sun in order to breathe. And suddenly that awareness made the idea of possibly meeting his family less fraught. In a strange way, they no longer mattered. At least not in the way I had imagined they would. On that trip, it was as though I married Saro again and also wedded myself to his homeland.

Still we remained hopeful for a reunion with his family.

The logistics of Operation Family Reunion went like this. Each morning we left word in town with Franca, telling her we would be at the hotel between 5:00 and 7:00 p.m., if anyone chose to come down the mountain and visit. Franca was desperate to see her brother in person. Since our arrival, she had been attempting to broker peace and convince their father to come with the family to meet us at the hotel. Family mores dictated that if his father refused to come, then his mother, as was the custom in the Sicilian patriarchy, would not come. And if her parents didn't come, Franca couldn't come. Going outside that ancient code of conduct would have been seen as a sign of disrespect, an act of defiance. Saro explained that it was a Byzantine arrangement, one that, if not handled carefully, could end in a jagged line down the center of the family, a war zone on both sides. Giuseppe, as was his right, was dictating the actions of the whole family, just as he had done two years earlier regarding our wedding.

In town, it was no secret that we were less than twenty miles away, patiently waiting in a hotel. News had spread, as it does in small towns. Saro's mom had sought counsel from the priest, she had talked to her closest friends. From what Saro told me, Franca and his mom "were working on it." We just had to give it time. Every time he tried to explain, I threw up my hands and told him to pour me more wine.

In the meantime, each afternoon we waited, sipping wine or espresso or both and biding our time in case anyone came to meet the prodigal son and his American wife. Those afternoons in the garden were surreal. We got dressed up. I put on makeup, styled my hair. I laid out the gifts we had bought as a gesture of goodwill. Then we waited like storefront mannequins with a Mediterranean backdrop until it was clear no one was coming.

I felt as though I were in a parallel universe. Sicily seemed a place where individual free will had been abandoned and a town of people was under the spell of something greater than them—history, tradition, fear of reprisal. I had never been witness to a culture so willing to pledge allegiance to the group over an individual. Saro kept trying to explain to me that it was about keeping the peace. That families were forever divided when a wife or a daughter or a brother-in-law went against the head of the family. A visit could happen only with his blessing. Otherwise, it would all be rancor and tension with a hefty dose of gossip. He didn't want that for his mom, he didn't want it for his sister. So we just waited. And I held my tongue as my plan to take the mountain to Mohammad was going up in smoke.

On the third afternoon of waiting, I looked out our hotel window onto the dazzling blue waters, and I broke. I finally allowed the disappointment, hurt, and rejection to wash over me. I had flown halfway around the world only to have no one stand up and do the right thing. No one was willing to put Saro and his feelings first. I had brought myself into exile.

"I'm not coming down to the garden this afternoon. I'll be in the room. Come get me if anyone comes."

"*Amore*, please. Come with me. If no one is here in fifteen minutes, we'll change and go to the beach. Then a sunset dinner."

"Saro, this is completely absurd! And I feel stupid for ever thinking this could work. I don't get this place, this culture, these rules. I mean, I love it here, it's beautiful, but I also hate this."

"I tried to explain it." He was hugging me. When he let me go, I could see the hurt in his eyes. But I also saw a new, clear awareness. "We did what we came to do; the choice is theirs. I love you. This is on them."

Fifteen minutes later no one had come.

It wasn't until the fourth afternoon that Franca told us we would have our first visitors, Saro's second cousins. The next day his dad's brother and his aunt would come. It had taken days, but Nonna and Franca had devised a plan. Each day small groups of the extended family would visit, thereby putting pressure on Saro's father. They were using Old World reverse psychology to create an environment that would make Giuseppe publicly seem like an obstinate, uncaring father, a man willing to watch his wife weep openly and refuse to attend Mass because he was keeping her from their only son. I liked the way these women worked.

Then came a shift. On the seventh day, Franca and Cosimo arrived with their girls. That was a sweeping gesture. Seeing her for the first time moved me to tears. She was so much like Saro, taller even, with a radiant smile and kind eyes. When she walked up to me and we kissed each other on both cheeks, I almost melted. I had given up on that moment ever happening. I instantly admired the woman who had been quietly working to achieve this moment. I knew what an act of defiance it was for her to be standing in a garden under a vine of bougainvillea, finally meeting her sister-in-law. She had chosen the love of her brother over continued allegiance to the way things were done. For that, she was heroic.

Still, Saro's irascible sixty-something-year-old father, Giuseppe, refused to come. He had made a decision on which he doubled down. By that point, the whole situation was brimming with Sicilian pathos, and frankly I feared for the well-being of a man who could relentlessly commit himself to disowning a son. Still I tried to humanize him. I tried to imagine his position.

I imagined that somewhere inside he must have known or at least considered that if he didn't see Saro then, he'd likely never see him again. America, distance, and a foreign wife who had done all she could might see to that. Somewhere inside, he must have known that by flying all the way to Sicily, we were extending perhaps the largest olive branch he'd ever see on an island with no shortage of olive trees.

In the late morning of the eighth day, Saro packed our Fiat rental and tossed me the keys. "Here, you drive. I want to find Polizzi Generosa. We'll drive until we're tired or too drunk on good food to turn back." Polizzi, he told me, was a town he had heard of as a child but had never visited. Sounded good to me.

As an unspoken rule in our relationship, I was the driver and he the navigator when we traveled outside of L.A., mostly because I had been driving since I was a teenager and he had not gotten a license until he was thirty-five years old and living in the United States. We had learned that one of us was notoriously awful as a passenger: me. With my impatience and commentary, I drove him to distraction and then anger, often a combo platter of both. He had learned to toss me the keys and content himself to lean out the window and ask for directions when needed.

Two hours after leaving our coastal hotel, we tumbled into the mountain town of Polizzi Generosa. I was hypoglycemic, carsick, and generally a wreck. I had not anticipated the remoteness and the steep, narrow roads with stomach-turning drops into rocky valleys below. One look at the stone edifices rising from the rocky precipice of the mountain, and you could immediately see why Polizzi Gener-osa (meaning "generous city") had been a high-elevation Hellenistic and later Norman outpost, strategic for defense. Getting there, even a thousand years later, was not easy. It took more than a notion.

As I clutched back and forth in the Fiat and left rubber on the road, I lobbed nonsensical threats at Saro, concluding with a prom-ise to never have his children if he couldn't find me a trattoria that could produce the best plate of local food and a liberal pour of the house wine immediately. He met my hyperbole and hypoglycemia with indifference and deflection. "You will thank me for this mem-ory one day." When I pressed him with more laments, he finally threatened to leave me in a trattoria to cool off while he watched soccer on TV at a local bar. It was the kind of irritated banter re-served for young married people who found themselves lost on an island that was both familiar and foreign. I finally put the car into park and hoisted my hunger from the two-seater.

It was maybe 2:30 p.m. Siesta time. The hours when a Sicilian village is a ghost town of shuttered windows and the faint sounds of dishes being put away before rest.

We sidled up to Pasticceria al Castello looking for two things: a restroom and a break from each other. From its open door, the intermingled aromas of vanilla, almond, and sugar emanated from within. I let Saro break the beaded doorway hang first. No matter how much we were annoying each other, I was still a black woman in the interior mountains of Sicily. Not that I expected anything to happen. But I always let Saro be the first point of contact, just as he let me be the first point of contact when we drove the back roads of East Texas to the sharecropping land my people hailed from. We are practical even when irritable.

The baker and owner, Pino, allowed me access to the restroom while Saro caught some of the soccer game on a small screen. We didn't hope for more than espresso and maybe directions to a still-open trattoria.

Saro and Pino began speaking in dialect. Within seconds it was established that although he was a native of Sicily, Saro in fact resided in Los Angeles with me, his wife, an actress. Pino's face lit up, and suddenly his eyes swung in my direction. "Do you know Vincent Schiavelli?" He spoke to me in a rough, rushed Italian that I could mostly follow. I knew that Vincent Schiavelli was the famous character actor from *One Flew over the Cuckoo's Nest*, *Ghost*, *Amadeus*, and *Batman Returns*.

"Yes, of course. Not personally, but I know him," I answered in Italian.

"This is his grandfather's hometown. He comes here often. You

have to take something to him from me." And before I could protest, he had disappeared into his lair of pastry ovens behind the
display case. Saro called after him, "Of course we will."

Pino reemerged with a round flat cake on gold-faced cardboard.
It was not just any cake but the traditional cake of Polizzi Generosa,
he explained. Cake made one way in one town in the remote mountains of Sicily, in a town that didn't see a lot of visitors. A cake Saro
had never heard of. A cake I didn't want but knew immediately
was coming with us. "Sure, of course we will," Saro redeclared our
commitment to deliver the cake as Pino wrapped it up in pink paper
and adorned it with gold ribbon, attaching a card with his phone
number. Before I could tell him that I didn't know the first thing
about how to track down Vincent Schiavelli, the cake was in my
hands and we were walking out the door. I turned to Saro and gave
him a look that said, "Really? You know this cake is never leaving
Sicily." To which he retorted with a nonverbal "Don't worry, I'll
carry it."

I don't know what happened between the time Franca returned to
Aliminusa and we returned from Polizzi. However, the next day, our
final day in Sicily, we sat down for our afternoon espresso, dressed
up, and were ready to receive guests when a car pulled into the
gravel parking lot and Franca filed out, behind her Saro's mom.

In the emotional overwhelm of Saro seeing his mother, I didn't
register the large figure walking behind her. Until Saro grabbed my
hand.

"Tembi, that's my father," he said. His grip was so tight it almost made me shriek. Then he quickly let go, rose from his chair,
and went to his mom. I couldn't take my eye off Saro's father.

Giuseppe had made his way to our hotel to meet the son he

hadn't seen in years under an arch of bougainvillea in the hotel garden. I let out an audible "Fuck!" I didn't know who to greet first, I hadn't even thought of what I would say. Before I could collect myself, he was upon me. There was a cordial hug. I offered a tentative smile.

"*Ti presento mio padre*—May I present my father." Saro was speaking to me as though we were on the floor of the United Nations.

Giuseppe was taller than I had imagined with a face weathered from a lifetime of field work. He wore creased dress pants and a collared button-up shirt under a suit jacket. He was dressed as if he were going to church. And he wore the same hat that he had worn in the photo I had seen of him. "*Salve*," he said simply, his voice gravelly with cigarettes and understated emotion.

At his side, was Saro's mother, Croce, wearing a dress skirt and floral top. She clutched a small black purse that looked rarely used. She broke loose from her husband and went straight to Saro. She beamed with joy at the sight of her son, overcome at being able to hold him again. There was relief in her face, too. I would later learn that it was she who had turned the tide and brokered the meeting. She had woken up that morning, our last day in Sicily, dressed herself in her Sunday finest, made her husband coffee, and announced that she was getting a ride with her cousin to drive down to the coast to see her son. She pointed to a plate of room-temperature pasta and told Giuseppe that he could stay or he could go but her mind was made up. She would not live a day in peace if her son got back onto the plane bound for America without her ever seeing him, without her laying eyes on the woman with whom he had chosen to spend his life.

After Croce finished hugging Saro, she turned to me. Her face broke open with a tender, toothy grin. Before me stood a determined woman who carried my husband's smile. She leaned in and said, "*Grazie.*"

That night we concluded our time in Sicily with our first family dinner at a roadside trattoria adjacent to the Greek ruins of Himera. It was a place his father could comfortably afford and far enough from their hometown that it would create no further gossip. We broke bread as a tenuous New World/Old World biracial, bilingual family.

I felt an intense relief that this was finally happening. But I also felt hyperaware of my every move. I was self-conscious about my Italian, my open displays of affection with Saro, even my choice of clothes: jeans, with a midriff-baring top. I wore a sweater to cover myself the whole way through dinner. I had never imagined that what they thought of me would matter. But it did.

Saro and his parents chatted in dialect; I caught fragments of what they were discussing. Saro turned to me periodically to translate. I held his hand under the table. I talked to Cosimo, seated on the other side of me, about the number of siblings I had, where my parents lived, the names of TV shows I had been on. When I wasn't making small talk with him, I focused on the two sweet young girls who were my new nieces. They were both under the age of five, and I could speak to them freely without worrying if I was using the wrong verb tense or using a masculine article with a noun when I should have used the feminine.

As we passed bread, no one referenced the previous years. There was no grand apology or even gesture of regret for time lost. We just ate and carried forward as if starting our relationship from that moment.

I ate pasta with local capers and a simple tomato sauce that pleased my palate like no other. I gorged on eggplant caponata and grilled artichokes topped with sprinkles of fresh mint. I had after-dinner espresso at his father's urging despite having recently discovered that it wrecked any chance of my having a good night's sleep. I willingly removed any obstacles that would come between me and this tentative Sicilian bonding session. I even bypassed my aversion to grain alcohol to take a sip of pear grappa. I wanted everyone around me to feel at ease. I knew I could never be one of them, but I could be the kind of wife who supported her husband's making amends with his people. That much I had proven. And it made me quietly triumphant, optimistic even. We had done it.

Back in L.A., I pulled a cake out of my suitcase. The cake from Polizzi we had carried across three continents. Pino had told us it was dry cake and could be kept wrapped and unrefrigerated for up to ten days. He assured us that once in Vincent's hands in Los Angeles, Vincent would know what to do with it. Something about a liqueur that could be poured onto it or about it being like a *panforte* or an American fruit cake, neither of which I had tasted or held much appeal. So Saro became the cake's custodian while I balked at the extra encumbrance when we boarded a train in Fez. I had pushed it to the back of our hotel room closet in Marrakesh. In my mind, there was just no way that cake would ever set foot on US soil. There was no way the acclaimed actor Vincent Schiavelli would ever eat a dessert brought to him by complete strangers.

We had barely finished handing over our customs form after landing in Los Angeles before Saro asked me, "So how are you going to get in touch with Vincent?" He asked it with a whiff of challenge, as if he had done his part and now it was my turn.

I let two days go by; then I called my agent to ask about Vincent

Schiavelli's agent with what I am sure sounded like a convoluted story about a cake and connection to Sicily.

Thirty minutes later, my jaw dropped when Vincent Schiavelli called our home phone. Two hours later, the actor was standing in our one-bedroom apartment, wearing round wire-framed spectacles and a pastel linen jacket on his six foot–plus frame.

"This is perfect, I am having a dinner party later tonight. This will make a delicious dessert." He was delighted, beaming with incredulous joy that he was about to share a taste of his beloved ancestral land with his closest friends. That a stranger had taken the time to bring him cake.

We made small talk about where exactly in Sicily Saro was from, how long he had been in the States, how we had come to have the cake, how Pino had known to give it to us. I didn't mention that I was an actor, too, which, in Pino's world, meant that naturally Vincent and I were colleagues and would know each other. After fifteen minutes, I snapped a picture of Saro, Schiavelli, and The Cake just before Vincent sauntered down our steps and back into his own life.

Saro and I told that story for years. He used it as evidence of the tenacity and determination of his people. He used it as a way of educating Americans on what it means to hold on to a piece of yourself when you straddle two cultures, calling two lands home. Each time he told it, he referred to the protagonist in the story not as himself but as "Schiavelli's cake." The cake was the connective tissue that had brought a Hollywood star into an immigrant's home. That's how he saw the story. I saw the story as emblematic of the way Sicily made me see how home is a place we carry with us in our hearts.

The story he rarely told was the one of his father, the family strife, and our exile. That story was harder to tell because it was hard to live. And for years, the renewed connection with his parents felt as fragile as parchment near a flame. When we did eventually visit Saro's childhood home for a vacation, then a family wedding and later a first Communion, I slept under Croce and Giuseppe's roof as a guest content to pass the time conversing as little as possible, being unobtrusive, burying my face in a book until the trip was over. I respected Saro's parents for the change they were willing to undergo. Many people never achieve that in a lifetime. But in truth, I also never expected to be close to them. The most I hoped for was a delicate reconciliation and civilized mutual respect. I could now expect to be notified if someone were sick or if there was illness. Little did I know that we would be the ones bearing ominous news.

VOLCANIC SAND

Two weeks into this monthlong Sicilian trip, our first without Saro, I boarded a ferry with Zoela in tow for the four-hour ride to Stromboli, a volcanic island and the farthest point in the Sicilian archipelago. I had been desperate to leave Aliminusa. The near-constant reminders of Saro—at Nonna's house, in the town square, at the bar getting espresso—became dizzying. Being in town elicited a twin experience, by turns soothing and then triggering big waves of grief. A couple of days at the coast and a trip to a remote cluster of tiny islands seemed just the thing to satiate my growing wanderlust and give Zoela and me time outside the confines of the tiny town.

I suspected that Nonna needed a little time alone as well. The three of us had settled into a quotidian routine of abundant meals, long naps, and early evenings spent on the bench in front of her house, retracing our loss. In the kitchen, Nonna and I talked over coffee. I watched her dry fresh oregano from the garden, then sieve it by hand using the same plastic colander she had used since the days when Saro was a bachelor in Florence. Summer was ripe with flavor and memory. And the only time either of us had away from each other was when she went to Mass in the afternoon.

The line of tourists boarding the boat was two deep. I grabbed Zoela's hand as we crossed the dock. "Sweetheart, we're going to sit inside the cabin, not on the deck. The winds will be too strong, and it's a long ride to see the volcano."

"Can I watch a movie?" she asked, grabbing hold of the straps of her daypack just as I had taught her.

"No, it's not like a plane, there are no movies on board. You can read or better yet, try to take a nap on my lap."

Halfway into our time in Sicily, and she had not developed any discernable sleep pattern. The jet lag was crippling. Since Saro's death, we had been sharing a bed. At Nonna's house it was no different. Zoela needed it. I needed it, too. At night, she hooked her body close to mine. Maybe she was afraid that if she migrated to the opposite side of the bed, she'd lose me, I'd die in my sleep like her dad. So she stayed close. And her small form kept me grounded. I reached for her during those nights just as much as she reached for me. We were testing each other's permanence. So having her sleep on the boat meant she would be less cranky when we arrived and I'd maybe have time to shut my eyes as well.

As we settled into our seats, I sensed that this was an important first, testing my ability to step into the old me, my adventurous self, the person who had traveled so much before cancer and caregiving. Did she still exist? Could I awaken that old self? With Saro, I had seen nearly every corner of Sicily, but there were some places, special places, that he and I had longed to go to but never could due to his illness. I had visited Stromboli twenty years prior as a single coed but never with Saro.

I told myself that in my new life, I would be the one to show Zoela the world. I would have to show her that we could still find kernels of joy or excitement in the midst of grief. I didn't yet know it to be true, but I wanted to test the idea. Stromboli seemed a symbolic, epic first step. But once we were on the boat and the engines turned and the underwater propellers set us into motion, I realized I had miscalculated.

My anxiety swooped in like a cleaver hacking down on a chicken bone. Five minutes into a nearly four-hour ride, and I was riddled with fear of the things that could go wrong, aware that I was now alone with Zoela on the open sea without cell reception until we reached land. Also, I had no real plan as to what we would do when we arrived. I had never traveled with her like this alone. In her daypack there was an envelope with the emergency contact info I had typed up back in L.A. It held copies of our passports from both nations, in case we got separated or something happened to me. If all hell broke loose, I wanted people to know to whom she belonged, whom to contact, and that this little girl with pigtails and brown skin was not alone in the world. I had spent hours on the Internet looking for tips on how to travel abroad as a single parent. That's how I had learned that when traveling abroad, solo parents who have different last names from their children, which I did, can experience challenges. I needed some document that united us on paper, something that reconciled our different last names. So in addition to the picture of the two of us together, I hyphenated my name to "Locke-Gullo" on the emergency contact list. Then I typed, in bold, *"PADRE MORTO 2012*—FATHER DECEASED 2012."

I didn't want to transmit all of my fears to Zoela, so as she fell asleep on my lap, I whispered into her ear, "Sweetheart, we're gonna get to climb a volcano and see lava."

Then I closed my eyes and tried to focus on the geological wonders of Stromboli, the memory of molten earth, sea, wind, and Mother Earth coughing up her inner core. The magnitude of a volcano and its constancy in the face of so much human frailty fascinated me. There was something so primordial about it, something about the way its aliveness contrasted my grief. The island was a magnet for a widow, adventurer, curiously creative like me. Or so I tried to tell myself.

As I caressed the top of Zoela's head, I conjured up joyous images of us happily trekking up a volcano, spending an afternoon on the black sand beach, watching lava set against the backdrop of the setting sun in a faint blue sky. I fantasized about the two of us being transformed as we set out on a kind of pilgrimage to a place where humanity had managed to make peace with the impermanence of life. The people of Stromboli lived at the base of an active volcano, for fuck's sake. Though it hadn't done damage in hundreds of years, if there ever were an emergency, there'd be no easy way out. Yet these people carried on their lives with that ever-present awareness, accepting throngs of seasonal tourists, then living in relative solitude in the off months. The idea of this place was both alluring and vexing. I tried to lull myself with the hum of the boat's engine.

But my anxiety was bigger than my *National Geographic* musings. It grew into a free-form amoeba, attaching itself to all manner of doomsday possibilities—from the boat sinking to Zoela getting seasick to my being incapacitated by heat to losing my American Express card and having to wash dishes to pay for our boat fare back to Cefalù. Suddenly all I wanted to do was get back to land, back to Aliminusa, back to the safety of Nonna's house. Then it hit, a reckoning of who this widowed me might be. I was either willful or naive or, worse yet, both. *What in the hell possessed me to do this?* I wasn't twenty years old anymore, I didn't have a partner to back me up. I was taking a young child for a long adventure with no adult companion. No extra set of hands. Suddenly I was hyperaware that we were away from Nonna's kitchen and community. We weren't surrounded by people who knew us, nor in a place where we instinctively felt protected. Where Zoela's whole well-being didn't depend exclusively on me. If anything happened—illness, accident, loss of documents—in Aliminusa I had a town at my disposal to help remedy it. And I'd certainly have to entertain Zoela at times, ply her with gelato when she bumped up against the inevitable boredom, and possibly carry her when she got tired. I had taken a grand adventurous leap and then panicked once my feet left the ground. So much so that I lifted Zoela's head off my lap, reached for my bag, and popped an Ativan.

German and French families sat around us on the boat along with some young Italian couples eager to brown their skin while lying on black volcanic sand. Zoela and I were among a handful of Americans, mostly young college kids with greasy hair and wrinkled shorts they had pulled from the backpacks they were using to hike through Europe. We were the only people of color.

Out on the open sea, in a boat full of strangers, I became acutely aware of my vulnerability and in turn Zoela's—the structural rawness in our lives and our inability to handle any additional upset. I pulled her closer and sent a prayer out into the horizon.

The first thing I noticed when we got to Stromboli was the port. It was much more built up than when I had been there twenty years before. The second thing I noticed was Rocco, my one-night stand, now two decades older. It wasn't hard to miss him. He was positioned near a bar at the port. The identifiers were all there—the Vespa, the same frame, the same face, each a little more worn. I let out an audible cackle. *Saro, you are heckling me from the heavens.*

Seeing Rocco at the port greeting throngs of tourists was like peering through a looking glass into an audacious parallel universe.

In that universe, the twenty-year-old me had made different choices. I had chosen Rocco, my one-night stand, and that romp on a black sand beach at midnight had turned into a life serving beer to tourists in the summer season and ironing his underwear in the off-season. Rocco was a 3-D, bronzed-by-the-sun, cautionary tale. For every romantic cliché—nice girl forever crushing on unattainable bad boys, Italian gigolos on the prowl for American coeds—we had been both. Only he was clearly still at it. One look at him, and I drew Zoela closer.

I wanted to warn her that men perched on a Vespa are like gelato that looks like pistachio but tastes like anchovies. But I decided that was a conversation for another time, a future way off.

Instead I was surprised by a feeling that crept over me, a subtle, almost indecipherable sense of injustice. How was this man still there after twenty years? A lifetime had passed for me with a breathtaking love, a marriage, a child, and death. So much sweeping change. Yet here he was, as fixed and constant as the volcano behind him. I felt a ping of vague resentment in my belly as I stared at Rocco. He was a sore point, a visual demarcating my life before Saro and my life after. His presence was a reminder of Saro's absence.

I took a deep breath, trying to relax and take it all lightly. *Okay, Universe, I get it. You are mercurial.*

Then I steered us along the length of the port hand in hand, away from any possible eye contact with Rocco. Within a few steps, I suddenly felt emboldened, invisibly stronger. I had brought my daughter this far. I had done it. Alone. My earlier doubt melted away, I felt capable. As though maybe, just maybe, I could navigate the complexities of my new life and not get completely lost. Or, at the very least, I could get Zoela and me onto and off of an island far from home. Or maybe it was the Ativan talking.

I squeezed her hand and pointed to the top of the volcano ahead. "Sweetheart, that's an active volcano. The first one you're ever seeing."

She took one look at it and then turned to me. "How long are we going to be here, Mommy? I'm hungry."

Of course, children have priorities that don't include volcanoes and memories of one-night stands.

I promised pizza and gelato, magic words that can shift the mood of any reasonable person. Then we started our way into town, following the narrowing ascending street that I remembered from years before. I knew there would be places to eat along the way because of the smattering of tourists headed in the same direction. If nothing else, we'd have a great meal on the island. Now that I was here, it didn't much matter to me that we actually trek the volcano. The trek, at least the one I was navigating internally across the landscape of loss, had already begun.

Half an hour later, we were seated at a restaurant perched in the foothills of the volcano with a head-spinning view of the Mediterranean. Zoela ordered *spaghetti alle vongole*—pasta with clams, fresh parsley, and red pepper flakes. When I was seven, on trips to East Texas, I had eaten canned Vienna sausage and drunk Tang by the gallon. She was her father's child, in all her culinary sophistication.

The clam dish was something that I almost cautioned her against. All I could envision was the shellfish hitting her stomach the wrong way and an ensuing disaster on the boat ride home. But she wanted it. And Saro, I knew, would have said, "Yes, go for it. Enjoy." I wasn't proud that I was becoming a mother more familiar with *no* than *yes*. So I encouraged her to have the pasta. "But maybe don't eat all the clams. Just a few," I advised.

A quick scan of the leather-bound menu, and I knew what I

wanted, *pasta con pesto alla siciliana*. What makes the dish stand out are the two ways it differs from its sniveling sibling, the pesto you find in every American supermarket. In Sicily, the chef uses almonds instead of pine nuts, and vine-ripe tomatoes are added. The almonds give it a robust body and a dense texture. The tomatoes add a rosy under hue and a fruity acidity to the dish. The whole entrée announces its presence in vibrant earth tones and a fragrant intermingling of basil and tomato.

Zoela and I ate in silence, something we had been learning to adjust to since Saro's death. When something so big has happened, chitchat seems banal. Even to a seven-year-old. Plus, in my experience, two adults were always better than one when it came to drawing conversation from the under-ten set. Saro had effortlessly found ways into Zoela's ever-changing topics of interest. That day I felt I had exhausted the conversation landscape. So I drank a local white wine from a quarter-liter minipitcher, the perfect amount to push through dinner and still have my faculties intact.

Zoela unpacked her My Little Pony figurines from her backpack and lined them up on the table as our additional guests. In another life, I would have told her, "No toys on the table." But we were in the kind of life where finding moments of joy was like finding a winning lotto ticket in an empty parking lot. You took them, and you didn't ask questions.

"How about we toast Babbo?" I asked after a few moments. All the books on grief and children suggested talking about the lost loved one, bringing him or her into everyday conversations.

"Do we have to?"

"No, I guess not. I was just thinking about him."

"I don't really want to toast him." She had lined up the empty clam shells on the rim of her plate. "I just want to know why he died."

Some kids ask Why is the sky blue? Why can't my tongue touch my nose? This was my daughter's *Why?*

"Sweetheart, he was sick, very sick, for a long time. What I know is that he fought to stay alive as long as he could because he wanted to be here for you."

"Well, I don't like loving him. It hurts." She didn't take her eyes off the clams.

"I know. It will feel that way for a long time. That's what people tell me."

She moved the pony that was wearing a periwinkle-colored felt wide-brimmed hat, which made it look as though it were attending a wedding at Windsor Palace. Then she said, "Well, I just miss him. So I wish I didn't love him."

She had said that before. She had also said she wanted to die, to join him. She had said she wished I were dead and not him. She had said many things, things that were hard to hear, harder still to push through. Things the therapist and books all said were very normal. When those moments happened, when the grief was too big and it threatened to buckle the frame of the house, we'd often go to the back yard of our house and lie on the grass, put our bodies prostrate on the earth. On the blanket looking at the stars, I would tell her to give her hurt to the stars. They could take it. I told her she could say anything to them. She could cry, she could scream, she could curse. Anything she felt. She often said only one thing: "Babbo, you should not have left me."

Now, seated at a table nestled at the foot of a volcano, I told her, "Not loving him would only make you feel a different hurt. It's because there was so much love that there is so much hurt. And he loves you always and forever."

"Well, I'm gonna stop loving him," she said emphatically,

convinced of her own power over love. Pools formed in her eyes. But she continued, "And being here makes me miss him, and I don't like that."

I felt seasick on dry land.

"Being here in Stromboli? Or here in Sicily on the trip?"

"Both."

She had said it, the thing that worried me. That I was a mother intent on opening wounds for which I had no salve.

The waiter appeared and poured more water. I started to order more wine and then realized I still had a few ounces left in the quarter-liter carafe. I had to face this as clearheaded as fermented grapes would allow. For a moment I watched the skinny, black-haired waiter move on to other guests at other tables—families who were actually on vacation. Moms and dads with cherubic toddlers and moppy-headed teens. People jovial and sun-drenched. People Zoela, Saro, and I had "sort of" been, could have been, might have been but for *il destino*—destiny.

"Angel Pie, to stop loving your dad is no more possible than to stop the sun and moon. His love is part of you."

She looked at me long and hard, penetrating me with her deep brown eyes. As though she didn't like my words, me, the conversation, her life. Then she cast her eyes outward and down to a cluster of stray cats gathered on the clay tiles of a roof below. She made the tiniest shrug of her shoulders and then asked, "Can I have another clam?"

Fuck, have them all.

The rest of the day passed uneventfully as we moved from tourist shop to gelateria and back to tourist shop. She wanted a dolphin figurine fashioned from the black volcanic rock that was everywhere on the island. It was tourist kitsch, but I was happy to comply. We passed Rocco again at the edge of a crowd in the port. He stood sun-drenched in too-tight shorts, schmoozing with tourists. I pitied the duo of twenty-something blondes in bikini tops he was talking to. "Get on the boat, girls," I wanted to say. "Trust me, he's not worth sand up your ass."

At sunset, Zoela and I climbed back onto the ferry. When it pulled out into the open sea, the captain allowed the vessel to idle as the sun turned the sky amber. From the crowded deck, we watched the volcano erupt. Incandescent liquid rock spouted into the sky, the earth's inner core in full purgatorial glow. To be bobbing on the open water and watch the earth cough up its molten core, expelling it into the sky, opened my heart as wide as the day Zoela was born. It was perhaps the most spectacular experience in nature I had ever had. I was glimpsing the earth in progress, bearing witness to geological history. I held Zoela tight, I held Saro close in the locket around my neck. I felt he was with us, bearing witness to his wife and daughter in progress. We were survivors of a kind. We held, between us, a kind of secret of life and what mattered most. And that secret, that deep understanding of the constancy of nature and its opposite, human impermanence, was what I hoped would eventually help us regain our equilibrium.

After the sun had set and we were traversing the water once again, Zoela fell asleep on my lap. I stared out a portal window of the lower deck into the *noir* sea, illuminated only by an undulating streak of moonlight. Though it was impossible to see anything, I kept looking. In the darkness I saw a sliver of the moonlight dance on the water. It was a visual metaphor of that precise moment in my life—a fragment of light and darkness. I hoped that the next path in my life would be illuminated the way the moon brought light to the waves.

BITTER ALMONDS

"*La lingua va dove manca il dente*—The tongue goes where the tooth is missing," Nonna said to me as we sat talking in the kitchen before her afternoon Mass. Zoela and I would be returning to Los Angeles in a week, and Nonna was telling me a story from her childhood about a boy who liked a girl his parents didn't approve of. One day he took the girl, unchaperoned, into the fields outside of town. They spent the afternoon in an old mule stable and then he returned her to her parents that evening. In the Sicily of Nonna's childhood, that was akin to eloping. It meant that the couple had to get married because the girl's virginity was in question. There would be gossip and shame.

When the boy returned home, his outraged parents barred the door, banishing him. They tossed his clothes into the street and set them ablaze. He never went home again. And the girl's family refused to let her marry him. He was destined to be alone. And he was until the day he died. Nonna concluded that ill-fated love story, a version of which existed in nearly every small town in Sicily, with a proverb about a tongue and a missing tooth.

I was intrigued as she recounted it to me. Its meanings were multiple, and coming from Nonna, given our personal history, it was undeniably significant. We had avoided the fate of that family, rising above lives that played out like characters in a Sicilian morality play. We had bridged estrangement; there were no clothes burned in the street. Where we stood that day, the piece of the story that was most relevant was that the boy had spent his life tracing what was gone: family, a girl, his dignity. She was telling me that throughout life, we revisit the empty spaces. That was her understanding of grief. That we are always trying to reconcile memory with reality. The tooth was a metaphor for all the missing things we lose in life.

Telling stories, particularly old stories and fables of Sicilian life, was a special connection Saro and his mom shared. They liked to revisit, through the oral tradition, a Sicily gone by. Now she was sharing a similar moment with me. And even though I had to ask her to slow down, repeat certain words in dialect, translate phrases into Italian, she was willing to do so. I wasn't her son, but I could be her listener. It gave us a way to fill the silence we were learning to traverse. Nonna liked to dole out wisdom in the context of old parables. I guessed that the unspoken wisdom of that tale also had to do with good-byes and living with goneness. In one week, we'd be saying good-bye to one another. The pending departure was foremost in my mind. Earlier that day, she'd asked me if I'd started getting the suitcases ready. For an American like me that seemed excessive, but each summer she had encouraged us to have our suitcases packed two whole days before departure. "Think about what you want to leave here," she had said. The statement dangled in the air.

After three weeks in her home, I had come to feel a new bond with her, one forged through shared circumstances and love for Saro. I had grown a tiny bit more comfortable with our periods of silence. I respected when emotions swelled up and she told me not to cry. "*Se cominici tu, non possa fermare*—If you start, I'll never stop," she had said several times during my stay. She wasn't denying me my feelings, but she was also letting me know that this was hard for her. She was doing her best. I suspected that she preferred to cry alone, as I had once seen her do while reciting the rosary.

I was not doing much better, often crying at night after Zoela had fallen asleep. Good-byes have never been easy for me. But the idea of Zoela and me returning to Los Angeles to an empty house, to the slog of commercial auditions and dinners alone, was almost crippling, even if I was also ready to be back in my own bed, ready to see my friends and family. I was still leaving one of the most peaceful places I have ever known and relinquishing a certain closeness to Saro that could be found only in this community, in the presence of his mother, in her home, at her table. That indescribable closeness was overrun with loss, but it was also comforting. Part of me couldn't take another day, part of me never wanted to leave. It was a duality that was difficult to make sense of. I kept thinking of something Vincent Schiavelli had once written of Sicily and L.A.: "It's a strange conundrum. When I'm in Sicily, I want to get back to L.A. When I'm in L.A., I long for Sicily."

The question of whether we would return to Nonna's next summer remained unspoken, mainly because I didn't have a definitive answer yet. A year seemed so far away. There would be finances to consider, a mortgage to refinance, auditions, and the ultimate reckoning of whether I could face another season filled with so many bittersweet memories for me, for Zoela. Who knew where I'd be in a year? Nonna had to be wondering if we would come back again now that Saro's ashes were interred. Sure, it had been our little family's summer tradition, but she of all people knew the ways widowhood changed one's ideas and plans for life. She also knew, I suspected, that although we had a strong tie that bound us to each other, we weren't exactly close. It would be up to me to decide whether I wanted to come back.

Nonna and I didn't have a shared language with which to explore all that. So we simply didn't talk about it. Instead what we had was our time together, especially in her kitchen, the place where her house came alive three times a day.

She stood up from her chair and adjusted the nylon stockings that stopped at her knees. Then she turned off the flame and put a mismatched lid onto a pot of stewing tomatoes. They had been picked earlier in the day by a neighbor. By afternoon, they were sweating themselves out of their skins, reducing themselves into an intense juice and fleshy fiber that would somehow play a part in the evening's dinner.

"It must have time to come together," she said, referring to the tomato sauce. I had begun to appreciate that in her world, nothing was rushed—love, grief, joy, or a pot on the stove.

Zoela played upstairs with Rosa Maria, or "Rosalia," as she liked to be called. She was the granddaughter of Giacoma, who lived at the edge of Via Gramsci. A year older than Zoela, Rosalia was easygoing and affable. The girls had met when Zoela was perhaps four or five, and they had been playing together each summer ever since. She was fascinated by a girl so unlike herself—American, black, bilingual, and with a mother readily willing to open her purse and dispense euros for gelato at the bar in the square. They were inseparable. They waited for each other at the front doors of their grandmothers' homes. Zoela had told Rosalia where to find candy in the houses of the women of Via Gramsci. Their friendship was as firm as the cement between the stone blocks of the church's facade.

Upstairs they made forts with sheets, acted out various roles with large puzzle pieces of zoo animals and a one-legged Barbie. They communicated like twins with a shared language only they knew—part Italian, part Sicilian, part English. They found a way to bridge the vocabulary each of them didn't know. When I had checked on them earlier, Zoela had told me to leave. She liked making Nonna's upstairs her play domain each afternoon as the sun began to recede and the town came to life after the siesta. And while Nonna was at Mass, Zoela had gotten accustomed to leading Rosalia downstairs to swipe the Italian version of Twinkies that Nonna kept in a cupboard.

Two days later, I met a farmer while walking through town to mail a postcard at the post office. He was unloading almonds in front of his house, hoisting them from his truck to the narrow sidewalk with a swiftness that made me look twice. He was Nonna's age. His face was both ancient and youthful, a network of lines etched around bright blue eyes that could have belonged to a movie star had he been born in a different place. I couldn't believe how deftly he lifted his harvest given his arthritic, bowed legs.

"*Signora, prendane un sacchetto*—Mrs., take a sackful." He motioned for me to come closer. "*Portine alla Croce*—Take them to Croce." Then he told me to tell her they were from her cousin. Before I could answer, he disappeared into his house and returned with a sackful for me to take home.

Until that trip, I had never had a soft, green almond, tender and fleshy with a sweet aftertaste. They grow on trees everywhere around the periphery of town. In summer, they jut from the branches, green with a soft shell. They are an edible gift for those willing to do the work of *il raccolto*—the harvest. Sicilians are known to eat them alone as a snack or after dinner with fruit. But he was giving me a large sack of the dried variety because, as he explained, he needed to make space for the green ones he would be bringing home in the coming days.

I took them and thanked him.

It was a rookie move to try to carry three kilos of almonds through town. Halfway up the last hill to Nonna's house my back told me to fuck off. When I drew back the curtains to enter her house, she shook her head as she watched the bag hit her kitchen table with a thud.

"*Che cos'è?*—What is that?" She was already opening it for inspection.

"*Sono mandorle*—They're almonds." I knew I had just brought more kitchen work to her home on an otherwise uneventful morning.

"*Dove le hai trovate? Ma sei pazza?*—Where did you find them? Are you crazy?" Her tone belied the fact that she actually liked that people gave me gifts to bring to her. It was a sign of consideration and respect. Even if it meant that there'd be work to do.

"I need my own mule when I walk through town," I quipped as I watched her take the bag and walk it toward her "cellar," the cool space under the stairs where she stored olive oil, a year's worth of homemade tomato sauce, jars of caponata and artichokes, and bulbs of garlic hung on a rope. It was also the place where she napped on the hottest days of summer.

The next morning I awoke to the sound of Nonna hammering steadily outside the front door. Looking from the door of the upstairs balcony, I saw wind snapping freshly washed sheets on the line. I tied my hair back, slipped on a linen dress, and went downstairs. I found her, mallet in hand on an upturned wooden crate, bearing down on the almond shells, a blanket of massacred shells at her feet.

"Can I help?" I asked.

"You'll only slam your finger." Her voice was neither low nor loud. It came from the distraction of some thought. I knew immediately that she wanted to be alone. "I left the coffee ready on the stove for you," she told me without looking up.

I watched her work a few seconds more. Steady, repetitive. Peeling, slicing, chopping, working was how she contemplated life's problems; prayer was how she turned those problems over to God.

Just before I turned to go light the flame under the *caffettiera*, she called over to me, "If you want to take them back, I have to begin now, no?" She was talking about the almonds.

Instantly I knew it was our forthcoming departure that was occupying her mind. It was on mine, too, as I drank my coffee, listening to the sound of cracking shells.

A vendor came by, Nonna continued to work. Her cousin Emanuela shuffled down the street to retrieve bread. Nonna kept hammering. Emanuela returned, and I took the bread from her. Nonna went on cracking nuts. I placed the loaves near the stove, next to stewed artichokes and a pot of zucchini pieces jostling lightly in a broth of mint and basil over a low flame.

Then I walked out into the morning wind. I got a brick from under the bench and placed it on the stone walkway. I took a second mallet, the one I could see had been next to her all along and began to pummel almond shells.

"They are delicious. Here." She gave me an almond from the shell she just forced into opening its heart.

It was divine, its flavor gentle with a delicate hint of sweetness. The flesh of the nut was somehow structurally firm but also tender with delightful elasticity. When left unattended to dry out, almonds became ever better, more robust. Those Sicilian almonds were nothing like the nuts in six-ounce plastic bags sold at gas station checkouts in the United States. They were a singular act of natural goodness. They reminded me that a thing can be tender or hard, depending on conditions and care, intended or otherwise.

I reached for another.

"*Non quella. È amara.*—Not that one. It's bitter," she told me. "There is nothing worse than a bitter almond."

Amaro—bitter—is the one flavor profile that is at the epicenter of Sicilian culture and cuisine. It is a flavor foraged for in wild greens. It is distilled into liqueur. With *amaro*, Sicilians get intimate with nature's lack of sweetness; they get up close to its marked intensity. In the kitchen, when Sicilians juxtapose something *amaro* with something *dolce*—sweet—they bring the contrasting flavors to life, make a stage for both, side by side. Bitterness, Sicilians understand, is an essential flavor both in food and in life. It has shaped the island's culinary identity. There is no sweet without bitter. The poetry of the island tells us that the same is true of the Sicilian heart.

Nonna showed me the moisture inside the shell I had just cracked.

"When there's too much rain, this can happen." Inside the shell I saw a small amount of mold and rotting. "Too much of anything can ruin. Even water."

I knew she was talking about almonds, just as earlier she had been talking about a tooth. But I couldn't help but feel that she was also talking about so much more. We had both been drowning on dry land in a sadness that seemed to stretch to infinity. One look at Nonna, and I knew she knew that life could be bitter—as could joy and love. She had lost her husband and her only son. She had had the taste of bitter almonds linger on her palate. She wanted to spare me the same.

I worked with the wind at my back. Gentle and silent, the wind was a persistent character in a town of characters. It caused curtains to billow, windows to shutter. Damp socks batted against stone walls on the laundry line because the wind compelled them to. It carried the rooster's crow above and across the bell tower, depositing a faint echo among the budding olive trees in the orchards at the edge of town.

I was aware that in four days that same wind would carry me off the island.

Getting into the olive grove wasn't hard. I found an opening past a large laurel bush where the earth was low and I could bend the rusted barbed wire without much effort. I squatted near a sprout of fennel, did a tuck and roll, and hauled my body inside the family land with only minor scratches on my legs, prickly spurs stuck to my pants. Small clumps of earth had made their way into my shoes, and my ankles were dusty, which I'd likely have to explain later. But I was in.

Standing, I could see that many of the trees had tiny fruits, baby green olives not bigger than a small grape. Saro had taught me that when they are that hue of green, with a yellow undertone, they are months from harvest. A line of black ants scurried on a diagonal along the gnarled trunk of the nearest tree. Their procession seemed urgent. Below the tree and throughout the sloping grove, it looked as though the ground had recently been cleared. That would make getting to the chosen spot easier; I could walk without worry of snakes or large holes that would otherwise have been hidden by knee-high *tumminia*—an ancient variety of wheat that sprouts everywhere after the wind sows its seeds back into the earth each season.

I moved deeper into the grove, carefully navigating the descending earth so as not to fall. Once I arrived in the center, I stood before the tree where I would scatter Saro's ashes. The late-afternoon breeze moving in from the Mediterranean refreshed and emboldened me.

The tree I chose was neither the largest nor the oldest. It was just one with the clearest view to the dazzling, ever-present blue sea, the one with enough level ground at its base for me to sit on because I felt the emotion coming on.

Taking the small wooden box from my pocket and opening it, my hands shook just a little. I removed the clear plastic bag meant for small jewelry and opened the seal. If I had planned better, I would have had a prayer committed to memory, ready to recite. But it didn't go like that. Standing in this sacred space of nature was the only form of prayer suitable to consecrating Saro to *terra firma*.

The ashes left the bag easily, falling gently but slowly to the earth. I watched them disappear into the grayish sienna dirt. Then the last almost imperceptible bits were carried away by the wind.

He was back, returned forever to the soil of his childhood, free between the sea and the mountains.

When I finally stood, my shirt was stained with sweat and spotted with tears. The cicadas had never stopped keeping time. They were a Sicilian symphony. Then a tractor engine sputtered in the distance below. Life in Sicily went on.

Part Three

SECOND
SUMMER

Casa quantu stai e tirrinu quantu viri.
Home for as long as you need it to be
and land as far as the eye can see.
—*Sicilian proverb*

HEIRLOOMS

Two days before the first anniversary of Saro's death, I felt woozy as I stood outside Stage 7 on the Paramount Studios backlot in Hollywood when I was struck with a surge of grief. I was about to audition for a police procedural, a television pilot. And I could barely hold it together.

It had now been fifty-two Wednesday mornings since Saro had died. Enough Wednesdays for Zoela to get taller, her baby teeth to become fewer. Enough Wednesdays for her to ask me again and again, "Why did Babbo die?" and have my answer still not satisfy. Enough Wednesdays to see just a little more peeling paint on our hundred-year-old house, enough Wednesdays to watch the apartment building next door empty and fill again. I had seen Wednesdays when I couldn't get out of bed and Wednesdays when I couldn't fall asleep, so weary and bereft I had asked other people to drive my daughter to school, pick up groceries at the store, stand at my dining room table and help me fold clothes.

I had stacked fifty-two Wednesdays on top of one another, at the base of which was that Wednesday morning that had changed everything. In that time, I had been guerrilla grieving—stealthily mourning out of public view, using any tactics necessary to get by. Moreover, I had an unspoken belief that if I just pushed through and kept everything from falling apart, at the end of the first year things would get easier. They hadn't, and I felt duped.

Instead, I had come to think of my grief as a character in my life, something I had to get to know, befriend, make peace with, because it was bigger than anything I had ever known. It pulled me down and sometimes propelled me forward. That day, I wasn't sure exactly what it was capable of doing.

As I walked across the lot to the casting office, I rehearsed my lines in my head once again: "I found the body," then "Perp never saw it coming." Later in the script: "I'm not sure I want to be on this job." There was a singular, personal truth in that last line. One year out, I still felt unsuited for the job of widow.

I looked up at the looming water tower above the fabled Hollywood backlot. I loved the Paramount Studios. It had been the home of my first television series, and I never tired of its Italianate and Art Deco architecture. But the water tower gave it a small-town feel. The first time I had ever driven onto the studio lot, I had used the water tower as the landmark to find my way back to my car. It was emblazoned with the Paramount logo—a mountain peak surrounded by stars. As I headed to the audition, I wondered what it would feel like to stand at the apex of a mountain. To have climbed so far and be able to stand above it all, above the mist and the clouds. I wondered what a reprieve from the hard work of grieving might feel like.

A golf cart passed me with a twenty-something assistant on *NCIS: Los Angeles* talking on a headset; a messenger dumped his bike by a palm tree before disappearing into the commissary. For a moment, I thought to stop inside and get an espresso. Then my cell phone rang. It was my mom.

"Have you landed?" I asked. She was set to arrive later that day from Houston. My dad and Aubrey were also coming to town to help mark the first anniversary. I had planned a gathering of friends at the house. No one wanted Zoela or me to be alone. Least of all us.

"What can I pick up from the store?" she asked. "I wanted to call now in case you're busy with Zoela later."

She knew I didn't usually answer my phone in the evenings. The end of the day was still unpredictable for us. Some days were still hard, especially as the anniversary neared. Zoela had returned to sleeping in her own bed, but we needed lots of lead time for her to feel safe and secure enough to fall asleep. Then I slumped into bed myself, worn down by single parenting while grieving. Often I would lie awake. When I did finally fall asleep, I was visited with a recurring dream of Saro and me making love on the beach, as we had done in Greece and Elba. In the dreams, there were sand dunes that formed around a tent on the beach where we met daily to wrap our bodies into each other. He entered me and I cried out, and then I'd look out to see the waves approaching. I could see that the shelter would be washed away. Us included. And in the dream I'd say, "Hurry, hurry, let's do it." Then I'd awaken to silence.

"I don't know, Mom. Can we think about groceries tomorrow? I'm actually walking into an audition."

"Great, break a leg." Although she ran a multi-million-dollar business, she loved the fact that I had made a career in the arts and always got excited about my auditions. "You'll do great. I'll pick up flowers. You deserve them."

Ten minutes later I was seated in a waiting room full of actors. Five minutes after that I was in front of the camera. Another five minutes, and it was done.

When I got home from the audition, the sun shone through

my kitchen window in a golden hue, bathing the hundred-year-old floorboards in a light that made me think of candy caramel laid in strips. I listened to the swell of silence that had descended on my house. I still hadn't gotten used to it. At times it was deafening. The silence seemed to bat against the windows, rattle the panes. Zoela was at school, but I called out her name and then Saro's to drown out the sound of nothingness. Then I pretended that Saro was calling from another room, lobbing easy conversation back and forth. It was a game I played to fill the emptiness, physical and emotional. Still, that day their names fell from my mouth onto the floor with a thud. Only silence echoed back.

In two hours, I could pick Zoela up from school. She would set the house vibrating with cartoons, card games, doll play, and music at the piano. She had recently written a story wherein a young girl had lost her mother because the mother had gone out "wandering" for the girl's father, who had died.

Over the last year, she had marked her first birthday without her dad. She had often asked me, "Who will take care of me if you die?" The question peppered our conversations at the dentist's, on airplanes, when she put her head onto her pillow.

"I am well, I am healthy, I am here for you. I plan on being here to see you grow old." My answer had become a mantra.

"But you don't know that for sure." At eight years old, she knew about life's trapdoors.

"You're right. None of us knows when we will die. What matters is that we are alive now. And I am here with you now. Right now." It was the kind of thing therapists and books had taught me to say to ease her anxiety.

With work done, the heaviness of the day was barreling down on me, and I was suddenly aimless and distracted. I needed fresh air.

So I went outside to Saro's garden, where fava beans were growing. It was the place in my home that lifted the heaviness from my heart. Resurrection, renewal, sustenance—the promise of this bean.

Standing in front of the central fountain, I remembered how the garden had originally come together in a January years earlier. By that spring, Saro had recovered from surgery and he was once again on chemo when I finally tasted the *pasta con fave* that he made directly from the garden. There was something about that first meal from his garden. He had found a way to transform anxiety, fear, and worry into something beautiful. It literally made me cry when I took the first bite. Right then, I vowed to plant fava beans every year going forward. When the season ended, we dried two handfuls of beans, and those were our seeds for the next year. It had been that way for five years.

Even this first year following his death, I had planted the beans again on a late-January day, the anniversary of when we had eloped in New York City.

As I surveyed the bounty in the garden, there looked to be five pounds of beans waiting to be picked. Saro had taught me how to eyeball a harvest. I wanted to make his favorite spring dish, *purea di fave con crostini* for the forty friends who were coming over to help me mark the anniversary of his passing. In two days, we planned to celebrate his life and raise a glass to the fact that Zoela and I had somehow made it through the hardest year of our lives. I had gone from being a caregiver, with its constant triage and putting out of fires, only to have that chaos give way to the melancholy of grieving wife. I wanted to acknowledge that transformation, that I was learning to survive. I wanted to get it right. So I started plucking the bean pods from the stalks.

As I picked, I felt grateful for those these beans would nourish.

If friends are the family you choose, I have chosen the best family on the planet. They are my tribe. Each one came into my life through some chance encounter—a freshman college class, the first day on a new set, looking for shoes in the sandbox that belonged to our barefoot toddlers at nursery school, Saro introducing himself to the parents of other biracial kids in the park with the sentence "My kid looks like your kid, we should know each other." My tribe comes from all walks of life, ages, interests, and professions—a mosaic artist, lawyer, teacher, therapist, investment banker, actor, writer, limo driver, cartoon artist. The common thread among all of us is a fundamental willingness to walk beside one another in the most uncertain and painful of times. They had come to me by chance; they had stayed by choice. I wanted them to have Sicilian fava beans. Beans that I had grown all winter in anticipation of this day. I wanted to huddle the team to let them know that their love and care in the preceding twelve months was the only reason I was standing upright.

Since this was my first time having people over to the house in big numbers, I was literally attempting to resurrect something—a tradition Saro and I had had of opening our home to friends for convivial connection and seriously good food. He had always been the magnet that drew people to our home. His company, his food, his rambling stories about his childhood in Sicily, where a teacher had once made the students walk home through town with "I am a donkey" signs pinned to their backs because they hadn't been paying attention in class. Friends loved those stories of a time and place that seemed to be drawn from outtakes of *Cinema Paradiso*.

After his death, I feared that our friends would stop coming over because I was not like him. I didn't have his easygoing, drop-by-anytime, open-door policy. I was more rigid, a woman who relied on making plans to the point of pathology. But I hoped that by hosting this gathering I could bring back both some of the spirit of Saro's conviviality and a house full of people eating, spilling wine on the table, and laughing at years of memories.

I went back inside the house and dumped a minimountain of fresh fava beans from the garden onto the kitchen island, ready to make his favorite spring dish, but I couldn't remember all the steps. I remembered the shelling and boiling part. But the rest was vague. Should I puree them with a bit of the water they were boiled in, or should I make broth? Should I add garlic or shallots? Garlic, I thought. Pepper? How much olive oil? Would butter work?

When in doubt, there was only one other person I could call. Nonna.

"How are things in town?" Apart from cooking tips, she was now the only person with whom I spoke Italian regularly. Our thrice-weekly conversations kept me somewhat fluent, a tie to my former life. It was the way we stayed connected and kept current with how each of us was doing in Saro's absence. He had talked to his mother daily after his father had died. It seemed natural that she and I keep up the tradition after Saro died. It had drawn us closer.

"Beh, the usual. I'm not going out much. There's no use taking my sadness on the road," she said, responding to me in half dialect, half Italian. "But I will be at Mass for the anniversary."

A monthly Mass during which Saro's name was read was her way of marking time. I hadn't figured out how to tell her that we were having a gathering at the house in his honor, a celebration of his life. "Celebration" seemed the wrong word to use with a woman for whom there was no such cultural ritual. I had had many moments like this with her, when I had worried that something I'd say would get lost in translation. It was another way that Saro's death kept reverberating. He would have known what to say, he knew the cultural ins and outs: what to omit, what to gloss over, what to explain in detail. In his absence, I was sensitive about how my language or misuse of it would create hurt or confusion.

"Zoela and I are having people come over. My family is in town. We will commemorate Saro." I had pulled up the Italian word for "commemorate" while I was on the phone with her. "And I'm making the fava beans from the garden."

She knew about the heirloom beans, passed down through generations in Sicily, that we had been growing every year. It made her happy to imagine them growing in foreign soil, feeding us thousands of miles away. She gave me tips on how to keep the beans creamy once pureed. Then we talked about Zoela and school. She asked me if Zoela still asked about Saro. And just before we were about to hang up, she surprised me. "Are you coming to Sicily this summer?"

"Yes, we will be there," I answered before my brain had time to calculate a response. The reflexiveness of my response surprised me. "I think it will be good for us," I heard myself say.

I hung up the phone and looked at the pile of fava beans. Some people have heirloom jewelry. I had fava beans.

Two days later, I put my energy into making an altar-like memory table in the room downstairs where Saro had passed a year earlier. Zoela and I lit candles around the room. I put on his favorite music, laid out his favorite books. We put a rosary around the statue of Buddha. Then I opened the pocket doors and said a prayer. An hour later, one after another, friends and family filled the house. I invited everyone who arrived to pass through the room, if they wanted, and leave a message for Saro. They could do it silently or openly or write it down in a book of remembrance.

Outside, the back yard was teeming with people, all in mid-conversation about Saro, life, current events, food. The fountain bubbled, the scent of jasmine filled the air. That day the Los Angeles spring sky was bright and giving.

As the afternoon moved toward the softening of twilight, we all went inside. Thirty or so people huddled in the living room around the fireplace, the piano, and the large picture window that looked out onto Saro's garden.

"Thank you all for being here. Saro would love that we are all gathered. He's gathered here with us. And I know he'd have some story to tell. But for today, I'd like anyone who wants to to share a story about him."

Zoela sat on my lap as the room came to life with stories of his friendship, idiosyncrasies, political rants, gentle spirit, hospitality, and food. And of course, people talked of his love. For me, for Zoela. A few of our musician friends picked up his guitars, and an impromptu jam session took hold of the house. Piano, bongos, acoustic and bass guitar filled the air. It was the most alive I had felt in a year.

When everyone left, well after 9:00 p.m., I was tired but still in the afterglow of so much love. As I put away the leftover food, I noticed that some of the fava bean puree remained in the fridge. I thought about my conversation with Nonna days before, the way I had been so worried about what I had said or not said. I had committed myself to seeing her again. There would be another summer. And just like I was still figuring out how to cultivate and prepare the beans on my own, I still had to figure out so much more—in life, in parenting, in the intimacy needed to stay close to his family across culture, geography, and the landscape of grief.

AT THE TABLE

"*You know,* you don't have to do this. People do leave," Julie said as we sat at The Ivy on Robertson. It was three months after Saro had been diagnosed with a soft tissue cancer that had metastasized to his bone, and he was in the midst of undergoing indeterminate rounds of debilitating chemotherapy. Julie was my acting coach, friend, and mentor. Even more relevant was the fact that her husband had died when she was in her early thirties, leaving her to raise a son all alone. She knew about grit, adversity, and making the best of the hand you are dealt. She had also faced life-threatening illness herself. "It can be too much, not what you signed up for," she continued, looking me dead in the eye.

Just two nights before, Saro and I had experienced the lowest point in our marriage. We were holding each other in bed after a particularly difficult week of chemotherapy. His immune system was reduced to so few white blood cells that we could practically have given each of them a name. The situation was dire. So I kissed him as we lay there and ran my hand along his chest.

He moved my hand away and said, "I think you should take a lover."

"What?" He had never said anything like that. I felt the room spin. "No, absolutely not. *No*, Saro. I love you and only you. We're in this together."

We hadn't had sex in months. He had been too sick, too weak, too nauseous. Neither of us had spoken about it directly. We just held each other each night and then rolled over, resigned to whatever sleep we could find.

"I will not take a lover. You are my lover. Period."

"I just don't want you to suffer so much. You have needs, and I can't meet them."

"If you say one more thing, I am gonna kill you. Stop it. Don't do this. We're fine." I put my hand back onto his chest and gave him a kiss. "We will be fine."

Then I turned from him with a private understanding that we were in new psychological territory. It wasn't just about fighting for his life; part of this would require fighting for our marriage.

I had just shared that with Julie. I thought she'd cheer me up, say something to lighten the moment, lift my spirits. I had never expected her to suggest I leave him.

"What are you talking about?" I demanded, an odd feeling ghosting up my neck, but before I could discern it another rushed in, anger. I pushed back my plate and clocked a room full of the strident celebrity hangers-on for which The Ivy was known. The setting was absurd to discuss cancer and leaving Saro. I suddenly felt weary. This lunch was the opposite of the easy, breezy girls' time she had suggested when she had convinced me I needed a moment of levity after months of intense caregiving.

"I'm serious. Leaving is an option," she pressed on, undeterred. She even poured herself more tea.

"No, there's no way. I would never leave Saro." Did she not get it?

"Then," she said slowly, "you have to choose this. And I mean really *choose* it."

She took another bite, sipped her Earl Grey, and leaned back. She had elicited a response from me, exactly as she'd intended. Then she continued, "Do your best and keep your heart open. Show up in the face of the unknown. And he, no matter how bad it gets, has to do the same. If you're in it, you're in this together."

I left The Ivy that day with the understanding that my marriage could go deeper than either of us had imagined. Or we could become strangers to each other as we fought a common enemy. That I would have to choose the path of caregiving. But even more important, I realized for the first time that what we were up against would require me to show up for Saro in a way I had not ever had to. That conversation with Julie gave me the awareness that it was my turn to be the kind of person who could stand in the rain for hours, steadfast and open, ready and available to this man, come what may.

Many rounds of chemo, three hospital stays, and a major surgery later, Saro still had not told his parents about his diagnosis.

"I want to see how the complete treatment goes first," he had told me in the days immediately after his diagnosis. "I want to wait for results. I don't want to worry them. It will kill my mother."

He didn't want to hear the worry in his mother's voice half a world away at the same time that he was barely able to hold his own life together. I understood, but still it bothered me. I had told my parents right away, I leaned on them. They encouraged Saro, even offered to help financially since he was no longer working and his medical costs were staggering. I didn't like having to withhold the incredible information from his family. We finally had open communication with his parents. Not telling them felt like a betrayal, a glaring lack of intimacy. But he had his reasons. Chief among them was that there was nothing they could do so far away and that the worry they would carry would be too much. He wanted to wait. So I made Saro a promise to say nothing, a promise that made me see the many forms of divisiveness cancer wrought. We were back to keeping things from the Sicilians.

However, as Christmas approached, Saro had completed more than four rounds of chemotherapy and had had his knee replaced with an implant prosthesis, rather than having his leg amputated at his femur as we had feared. He was still walking on crutches. We had been told that his femur and tibia would take months to heal around the prosthesis and months would go by before he could walk on his own again. In the meantime, I helped him to be mobile and he had in-home physical therapy as we waited for his immune system to recover before he could receive more chemo in the new year. He chose that as the time to finally tell his parents that he had been diagnosed with cancer.

"*Il cancro non c'è più. Sto molto meglio.*—The cancer is gone. I'm much better," he said in the most real and honest conversation he'd had with his parents in months.

I heard the quivering in his voice as he responded to a barrage of questions from his mother and father, who were both on the phone. His mother said, "Rosario, Rosario!" with such lament in her voice that it frightened me. It made me nauseous. It brought back all the doubt. I instantly understood exactly why he had waited to tell them. There was no way we could have navigated the previous months with the additional responsibility of managing their anxiety.

Saro cried when he hung up the phone. I left him alone. We were learning something new in our marriage—when to leave each other alone to allow space between us and when to draw closer. It had been five months of him being at home every day, not working, me caring for every aspect of his physical needs as well as the needs of our household. We were with each other 24/7, in the trenches. We were forming a new way of being that included allowing him to cry alone.

The day after he broke the news to his parents, Franca called to say his parents were coming to L.A. to visit him for Christmas. She had purchased the tickets on their behalf. She said the tickets would be cheapest if they stayed for a month. No one had discussed it with us. It seemed that a mother who had missed her son's wedding would not miss being at his side during cancer. The idea of a month of my in-laws being with us in L.A. nearly stopped me cold. When I tried to suggest to Saro that it might be too long, too stressful, he said, "Tembi, let them do this. They want to help. I don't know if it's the right thing for us, but nothing is as we would have it in this situation." Lying in bed, he rolled away from me to face the window. "Plus I don't know when I will see them again."

His parents were on a flight two weeks later. Since our first meeting five years earlier, I had been seeing them roughly once a year. We interacted the way distant relatives might do at an annual family reunion: exchanged pleasantries and hugs, smiled at one another throughout the day, and broke bread together without ever really scratching the surface of intimacy. I had accepted that I would never be close to his parents. Just being in one another's lives was a huge enough hurdle to overcome in one lifetime. I had never imagined them coming to Los Angeles, seeing our life in person. Cancer had changed all that.

The morning of their arrival, I was getting the house ready while Saro rested, still too ill to do much. But not too ill to hide his anxiety or keep him from directing me through what needed to be done.

"Have you been to the store?" he called out from his resting place, our bed, surrounded by books and two issues of *la Repubblica*, his Italian paper, to keep him occupied.

"Yes," I responded from the guest room across the hall, where I was making the bed and putting out towels for them.

"Did you get an iron?"

"What? An iron? Why? I don't iron," I said, walking to the entrance of our bedroom to make sure I had heard him correctly and to get a good look at the husband who was suggesting that our house suddenly needed an iron.

"Yes, an iron. My mother will need to iron."

"Really, Saro, you want me to go out and get an iron on top of everything else? Seriously?"

"Tembi, she's going to need something to do in the house. She can't drive, she doesn't know English, so she's not going to watch TV. She's going to want to do housework to pass the time. She will want to iron."

For fuck's sake, I thought. "Fine, Saro, after I finish cleaning and picking up your antinausea prescription, I will pass by the hardware store for an iron. Does it have to be a certain kind of iron?" I asked, my resentment on full display.

"Don't be that way. You know I would do it if I could. I can't even leave this fucking bed without your help. I just want things to go as easily as possible. They will need to be taken care of. I want this time to go smoothly."

I knew he was right, and I also wanted peace and ease for him. He deserved that. He deserved time with his parents, as his life still hung in the balance.

We gathered them at Los Angeles International Airport. Saro's mother greeted him tearfully; his father kissed him on both cheeks.

They were seeing their son for the first time postchemo and post-surgery. The change in his appearance startled them.

As we drove through the Westside, past downtown, into Hollywood, toward our house, they looked out at the city lights, the endless flow of cars, the different styles of architecture, the proliferation of billboards, including one with the L.A. icon Angelyne. The cityscape was immense. In the back seat, Saro's mom clutched her purse.

"*Ma dov'è il centro?*—But where is the center?" Saro's father asked, looking out the passenger-side window.

"There isn't one," I said in Italian. "It's a decentralized American city." I didn't know if he knew what that meant; part of me didn't care.

"There are just lots of little neighborhoods," Saro said in dialect, covering my rudeness effortlessly.

I heard Saro's mom let out a sigh from the back seat. She was visibly distressed. This was all impossibly new to her: the trip, the city, the circumstances. Her concern for Saro was formidable.

Forty-five minutes later, we pulled up to our house. I turned to Saro. "Show them the way." Then I sat in my car alone. I needed time to process what was happening. In the silence of the car, the tears hit me. I cried from being overwhelmed and exhausted by what life was asking me to do. The ways in which love required more than I felt I was capable of doing. Spending a month with my in-laws at a time when Saro and I felt so fragile felt far outside what I had signed up for. I wanted to run, I wanted my life back. Instead I wiped my face, took a deep breath, and opened the car door.

When I went inside to join the Gullo clan, the first thing I saw was Croce and Giuseppe wandering around our home, touching the handrails along the stairs, opening the fridge, looking at the fountain in the atrium. Giuseppe tapped the copper-pipe railing that led upstairs. He stuck his face into the dryer. Croce took her shoes off and sunk her stockinged feet into the carpet.

By the time I took them upstairs to the guest bedroom, it was obvious that they were proud. Not because the house was particularly big or opulent in any way. It didn't matter that the beds still didn't have frames or that we had Ikea side tables. It was their son's house, something he had managed to own as an immigrant in a country that they themselves had found overwhelming and inhospitable.

When I suggested that they should rest after more than twenty hours of travel, they balked.

"*Abbiamo portato da mangiare*—We brought food," they said in unison. "We need to unpack it."

Within a matter of minutes, two of their three suitcases were open in the hallway upstairs, and they began arguing over what to make for dinner from the fresh produce they had brought.

Then Giuseppe took off his homemade money belt, an old undershirt Croce had stitched with muslin and fashioned with a draw tie. I could see a stack of euros inside, enough for a monthlong stay. That kind of money was the result of years of harvests, years of savings. He handled the money belt carefully, resting it on the floor so that he could freely unpack the food, unencumbered. Then we went downstairs to where Saro was waiting, still unable to navigate stairs unassisted.

"*Passami il cibo*—Pass me the food," he yelled up to his mother.

Over the railing, Croce handed him eggplant, winter cardoons, a string of braided garlic, and artichoke bulbs for planting followed by bottles of tomato sauce, a two-gallon tin of olive oil, jars of marinated artichoke hearts, a small wheel of cheese, dried oregano, and plastic bags containing chamomile flowers still on the stalk and bundled with a tie.

I learned two things about them in that moment. One, that my in-laws were wholly unaware of the fact that transporting fresh produce into the United States was illegal. I was shocked, staring at a suitcase full of food directly from the fields of Sicily. How they had gotten bulbs of garlic, winter greens, and cheese through customs, I will never know. And two, that they had no faith in American grocery stores. If they were going to a foreign country, they wanted to bring what they knew: good olive oil, tomato sauce, caponata, garlic they had grown with their own hands.

I helped the process along by taking the remaining items down to Saro. I was ready to laugh with him about how absurd it all was. Instead, he met my sarcastic smile with genuine excitement. "*Bellissimo! Facciamo una pasta?*—Beautiful! Shall we make pasta?"

It was nearly 10:00 p.m.

Half an hour later, Saro was talking to his father in the living room and I was showing my mother-in-law around our tiny kitchen. I shoved cardoons with the roots still intact into the lettuce crisper alongside my California rolls.

She started cooking that night and didn't stop for the next month. The house always smelled of something simmering, sautéeing, or frying. Once again it had the familiar noises of clattering dishes, flames clicking into action, the opening and closing of the oven door. Croce seemed happy to do it. It gave her purpose each day.

We got Italian stations on satellite TV for Giuseppe, and when he wasn't yelling at then prime minister Silvio Berlusconi on the screen, I was tasked with entertaining him on trips to Home Depot. He walked the aisles, marveling at all the choices, American surplus on display. He wanted me to translate everything from drills to drains to screen doors.

After a week, it was clear that I was to be Giuseppe's bread runner. I taxied him to the store each day for daily loaves. After a week of going there twice a day, as he would have if he had been in Sicily, I was exhausted. I had a husband at home who was still going to regular doctor appointments and still taking powerful drugs to help repair his immune system and promote bone growth before starting chemotherapy all over again. I had in-laws who didn't drive or speak English. They had no interest in museums or restaurants or retail stores. They wanted to be with their son. They wanted bread. They wanted to make sure their love stood guard over cancer.

One night, as Croce and I cleaned the kitchen while Saro rested and his father watched television, Croce asked me, "What do the doctors say?" Her voice was gravelly and full of tamped-down emotion.

"They don't give definitive answers, but so far he has responded well. Some people have years with no recurrences," I responded.

"But it comes back?" she asked, abandoning Italian and speaking to me in Sicilian. I hated the question. To answer it, I'd have to reveal the reality of the worst possible outcome.

"I don't know," I responded in Italian.

"Saro would have more to live for if there were children," Croce said almost under her breath. I nearly dropped the plate I was drying, struck as I was with shock. Her words had hit like a gut punch in the place I was most vulnerable. *How dare she? What does she know?* We were fighting for life, and we had preserved the possibility of a future life with kids. But I didn't have the words, energy, or desire to express all that. Even in that moment, I knew her statement, typical of a concerned Sicilian mother, was not meant as a rebuke of me as a woman, as a wife. Still, it made me feel that I had failed Saro. I wanted to cry, I wanted to scream. More than anything, though, I wanted her and Giuseppe gone. I left the plate on the counter and went up to my room, shut the door, crawled into bed, and didn't speak to anyone until the next morning.

By the eighth day of their stay, I had reached my limit. Saro and I were strained in our interactions, both fatigued for different reasons. I was tired of hosting and assisting, feeling subtly less than because I wasn't a wife who bore children and ironed her husband's underwear, as Croce did for Giuseppe. Saro was emotionally exhausted from constantly reassuring his parents that he would be okay.

"We have to get out of here and go to Houston, or I'm going to lose my mind," I said as we lay in bed that night. His body was tender, undeniably fragile. Even his hands, the hands that had once labored to create magic, even they were soft. Attempting to process it all brought terror to every cell in my own body. I hadn't said anything about the kid comment and had decided I never would. No good would come of that. "I need to see my parents. I can't face Christmas morning with all this." I pointed to his medicine on the nightstand and the crutches in the corner. But what I also meant was the presence of his parents.

"Okay, *amore*. If you want to go to Houston, we can go." He leaned in to kiss me. Then he pulled me close. "It's going to be fine. It's all going to be fine," he said. He wanted to believe it, he needed to believe it.

Neither of us said it aloud, but I believe that somewhere in that discussion was a desire for our families to meet for the first time. I think we both feared there might never be another chance.

• • •

That trip to Houston has become a composite of key moments, captured in photographs that help me remember the early period in his illness when I was so exhausted and traumatized that memory is hard to access. I remember taking Saro's parents to see the Gulf Coast; Giuseppe casting a fishing pole for the first time; his parents giddy as they held up the gold medal my uncle Frederick had won for track and field in the 1976 Olympics; my dad taking them to a Texans football game and his dad waving a pennant when the cheerleaders took the field. I have a flash memory of Saro's mom standing in a buffet line staring at trays of barbecue and shaking her head. That memory is the clearest because it happened just before we sat down to dinner together as two families for the first time. We ate at a large communal table at my aunt Rhonda's house. Croce said in genuine bewilderment, "I don't understand why Americans pile so much food onto one plate."

"I don't know if all Americans do, but Texans do," I said with a smile, happy to be with my family and have her sitting at their table.

A tray of ribs was being passed around. "Mamma," Saro said, "you don't have to eat it all." Then he took a rib just as my father offered him a glass of tea. The table was full of the southern soul food that nourished my family and told us who we were culturally. Food my family was always happy to share with others.

"I'll try it," she said. Then she stealthily took the meat off her plate and foisted it onto Giuseppe's while he sat speaking Sicilian to my uncle. My uncle in turn looked to me for translation. Giuseppe was asking how much land it took to graze one head of cattle, a conversation that surprisingly was right up my uncle's alley, because he was a rancher.

Nonna sat quietly observing the room, taking in the faces at the table, noting the gestures and interactions of another foreign language so far from her home. But mostly she kept looking at her son. Since her arrival, I had caught her casting long glances his way. I imagined that she was trying to process his physical changes: weight loss, thinned hair, the need for crutches. But in Houston at the table, she was looking at him in a different way. She finally spoke up sometime between the potato salad and peach cobbler. She turned to my sister, who was sitting next to her. *"Non lo sapevo che mio figlio avevo tutto questo, questa vita, quest'amore qua."*

My sister called to me across the table to translate. But it took me a moment before the words could leave my mouth. I looked back at Croce, who held my gaze as I translated.

"She said, 'I had no idea my son had all this, this life, so much love here.'"

Saro had built a life for himself abroad, she could see that for the first time. A life that included a family that claimed him as their own. I saw the relief in her eyes.

And as I sat there with everyone eating—not just consuming food but sharing our dreams, our aspirations, our histories—I could see how the stakes, the specter of illness, had changed all our lives. What was important had changed. We were far from the wedding in Florence, reading telegrams from the half of our family who had refused to come because of race and fear. That trip to Houston was the first time we didn't have to wonder what it would have been like to have both parts of who we were together in the same room.

I read somewhere that a wedding is more than just the joining of two people in unity; it is a symbol of the conjoining of two families.

That had not happened for us at our wedding. It had taken a rare cancer to bring these two very different families together.

RICOTTA

"*La famiglia Gullo è tornata*—The Gullo family has returned," Nonna said, using the family name to call us one, to claim us all. She had never done that. She was wearing the same earrings she had worn for more than forty years and the same wooden cross necklace that her sister Carmela, the nun, had brought her from the Vatican. She rose from the bench outside her front door. Her wedding ring sat snug on her arthritic hands as she put her hand on my shoulder.

I smiled and put my arms around her for an American-style hug. We were in the middle of our second annual arrival ritual. The widows and wives of Via Gramsci had surrounded the car once again, their usual chorus of salutations and physical evaluations in full swing: "Zoela is taller." "Your hair is longer." "You look tired." "You look nourished." "You need to rest."

The first greetings were always an evaluation of how we looked. It was the Sicilian way. "Nourished" was shorthand for well fed. It was true that I had gained back some weight since the previous summer. And Zoela was now chest high. She had breast buds. I was happy they didn't mention that.

Within an hour, we were seated at the table, ready for our first meal together in a year. Nonna ladled *ditalini con le lenticchie*, tiny tube-shaped pasta with lentils, into a shallow pasta bowl. There was cheese infused with large, jet black peppercorns. They reminded me of mini black-eyed peas in a sea of pecorino. I'd always enjoyed that variety of sheep cheese, its outer ring so salty, it made my palate spark to life. It had all the characteristics of Sicily, strong but inviting. Nonna had sliced it into wedges that rivaled a small filet of beef.

It was as if no time had passed. My seat was where it usually was. Nonna positioned herself nearest to the stove so she could serve without standing. Zoela plopped down to my left. One bite and my heart eased, my stress lowered. Los Angeles began to fall away as if it literally existed in another time and place.

"*Mangia*—Eat," Nonna said to Zoela, who, after twenty-six hours of travel, was more tired than hungry.

I put my spoon to the bowl once again, consuming fortune, fate, and grief. All of it. Then I grabbed a roughly sliced piece of bread from the pile that lay on the table.

"How are you?" I asked, aware that Nonna would be inspecting me for signs that being in her home, eating her food, was in fact restoring me, putting me back together.

"I'm as God wants. No more, no less," she said, shrugging in her shoulders and simultaneously reaching for the stack of napkins that lay just beneath a statue of the Virgin Mary.

Over the past year, I had received reports on who had become ill in town, who had been born. I had gotten a blow-by-blow of the contentious local election in which Nonna had refused to vote because two cousins were up against each other for the same post. I knew of her high blood pressure and diabetes. I knew she had nerve pain in her shoulder. I knew my nieces were studious and Franca and Cosimo were toiling in precarious work that left little for any of life's excesses, let alone luxuries. And just days before I arrived, Nonna and I had talked about the raging wildfires that were engulfing parts of the island.

I turned to Zoela, who had eaten only a few bites and was about to get up from the table to go sit in the small living room to watch Italian soap operas, her favorite pastime when there was nothing else to do. Before I could ask her to, Nonna intervened.

"*Mangia, Zoela, amore. Mangia, perche ti devi fare grande.*—Eat, Zoela, my love. Eat because you need to grow," Nonna implored. She wanted the pleasure of seeing her grandchild eating vigorously at her table. She put another filet of cheese on Zoela's plate.

"Zoela, Nonna is happy that we have returned," I said to her in Italian in the hope that the three of us could have a shared conversation. In our common language.

"I know, I heard you," she responded in English. Then she got up and walked to the adjacent living room.

"Well, do you want to tell her something about how you feel about being here?" I pressed.

"Sure." She plopped herself onto the couch and began to take off her shoes, never taking her eyes off the TV. Eight years old was the new eighteen.

"Okay, why don't you come back here and say it to her personally? Or give her another hug." I switched back to English suddenly and in a tone that I failed to make sound easy breezy.

Nonna sensed that something was amiss.

"*Picciridda mia.* I know how happy she is. I can see it in her face and how she liked the lunch." The way Nonna said "*picciridda mia*—my littlest one" in Sicilian as an emphasis of affection made me suddenly have to hold back a torrent of tears. Grief was still like that. The tenderness brought it all forward. We were a trio of different ages and languages trying to make it work. The little things meant a lot.

Zoela came back into the kitchen all smiles and kissed Nonna on the cheek. Then she pivoted on one foot and trounced out again.

"Barefoot like a gypsy," Nonna said, smiling, an affectionate reference to Zoela. "Let her be."

When Zoela got to the other room, she turned and called back to me in English, "Mommy . . . how come there are no pictures of you and Babbo getting married on Nonna's wall?"

It was the last thing I had expected, but she was eight and seeing her world differently with each passing day. And it was the first time I realized I'd eventually have to answer the question. But not yet.

As Nonna had begun to clear the table, I responded carefully, "There are no pictures of our wedding hanging, but there are many other pictures of us in the house." And she didn't press me anymore.

She wasn't old enough for me to tell her the details of the ways in which families can hold back on accepting whom their children love. I didn't want to create any division between her and her grandparents. A full answer would require context first. And to provide a context would require breaking down the long-ago past.

One day I would have to articulate what at the moment remained unspoken: that we were a family stumbling toward connection and the process of forgiveness is sometimes graceless. I would tell her about the drive for love, the capacity for human change, and a reunion in a hotel garden by the sea. I'd have to try to illustrate how life required constantly repairing and rebuilding relationships. How her dad's illness had brought us closer. And how her birth had changed everything.

She would know these visits as fixtures of her childhood. She had been coming to visit her "Nonno Pepe," as she had called Giuseppe, and her nonna since she was six months old. Her relationship with them happened in fleeting moments, vignettes of connection. Like the summer when she was four and she had sat on her grandfather's lap every afternoon, unaware that it was his final summer. He had been too ill to take walks with her, sick with cancer in his kidneys that had come on suddenly and aggressively. So she had blown bubbles in his face and tickled his neck to make him laugh. Their conjoined laughter in the air had made Saro cry. He was six years into his own battle, and he knew that was the last summer he would ever see his dad. That summer Nonna had seen both her son and her husband slipping away because of *il male*— cancer—at the same time. It had made her weak and desperate with heartache. After Giuseppe had died, she had donned her black widow's weeds and would wear them the rest of her life, as was the traditional way. It reminded the community of her loss, that she carried mourning with her. It gave her a public role to play, the carrier of the stories and memories of the deceased. I'd have to tell Zoela all of that one day. And that the beginning of our story as a family did not foretell the ending. That time forgives.

All she had ever known was the love of two grandparents who had welcomed her with open arms because she was the beloved daughter of their only son. Whatever had come before was, as my own grandmother would say, "the road that got us there."

And it struck me clearly in that moment that now Nonna and I were the ones standing at the end of that road. And we were starting down the beginning of another.

Zoela continued watching TV, seemingly satisfied with my answer/nonanswer. Nonna dried the last dish and moved to put the after-lunch espresso on the stove. I brought my attention back to the cheese and took one last bite of the tender, firm slice. Nonna saw me as she twisted the top on the *moka macchinetta*.

"It's from the cheese maker across from the bar in the square. She and her husband make it. She has a daughter about Zoela's age," she said.

I had always been on the hunt for social hookups for Zoela while in Aliminusa. Now more than ever, providing her with peer interaction was the only way to get her to settle in, speak the Italian that I knew she could, and have unexpected moments of joy and spontaneity. Her cousins Laura and Giusy were much older, finishing high school and entering college.

"Zoela, do you want to meet the cheese maker's daughter?" I asked her in Italian as I pulled another piece of bread off the loaf, topped it with cheese, and brought it to her. "We could sample everything in their shop."

"Not really," she said, indifferent to my efforts to expand her circle of friends.

"Why?"

"Because I don't." She shrugged, a sign that she was wholly uncommitted to anything beyond the moment right in front of her.

"But I'll be there with you. Maybe we can get Rosalia to come with us."

I was trying hard. It was something that I had been doing in L.A. as well. At home I struggled to keep her socially active. Being alone at home, just the two of us, was often the hardest parts of our days. I rarely had the energy after a day of auditioning, prepping meals, doing laundry, and car pooling to entertain her beyond just sitting together, curled up watching TV. We missed the way Saro had played guitar while she sang her lungs out to Aretha Franklin's "Respect." Instead, we watched *Chopped* and *The Voice*. Walking together to get ice cream was a significant outing most weekends. I knew she needed more. So my in-box and text threads were full of seven to eight exchanges with other kids' moms trying to coordinate scheduling, figure out activities, discuss meal preferences. It was exhausting being a kid's social planner. But hanging with friends was better than relying on me, her grieving mother, to be wholly present. I knew that if I didn't actively step up the role of social coordinator, the two of us might get swallowed up in inertia and sadness. Worse yet, she'd be some modern version of Laura from *The Glass Menagerie*.

In Sicily, it was easier. Every kid ate pasta; no one was gluten free. If they wanted to play, they went outside and played. She could move around freely with a friend, buy gelato at the town bar without fear of getting lost. In L.A., though I was not a helicopter parent, she certainly didn't make a move without my knowing her coordinates at all times. Here she roamed according to her own curiosity and interest. I was thrilled for her. And I was determined that we'd make cheese.

Later, as Nonna and I sipped espresso in the kitchen, I let Zoela shake out the tablecloth in the middle of the street. Then I walked four houses down to Giacoma's, Rosalia's grandmother. I asked about Rosalia's whereabouts. Within ten minutes she was in Nonna's kitchen and we made a plan to visit the cheese shop.

Two days later, Rosalia, Zoela, and I walked into Donatella's cheese shop at 6:30 p.m. One glance, and I could tell it wasn't like my favorite cheese purveyor and hipster haunt back in L.A., the Silver Lake Cheese Shop. It was not a swanky retail outlet replete with a tasting table and jazz piped in through Bose speakers. This was a real shop in the truest sense of the word. I knew from the minute

I stepped down from street level onto the tiled floor and saw the larger-than-life stainless-steel cauldron in the room to my left that the work of making cheese happened there. Retail was secondary. Sure enough, there was only a small glass display case holding just two medium-sized wheels of cheese, and the case wasn't even illuminated. There was no one manning the counter. The calendar on the wall was from the previous year. The shop was dark. Clearly cheese was made and purchased quickly in this shop. There was no need for copper-patinaed presentation plates straight out of *Elle* magazine or John Coltrane.

Nonna had told me not to go any earlier than 6:00 p.m. She explained that Donatella's family rose early, 4:00 a.m. They herded their flock of sheep from the fields above town to the valley below where the animals grazed openly along the creek that ran to the sea. Then they tended and milked the sheep and took the milk to market. In the early afternoon, they transported the milk back to town for the afternoon and evening work of making cheese. Wednesdays they made fresh ricotta. Families in town placed their orders the day before and picked the cheese up, still warm, around 7:00 p.m., in time for the evening dinner. It was not Wednesday, so Nonna wasn't sure if I would be able to find Donatella in her shop. They lived in the house above it. She told me to call out to her in the street if no one was there. As Old World charming as that sounded, the American in me found the idea a little pushy since Donatella and I had never met.

Nonna had also told me that before moving to Aliminusa, Donatella and her husband had sold their cheese at the market. Donatella had thought it wise to teach herself the art of cheese making because she had married into a family of herders. She thought it was stupid to waste the milk they didn't sell or, worse yet, sell it cheaply to others who would turn it into cheese, making a bigger profit than they ever saw. The more I knew about Donatella, the more I wanted to meet this female cheesemonger and flavor visionary.

Zoela and Rosalia giggled in the corner as they took turns trying to sit on top of an old wine cask. I was happy to see Zoela smile effortlessly. I wanted to bundle up such moments. And I wanted to reward Rosalia with anything her heart desired because she was making my child smile. She also had Zoela speaking Italian, something with which I had had middling success since Saro's death. I watched them for a minute waiting. Then I asked Rosalia if she knew where I might find the cheese maker.

Rosalia had become my pint-sized intel agent. In past summers, she had been my go-to person when I wasn't sure about the time or location of minor happenings in town. She had reminded me when Mass got out. She had informed me when the bakery closed. She had told me which street to take if I wanted to take Zoela to see the last donkey in town. With her red-rimmed glasses and head of thick, dark hair, she reminded me of a kid version of a public radio host. Her raspy voice instantly made me a sucker for all things Rosalia.

"We can ring her bell. She may be upstairs," she said to me in Sicilian. And before I could answer, she was out the door with Zoela in tow.

I stood alone inside Donatella's cheese shop, and it hit out of nowhere. Suddenly I missed Saro anew. It happened like that in Aliminusa: I would be moving through the day, and his absence would come to me in the faces of the people I met. I would feel a sudden sense of loss so acute that it would momentarily destabilize me. Now his absence was in the sound of a kid taking our daughter to ring the bell of a woman I had never met because that was the way things happened there. The way they always had. The way Saro always believed was intuitive and superior to the American way. Very little happened in Sicily because of adroit planning; everything happened *all'improvviso*—on the spur of the moment. It was about being in the right place when an opportunity presented itself, and suddenly it seemed like the most obvious thing in world. Saro would have loved that Zoela was knocking at the door of someone she didn't know. That within a matter of minutes, I would likely be asking that person to let us help her make cheese. That was the part of Sicily he had wanted me to love.

I thought about what he had always said of the island: "*Li ricchi cchiù chi nn'hannu, cchiù nni vonnu*—The more you have, the more you want." I collapsed onto the wine cask to take the weight off my bones.

Rosalia returned with Donatella at her heels. I jumped down off the wine barrel just as our eyes met. She was a stout woman in her late thirties with red cheeks and a short bowl cut tapered at the neck. Flushed from the summer heat, she wore an apron that suggested she had likely been doing housework when Zoela and Rosalia had called to her.

I extended my hand. "I'm the daughter-in-law of Croce," I said in Italian while I scanned her face for recognition. I found none. "My husband was Saro. We live in the US, in California." I was giving out identifiers, letting her know I wasn't a complete stranger.

"I know of you. Saro's wife. I never met him, but I know your mother-in-law." She wiped her hands on her apron before reaching out to shake mine. She was almost two generations younger than Nonna; her Italian was effortless even behind a Sicilian accent. She, like others her age and younger, had been taught Italian in school and grown up hearing it on television. Some members of the younger generations now had to be encouraged to learn and speak Sicilian because they considered it an inferior language. Teens sometimes made gentle fun of their grandparents, who spoke an even older dialect. This complex, beautiful oral language dies a little with each generation.

I shifted my feet and nodded. Of course. I was the only black American woman in perhaps a thirty-mile radius. Zoela and I needed no introduction.

"My condolences," she offered. "It's nice you came to visit. Za Croce must be happy." "*Za*" is a familiar Sicilian title given to older women, like saying "Aunt Croce." "How can I help you?"

"I want to buy some cheese or place an order. And I am also wondering which day you make cheese here in the shop." Donatella raised an eyebrow. "My daughter, Zoela, has never seen it. I want her to know where the food she loves comes from." Across the room, Zoela perked up at the mention of her name.

"Of course. What kind of cheese do you want? I just need to know the size and flavors."

"I will be eating it here and then taking some back at the end of the month to my home in Los Angeles. Small wheels for travel."

"Two kilos?" she asked, moving to the display case and retrieving a small notepad from underneath a dusty cash register.

"Sure," I said, unsure exactly how big two kilos was but figuring she knew best.

She wrote a note to herself in the notebook and then looked back at me. And then across at Zoela and Rosalia.

"Are you sure you want to make cheese? Most people here don't want their kids to get dirty doing something like that. They want the cheese at the table, but they are not interested in how it gets made." She looked at me with skepticism.

"I live in Los Angeles. I don't have a cheese maker down the block. And Saro would love this. I can always wash her clothes."

Donatella nodded. "As you like." She seemed pleased by if not curious about this American woman standing before her.

After all, I was a visitor, not a local woman with a home to keep, a husband and children to cook for. I had time to be curious about things that other women saw as the work of someone else.

"Well, it's my American curiosity," I said, making a joke that I suspected was both unclear and lost in translation the minute it left my mouth. "What day should we come?"

We set an appointment for two days later in the late afternoon. She would be making fresh ricotta. Zoela could make a batch to take home to Nonna. We would make small wheels of salt-cured pecorino that would mature in her shop. The whole endeavor seemed exciting, educational, and full of savory promise.

"We'll bring aprons," I said to Donatella as Zoela, Rosalia, and I spilled out into the street and the afternoon sun. The main street had come alive in the late afternoon. We waved hello to a brigade of old men gathering in front of the bar and in the piazza alongside the church to play cards before dinner. Each one had a face tanned by work in the fields and was wearing a starched shirt and a well-worn *coppola storta*, the traditional Sicilian cap that makes people outside Sicily think of the Mafia. Again I thought of Saro and how he had once told me that his father had lined the top of his *coppola* with newspaper in the winter to keep his head warmer. It was a detail that had endeared Giuseppe to me.

On the appointed day, I stood in the cheese shop as Donatella taught me that there are two critical times when making fresh ricotta: first, when you stir the sheep's milk, waiting for it to curdle, and second, when you put the freshly curdled cheese into the cheese basket to give it form. At either of these two junctures, the cheese can go to hell and with it hours of work. To say nothing of wasting the generosity of animals who let down their milk so that we can make dishes such as *linguine con funghi e ricotta* and *fusilli con ricotta, limone e basilico*.

As the girls began making ricotta cheese at Donatella's, something so deeply entrenched in the Sicilian culinary tradition, I couldn't escape another wave of longing for Saro. In the low light, I watched Zoela's small hands hold a large wooden spoon to stir the ricotta in the large stainless-steel industrial mixer. She had Saro's focus, his precision. The open window behind us let in the sounds of a tractor rolling by and church bells ringing. I wanted my husband.

"This batch that we are making will take days to salt cure. It will need to be pressed, and pressed, salted again and again to release liquids and then left to set in a wrapped cloth at room temperature," Donatella explained to Zoela and Rosalia. She spooned three ladlefuls of the liquid into a plastic mesh mold, then pressed on it again and again, forcing the liquid to take the form of the mold. I watched the excess liquid drain off and run into the drain on the floor in the center of the room.

As I watched Zoela in a white, floor-length apron, stirring the cauldron of milk with a huge wooden spoon, gently separating the curds into coarse grains and letting the whey settle below, I was fascinated. I realized how little I knew about making cheese. In my complete ignorance, I had thought it was formed by simple stirring and pouring. I kept looking to Donatella for guidance and affirmation that this was all going right. I was suddenly very attached to the idea that the cheese must be good, that Zoela be proud of the cheese wheel she made. I stood back and took pictures.

"Babbo would love to be here to see you," I said to Zoela in English. I knew he would be so proud of Zoela, her little arms stirring with all her might.

I thought then of the etymology of the word *ricotta*. In Italian, it means "recooked." The process of making it requires that the whey be recooked, which is what makes the cheese distinctive. It's what gives it its flavor characteristics. The process is in the name.

I continued to watch the girls take turns stirring and then straining the curds into waiting baskets, using tools to apply gentle pressure to drain the new, still warm cheese. I couldn't help but feel that I, too, was being stirred and molded and then shaped again. A grief metamorphosis. Now past the one-year mark, I had begun to filter out the unneeded parts of my life. Life was separating my curd from my whey. I began to understand that cheese making, especially making a wheel of infused pecorino, is a lot like dealing with grief. It requires time, labor, attention. It also needs to be left alone for a time. It requires gentle hands but also strong intentions. And in the process, there is pressure, there are the curing and solidifying. In cheese making, the curing comes from the earth element salt. It requires pressure and the addition of time. But grief also involves pressure and time.

Standing in a cheese shop far away from home, I realized that life was recooking me and it would change me, as surely as the milk curdling in the cauldron stirred by my daughter would become something else. I just didn't yet know what my something was. I only knew that another summer in the Mediterranean, making cheese in a mountain town in Sicily, was but one of the ways I might get there. I knew that spending time with Nonna was part of it, too. Whether I openly acknowledged it or not, she was the heart of the reason I had come back.

THE PRIEST

Each day in Sicily, when it was time to clear the table of what remained of the pasta, artisanal cheese, fresh bread, and home-cured olives, Nonna had one objective: to change the television channel from Zoela's favorite program, *Don Matteo*, to her own favorite show, *Tempesta d'Amore*, a German-produced soap opera dubbed in Italian. When it came to soap operas, Nonna liked a good healthy dose of love, family betrayal, out-of-wedlock pregnancy, an occasional kidnapping, and, of course, young lovers unsure of whether or not to consummate their relationship before marriage. Throw in lies, opulent villas, and sweeping aerial shots of European coastlines, and she was set.

Zoela, however, liked one show and one show only: *Don Matteo*, a moralistic telenovela whose protagonist is a crime-solving priest with piercing blue eyes contrasting with his black robe. In every episode, the priest, Don Matteo, whips a cell phone out of what Zoela called his "dress" whenever an important plot development transpires. The show is an Italian hybrid of *The Mentalist* and old-school *Columbo*. In particular, the scenes in the confessional booth riveted Zoela. She especially loved the scenes when Don Matteo went undercover and changed into jeans and a polo.

"He looks like he could be Justin Bieber's father," Zoela said, looking at the TV one day as we were finishing lunch.

Nonna looked up from the sink, where she had gathered the lunch dishes, and then toward the screen. She clucked her tongue behind her teeth and said, "Only in the north do priests go around like that."

She had no love for Zoela's show, and I could see she was ready to change the channel to catch her soap opera just as *Don Matteo* was coming to a conclusion.

"Zoela, why don't we let Nonna watch her show and you can watch a movie on the iPad upstairs?" I said in English. I had become the intergenerational programming intermediary.

"But, Mommy, I want to know how it ends."

"Yes, I know. But Nonna just made us lunch, and she likes to watch her show as she cleans the kitchen. I can tell you how it ends . . ." I had seen many such shows and read enough scripts to know their predictable conclusions.

"No, don't tell me!" she said, horrified that I might give away the plot. "I want to watch it."

"Today you can't, sweetheart. Maybe tomorrow you can finish the episode across the street at Emanuela's house while Nonna washes dishes. But today, watch a movie upstairs."

Emanuela was Nonna's widowed first cousin who lived across the street. She was recovering from a recent hip surgery and would welcome the company. Zoela seemed nonplussed about the idea. She pushed her chair back, handed her plate to me with just a touch of side-eye, and then went upstairs.

"What happened? Why is she going upstairs?" Nonna asked me in Sicilian.

"Because she wants to watch a movie," I lied.

Nonna shrugged, turned off the running water in the sink, dried her hands, and reached for the TV remote. She turned to *Tempesta d'Amore* just as the opening credits were finishing.

I helped her clean up, momentarily stepping out in the midday sun to shake out the tablecloth in the middle of the street, away from the front door, so that ants wouldn't be attracted to the crumbs and make a trail into the house.

When I came back inside to fold the tablecloth and put it away, Nonna lowered the TV volume during a commercial break. She had other things to tell me.

"*C'è un prete di colore*," she began. There was an interim priest "of color" in town.

She had my full attention. Except for the immigrant men who passed through twice a year selling items like those found in the 99 Cent store at home, I had never heard of a person of color in Aliminusa, let alone a priest.

Nonna wasn't sure exactly where he was from, but, based on her description, "*africano*," I suspected he was likely a young priest from a developing nation sent to town as part of his seminary requirements. Suddenly I looked forward to meeting him. The whole idea of the parishioners of Aliminusa being led by an African priest, even for a few weeks, was the kind of cross-cultural moment I couldn't pass up.

Nonna had mentioned him before, when we had spoken around the time of Saro's one-year memorial. He had spent a week in town at Easter. Now he was back for the summer season while the resident priest, Padre Francesco, was away doing a sabbatical in the north for some months. The new priest had been met enthusiastically. That he was "of good heart" was the consensus. However, his Italian was not good. He had mixed up his words after a Mass for the dead and offered the bereaved heartfelt congratulations instead of condolences.

"Now we need a wedding so he can offer his condolences," Nonna quipped. She loved a good joke. But her laughter quickly subsided. She was onto a serious matter: the new portable fans that had appeared in church.

Unlike some churches in Italy, during the summer months the small church in Aliminusa was not cooled by marble walls and vaulted ceilings. It was narrow with stone walls and no windows. In the summer, afternoon Mass was like a sauna. During the winter, Mass was the best ticket in town, as few people had central heat. But at the moment, winter was a long way off, and we were in the dog days of summer.

"I have to get to Mass early today," she declared, having just finished ironing the clothes she had mended earlier. "Yesterday the fans were off and my clothes were drenched."

There had been an ongoing battle of late among parishioners about whether the new fans should be on or off during Mass. Some said the wind troubled their rheumatism, while others, like Nonna, were labeled "wind lovers." Today she was armed with a plastic ice cream container lid to cool herself between the rosary before the start of Mass and singing at the end of it.

"After Mass, come to the church. I want you to meet the priest," she said. "He's very nice, and I told him about you. Bring Zoela."

Later that afternoon, as Nonna was preparing to leave for Mass, Zoela was out roaming with Rosalia and Ginevra, the cheese maker's daughter. I asked Nonna where she was. Nonna stuck her head out the window and called to Giacoma down the street. Giacoma, in turn, stuck her head out of the door and shouted back that she'd call Rosalia's mother. Ten minutes later Zoela was back home.

I convinced her and Rosalia to come with me to church just as Mass was ending. I told Zoela to make sure that her hair was combed and she had on a clean shirt. We would be representing Nonna, and although her free-spirited gypsy look would be totally fine back home in the hipster confines of Silver Lake, in Sicily a granddaughter meeting the priest had a certain formality to it. I promised there would be gelato afterward for all her effort.

As the sun had just begun to settle below the mountain range on the other side of the valley that ran to the sea, we walked into the sacristy. Parishioners were beginning to rise from the pews and file out. We hung toward the back by the holy water font and two fans going at full blast. Nonna spotted us and bade us to come forward. A minute later, we were in the parish office and I was shaking hands with the African priest.

"It's a pleasure to meet you," I said.

"The pleasure is all mine," he said. His Italian was tentative and spoken with a wonderful accent that I couldn't place. When I shook his hand, I got a warm and open vibe. I felt a kind of unexpected pride in this man I was just meeting. Here was a fellow person of color. Here was a man acting as the spiritual leader of a town of people so culturally foreign to him. He was doing it in Italian, bridging language, geography, nationality, and race. I imagined that we both knew something about being both foreign and a non-Italian in Italy—he perhaps more than I, given his vocation, the intimacy it required. I wanted to secretly tell him that he was doing "God's work" in more ways than one by simply being in Aliminusa. But we couldn't cover all that ground so soon.

"It is wonderful to have you here," I said. There was a line forming behind us. There were other parishioners who had special requests or needed to speak with him privately. But he didn't rush us.

"Where are you from?" he asked.

I recognized the curiosity in his eyes. I had seen the same look when I had lived in Florence and bumped into newly arrived Senegalese immigrants. We were two people of African descent meeting across the diaspora, an event that forges an instant sense of community with another black person anywhere in the world.

"I come from California. Los Angeles," I responded. His face broke open in a smile of wonderment, as if I had spoken of an alternate universe full of fantasy and whim. I wondered how many films he had seen with palm trees and bikini-clad lifeguards. "Where are you from?" I asked in return.

"Burundi," he said. My geography was shameful. I couldn't picture the country on a map of the continent. But I did conjure up a tableau of a family who surely missed him, people who were sharing their son with the Catholic Church.

Next to me, Nonna beamed. As a deeply devout woman, introducing me to the priest was a sign of respect for him. During our conversation, she had been going into her purse to retrieve a private offering. Now, with money in hand, she put her hands on Zoela to gently nudge her to say hello.

"This is my daughter," I said. Zoela came forward and shook his hand. She said, "*Ciao*," and looked at him in wide-eyed wonder, as if he were a black version of Don Matteo.

"It's a pleasure to meet you." He smiled and took Zoela's hand. "You are the American granddaughter." He took a half step back and took her in. "May blessings be with you," he said, putting his other palm on her shoulder.

Zoela smiled, slightly embarrassed by the attention. Then she looked back to Rosalia, who was waiting a few feet away near the confessional booth.

"How old are you? What grade are you going into?" he asked.

"I'm eight, and I'll be in the third grade," she said shyly in her best Italian.

"Do you like Sicily? It's good to be with your grandmother, no?"

"Yes." The one-word answer covered both questions. I could tell that she had lost interest in the priest. She was eager to link back up with Rosalia and meander through town until dinner.

Nonna handed the priest her donation. He smiled, nodding a thank-you.

An impatient line had formed behind us, a formation of women with their handbags at the ready, poised to ask for special prayers, request a confession, make a donation on behalf of themselves or some loved one. Nonna put her hand on my elbow, the universal Sicilian gesture communicating that it was time to go.

"I hope to see you again before I leave," I said as Nonna and I peeled off from the standing-room crowd.

When we got outside, we stood on the marble steps in the midst of the sunset hour. Benedetta, who lived two doors down from Nonna, came up behind us and offered to walk with her and the kids back to Via Gramsci. I, on the other hand, wanted to take a walk to enjoy the first moments of the day without unrelenting direct sun. I wanted to walk the hills outside town, pick blackberries off the brambles. Be alone for a moment in the silence that could be found only once I left the stone buildings and cobblestoned streets.

I started into the low hills above town that were lined with small plots of cultivated land because it was the walk I had always taken with Saro. The cicadas were nestled in their posts among the almond trees. Nature was magnificent here. It created a kind of inner stillness I couldn't find in L.A., where I was in constant motion. Now I could slow down, I could just be. As I listened to an orchestra of cicadas, I could smell jasmine. I turned toward the wind so I could see the land outstretched to the blue sea.

I didn't see things like that in L.A. A haze always hung over the city, separating the lives we led from the open sky. I moved through urban stretches without ever looking up or even out. Still, occasionally such vistas came to me. Driving from Pasadena to Silver Lake, I would see the sky stretching toward the ocean—a narrow, fleeting view because I was moving along freeways and thoroughfares.

With each curve my ascent was more pronounced, the town of Aliminusa receding into the background. A view of the sea emerged peekaboo style when I reached the first flat plain. Then the Mediterranean was in full view. I stopped in my tracks. I turned my body in every direction, not wanting to miss any of the landscape. From that spot, it was all cultivated plots of land that, depending on the season, yielded tomatoes, artichokes, fava beans, peppers, eggplant, zucchini, garlic, potatoes, lettuce, chard, fennel, cardoons, chamomile, oregano, basil. Olive, fig, almond, pear, and apricot trees were my companions. Each inhalation cleansed my soul. Looking out over the land, I felt no inner division too wide or too difficult for me to cross.

There on the outskirts of town, my *lutto*—my mourning, the thing I carried with me, invisible to others—was freer. I didn't have to hold on to it so tight. I knew I wouldn't lose it there. And I was comforted to know that I wouldn't lose Saro there, either. There were a town, a history, a culture that would ensure that wouldn't happen. Saro couldn't be forgotten there, and for my still-grieving heart that allowed me to breathe deeper. In some way, I felt his heartbeat there, pulsing through the magic of the moment, as if it had been waiting for me to take myself there, our quiet place in a hurried world. There is a saying in Sicilian: "It can't get any darker than midnight." Life some days, more than a year later, still felt like an ever-present midnight. But as I walked, I was willing to lean forward into what little light I was given—the light of the Sicilian summer sun. I wanted to stand naked in it.

An hour later, I made the descent back into town and found Nonna ironing upstairs, something she never did at that hour of the day.

"I'm ironing Emanuela's nightgowns. Since her recent hip surgery, she needs the help. Come. Here." She led me from that room into the next, leaving her cousin's sleepwear and intimates on the ironing board. "I want you to see this." She was pointing to the dresser in her bedroom.

At first I didn't understand what was going on as she began to show me the contents of her dresser drawers. Then it became clear.

The top drawer of the dresser contained nightgowns—six sleeveless summer shifts in floral prints, never used. She told me that they were for if and/or when she had to go to the hospital. Hospitals in Italy (and in Sicily) do not provide gowns. She had prepared enough for a six-night hospital stay. That way, Franca would not have to wash and iron them every day of her stay.

The second drawer held the same contents but for a spring hospital stay, when the nights are cooler. The third and fourth drawers held clothing for a winter hospital stay. They contained fleece garments, wool nightshirts, even pajama bottoms, something Nonna had never worn, but they had come with the fleece set and she was willing to wear them because the hospital might not have enough heat on a coastal winter night. The fifth drawer contained handmade lace pillowcases. Pillowcases, too, I learned, were not provided in the hospital.

When we came to the final drawer, I had to kneel down on the hand-painted floor tiles to help her open it. It was low to the ground, and it strained her back to reach there. Outside the window, I heard the fruit vendor bringing his car up the narrow street, shouting for us to buy the sweetest melons, the tenderest plums. We ignored him. I peered into the contents of the sixth drawer.

There, alone, was a single clear plastic garment bag. Inside it, there was one pressed and folded white floral-printed nightgown. "Take that out, I will show you," she said.

As I reached in, I focused on a detail inside the clear plastic. There was a photograph set on top of the pristinely folded nightgown. It was of her and Giuseppe, my father-in-law, taken some fifteen to twenty years earlier. In the photo, she is standing behind him and they are both smiling. I could see presents on a table in the background. The two of them were dressed up. It had probably been taken at someone's wedding. I handed her the bag, and she set it on top of the dresser. Slowly she removed the photo, set it aside, and held up the clothes: a nightgown, undergarments, stockings.

"These are for when I die."

Then she patted the clothes, straightened the stockings, and carefully put them and the photo back into the bag. I was directed to put the bag back into the sixth drawer. "I have to have all this. You don't want anyone saying at the end of your life, 'She didn't have enough to have fresh gowns in the hospital and a decent gown to take to the cemetery.'"

I told her I understood. She shrugged her shoulders, as if maybe I did, maybe I didn't, but at least now I knew. Then the fruit vendor's baritone interrupted the moment as he made his way up the street. Nonna took that as a cue to return to ironing Emanuela's nightgowns. "I do this because her daughter-in-law doesn't like to iron. But people come to visit each day. It is needed."

She left me standing in the bedroom alone as she went back to work. I was caught off guard, moved by what had just happened. She had shown me her most vulnerable self, invited me to see and contemplate her own mortality. I felt soft inside, as though I needed to sit down. We had never had openness between us like this before. In one day, she had shown us off to the priest and shown me her death clothes. I wasn't sure how to respond to such an invitation of closeness, to being included in parts of her previously unknown life. In all our years together, this was perhaps the most intimate moment we had ever had. She had literally opened up hidden places, shared with me her wishes for what would happen when she no longer had the ability to make decisions. This was end-of-life planning, Sicilian style. But I also felt trusted, as if she had invited me into a new chamber of her heart and was encouraging me to stay. I felt like her daughter-in-law in a new way.

When I left the bedroom and passed her at the ironing board, pressing the creases out of Emanuela's smock and bras, I was struck by something else. I realized I was witnessing another example of the way community functions so tightly here. For better or for worse. Each of the women on this street will be called upon and expected to participate in the illness or death of the others. They held one another up. It was a custom as ancient and alive as the ruins of Sicily's Hera Temple—where Zoela and I were headed next.

HERA AND THE
SAPPHIRE SEA

The ride to Agrigento devolved into a nearly four-hour, mapless road trip full of road closures and detours. Cosimo had offered to drive us, I think because there was a collective concern on the part of my in-laws that Zoela and my bisecting Sicily's desolate interior without a local was a potential shit show in the making. Franca came along, too. Frankly, having endured many road trip mishaps in Italy and Sicily, I was relieved to have them with me. Most memorable had been five years earlier with Saro, when a gas station attendant had pumped leaded gasoline into the diesel engine of a car we had rented in Rome. Twenty minutes later, the transmission had gone out on the autostrada. It was the middle of the day in August. No AC, limited cell service, cars zooming by at ninety miles per hour; we couldn't even let the windows down once the engine died. There was no AAA to come to our rescue. The Numero Verde, Italy's national emergency response number, was a Kafkaesque nightmare of a single prerecorded voice telling me to "press one" for assistance over and over again for hours. Saro cursed the nation and declared Italian inefficiency a plague on mankind. I prayed for a miracle and peeled the oranges we had just bought to keep Zoela hydrated. We waited for help for four hours. Spending four hours stranded road-side on the loop around Rome in summer is like idling a diesel engine inside a sweat lodge. At the end of that trip, I declared Italy insufferable and threatened never to come back.

That memory was fresh in my mind as I planned our trip to Agrigento and considered the two major things that were happening in Sicily that summer: raging wildfires (likely due to arson) and the closure of a portion of highway A19, which leads from the northern coast toward the southeast to Catania. Still, Cosimo wanted to begin our journey on A19 because he was familiar with it and he wanted to avoid Palermo traffic before connecting to the main highway that leads to Agrigento. This meant that in order to get from Aliminusa to our destination, we'd have to go through the island's interior on secondary roads. It was a trip that would take an hour and a half on a California highway, but in Sicily, traveling that same distance would take four hours. Still I was undeterred.

I had chosen Agrigento because Zoela loved tales of the gods and goddesses, their virtues, struggles, laments, humor. Saro had taught her about all of them, and she had readily entered into his deep thinking about the big struggles of human behavior. I wanted to travel with her there to the Valley of the Temples, the greatest archaeological site in Sicily. Saro had taken me there years before. We had kissed among the pillars of the Temple of Hera, the goddess of marriage. It was a place where my past and my present could perhaps meet. Closer to North Africa, the Valley of the Temples was sacred, ancient, evocative, a place where visitors must wrestle with the construct of time. Standing in the presence of the temples, you can't help but contemplate what has been lost while also seeing the continuity of life. It was just the kind of place I needed.

When our carful finally arrived in Agrigento, I was a little carsick yet nonetheless optimistic. It was hotter than I could have imagined. When we filed out of the car at midday, the air felt like the inside of a pizza oven. To make matters worse, Zoela and I were both on the verge of crippling hunger. I wasted no time pulling crackers from my purse, along with a pear I had swiped from Nonna's house for this exact moment.

My in-laws and I differ in many ways but none so much as the fact that I am more than willing to stop at a trattoria for a hearty lunch or a snack. I'll even stop for a bit of respite before venturing out into a sweltering afternoon of monuments and tourist attractions. I am of the easy-does-it school of tourism. They, on the other hand, prefer to power through, inhale a home-packed sandwich, see the sights, and then hit the road home in the hope of arriving before dark. They will always choose to eat dinner at home. They rarely dine at a place they don't know. Practically never. That day I was on their schedule.

As they surveyed the parking lot of Agrigento's archaeological ruins, clearly hungry, hot, and thirsty, I suddenly felt bad. I could see from their general lack of interest that I was putting them out, taking them from their routines, albeit bringing them to one of the most beautiful historical sites in Sicily, but one that I think neither of them cared much about seeing. We had all just spent nearly four hours in a cramped car. I had the subtle feeling that they couldn't wait for me and my demanding American predilection for journeying here and there to wrap up. A lifetime could pass for them, as it had for Nonna, never seeing Agrigento. I, on the other hand, was pulled by desire, loss, hope, mystery. I wanted to know more and more about the island that I was now claiming as part of me, my past, my present, perhaps even my future.

"Zoela, come with me." I pulled her close to me as she took a bite of the pear. I felt as though everyone else was on a short fuse and, except for me, had little interest in seeing ruins. Heat was the enemy. I was the only one who was willing to challenge it head-on. So Zoela and I began walking. I quickly decided that I'd start with the biggest and largest temple, the Temple of Hera. Everything else, if I saw it, would be a bonus. We'd leave my in-laws to wander at their own pace.

"Mommy, it's hot." Zoela hated heat, always had.

"I know, sweetheart." I was conscious of the fact that she would be able to handle the heat, the sightseeing, for only so long. I'd need to spin this. "It's hot because this is the place where Icarus fell after flying too close to the sun." She loved the story of Icarus. Saro had read it to her countless times. She loved fingering the pages of the story in her book on Greek myths.

I delivered my version of the tale with the same enthusiasm that I used to perpetuate the fantasy of the tooth fairy and Santa Claus. "I think we can actually see where Icarus's body fell." If I couldn't fool an eight-year-old, then someone should revoke my Screen Actors Guild card. I'd find a hole in the ground and point to it, if I had to. I needed to hold her attention just long enough for us to approach the Temple of Hera and touch the pillars. That's all I wanted. And maybe to take a few pictures. And if I were lucky, I'd get to say a silent prayer into the waters facing North Africa.

Prayer at the seaside was the one thing I had taken from the twenty years that my mother had been married to her third husband, Abe, the Senegalese eldest son of a Muslim family who had grown up in Dakar and been educated at the Sorbonne. He had introduced me to the tradition of saying a prayer at every shore you visited. It was something he did without fail. When he came to Los Angeles for visits, he would travel to Santa Monica to honor his ancestors and the dead by offering a prayer into the water. Whether that tradition was a by-product of his faith or his culture or a personal affinity, I could never tease out. Frankly, it didn't matter. I loved the idea and spirit of it. During Saro's illness, it gave me peace to leave the oncologist's office in Santa Monica during his treatments and drive two miles west to pour my worried prayers into the ocean. In the two years since his death, prayer at the seaside had become one of my rituals. That day in Agrigento I hoped to say a prayer that might reach the shores of northern Africa, which Saro and I had once visited. It was an illogical but heartfelt notion that if my grief touched all the places where my love had traveled, it might somehow help heal me.

"Franca, Cosimo," I called back as Zoela and I were ascending toward the ruins. "Take your time. Zoela and I will go ahead. We can meet back here in an hour." They were trying to figure out if the car needed a ticket to park in the attendantless, dusty gravel lot just below the archaeological site.

I took off without waiting for an answer.

For the next half hour, Zoela and I wandered among the pillars of the Temple of Hera. We touched a five-hundred-year-old olive tree. We circled an art installation of the fallen Icarus. An artist had rendered his bronze torso as large as a pickup truck, lopsided and fallen, sprawling on the ground. And there somewhere between the fallen Icarus and Hera, I started to feel a duality that was becoming familiar in my grief. Part of me was exalted by getting to experience this place again many years later; another part of me suddenly wanted to plunge myself into the sea. Grief did that still and often: it left me to wrestle with two contradictory feelings at once. In that moment, I felt a little like another character from mythology, Sisyphus, forever pushing his boulder uphill. My boulder was loss. And life after loss could be a repetitive loop of heavy lifting, pushing, and struggling to move to higher ground even while enjoying a view of the sea.

As Zoela and I wandered the archaeological site, the internal questioning grew deeper, darker. Had Saro and I been too ambitious in our love? Had we flown too close to the sun? Was cancer some cosmic challenge assigned to us by the gods? The randomness of life made no sense, giving and taking in equal measure. Though I knew we'd had a great marriage, a brilliant and dynamic love, I still wanted more and I felt cheated. Cheated of companionship, lifelong love, the joy of someone who had known me well enough to know that standing at the temple of the goddess of marriage would make me feel a little insane.

Then it was as if someone had turned on a blender and all my darkness began to churn at rapid speed. I felt jealous of all the couples around me on vacation in their shorts and sunscreen, celebrating new and old love. I was jealous of Cosimo and Franca, who still had each other. I was jealous of all the women who still had spouses, maybe even the ones in unhappy marriages, because at least they had help, their children still had dads. I had come to the southern side of Sicily only to be mad at Saro for dying. I had driven four hours to find a feeling as ancient as time: anger. There in Agrigento I quietly raged at Saro for being dead and leaving me to move through a morass of memory, questioning, a middle-aged woman who was desperate to stand in the presence of ruins in the hope of finding myself again. I was at the gates of an ancient temple trying to retrieve parts of my soul.

Suddenly I realized that I had had three marriages to Saro: the one we had experienced as newly-in-love married people; the one we had spent in the trenches of surviving cancer; and the one I had with him now, as his widow. In the decade that I had cared for Saro, I had lost parts of myself, my natural effervescence, my sense of my own sexuality, my sense of optimism. The ups and downs of years of cancer caregiving seemed to have leached those things from my life. And although caregiving had taught me how to draw from the well of my strength, how to love deeply and unconditionally, how to see the big love that exists all around us at all times, it had also dimmed my everyday light a little, grief perhaps even more. I was tired of being tired. The thing that terrified me was that I felt I might never be able to laugh effortlessly again, so hard that it hurt my sides. I worried privately that it might be years before I made love again. Things I had once done regularly that now felt outside of my reach. Nobody had told me that widowhood would be so full of fear for what might never be. I was terrified that this aspect of my grief might have the solidness of a temple's stone pillars.

I was beginning to understand that the last marriage with Saro would ultimately be our longest. He was no more gone from my life than the moon is gone from the sky in daylight. He was everywhere, yet unseen. Learning to exist in that kind of love would take time. Time is maybe the most critical aspect of loss.

On the drive back home through Sicily's rugged interior, I looked out the window, feeling as though I'd lost track of how many days we had been there. Time had a way of eluding capture. Much like the Sicilian landscape, it played tricks on my mind, giving me valleys of verdant groves one moment, then taking it all away, leaving barren, jagged mountains. Since I had arrived that summer, more than ever I couldn't attempt to measure time in nice neat half and quarter hours. There were days with long stretches of endless sun and nothing to do but observe that morning and afternoon were petulant twins, each demanding their time. Then there were the twilights that came on quickly and lingered as if they were loath to submit to night. I realized then that I'd have to take the remaining days slowly, just as I did Sicily herself.

I craved the taste of sea salt at the edge of my mouth and sand between my toes. I wanted the gentleness of the Mediterranean to take me as I floated on my back, belly to the sun. I needed to feel my body become light, effortless, drifting wherever the water would take me.

So two days later, Cosimo let me borrow his Fiat, and I drove Zoela from the foothills to Cefalù by the sea. As we moved along the two-lane coastal road going into town, we passed the turnoff for Hotel Baia del Capitano. For a fleeting moment, I almost turned to Saro to reminisce about when we had sipped espresso in the garden and waited for his family. Memory is tricky that way. But I kept driving, imagining the feel of his palm on my knee and focusing on the moment at hand, a day in Cefalù with our daughter. His life was being lived through us now.

When we arrived in Cefalù, two things usually happened. Zoela and I would stumble up to Lido Poseidon because the place had three wide, deep freezers of eye-popping gelato, and I would order pinot grigio or an espresso seaside, depending on how my day was going. That day it was wine.

From our many trips here before, Zoela knew the drill. She swaggered right up to the hostess and requested two lounge chairs and one umbrella. She paid the twelve-euro rental fee and then told the twenty-something cigarette-smoking lifeguard in a red Speedo exactly where she wanted our chairs to be in relation to the sea. "*Mia mamma vuole leggere*—My mother wants to read." What she meant was that I wanted a chair close to the shore so that I could watch her as I rested.

We were fortunate to be assigned chairs one row back from the shoreline, and then Zoela took off for the sea, periodically turning back to make sure I was following her.

I set off behind her, trailing. When I reached her, we stood together in the shallow waters. I told her, "In my dreams, I will tell Babbo how absolutely beautiful and spectacular you are. You are the pearl of his beloved sea."

She splashed water into my face and asked, "Do you think he can see me?"

"I believe so."

"Would he be proud of me?"

"Absolutely."

She smiled. My words seemed to ease her. I resisted an urge to take her little body in my arms and call on the gods to suspend time, help me hold on to the grace of that moment. Talking about her dad and making her smile at the same time was rare in our new life. I submerged my body. When I came up, the air felt new, warm.

Around us were intergenerational families; bronzed, high-pitched children; flirtatious couples; duos and trios of friends from seemingly all over the world. They swam, they relaxed. They, too, were drawn to the sea. On the beach, North African and Bangla-deshi immigrants walked among the throng of visitors selling their wares: towels, sunglasses, cell phone cases, swimsuit cover-ups, in-flatable plastic dinghies in the shape of dolphins. A pair of Chinese women offered massages beachside. The world had closed ranks here. Our countries of origin and economics aside, we were all part of a seaside tableau. I thought of all the invaders, conquerors, quest seekers who had come to these shores over the centuries. I thought about the refugees coming from Syria, Libya, North Africa, and sub-Saharan Africa to Sicily each week. They were fleeing civil war, and the ensuing humanitarian crisis had brought people with many stories of unforgettable pain. It was the migration story of our time. Sicily was changing, but it always had.

Zoela swam up to me. She locked her body around mine, her legs around my waist. "Mommy, why do you think there are no other brown people in Aliminusa?" Our surroundings were not lost on her, either.

"Sweetheart, Aliminusa is a small town in a part of the world where people have not immigrated. It's not like Los Angeles or big cities. For a long time, it has just been full of people who were born there, married there, and had kids there. Not a lot of outsiders." I stopped myself before I descended further into a historical and geopolitical diatribe. I couldn't even begin to address the refugee crisis with her. I didn't know quite how to talk about the children, mothers, and fathers who were crossing the Mediterranean to get to the island on which we stood and the circumstances that also made this place a sea of tears.

"But why aren't there brown people like us?" she asked again, sea salt forming at her hairline.

"Because people like us, black and brown people, did not originate in Europe. People like us were brought to Europe and throughout North America and even South America hundreds of years ago as slaves." At once I saw myself as the overanswering daughter of people who had answered my own childhood questions with complex adult narratives. If we had been on shore, I probably would have started arcing out the slave route with lines in the sand.

"But are we the only brown people they know?" She asked as if the question and its answer had just reached her consciousness at the same time.

"Maybe. Yes. It's likely, aside from the priest," I said.

"I don't want to be the only brown girl." I knew what she meant; being different, being the only one, standing out because of skin color was hard. I suspected it made her feel "other" or, worse yet, less than. She certainly wouldn't be the first black or brown girl who at some point hadn't wanted to move through the world in a different packaging. Hell, untold numbers of books have been written and award-winning documentaries made delving into the psychological complexities surrounding identity and race for little black girls in predominantly white environments. And although we weren't in the United States, I knew I had to triage any psychological damage that might be festering. I knew I had to do what black mothers have been doing for centuries: remind my daughter that she is valuable and beautiful in a world that often says otherwise.

"Being brown is beautiful." I spun her in the water, brought her face close to mine. "Baby, a part of the gift of travel is going places where people are not exactly like you. Life would be boring if we never did that. And one day, I imagine you'll travel to many places. Not everyone will be like you, but you will have fun and learn about all kinds of new things."

I concluded the conversation with the reassurance of a kiss. It seemed enough in that moment. Then she reached for the locket with Saro's picture that I still wore around my neck.

She rubbed it as though she were making a wish. "Can I have gelato before dinner?"

"Yes," I said, relieved that we had stepped back from the conversation before I had to answer the question that I suspected was underneath the question: Do I belong here?

It was a question I had spent the better part of two decades trying to answer—to strangers, to the world, to myself. The question could be traced in a straight line back to my first trip to Sicily with

Saro. But I had learned that identity is prismatic, that belonging requires claiming.

Later, after a dinner of grilled swordfish drizzled with a blood orange reduction on a bed of arugula, an ancient pairing of sea and fire, we walked from the restaurant along the seawall. I thought about Stromboli and our trip there last summer. Zoela was looking out onto the water as well. She turned to me.

"I want to know what is out there . . . Where does it end? . . . How does the water stay on the planet if it is a circle but also a flat line? Gravity, but still." Her forehead was tensed in a fixed gaze.

It was the kind of rapid-fire, big-picture questioning that made me proud to see my tuition dollars at work.

"Sweetheart, those are the essential questions that prompted human exploration of the natural world," I told her. She looked back at me as if she got about 70 percent of what I was saying. "You have to want to know first, before you can take a journey."

"Well, I want to know!" she exclaimed. Sicily was having an additional impact, beyond just family connection.

As she said it, I considered my own journey. Some part of me desired to know what would become of me. That was keeping me going. Grief exhausted me, but it also made me want to live. It made me appreciate the brevity of life. I wanted to be around. I wanted to know how things would turn out for Zoela, the extraordinary human being who called me her *mammina*—little mother. I wanted to hear the voice of the woman she would become as she remembered the Mass in the tiny Sicilian church with the African priest and how worried she had been for him because "it is hard to be a priest if you are still learning Italian." I wanted to know if she would remember that she had sung the word "Hallelujah" right alongside Nonna when the priest had said her father's name during

Mass. I wanted to be there to remind her one day—perhaps in some early spring or perhaps on a gloomy afternoon as fall turned into winter—a day when she would need to be reminded of who she was. I wanted to be there to see the recognition in her eyes when I recounted that story. I wanted to be there to share the details of her life, because I carried her story. I wanted to eat dinner in my daughter's kitchen, lick the sauce from the spoon, and taste the influence of her father's hand. I wanted to read a letter she might write to me from some place in the world I had never seen. I wanted to run my finger over the stamp and picture her there in my mind's eye. I wanted to know whom she might choose to love. I wanted to greet her at a train station and have her ask me glee-fully, "What took you so long?" She would take my hand, make me laugh, as we exited out into a busy street of a busy city and she'd hail a cab and I would hear her voice keeping time to the meter as we traveled along. I wanted to know what my hands would look like at eighty-five, what shoes I might like to wear, if I will prefer straps to laces, if orange will still be a favorite color. I kept going because I wanted to know how one puts one's life together again, making up the bits and remnants into a new whole. I wanted to lose myself many times and find my way again. I wanted to know even more ways to carry love forward in the tiniest of gestures, how to see love in the smallest of things. I wanted to someday stand on a stage and thank Saro, my best beloved, without whom life would be a lesser, blander thing. I wanted to see the sand in the Berber mountains once again. I wanted to pick mulberries, eating till I felt drunk with the joy of what nature gives so freely, so completely. I wanted to hold another person's hand when he or she dies, for that is such a great honor. I wanted to know what will become of the people, places, and things that have meant something to me. I wanted to learn something new from someone I have yet to meet. And I wanted to be able to know that I could see unspeakable pain and know that it, too, would change me but not undo me. I wanted to journey to beyond where my eye can see and greet the self who carried me forward to get there.

The next morning, Nonna lit the fire and cooked *arancini*—rice balls with mozzarella at the center. As she made them, she told me the story of Saro's birth. I didn't know exactly what prompted it. But I had enough experience to respect that memory comes unbidden and it has to make its rounds to completion.

"He had the mark of a strawberry where his hairline gave way to his forehead. *Com'era bello. L'ho baciato ogni giorno.*—How beautiful it was. I kissed it every day."

She was uncharacteristically open and forthcoming. I sat silent. Whatever would come next needed to be said.

"He had a birthmark, the stain of coffee, on his butt, the right cheek," she continued, wiping her eyes with the back of her hand before getting back to mixing the rice balls.

Suddenly I remembered part of the man I loved, a detail I had forgotten. His birthmark. I had loved that birthmark on his ass. How had I already forgotten that?

She told me how when she was pregnant, in the last stages, it was voting day in town. She had gone with Giuseppe to vote, and someone had offered her a coffee as they waited in line.

"I was too ashamed to take a coffee in public. Back then decent women didn't do that. Only men drank espresso in public. I wanted it, but I refused and I sat down. I leaned on my right side for comfort." She pointed to her right hip. "That's how he got the birthmark."

Saro had been marked by her unrequited desire for coffee.

She told me all this while adding mint to peas that looked fresh from the fields. Then she was done talking, and she returned to the repetition of small domestic things that made the big world outside seem somehow petty with endless ambition. A world that held little interest for her, except in the ways it affected her family, the price of bread, or a tax increase on television services.

Then she switched gears. "Tomorrow morning you're going to see the attorney."

I thought I had heard her wrong. "Attorney? What attorney?"

"I am giving this house to you and Zoela. Franca will take you to sign all the papers."

I was standing at the landing of the staircase, star-crossed lovers on the TV next to me making a stilted but soap-operatic declaration of their love for each other. I turned back to Nonna, who was still in the kitchen, still processing what I thought I had heard. "What did you say?"

"The house. It's yours. I want you to have it. It would have been Saro's, and now it is yours."

TERRA VOSTRA

The arid Sicilian countryside rolled by as we drove to the *notaio*—notary—three towns away. I sat in the back, silent and hot. Cosimo flipped through radio stations. Franca was quiet. On my lap were all the pertinent documents: my passports (American and Italian), marriage license translated and stamped, Saro's death certificate, his passport with a stamp from the Italian government declaring him deceased. If Italian bureaucracy maddened me, Sicilian bureaucrats could bring me to the point of tears. I had learned that the law required that this sort of land transfer must happen within one year of the death. However, because I lived in another country and hadn't known that, we were four months past the official cutoff date. To my knowledge, we'd have to plead our case, outlining the extenuating circumstances to the notary, who functions as a probate attorney. I wondered how we would handle the logistics, what I needed to say or not say to move the process along. As I looked out on the hills, I decided it would be best to say nothing. I may have been becoming a Sicilian landowner, but I was far from home, way outside my sphere of knowledge about how any of this worked.

Franca, however, was a veritable master at surmounting bureaucratic intricacies and the cultural nuances they necessitate. She knew when to push, when to deflect, how to defer, exactly the moment to pay respect, lie, or exaggerate, if needed, to move the whole thing along. Cosimo acted as her wingman. Years earlier, I had seen him stand just behind her opposite an official's desk, arms crossed, waiting to pounce with a brisk "*Scusi*" if the official used the wrong tone or pushed back where not warranted. They were a dynamic duo, alternating good cop/ bad cop when the situation called.

Saro always said that his sister had a quiet but fierce stubborn streak. When they were children, if a family decision was made that she didn't like, she had the capacity to batten down the hatch and prepare for the long haul. She could easily (and seemingly effortlessly) go three weeks without uttering a single word to anyone in the house. Her protests had become another character in the house. Her silent streaks with her father were infamous. Saro had often chided her about that when they were adults, the way only a sibling can. They'd laughed about it, and she had reminded him that his response to family difficulties had been to leave. "What do you remember from up there in Florence?" she'd ask. I suspected that she'd gotten the residual emotional fallout of two parents who didn't understand where they had gone wrong, why their son was so hell bent on being different from them. Whereas Saro had set himself free in far-flung places, Franca had rooted down deeper. The daughter. The quiet one. The one who lived in the same square kilometer she had been born into. Now she sat in front of me, doing the work of family, helping her brother's widow once again.

I was so taken aback by the abiding love shown by this unexpected gift that my heart broke open, tender and raw with a mixture of gratitude, stupor, joy, even a tinge of an inexplicable feeling that came close to guilt. The latter feeling surprised me. *Do I deserve this?*

My mind raced all night. The echo of Nonna's words, "It would have been Saro's," lingered. There was a restless tension between my longing and wanting to belong and a deep sense of how bittersweet it was. Then, when I felt exhausted by the odd collision of competing feeling and mind churning, my heart would pop free with gratitude once again.

Still, I had wondered the whole night before about Franca and her kids. How would they feel about me getting the land? She and Nonna had definitely discussed this, because Franca was designated as the intermediary, the one taking me to the lawyer's office that afternoon. Thus, I guessed, it was okay with her. It was no secret that the taxes Italy levied on homeowners with second properties were debilitating for many in rural Sicily where unemployment reached upwards to 50 percent for young people. Leaving the house to Franca would someday make her a second-home owner. To my basic understanding of Italian tax law, that could possibly be more of a burden than a gift to her, especially if she needed to support her daughters into adulthood with her already precarious work. In my name, it might be easier. The taxes would be minimal for me compared to what I paid in California. Still, a tax work-around didn't really seem to be the reason for the gift. Perhaps this had been Nonna's plan all along? The wedding gift her son had never gotten.

Before I left the house, Nonna had been outside hanging out laundry. Inside, I saw where she had laid one of her widow's black skirts on the table with a needle and thread. She would be mending it while I was away handling the land transfer. When she crossed through the front door, momentarily balancing herself in the doorjamb, she began speaking as if in midthought: "If the land doesn't belong to you, it belongs to no one."

"*Grazie*," I had responded. I felt tears coming on. She didn't like morning tears.

"If we start now, we won't stop. The day is long."

Then she put magnifying glasses on top of her regular glasses and sat down to work.

As Franca, Cosimo, and I continued downward on the winding road, passing abandoned farmhouses and the little-used Cerda train station, I realized I hadn't called my parents to tell them the news. I hadn't told my sister. It had happened so fast, so unexpectedly, I had been too overcome by the turn of events. I needed time before I knew how I felt about it all, before I could feel in any way celebratory. At that moment, it was bittersweet. Saro and I had often dreamed about owning a house in the Sicilian countryside, surrounded by an orchard of olive trees. Now the possibility of that was happening without him.

With the house also came responsibility. *Will I be able to afford it in the future? Who will help maintain it? Will I even want to keep coming back once Zoela is grown?* All that felt hard to explain to my family all at once. Still, I knew they'd appreciate the significance of landownership. Since slavery and Reconstruction, landownership had been the way my family (on both sides) had charted their progress, wrestled with the past, and stayed connected with one another. Now it was my turn to stay connected, albeit in an unexpected place. As Cosimo slowed the car to a near stop behind a moving tractor carrying large bales of wheat, I contemplated what family land meant to me.

By the time my maternal grandmother was a teenager in an area of rural East Texas between the black post-Reconstruction settlements of Piney and Nigton, her family had acquired several hundred acres of timberland. They had farmed it and labored on it. The land had come to them bit by bit, in minor acquisitions. It was low-lying and difficult to farm but affordable to people born the children of slaves, without education. Whites with an eye to ownership looked to the areas with better farming land surrounding Nigton, leaving a small community of blacks, like my family, to quietly begin buying some of the land on which their ancestors had been enslaved. They had eked out a living in a territory surrounded by Klansmen, somehow surviving in a social system committed to Jim Crow.

Still, that land was theirs. And it was enough to farm and rear four children, sending one—my grandmother—to college and on to earn her master's degree. By the time she was married and raising my mom in a nearby town, the land was being worked less. Meanwhile, the local timber industry prospered, often by claiming eminent domain on black-owned properties. Later, the vacation spot of Lake Livingston went from a glimmer in some developer's eye to a destination spot for Houstonians. The development stoked the interest of local speculators, who systematically swindled land away from absent owners.

In a storied tradition as American as apple pie and cronyism, a local white landowner "Dusty" Collington and his family had successfully misappropriated the land of many black farmers by manipulating records at the county clerk's office. He had preyed on the absent generation of Nigton's descendants, those who had moved to other parts of the country during the Great Migration, those who had aspired to greater opportunity.

Between 1960 and 1980, while my grandmother had been a county away, Dusty had asserted that family members had sold him the land for a price. He even had "records" to prove it, a forged deed of sale signed with an *X*. The *X* was meant to substantiate his claim of illiteracy on the part of the seller. He claimed that my great-grandmother had signed with the *X*—proof that she was herself illiterate and had sold the nearly 150 acres to him. I don't know which galled my grandmother more, the fact that Collington said her mother was illiterate (even though her signature was on other documents in the county clerk's office) or the fact that he was suggesting that she had sold off the family land without mentioning it to her daughter. By the time my grandmother died at ninety-seven, the year before Barack Obama would become president and the year Saro was too sick to travel to her funeral, the family land had dwindled down to less than a hundred acres despite only a tiny percentage of the original acreage having ever actually been sold.

I had watched my grandmother's struggle to reclaim the land and legally contest Dusty at a distance as I went off to study in Italy, then get my first apartment in New York City, and later move to Los Angeles. The injustice incensed me. Still, I loved the scent of pine, and the winding red clay roads were in my blood. I literally knew their taste in my mouth. That land was a place as real and alive to me as my skin. Even if I never wanted to be dependent on it as my ancestors had, I loved it in the way you love a place you know in your soul and in your heart you can't let go.

Once we arrived at the notary's office, I knew my role was nothing more than to play the American wife who barely understood a word of Italian. I would sit back and let the legal transfer unfold. And I would step in if, and only if, an old-fashioned show of Sicilian emotion or pathos was needed to get the job done. Because amid everything else that I had learned, I knew Sicilians would move mountains where the pain of grief, death, and loss was concerned. They felt it was their cultural duty. It was what made them Sicilian and not Italian.

The interior of the office struck me as the work of a cinema production designer. It was a cross between a Harry Potter–like reading library, with floor-to-ceiling volumes of bound files embossed in gold, and the private home of some local aristocrat who favored plush tapestries and floor-length silk floral drapery complete with an ornate valance. When we walked into the salon-like conference room, I was invited to sit at a large, antique lacquered table with ball-and-claw legs. A crystal pitcher of water was put before me along with a tumbler on a hand-crocheted lace coaster. The presence of water suggested that we would be there for a while. Then the notary, a suntanned man in his fifties with a George Clooney head of hair, a nautical blue polo, and leather Gucci driving shoes, laid before me a large folio, bigger than 11 by 14. The paper was lined, full of meticulous fine print. It looked to contain the registry of landownership, heredity lines, titles listing parcels of places I recognized, some I didn't. Then he asked to see my passport and Saro's. As I passed them to him, he offered his condolences.

Minutes later, I saw Saro's name in fresh ink on what I presumed to be the Gullo family document of ancestry or heredity. The legal terms were in a cursive that looked as though it were from the eighteenth century. My eyes landed on Saro's birthday, his national identity number, his birthplace, our address in L.A. Below that, I saw my name and farther down Zoela's name, more dates, locations, the coordinates of dual citizenry and language.

On the page, Saro's existence had been reduced to the key places and major events that were the broad outline of the life he had lived: birth, residences, marriage, child, death. As I looked at the words on the page, then back up at the notary, I began to cry. The notary passed me a tissue with tobacco-stained fingers, and I signed my name.

When we emerged back onto the streets of Termini Imerese, in the midst of rush-hour chaos, I was hit with a rush of Vespa fumes, sea salt, eucalyptus, and oleander. I squinted my eyes in the midday sun, temporarily blinded. I now owned land in Sicily.

I didn't have a copy of what had transpired or a receipt of the transactions. Franca was handling it all, including the two remaining trips there to conclude the land transfer. My part was done. I didn't worry; I trusted Franca completely. In Sicily, so much happened this way. I was instead grappling with living at the edge of my wildest imaginings of what life could still offer.

When we returned from the notary, Nonna was making caponata. The smell of onion sautéing with a faint aroma of mint was as familiar as that of salted water for pasta. The dish was sweet and savory, quintessentially Sicilian. Just one mouthful told the island's entire sensuous story: sun, wind, earth, Moorish, and European, it was fantasy brined in reality. Fragrant and textured, caponata has the color of darkness and the taste of paradise.

"How did it go?" she asked me, putting down her wooden spoon.

"Well, I think well. Franca handled it all. She knows all the details."

"Good." Nonna returned to cooking.

I watched her put the ingredients together. Eggplant, olives, celery, carrots, tomato sauce. Alone, each is an everyday item, not particularly rich in value. Together, they are a wealth of flavor.

"Nonna, are you sure I can't help pay the legal fees? I know it was expensive to do this."

"If you can't afford a gift, then you don't give a gift," she said. She put a lid on the pot to punctuate her point and let the flavors of the caponata meld.

As I watched for a moment longer, Nonna seemed as rooted and grounded as any ancient olive tree on the island. I realized that I was standing in the shade of her tree, whose taproot was anchored in the Old World understanding that in order for me to go forward, I'd need a place where I could look back. In giving me the house, she would hold that place for me, for her granddaughter, draw us closer, keep food on the table. Her gift was her way of allowing me to stand in her shade until I was able to walk out into the sun.

Later, there in Nonna's kitchen, the warmth of the waning but persistent sun came through the lace curtains that separated her home from the outside world. Even inside, I felt the touch of wind cut gently by sparrows dancing low in the street. I now had a place in Sicily to call my own, a place to return to next summer and beyond.

Part Four

THIRD SUMMER

Nun c'è megghiu sarsa di la fami.

Hunger is the best sauce.

—*Sicilian proverb*

WILD FENNEL

I awoke the first morning of my third summer in Saro's family home hot and jet-lagged but in the pleasant stupor of a long-forgotten memory—my first trip to the island, when Saro and I had stumbled into a rural trattoria on the northern coast. This memory could have been revived only in Sicily, where the sights, sounds, and smells served as conduits to parts of Saro, events and details that I couldn't seem to access in Los Angeles. Life after loss was confounding in that way: memories lapsed and then resurrected themselves unexpectedly, almost magically. But that morning, as I lay in the soft morning light in a semi–dream state conjuring up a bygone memory of fennel, I grabbed hold of the magic and held on.

"Let's stop here," he had said after we had spent the better part of the day exploring the secondary roads and towns around Hotel Baia del Capitano.

We pulled into a gravel parking lot off the two-lane road parallel to the autostrada.

"It looks closed." I was a little grumpy, a little hungry, a lot unsure about where I found myself.

"It's not closed," he responded.

"How do you know?" I challenged.

"Because it's 3:00 p.m. And look behind the building. The owners live here." He pointed to a side building with a laundry line and geraniums in terra-cotta pots flanking the front door. Apparently, those were all the visual clues I should have needed to puzzle out that a chef was inside and the place was not closed.

Moments later, we pushed the door open and found an empty restaurant of ten or so four-top tables. It was simply decorated with a small hand-painted vase on each table, yellow walls the color of the frescoed suns in sacristies all over Tuscany. The guitar riffs of Pino Daniele came from the kitchen. The owner/chef stepped out. He was short and stout, with a face that looked like so many of the faces dotting all the isles of the Mediterranean.

"*Salve*," Saro said, greeting him before he could greet us. "*Siamo appena arrivati dall'America, possiamo mangiare qualcosa?*—We've just arrived from America, could we have something to eat?"

It was spring, and the owner/chef explained that he was waiting for swordfish to be brought in by the local fishmonger in anticipation of the dinner service later that day. "We're not open yet, but since you've come from America, I'll make you pasta. *Sedetevi*—Sit down." He pulled back the wooden chairs, turned over two glasses, and reached toward the bar behind him for a liter of Ferrarelle mineral water.

"*Di dove siete?*—Where are you from?" He pried the top off with an opener from his back pocket.

"Los Angeles."

"Well, then, how about a plate of wild fennel? I have some growing in back."

"That's all we need," Saro said.

Two plates were placed in front of us. I saw greens, wilted briefly, sautéed in olive oil with a little onion, salted, and then braised in a tomato sauce. The plate was dusted with a shaving of *ricotta salata*.

"This is Sicilian nature on a plate," Saro said as he turned his fork, whirling spaghetti into perfect barrel-shaped clusters ready to heave into his mouth. "This dish is spring. Wild fennel makes us know we are alive, no matter what is happening."

That morning I wanted nothing more than to know that it was possible for me to feel alive, fully alive again. The half living of life after loss was shifting. I wanted to be reminded of the bounty of life. I ached with desire, the possibility exhilarated me.

In the quiet of that morning, I wanted to reach across to Saro and feel the curve of his back. His skin was a thing of shameless softness, a rich sensuality. I wanted to inch closer, near his inhaling and exhaling. I wanted to raise the back of his shirt and reach closer to kiss my favorite landing spot, the skin between his shoulder blades. His back was a constellation of moles. I wanted to dive into Orion's belt.

I imagined he'd then awaken.

"It's too early," his voice would say, gravelly sweet. I poured rich details into the fantasy: a vendor outside our window selling swordfish, just caught, steaks by the kilo; the light of late morning penetrating the shutters of our stark marble room. In my fantasy, the space was cool, but I wouldn't be fooled. I was imagining us in Sicily in July.

"We have to get up," I'd say, thinking of breakfast and its ritual of brioche, cappuccino, and inky newspapers. "Saro, you know I hate an empty pastry case."

"You have to ask the guy to save you one, no?" Saro always believed in befriending the guy at the local coffee bar.

I lay there in bed a little longer, summoning my deepest desires. I imagined his body rolling toward me. How he had smelled of salt and earth, with a hint of cardamom. Thoughts of breakfast receded into the pale stucco walls. "How do you do that?" I wanted to ask him.

"Do what?" he'd say.

"Make me think of dinner before I have had the day's first coffee?"

"*Amore*, you would think of dinner with or without me. I just make your dinner better."

I'd laugh and he'd kiss me. Making love in Sicily had been full of ecstasy. I would demand seconds. Instead, I pulled myself back to reality.

When morning broke, it was time to rise and start my third year of Sicilian July mornings as Saro's widow. But my mind was still thinking of the dream. I was more aware than ever that I hadn't had sex in nearly three years. On my annual visit to the gynecologist, she had joked that my lady parts might atrophy. The conversation had disturbed me so much that I had looked up the definition of "celibate" while still in the parking lot. Celibacy was for nuns, grandmothers, and women in a coma. Sure, I knew women my age who had lived through periods of celibacy. But they had been coming off a bad relationship or trying to heal a sexual addiction. Honestly, I felt like a forty-year-old virgin with twenty years' experience. One of my married girlfriends had suggested masturbation. I told her that that was like telling someone who wanted a five-course meal to grab a can of Spam out of the bottom of her earthquake kit. Sure, it would do in a pinch as a bridge to get you out of disaster, but it is no substitute for a well-balanced meal. After that visit to the doctor, I had started doing Kegels in the car pool lane and while I stood at the stove in case I ever wanted to take my lady parts for a spin again.

Maybe Saro appearing in a dream was his way of reminding me about a part of myself with which I had lost touch since his death. Maybe he was inviting me to be open to the possibility again.

As I lay in Nonna's house, Zoela asleep next to me, I knew I had spent a good deal of the last year of my life in the process of continually making peace with loss, taking wobbly steps forward. In two years, my disorientation had eased, but the sadness was still there. And although I felt a little more stable in the world, more comfortable navigating the changes that come with loss, my life still felt misshapen in many of the unfamiliar places. The waves of grief still came; I just had a better sense of how to ride them out. It was the reimagining and rebuilding that didn't come easy. Before, the grief had been like being caught in the undertow. Now I felt I had fought my way to the top of the water. I could see the sky, but I had neither the energy nor the inclination to swim in a new direction. I was just learning to breathe again.

I know that people rebuild their lives all the time after divorce, job loss, death, illness. We are destined to have to remake our lives at least once or twice in a lifetime. I had come to accept that reconfiguring the pieces of my life, as both a solo parent of a still grieving child and a forty-something actress was something that would take time. And time was what Sicily gave me. So I lifted my feet from the bed and put them onto the marble floor.

The day stretched out ahead of me like an open field. I emptied my bags while Zoela slept the sleep of a child between time zones, languages, and worlds. Then I went downstairs to share a first espresso with Nonna.

I took her in for the first time since arriving the day before. She was doing well, was more joyous. Her smile met me like a familiar friend. She put a basket of fruit on the table, poured sugar directly into the *moka caffettiera* just as I set the demitasse cups on the table.

Before we could speak, Emanuela poked her head through the lace curtains that hung in the open doorway.

"*Mi' nora è tornata*—My daughter-in-law has returned," Nonna said, releasing a guttural laugh that could be heard two houses away. The word daughter-in-law in Sicilian is *nora* or *nura*, which, to me, is similar to the Italian word *onore,* meaning "honor." It gave me an indescribable sense of warmth to be referred to as something that might in some way honor her.

She and Emanuela gossiped for a minute about the statue of the Madonna at the entrance to town. From what I could gather, it needed to be cleaned and adorned with fresh flowers. They felt that leaving the Madonna with the faded plastic ones left over from winter would be a sign of disrespect.

"But eat breakfast first. I'm going to get bread. How many loaves should I get you?"

"Two, the long ones." Nonna gave her two euros from the stash under the vase of carnations sitting beside a picture of Saro and his dad. With that, Emanuela pivoted and was out the door nearly as quickly as she had entered.

Nonna and I went over the particulars of our lives since we had last sat down together: her blood pressure, my garden in L.A., work. We still talked on the phone weekly, but rehashing the news in person made it fresh and new again. I entreated her to report any new gossip, regale me with stories of local politics, tell me who was ill or shut in. It made her feel good to tell me about her world and listen to bits of mine. We both wanted to assure the other that we were fine. Pulling ourselves forward.

"That movie I filmed in Atlanta will come out in the fall." I knew she would never see *Dumb and Dumber To* or any of the other work I had done that year. She certainly had no idea who Jim Carrey was.

She listened intently. To her, my work as an actress was magical, as if I pulled each job like a rabbit out of a hat. The unemployment level in Sicily was so high that the idea that I was working—even if she couldn't quite understand what I did other than to describe it to strangers as "she works in the environment of film"—gave her satisfaction.

She folded her soft, fleshy arms across her chest and looked toward the calendar of saints on the kitchen wall, "After health comes work. In life, it's good to have both." Then she took off one house shoe, to give her foot a vacation from the straps of leather that left an impression across her instep. "And school, are you able to pay for Zoela's school?"

I thought she was going to ask how Zoela was doing in school. But she was fast-tracking the practical matters. There'd be time to talk about reading, writing, and arithmetic.

"*Mi arrangio*," I said. "I manage."

It was true, I was managing. My financial stability depended on a steady stream of new acting work; residuals from old jobs; the remainder of Saro's small life insurance policy, which I used for large unexpected expenses and inevitable employment downturns; and finally, the reduction of his medical debt. It was a high-wire act, no doubt. But I had seen myself through worse. We still had our house, I could still send Zoela to the same school. We had not suffered the secondary losses that so many widowed families do. I counted my blessings. I crossed my fingers.

Then I asked her how she got by. "I keep the lights off. I reuse what I can." It was true. She kept only two bulbs in the six-bulb light fixture that hung above her bed. "I have to save for when Franca will need help taking care of me." She was practical to the bone.

Then we joked about how my being with her in Sicily during the summer actually saved me the cost of Los Angeles summer camps and offset the daily carrying costs of life in L.A. At the end of our time on the bench, we had gone so far as to agree to enroll Zoela in the town's half-day kid camp. She could socialize with kids when she wasn't running in the streets with her bestie, Rosalia. The enrollment fee for the entire month of July was a total of 15 euros, or $18.00. I could spend more than that in a single afternoon of snacks at Starbucks.

"Here there's nothing to spend. We have food, we have shelter, you don't need a car." She said it so convincingly that for a nanosecond, I considered dropping off the grid; homeschooling Zoela; donning a kitchen smock; and getting my annual checkups compliments of the Italian government.

Then she asked me about my plans for the upcoming weeks of our visit.

"Well, at the end of the month, for my birthday, my parents will be coming to visit." I had mentioned a while ago that they might come, and now it was confirmed.

"Good. Then they will get to see the town feast!" She said it with such enthusiasm.

On the second anniversary of Saro's death, my dad had told Zoela that he would see her in Sicily one day. It had been another emotional milestone, especially for Zoela. Getting older for her meant more life being lived without her father; each year she remembered a little less, and it pained her. That day all my parents had come to visit me, and we had gone to the cemetery in Los Angeles. Attica had read a poem she had written for the occasion. Zoela had laid flowers and danced around in circles with her cousin. I told her to let her instincts lead the way. Dancing was a way of releasing energy and physicalizing what she couldn't say. In that intimate group, we had found people who could hold space for us as time went on. All touched the memorial tablet and said a silent prayer, and later my dad told Zoela he would come visit her in her grandmother's home. She had never had those grandparents in the same room together. The last time they had all gotten together was two years before Zoela had come into our lives.

Now it was happening. My dad and Aubrey would arrive on the day of the festival of the town's patron saint, my birthday.

Nonna hadn't seen them since her trip to Houston more than a decade before. "I have the house at the edge of town ready for them. Does your dad still like sausage?"

"Maybe even more," I quipped.

She told me the plan was that they would stay across town at Saro's aunt's house, the same aunt who resided in Switzerland, who had come to our wedding, and whose husband had waved a napkin in the air with my relatives to Aretha Franklin's "Natural Woman" at our wedding. Her husband had since passed away, but not before building a house in Aliminusa where they were supposed to have retired. It sat empty at the end of town, save twice a year, when she came down by train in the fall for the olive harvest and again in the summer for Ferragosto, the national Italian holiday on August 15, when half of Italy shuts down and goes to the sea.

"I hope it is not too simple for them, but it's got a cross breeze and it's quiet," she said.

"It will be perfect. They will love it. Thank you."

Excited and moved by the thought of our families connecting once again, I left her at the table and went upstairs to wake Zoela. We had roughly a month of mornings to enjoy being with Nonna. I didn't want her to miss even one.

THE PROCESSION

Three days into our trip, I prepared myself to head to the edge of town, to a place where *il silenzio parla col vento e ti porta ricordi*— silence converses with the wind and brings memory. Outside Nonna's house, a sparrow drank water from the topsoil of basil potted in crumbling terra-cotta. The leather-faced fishmonger drove away, a swordfish's spear pointing west out of the back of his wagon. I lingered at the kitchen table.

I had not been to the town cemetery in a year. This year I was starting a new tradition: taking a stone with me each time I went. Back in Los Angeles, I had come across Carlo Levi's *Words Are Stones: Impressions of Sicily*, a book on Sicily and the indomitable spirit of everyday people all over the island. Saro had it in his collection of books in our living room. The title reminded me that when Zoela was a toddler, Saro had passed time on the beach with her looking for stones. Ones shaped like hearts, one shaped like Sicily itself. In the years since his death, she had done that on her own at beaches everywhere. The previous summer in Sicily, she had found a heart-shaped stone and written "I love you" on it. Then I had taken it to the cemetery on her behalf. Now I wanted to take a new stone, and I imagined that in time, with many visits, there would be a collection—a little like the Jewish tradition of taking stones to the grave of a loved one. I was sure I would find one along the road on the way to the outskirts of town.

I started at the top of the first street in town and began the slow meander down the cobblestoned thoroughfares. It was a Sunday nearing lunchtime, hardly a wise hour to set out on such a pilgrimage. Everyone's windows and doors were shuttered tight as a defense against the heat. The relentless summer sun hung high.

There is a sudden wind in Sicily that swoops in dry, determined, and carrying with it air from the mountains of North Africa. It is called a scirocco. And although I had lived through two scirocco summers, that day it was different. It was gentler, bringing with it little to no dust. There was no sand covering the cars, and its gusts did not carry grains miles away, effectively destroying crops.

Along the descent, I passed street after street of contiguous, centuries-old stables, stone structures that with the passage of time had evolved into modest stuccoed houses. Within their thick walls were the rooms where generations of family had been born. I descended farther, passing the abandoned grain storage building that had served as Saro's first-grade schoolroom. Farther along, I passed defunct communal fountains where his grandmothers had collected water for laundry, cooking, and bathing husbands after a day in the fields. I passed the public square where tomato paste had been sent to dry. With each descending step, the past and present separated effortlessly and then came together again. The hot air was pregnant with jasmine and eucalyptus.

I passed the church steps. I greeted the butcher, the baker, the cheese maker. I passed a mule tied to a tree, scratching his hooves near a dwarfed palm. His tail swatted flies. As I walked, the town began to recede, opening up into fields that unfolded toward a distant valley. I looked out on the byzantine network of hereditary strips of farming land, impervious soil that, for centuries, had required rigorous cultivation. Still the land spits up wild fennel, almonds fall from trees, and capers grow unbidden from under rocks. Fennel and the dry North African wind were my pilgrimage companions.

Once I arrived, it took little effort to push open the iron cemetery gate. As easy as picking up a book. As if I were there to reread the particular sections where my old story line had ended and an unpredictable new one had begun.

On the other side of the gate, the sun was hidden by walls and the air was cooler. Corridors of marble walls shadowed me. They tamed the winds that came up from the sea. For a moment, summer was all but gone. It could have been spring, fall. This entrance to the cemetery was a seasonless place. The only thing certain was that at the cemetery I was wife, widow, the lover who had brought a husband's ashes halfway around the world because he asked.

I continued farther away from the gate and smiled as I wondered if some part of the poet-chef husband who still made love to me while I slept had foreseen this moment. If he had envisioned me, perfumed by the Sicilian summer, walking the stone ancestry to reach this place at the edge of his town. His easy, wise laugh came to mind. He knew. He wanted me to do exactly what I am doing. He wanted me to stand amid marble smoothed by time and find him again here, in the foothills of a foothill town. He wanted me to find him on an island in the heart of the Mediterranean.

As I stood in front of the tomb, my first act was to move the sturdy but weather-worn wooden stepladder into position against the mausoleum wall. However, at that hour, there was no one around to help me. It was a Sunday nearing lunchtime. Any native informant would have told you it was the worst time of day to go searching for memories. High noon in a Sicilian July only intensified everything. Other women, wiser widows than I, were somewhere else. They were at a stove top, putting the finishing touches on a lunch of eggplant and just-picked zucchini. They had set the table and sliced the bread. But I didn't cook in Sicily. So I continued to move the cumbersome stepladder slowly, dragging one side diagonally across the cement and then the other until I succeeded in positioning it against the wall bearing Saro's name.

My first step up always felt unsteady. I looked down to see a few loose nails holding the boards of the stairs in place. But I knew it wasn't loose nails that were making me shaky.

Once at the top, I saw the stone bearing Zoela's handwriting on the ledge. I was eye to eye with Saro's headstone picture, next to the one of his dad. The expression on his dad's face, posed for all eternity, reminded me of one spring visit in the first years of the family reconciliation.

Saro's father had just come home from working the fields and handed me a large string of garlic, a gift. "*Puoi fare una foto*—You can take a picture." He liked it when I photographed him or the fruit of his hard labor. So we stood in the middle of Via Gramsci, centered on the cobbled stones. The African American daughter-in-law, educated and urbane, taking a picture of the garlic-farming father-in-law, a man who stitched money into the waistband of his pants so he could have the feel of it against his skin while he labored in the fields. In the picture, he is clutching a kitchen knife with a weathered, arthritic hand, holding it at the center of the string of garlic. As though he could break it in two or leave it whole. The choice was his.

We kept that picture framed at home in Los Angeles. In the

weeks before Saro had passed, he had asked that I bring the photo downstairs and place it on the entrance table in the foyer. They say when a person is nearing death he will speak of deceased loved ones, recall them, even ask to see them. I hadn't known that at the time, but now it was all I thought of when I saw his father's picture.

I whispered a love message into the stone I'd found and placed it on the ledge. It was not a remarkable stone in any way, just flat and gray. Though stones of antique yellow, black lava, and red *agata* could be found on the island, gray-colored stone I had heard referred to as the pearl of Sicily. Finally I stepped back down to earth, sensing it was time to get home for lunch. I was sure Zoela was up. Nonna would be poking her head out the front, waiting to see me making my way up the street so that she could launch the pasta into the boiling water.

I moved back from the mausoleum wall, closed my eyes, and turned to begin the walk home. I didn't attempt to put the stepladder back. Leaving it was a sign that someone had been to see the dead.

The next morning, I found Nonna, Emanuela, Benedetta, and Crocetta seated around the kitchen table talking in thick, hushed Sicilian. Their faces were downcast. Nonna was using a sale circular from the morning mail as a fan. A seventeen-year-old resident of Aliminusa had died.

From what I could gather, the girl's illness had come on suddenly at midwinter. It was clear to doctors in neighboring Cefalù that her case was out of their league. She had immediately been transferred to Rome, where her parents had been living out of her hospital room for the last six months. Nuns from a neighboring church had fed them out of the convent cafeteria. Doctors from all over the world had come to visit her, because apparently she was one of thirteen people in the world known to have come down with the same symptoms; a rare, strange, mysterious malady with no name.

For months the priest had updated her case at Sunday Mass each week, asking for prayers for her and her family. Now word had arrived that she had made her transition. There was a pall over the town. Everyone had been rooting for her, "so young." Grown men cried openly at the mention of her name. At the tobacco/newspaper stand, at the bar, in the piazza, among the overflowing file rooms at city hall, her death was the only conversation in town. The tragedy seemed to be compounded by the mystifying nature of what had happened, the inability even to name the murderous illness.

"Her family, the poor mother, she never left her daughter's side," said Benedetta.

"The pain of not knowing," Emanuela said.

"Three babies were born, and thirty people died last year," added Benedetta.

Those were the genealogical facts of Aliminusa.

"The scale has turned upside. Who knows what will become of us . . . this is how we found this world, and this is how we will leave it," Nonna added. It was a saying as old as any of them could remember. Then they let silence fall over them, presumably contemplating the loss of a young life.

My heart went out to her family. I knew something about fighting rare and invisible enemies. I thought about how after ten years of caregiving I should have been prepared for what was to come. The specter of Saro's illness had hovered above me at all times, but I had never been ready to deal with its whims. His cancer was constantly reinventing itself, and acute crisis was as close as the air

I breathed. I had seen a calm Sunday breakfast of tea and fresh-baked croissants erupt into chaos due to an adverse drug interaction, which had resulted in a trip to the ER. I had seen him rise from the dinner table, saying he wasn't feeling well, only to pass out in the bathroom moments later, his head hitting the sink on the way down. I had seen his moods careen and collide in manic spectacle, turning to sullenness or anger in a matter of seconds. I organized our lives around that fickle mechanism known as his immune system. Under assault, it might make a dramatic appearance one week and then retreat without warning the next. I had watched him crack a tooth while eating a baguette one day, his teeth brittle and fragile from radiation therapy. That was the kind of stuff for which I could never prepare myself.

"We need to take fresh flowers to the cemetery. The procession is tomorrow," Nonna said to me.

"I will get them, of course," I said, suddenly feeling faint. Maybe it was the heat, the mountain's dry winds, maybe it was the emotion. I had been in Aliminusa for many occasions, feasts, weddings, hostile elections, but never a birth and never a full funeral. This was another important first.

After leaving the fresh flowers on Saro's tomb the following day, I walked the forgotten road back from the cemetery, the one used long ago for mules. I was aware that I was on the road that Sicilians say makes a person seem like *un'anima persa*—a lost soul. But that was exactly what I wanted. I didn't want to see anyone, just me and the wind. However, as I neared the last remaining working fountain in town, the one near the steps widened for mule and cart travel a hundred years before, I looked up to see that the processional for the young girl's funeral had begun. The mourners had just started the march toward the church from the statue of the town's patron saint, Sant'Anna, that greets visitors at the edge of town. The clock struck 11:00 a.m., and the wind made another push.

I continued my slow ascent up the steps, deciding midway to lean against the wall in the shade for support and respite. I was not dressed to go any closer. In red pants and a floral top, I was nobody's mourner.

I watched the slender coffin pass by, carried on the shoulders of six of her classmates, teenage boys with pimples, gelled hair, and cell phones bulging in back pockets. The white-robed Padre Francesco walked in front of the coffin; her parents, slumped over but somehow on their feet, walked behind it. Behind them came a mass of townsfolk, each carrying a single white rose. The older women sang the lament while incense permeated the already summer-pungent, restless air.

When the last of the mourners had passed where I stood, I peeled myself off the wall and took the remaining steps up the main street. Some older women, those in black frocks and orthopedic socks, receded from their viewing place at the front windows of their homes. They knew how the rest would unfold, and presumably they would return to their straw chairs and pray some more.

By the time I made it home, Nonna was seated at the table. Tears were in her eyes, too. She had watched the scene from her doorway high above the main street.

At the sight of her, I suddenly felt faint. She perhaps recognized the look on my face and had already pulled out a chair for me to sit next to her. So I did.

Grief in Sicily is not an individual experience but a communal one where people are called upon to witness and support one another. The way certain African cultures use drumming as an active means of dealing with their grief—the rhythm is played continuously for days, day and night, over and over, as a constant reminder to the community of its loss—in Sicily the story of the deceased is told over and over. I was prepared to sit and listen to Nonna bear witness.

But instead we sat in silence for a good long while. Nothing needed to be added to the moment.

Then she asked, "Did you get the flowers?"

"Yes, and then I walked back the long way."

"Nothing will be longer than the walk her parents are making today."

"I know."

The wind blew the curtains hanging at the front door.

"Plus, with this wind, they will be weaker still."

The afternoon wore on. Nonna sent Zoela and me upstairs to nap.

"Go rest. Too much sun and too much death in one day."

As afternoon gave way to evening, the sun had relented and the wind had calmed. Zoela and Rosalia disappeared into play and friendship, making water "balloons" from plastic sacks and tossing them up and down Via Gramsci. I left to buy more bread and passed the *edicola*, the newsstand that also sold pens, toys, batteries, and sunscreen, then stopped by the cheese shop to put in an order for *ricotta salata*. I wanted to order it early because I knew it would need time to cure during my stay, before I could take it back to L.A. when the time came. On the way back, I bumped into an older woman with piercing blue eyes and crooked toes in orthopedic sandals. She was one of Nonna's distant cousins, a gregarious talker. Her name slipped from me like soup off a fork. So I called her simply "Zia," which made her smile.

After reciting her maladies and her displeasure at the ten-cent increase in the price of bread, she asked about my family in the States. I told her they were coming for a visit and would be in town for the feast of Sant'Anna. She clapped her hands together at her chest in an expression of pleasure and surprise. Then she grabbed my face in the palm of her hands. "The connection you are creating here is like a flower. It requires soil and sun, things that, thanks to God, are given freely. But it is you, all of us, who has to water the flower to make it grow. Without water, all relations remain small. They can't open, and eventually they die."

She took my face again and kissed it twice good-bye. Then she started up the steep cobblestoned street to her house.

Zia had been talking about family, Zoela, connection, and nurturing relationships. But I had dared to read something else into her words. What if my own life was like a flower, something I had to continually tend to and nurture? Sicily was the water and sun that fortified me to stand stronger in my life after loss. And maybe my leaving a rock at the cemetery as an act of remembrance had additional meaning; maybe it was a symbol of the lasting permanence of Saro's love. His love, life, illness, and death had taught me so much, but it was the undergirding of his love that was my salvation in loss.

I continued back home, and when I passed the stone walls lining the street, I released a dream into mortar and crevices, into the stone diary that was my summer in Sicily. I will use the love of this place to fortify me. It is my stone inheritance, the gift of Saro's life.

THE SAUCE

The days in Aliminusa moved at a repetitively graceful pace, and by our second week back Zoela and I had fallen into step with it. Each afternoon she devoured warm milk and two fistfuls of cookies and took off down the street.

"Watch out for cars in the piazza, and don't go past the bridge at the edge of town," I'd remind her.

I kissed her good-bye, secure in the knowledge that she would reemerge at lunch for hearty dishes of olives, pasta with fresh string beans, cheese, and bread. Then surely she would take off again after settling in for an afternoon siesta.

Meanwhile, my dad kept calling me in Sicily to update me on their arrival. Our conversations went like this:

"Wi-Fi access?"

"None."

"What about an American coffee maker?"

"Dad, bring instant."

"We're renting a car."

"Oh, no, you're not. Let me come get you."

"Tembi, I've driven all over Europe and East Texas. I can do this." My dad's enthusiasm for road trips was almost evangelical.

Aubrey jumped on the line and began their favorite back-and-forth teasing, "Drive, huh? In Sicily? You going to do that like the way you speak Portuguese?"

"No, this is for real. I can handle the roads in Sicily. My Portuguese is just for show." It was a running joke in the family that Dad claimed to speak three foreign languages: Portuguese, Swahili, and "East Texas." He claimed to have learned Portuguese in Mozambique, Angola, and Guinea-Bissau while traveling with Stokely Carmichael; Swahili while in Tanzania helping freedom fighters in 1974; and "East Texas" while picking cotton on the land near his grandparents' homestead. Everyone in the family agreed that he could butcher five words in each language, at best. That is, with the exception of "East Texas." He was absolutely fluent in that.

"Dad, it would make me feel better if you simply got a driver to bring you from the airport. Sicily is a challenge to navigate. Frankly, it's not set up for tourists or non-Sicilians. Let me talk to your travel agent."

"Yes, Gene, please. Let's make this easy." Aubrey was the sensible yin to his adventurous yang. Then she continued, "Actually, Tembi, we called because I need to know what we should bring for Nonna and Franca and Cosimo."

Gift giving was Aubrey's forte. In another life, she could have started a business buying insanely intimate gifts for the people in other people's lives. She had a rare skill, like being able to sing above five octaves or juggle flames while walking on stilts. It was a skill I lacked. She wanted my Sicilian family to know how much the Texas family had loved Saro and appreciated their hospitality. I ran through a list of possible options for my nieces and brother- and sister-in-law. Then I got to Nonna.

"Bring her something for the house. Something that honors the memory of her son. That is all she will want. And maybe a black scarf."

It was vague, and I was embarrassed that I still couldn't figure out what to get the woman who was now like another mother to me.

My dad piped back in, "Also, we arrive the morning of your birthday. What do you want to do to celebrate?"

"Ah, Dad. I don't know."

I honestly didn't. It wasn't just my birthday, it was my anniversary. Two life events forever linked. Now, nineteen years after my nuptials in Florence, my parents and Saro's family would be together on the anniversary of the day when a world of difference and mistrust had kept them apart. Now they would be together without the person for whom their togetherness, especially in Sicily, would have meant so much.

Summer was sauce-making season. The air smelled of wood smoke and tomato sauce. Around town empty dark green mineral water bottles and brown beer bottles were drying on racks and in crates on the sidewalks in the front of homes and *i magazzini*—the cellars and town garages that were used to store tractors, farming equipment, and cauldrons for the tradition of making tomato sauce. Tomatoes, the signature of summer, deep red San Marzano plum tomatoes straight from the fields, were made into sauce, as had been done for generations. Storage spaces and cellars all over town would soon be lined with enough tomato sauce–filled bottles to last the residents through winter. Sicilians say, "The greatest joy is knowing that in the dead of winter, you can open a bottle and make a pasta that tastes like the height of summer."

Nonna had not made sauce in the years since Giuseppe had

died, six years before. Her hundred-year-old copper cauldron sat wrapped in wool blankets next to Giuseppe's tools for cutting artichoke and stringing garlic in the attic-like space between the tiled roof and the second floor of her home. She left the sauce making to Cosimo and Franca. Every year they made enough for her, thirty to forty one-liter bottles. But that summer Cosimo's work schedule dictated that he wouldn't be making sauce for another two weeks, after I would be back in Los Angeles. Instead, her cousins at the base of Via Gramsci were making it that very afternoon.

At the breakfast table that morning, Nonna made sure Zoela didn't discard her single-serve bottles of pear and peach juice. She would wash them, boil them, and store them.

"We can use them for the sauce. These little bottles will fit nicely in your suitcase. They are perfect for a meal for two. When you come home from work, open one, and you and Zoela will have a meal."

"I do the same for myself," she continued. "The small bottles are all I need since I am alone."

"If you want to see how it is done, go to Nunzia's later today. Take Zoela." I suspected that Nonna liked the idea of Zoela spending time with another of her cousins who lived on the main street that went through town.

Three generations and two tributaries of the Lupo family would begin the work of lighting the fire with wood collected from the fields, peeling the tomatoes, salting them, cutting onion, preparing the basil, manning the cauldron, then bottling and storing. The process took three days of prep (cleaning and sterilizing bottles, harvesting tomatoes), a long day of sauce making, then another day or two for the sauce to cool. Unlike other families in town, who began the work at 2:00 a.m. and worked until 10:00, the Lupo family made their sauce in the late afternoon and into the night because their cellar faced southwest on a hill. So by virtue of geography, they were spared the oppressive afternoon heat and received a cross breeze when they opened all the windows.

The "take Zoela" part of Nonna's plan was tricky. Tearing her from Rosalia would take a mammoth effort. In general, the kids in town did not like making sauce. And they didn't make it with any other family than their own. Making sauce was a family tradition that came with risks. It was incredibly labor intensive, and they were often not allowed to be near the cauldrons. Plus they often got tired and complained. It was one of the reasons so many families made the sauce in the night while the children slept.

As I washed out the small single-serve bottles, I poked my head out the door to chat with Zoela and Rosalia.

"Ro-zaa," that was the nickname the women on the street called her, so I did the same. "Zoela and I will be at Nunzia's house later today, making sauce. Want to come?"

She and Zoela were seated on the bench outside Nonna's house, killing time making movies on Zoela's iPad. The latest was a thriller about the coffins stored next to Nonna's house.

"No, I can't come. I have a clarinet lesson."

"That's right." In the last year, she had graduated to a spot in the town band. With the upcoming procession for the feast of Sant'Anna, she had to practice for the next few afternoons. "I can't wait to hear you play." Secretly I was thrilled, because it meant I would get little resistance from Zoela. I really wanted her to see where the tomato sauce she enjoyed almost daily at Nonna's table came from. And I wanted to try my hand at this oldest of town traditions. It felt like the perfect culmination of summer.

The afternoon seemed to be moving at a snail's pace. Rest after lunch, reading. I even had a plan to collect caper buds from the vine growing in the cracks at the top of Via Gramsci. It was Gianna, who lived in the house above the encroaching vine, who had told me what they were. I had never seen capers growing. She told me that some years the winds carried seeds, depositing them between the cobblestoned steps. I had plans to gather at least two cupfuls, salt them, and let them dry in the sun next to the tomatoes in front of the house. I'd be taking all of it back to L.A. when the time came to close my suitcase.

Then, in the early afternoon, the phone rang.

Nonna answered, irritated at having been roused from her nap. I could hear her clipped "*Pronto?*" bellow all the way upstairs. Seconds later, she called out to me, "*Pigghia u telefono.*" She was using Sicilian to tell me to pick up the phone. Not Italian. Whatever it was, it felt urgent.

There had been a car accident one street over. No one had been hurt, but one of the drivers was an English tourist. He spoke no Italian, and I was the only person in town who spoke English. A neighbor had called because they needed me to talk to the Englishman and hopefully translate and de-escalate a tense situation.

When I arrived, I found a forty-something man in slim jeans and a white linen shirt. He seemed shocked to see me appear from behind the wooden door of the pass-through between the two streets. He was in the middle of the street, visibly tense and surrounded by Sicilians. A scene was forming.

We quickly exchanged pleasantries and intros the way people of the same tongue in a foreign land can do. He was a music producer in rural Sicily on holiday with his young family. They were renting a farmhouse nearby. He had come into town to get bread, only to find that everything was closed. The man whose car he had hit, I soon discovered, was Calogero, the same affable farmer with a hearty laugh who gave me lentils each year from his field to take back to L.A.

As soon as Calogero saw me, he jumped to the quick *"Parla con quello!*—Speak with that one!" Then he threw his arms up in the classic Sicilian gesture signaling frustration, resignation, and rising indignation, a movement that told me everything I needed to know.

Before I could translate, the Englishman rushed to his own defense. He was adamant that Calogero had been at fault. One look at his Audi station wagon, and it was clear that he was probably right. Calogero had likely backed out of his driveway without looking. People rarely used that street. The Englishman was probably not expecting a car backing out of the shallow driveways and house fronts.

I asked the Englishman if we could speak away from the growing crowd.

"The man you are accusing of hitting the car is the mayor's cousin," I said. I was jumping to what seemed to me the most salient piece of information he needed to know.

He looked at me confused and irritated, as if to say, What the fuck does the mayor's cousin have to do with anything?

But I was thinking like a Sicilian, which means considering the social hierarchy of a particular situation before the facts.

"Do you have rental insurance?" I asked.

"No. I didn't think I'd need it. I just want him to sign the form in the glove box saying he hit me."

It was hot, the middle of siesta. The scene grew louder, and the crowd outside the house grew larger. It seemed that everyone was eager to tell me what they had seen.

"Let's go inside," I said, pulling him toward Calogero's front door.

Inside Calogero's intimate, immaculate kitchen, three generations of my lentil connection's family gathered at a kitchen table to testify to the innocence of their relative. We all sat at a plastic-covered table for four. The others hovered over us. A traditional Sicilian ceramic light fixture with a painted illustration of Moors and grapevines hung above us. A crate of tomatoes sat on a nearby chair, likely waiting to be boiled into submission.

I went back and forth between English and Italian, translating both language and culture for an Englishman who was suddenly realizing that the deck was stacked against him. In Sicily, fault is relative. Facts are always subject to how you see the events of the world. Still it took twenty minutes of back-and-forth illustrations on the back of napkins, attempting to re-create what had happened, before the Englishman gave up his pursuit of logic and submitted to the fact that he was in a town of Sicilians. People who would never betray one of their own. Whatever had actually happened was, in fact, irrelevant.

"You are not in Tuscany, you are in Sicily," I said, reminding him that Italy was not a monolith and Tuscany was not a stand-in for a whole nation, despite what cinema might suggest. Tuscans had been welcoming tourists for half a century, absorbing hundreds of thousands of visitors with all the issues, questions, and unexpected mishaps that can happen on holiday. Sicily, especially the rural interior, had scant tourist infrastructure. English was not prevalent, and locals were not casting their gaze outward, inviting the world in.

"I see that now." It suddenly struck him as a fact as clear as the Sicilian July day.

Then he turned to me, and, perhaps for the first time in the hour we had been together, he saw me—a black American woman seated at the table among the faces of people she neither resembled nor defended but whom she seemed to understand.

"How the hell did you get here?" he asked.

I gave him the only answer that would explain it all: "I was married to a Sicilian man. I'm now his widow."

He lingered for a moment, as if trying to process the sequence of life events I had laid out that had brought us to this moment. Then he offered his condolences. Ten minutes later I got him to agree not to pursue the insurance claim issue any further.

"Tell them your car was hit while it was parked. No one's fault. Pay the fine, and enjoy the rest of your vacation," I said.

"It's a beautiful place," he said referring to the rolling fields that led to the valley below. "Too bad about all this. I can't say that I will be coming back. These people don't make it easy." I wanted to educate him about the fact that he was on an island that has been conquered and ruled by many outsiders throughout history. That the Sicilian instinct isn't always to make it easier for an outsider.

I watched him drive away, up the winding road past the blackberry brambles, taking the series of curves that would lead to the country house he was renting. I was ready to go back home. The whole thing had been rather exhausting.

When I got home, Nonna made us afternoon coffee, and she shrugged her shoulders as I recounted the story of Calogero and the Englishman. Her purse was on the table. She was going to Mass soon. The priest from Burundi was back, and she wanted to get to the church to get a spot near the fans.

Calogero's wife had stopped me as I was returning home and had given me a bag of dried garbanzo beans from the spring harvest in gratitude for my help. Nonna and I decided to clean them while we waited for the coffee to rise to the top of the *caffettiera*. The beans still had remnants of earth and bits of straw on them. Nonna rinsed them to remove the unwanted parts; I stood ready with the colander and a floral dish rag to dry them. We worked in silence, the smell of brewing coffee permeating the kitchen. I had a feeling that something was on her mind. After I dried the last colanderful of beans and put them into a shallow bowl to dry further in the sun, the coffee was finally ready. That was when she finally spoke up.

"Did you side with Calogero?" She poured a thimbleful of espresso for herself, a full demitasse for me. "Because others come and go, but we are here together."

It took me a moment to register the full spectrum of what was being said—both a statement and an invitation, a moment as quintessentially Sicilian as the earth on which we stood. Nonna saw this as *us* versus *them*. At the same time, she was testing my allegiance and sense of belonging to this place, this community. Behind it all, she was asking if I was a part of her *us*.

The answer had been unequivocal for me.

"Yes, I did," I assured her. "You won't have any problems. Calogero will probably bring you lentils and garbanzo beans all year."

She laughed and wiped down the sink and countertop, wiping away dust or problems no one could see but her. I hoped she was also wiping away any doubt about how I felt about her and the place she called home. Soon afterward she dressed in her formal widow blacks, sprayed her hair in case the wind picked up, and left for Mass.

While Nonna was at church, I peeled Zoela away from her iPad and told her a boiling cauldron was waiting for us. It was time to make the sauce. We closed the front door and followed the scent of burning wood and velvety plum tomatoes.

When we stepped into the cellar, we found all the members of the Lupo family in full swing. One duo supervised the washing, another duo added onion and coarse sea salt from the flats of

Trapani. There was a milling station where boiled tomatoes were put through metal sieves to separate the pulp from the seeds and skin. It was there that the tomatoes were reduced to a puree. The smell of smoke that permeated the town was almost ethereal up close. In a second room, the oldest member of the Lupo family, Pina, stirred a second cauldron exclusively for the puree. She used a wooden spoon the length of her body, toe to breast. Her job was to constantly stir the sauce in a gentle motion so as not to let it stick to the bottom. Nearby, the oldest men scooped out small pots of the sauce and took them to the bottling station. Then Maria Pia filled each bottle, capping it with a bottle cap. Lastly, there was an area of the cellar where hundred-year-old straw *cesti*, large baskets, rested on the floor. They were the kind once carried by mules. Full bottles were put into the baskets and wrapped in blankets to cool.

Zoela and I looked at the ancient, efficient, precisely timed and rhythmic operation with no idea where to jump in. For a moment, I accepted that our role might be to stand and watch at the periphery, outsiders looking in. I worried that all my buildup to Zoela about making the sauce had been a letdown. I knew she would be bored in about five minutes if all she could do was stand around a hot cellar and watch other people work. But then she spoke.

"*Posso aiutare?*—Can I help?" The room lit up in surprise and enthusiasm for the little voice asking to join in.

"*Certo*—Of course" was the response that came back in unison. "Get her an apron," someone urged.

"*Voglio mescolare*—I want to stir." Zoela was pointing to the first cauldron over a bright orange-and-red wood flame. The wooden spoon was taller than she was. "I can do that."

"You must stand back. Or the smoke, onion, and steam will hurt your face. You have to stand back and stir."

Zoela took the spoon with a kind of glee that seemed unique to the moment when a child is invited by adults to participate for the first time in something previously unknown to her. She looked to me for approval. Despite the obvious risk of fire, smoke, and scalding liquids, there was no way I would have denied her the moment.

I hung back as everyone worked in silent ritual. Zoela's nine-year-old hands were doing something her grandmother had done, her father had likely done. It was collaborative, practical, healing in the sense of the continuity it provided. This went on for a while, and then Marianna broke the silence.

"*Tutte le cose in questa salsa vengono da qui*—Everything in this sauce comes from here." She put an emphasis on *here* and then pointed to the open window just beyond the cauldron, to the fields in the distance framed in a picture window of stone. "*Tutto viene da questo terrano*—Everything comes from this land."

Zoela looked up and out. I followed her gaze. The valley was visible, the mountain range some twenty miles in the distance. The hills were streaked in crimson, the color of summer tomato harvest.

"It is our little piece of earth," Maria Pia continued, moving closer to Zoela. She stood behind Zoela and put her hand on top of Zoela's to help her stir. The work was hard and fatiguing. I had been ready to help, but Marianna had sensed it, too. Zoela was relieved for the assistance but not at all ready to relinquish her post.

She stood stoic, her nine-year-old body as determined and committed as that of any other person in the room to making the sauce. My heart swelled. I admired this soul. She was the kind of child I imagined might become a woman who was not afraid to face life's heat and fire and still stir the pot. Who could appreciate the earth on which we stood. Who knew that she, wherever she might go, was a part of our shared *terra*. It was embedded into the meaning of her name, Zoela—a piece of earth.

We stayed another hour. I bottled, I stirred, I salted tomatoes, I learned to open the heart of the fruit the ancient way, plunging my thumb into the center where the stem once stood, getting access to the core. Zoela and I left smelling of smoky eucalyptus wood, basil, onion, and sea salt. It was in our hair, in our clothes, it had seeped into our skin. I was reminded of the way Saro had smelled when he had returned to that tiny apartment in Florence each night after working at Acqua al 2. It was a beguiling, living smell that I didn't want to leave me.

I went to bed that night tired but with the vision of plum tomatoes dancing in my head. The child, the daughter of the chef, stirring the pot. How I wished that Saro had been there to see it. Yet somehow I felt he had. I felt it the same way I had felt that he would be waiting for me the morning we said good-bye.

SAGE AND SAINTS

I woke on my forty-fourth birthday thinking of fennel and Saro's poetry. It was the last morning I would have alone with Nonna that summer, before my parents arrived by lunchtime. A few days later, Zoela and I would head to Rome, then back to Los Angeles. I heard the unmistakable sound of the water tank being filled above the rafters in the bedroom. Water arrived in town once a week from the mountains, and residents were allowed to fill their household tanks for the week ahead. The flow of water echoed through the stone walls and bounced off the marble floors. It was loud, thunderous enough to wake me. Zoela was still asleep.

The smell of household cleanser rose from downstairs. I heard Nonna moving chairs. It was likely that she was vigorously mopping the floors. Cleaning was her meditation, her tradition on our final days. My parents would be arriving in a few hours, and we would surely have a steady stream of visitors. Her cleaning time might be my final chance to talk with her quietly, just the two of us, face-to-face.

I readied myself, tying back my hair and slipping on a pajama cover. We would likely be interrupted by some passersby—the residents of Via Gramsci on their way to get bread, bringing fresh vegetables from the fields, hanging laundry out to dry, vendors selling their goods. They would poke their heads into the kitchen door with local news or gossip or to share whatever ailed them. So I wanted to be presentable, but I wasn't ready to dress fully. And after three summers, Nonna knew that when I sat at her table in my pajamas I was in no rush.

When I hit the final step of the landing that led into the modest living room, I was careful not to slip on her wet floor.

"*Stai attenta!*—Be careful!" she said. "I heard you above. The coffee is already on. Sit down."

I did as I was told. She checked the flame under the *caffettiera*, handed me my usual demitasse cup, and passed the sugar right behind it. It was a smooth, effortless action, simple kitchen table choreography we had done countless times before. I settled in.

"Mamma." I ventured to call her that, it felt natural in the moment. "You know how I feel about good-byes." I suppose I felt emboldened by the first light of day, my thoughts of Saro, my birthday, the impending guests, and the unspoken awareness that another summer was not promised to us.

"You don't have to tell me, since yesterday my heart is heavy. And for the next few days I won't be well," she said, lowering the flame on the stove-top espresso maker. She took a seat.

She went on to ask me about my plans for the day. I told her I'd be going to the cemetery one last time. She reminded me to weigh my luggage and to travel only with what was necessary. She told me we still had six bottles of tomato sauce to wrap and put into the suitcase. We continued with that small talk for about ten minutes.

Then we sat just silently. The bubbling sound of espresso perking to the top of the *caffettiera* broke the silence. She poured us both a thimbleful to start. Then she spoke. "What you have passed, the years you stood at Saro's side, you deserve to be rewarded for that."

She was speaking with rare, unbidden intimacy about my life away from her home, away from our moments at her table. I downed my coffee and looked out the door. It took a minute before I realized the various things she might be suggesting. Then, without a second more, I walked through the opening she had made in our conversation.

"In my own way, I am trying to pull myself forward. Raising Zoela to the best of my ability. I'm trying to build a new life," I said, feeling suddenly exposed, like a melon split open. "I hope for a life that is expansive for both of us. Zoela and I need that. With any luck, I have some forty years ahead of me. I'd like them to be filled with joy as well."

She shrugged her shoulders, "*Ma come no?*—Why not?" She went to take another swig of coffee, but her cup was empty, so she looked out past the hand-sewn lace curtain that hung at the front door. She wiped her mouth with a napkin and continued, "Going forward no one forgets." Then she turned and looked at me. "I don't know if I'm making myself clear."

I held her glance. I wondered if she was talking about my opening my life to another love.

"Yes, I think I understand. My heart will never forget while I carry this life forward."

She nodded in response. The air about us was full of what wasn't being said. She was, in her own way, telling me I was known and loved. That wherever my life might take me, there was a love that was unshakable.

She pushed back her glasses and used the same napkin to wipe her eyes. Then she pushed a pastry of apricot and brioche in my direction.

I knew we had passed another milestone as friends, widows, mothers.

"Now let's call my cousin in Petralia. That one will sink her teeth into me with a strong bite of guilt if you don't say good-bye to her personally. Hand me the phone."

Fifteen minutes later, I was dressed and out the door. I left Zoela, still asleep, to walk the hills one last time. I decided to go to a place I had once visited with Saro and his father. I walked down Via Gramsci and hooked a left. Sheep bells clanged behind me as the herder brought his flock down the main street to graze in the valley below town.

I felt a wind off the sea and looked toward the outward-stretched sky. In that moment, I couldn't think of a better birthday present. I didn't see sky like that in L.A. There the sky felt as though it was a dome over the city. And most days, I moved hurriedly along urban stretches without ever having cause to look up or out.

At the far end of a narrowing hillside was our family mulberry tree. Surrounding it were four pear trees that produced miniature, densely flavored green pears. It was where I would go to get away.

Silence was guaranteed.

The mulberries didn't disappoint. It was late in the season. Many had been taken by birds and fallen to the ground. I could never reach the high fruit without a ladder. So I settled for the berries left on the low branches. Everything about my life with Saro came rushing back to me. I remembered artichokes in spring and salt under his fingernails. I basked in that tiny detail. All the while, I let the tart, sweet fruit burst in my mouth once again.

Then I walked back toward town. I detoured and passed the road that led to the oil mill. A day earlier, I had sat with Saro's distant cousin Epifanio. He ran the olive mill located just outside of town, and he had given me an impromptu lesson in *degustazione dell'olio di oliva*—olive oil tasting. He had said that the key to tasting oil is to let the palate awaken to it, wrestling with its peppery, grassy flavors while also recognizing its smooth quality.

Around the mill, Epifanio had been cultivating heirloom varieties of mint, sage, and basil, ancient varieties that were common centuries ago but that were little known by modern Sicilians. All of it, he instructed me, was due to nature's organic cross-pollination; man need not interfere.

The thing that I focused in on was *salvia all' ananas*—pineapple sage, distinguished from the classic variety by its variegated color. In more than forty years on the planet, I hadn't known such a thing existed. The island, still twenty years later, was showing herself to me. When I rubbed the sage between my palms, it emitted a delicate scent reminiscent of pineapple. Epifanio told me I couldn't buy seeds. That it grew from clippings, letting a piece of one plant give birth to another.

I had stood there enjoying the aroma of pineapple jump from my palm, realizing that life was still revealing itself to me, I just had to stay open to it.

I meandered back home, passing clusters and clusters of wild fennel. I hadn't seen it before, but there it was, growing enthusiastically along the side of the same road I had passed earlier, accessorizing the landscape, the white stalks knee and waist high, rising with bushy green tops that looked to the casual eye like weeds. Fennel is a delicious thing that can sprout up among weeds along the road of life. As Saro had said, "It's there to make you know that you are alive."

When I got home, Zoela was awake and seated at Nonna's table.

"*Ciao, mammina*—Hello, little mama," she said with a grin.

Each summer in Sicily had marked her growth. Walking the streets on her own each morning to get the daily bread from the *pasticceria*, learning the ancient craft of making fresh ricotta cheese, frolicking in the family's orchard, Sicily had become a gift to her, the place where she would always know her father. Her independence was breathtaking, her friendships deeper, her Italian charming. She now made jokes in Italian, making me believe that Italian Zoela was American Zoela's alter ego. I rather loved them both.

She was writing a postcard. It was something I made her do every summer, write a postcard to herself telling herself what the summer had meant to her. Then we would send it back to L.A. This postcard had a nightscape of Cefalù. I thought about how we had walked the streets until well after midnight a week earlier. We had let the sea air fill our lungs, we had slurped granita in the cathedral square. She had found *il Gran Carro*, the Big Dipper, in the sky and had talked about her dad.

"Do you think he can see us here?" she asked.

She knew the close of our trip was drawing near. So we talked about saying good-bye to Nonna, her cousins, and her friends. Her grief sat right at the surface. I could see how she pushed for and pulled from the conversation. She talked about Saro's hair the day he had died, she asked about Nonna's age. Then later, as we were falling to sleep that night, she made me promise to do my best "to live to be a hundred years old."

I told her what I always did when fear and loss left her quiet and pensive: "I'm healthy. If I can help it, I'll be here long enough to see you become an old lady." It made her smile.

"But I won't live at home then, you know," she was quick to point out.

"I'd be surprised if you did," I said.

"Maybe I'll live here."

"If you do, make sure I have a room to visit."

After she finished her postcard and cleared away breakfast, she started to help Nonna prepare lunch. This was a first. Zoela called to me in the next room, where I was wrapping bottles of tomato sauce in newspaper and slipping them into old socks Saro had left there years before. "*Guarda, Mamma*—Watch me, Mom." She was grating cheese with a vertical tabletop grater that had a crank as large as her hand. It was the oldest kitchen tool in the house, purchased not long after Nonna's wedding.

A quick survey of the kitchen, and I could see that Nonna was preparing three courses—spaghetti with a classic tomato sauce, eggplant parmigiana, sausage from the butcher, plates of cheeses, and a leafy green salad, dusted with sea salt and tossed with her hands. She would add the vinegar once my parents arrived. Dessert would be fresh melon from her cousin Stefano's land.

Food was the center of her family life. Cooking was her second nature. There were no formal recipes; the ingredients, quantities, and steps were all in her head. I had asked her once to write down a recipe, and it had been like asking her to write down how she breathed or walked. "*Non ti posso dire. Faccio come si deve fare.*—I can't tell you. I just do it as it should be done."

The food from Nonna's kitchen told a story, an epic and personal story of an island and a family. It told the story of poverty, grief, love, and joy. It spoke forthrightly of people who had, at times, survived on bread, cheese, and olives while foraging wild vegetables from the rich orchards dotting the foothills near her house. Her kitchen always told me what was in season. It reminded me of my proximity to North Africa, to the East. It told me of the people whose cultures had passed through the island and the ways they had left traces of themselves. But what I loved most was that her kitchen showed me how one ingredient can be made into many different dishes. Her food spoke of malleability and resourcefulness in loss, in love, and in life. She had learned how to turn subsistence living into abundance.

Sicilians say that when you open a bottle of olive oil, you should smell the earth inside. Antioxidant rich, verdant, it should sing of life in a bottle. I grabbed a bottle of olive oil that sat on the table and poured some over fresh bread. I could taste the aromatic legacy of the artichokes, tomatoes, and eucalyptus that grew on the periphery of town. Their essence had infused the life of the olive trees nearby. Being near Nonna had done that for me; every dish she made would be a culinary afterimage.

Just before noon, my dad rang my cell to say that the driver had just pulled into the entrance to town.

"Stay there, I'm coming," I said, feeling strangely giddy.

"Well, where else I am gonna go? I don't speak a word of Italian and don't even know where I am," he chided. I could hear the excitement in his voice.

"You're in Sicily, Dad. You made it to Sicily."

I called to Zoela to come down from the upstairs bedroom.

She shot down the stairs with Rosalia in tow. "*Vieni con me*— Come with me," she commanded her friend. Zoela was full of agency. "*Ti faccio conoscere i miei nonni dall'America*—I'm going to introduce you to my American grandparents."

Within minutes we were all headed down Via Gramsci on foot, Zoela running ahead of me, Rosalia keeping pace.

I had waited two decades for this moment.

After we all exchanged hugs there in the street, couplets of on-lookers came up to the car to say "*Benvenuti.*" It seemed that news of their arrival had already begun to circulate.

Then we made the trek back up to Nonna's house. All the widows and wives of Via Gramsci poured out of their front doors to say "*Benvenuti*" as we made our way up the street. But the vision that took hold of my heart was Nonna standing proudly in her doorway.

"*Ciao, Gene. Ciao, Aubrey. Venite*—Come," she said as she pulled back the lace and invited them inside.

This was what she had not been able to do when her son was alive. But she was doing it now.

"Tell her thank you for having us," my dad said to me.

"Already done, Dad," I said with a smile and a wink. "I got this."

My dad had never seen me speak so much Italian. He was watching me carefully, as if from on the other side of an invisible partition between us that until now he hadn't known existed. His little girl had made a place for herself as far from East Texas as one could imagine.

"Ask Nonna if we can help her prepare anything," Aubrey said, pointing to the pot boiling on the stove. Aubrey was ready to dive in. They did not want Nonna to have to do everything.

"It's already done," I said.

"Yeah, Nonna will never let you do anything in her kitchen," Zoela piped in. "You are her guest, you just eat. That's the way it is here."

Thirty minutes later, we were seated at an abundant table. I was translating furiously as I twisted my fork around strands of pasta delicately coated with a sauce as unpretentious as the woman who served it. She wanted to make sure that my parents liked the food, that they were happy. I noticed Nonna zero in on Aubrey, who appeared to her to be eating very little.

"*Lei non mangia tanto*—She doesn't eat much," I said quietly into her ear to preempt any hurt feelings.

Nonna threw her hand back and turned directly to Aubrey, "*Mangia!* Eat more, we have lots of food here." She began lifting plates in Aubrey's direction. "*Mangia!*"

We toasted to Saro. I made sure my dad tasted homemade Sicilian wine left over from the days when Saro's dad had made his own vintage: remnants of pulp and sediment on the bottom, sharp tannins on top, the robust flavor of fragrant grapes in the middle. Nothing passed through; it was unprocessed, home distilled. The kind of stuff that my grandmother used to say could put hair on your chest.

"Think of it like a Sicilian Ripple," I joked, referring to the cheap alcoholic drink famous in 1970s black sitcoms and blaxploitation movies.

"Then I'll have a sip but not more. You don't want me speaking Portuguese, do you?"

The Sicilian novelist and essayist Leonardo Sciascia once said, "Translation is the other side of a tapestry." It was something Saro had told me one day when he was attempting to translate a poem from Sicilian into English.

There at the table, it was clear that being with Saro had been like weaving a beautiful, complicated tapestry. After his death, being with his family was like looking at the flip side of that tapestry. The stitching showed, the bulky knots, the places where the fringe had frayed. But it was still part of the same beautiful piece.

• • •

After lunch, I walked my parents to Nonna's sister's house at the end of town, where they would stay. We passed people all along the way, each stopping to greet us and exchange hellos. They kissed dozens of cheeks and shook dozens of hands with the people who seemed as much to me like family as my own. Each offered advice to my dad and Aubrey, told them what it meant to be from Aliminusa, and I translated for them.

My favorite was the man who lived above the bank and had a bird's-eye view of the comings and goings in the piazza. "We are all the children of God, just look at our hands." He held up his hand, palm facing my dad. "But notice, each finger is different. One is short, one is long, one is crooked. They each do different things. But we are all part of the same family."

Later, we passed Signor Shecco, nicknamed "Mister Mule" because he had one of the last remaining mules in town and often took her for a walk draped in colorful fringe, a tradition from the turn of the last century. He said to my dad, "*Siamo quattro gatti qua, porta a porta col cimitero*—We are just four cats here, door to door with the cemetery." He held up four arthritic fingers and waited for me to translate. "We are four cats" means "Our numbers are small"; "door to door with the cemetery" means "old and dying."

Then Signor Shecco continued, "*Ma siamo buoni, buoni e stretti. Capisce? Sua figlia è una di noi.*—But we are good, and we are close. Understand? Your daughter is one of us."

My dad smiled and thanked the man.

As we walked away, Dad looked back at the man with the mule, he looked around town at the cobblestones and buildings seemingly as old as time, and he said to Aubrey, "Being here, I understand my son-in-law in a whole new way. But I really understand my daughter more than ever." I was overcome by his words.

Late afternoon turned to dusk, and we readied ourselves for the procession of Sant'Anna. In filmmaking, we call that time of day "magic hour," the moment when the diffused rays of the sun make everything more beautiful. Here the faded stone walls of the town become a canvas upon which every color of the Mediterranean can be celebrated. It is that time of day that gives Sicily its timelessness.

Zoela and I collected my parents and took them to the town square, where a crowd of townspeople gathered around the church steps. It was time to bring out the statue of Sant'Anna. I looked up at the church, the marble-and-limestone facade, the Roman-numeral clock, the bell tower. It was the same place where two summers earlier I had stood unsure if I could make sense of my life, let alone reimagine it, while the priest blessed Saro's ashes.

Sant'Anna, I had since learned, was the mother of Mary, the grandmother of Jesus. In Catholicism, Anna is the matriarch of matriarchs, the embodiment of female wisdom. She was perhaps absorbed into Christianity from the pagan goddess of fertility, Anu, whose name means "grace." Once a year, her statue is taken from the church in Aliminusa, hoisted onto the shoulders of men, and carried through town, a procession of townspeople trailing behind her. Women who are able to walk the length of the town proceed barefoot on the cobblestones immediately behind her with her shadow cast upon them in the setting sun. These women pray to her in times of difficulty and times of celebration. I had also learned that she was the patron saint of widows and travelers. I was born on her day, July 26. I was married on her day. For the people of Aliminusa, that meant she was my personal saint. "You drew a good card," Nonna told me.

I stood on the street in front of the church, my parents and daughter at my side as the priest said the prayer and the band began to play. Zoela waved to Rosalia as she played the clarinet. The saint emerged from the large double-hung carved wooden doors. It was indeed magic hour.

Coincidence and *fate* are two words for the same phenomenon. The coincidence of a chance meeting in Florence had fated me to stand here decades later, thousands of miles from my home of origin but simultaneously in a home I had chosen, tasting my first flavors of renewal. Saro's love, his life, and his loss had forged me, softening me to life and strengthening me in the broken places.

As the statue was carried down the steps and the procession began, I did not move. There was nowhere to go just then; the journey for the moment was complete. Inside me I felt a bittersweet evolution. I would leave this place aware that there was a lot of living to come. The wound of loss had become a scar of love. I knew that in whatever experience was yet to come, I would be ever more in love with the poet-chef in elf boots who had lit the fire for a lifetime.

I closed my eyes, held Zoela's hand, and asked, "Anu—Ana—Grace" to follow me—one mother, one widow, one traveler, wherever I would go next.

RECIPES

FIRST SUMMER

*Carciofi con Pomodori e Menta (Artichokes
Braised in Tomatoes with Mint)*

*Pesto di Pomodori Secchi, Oliva e Mandorle
(Sundried Tomatoes and Almond Tapanade)*

Spaghetti con Pesto alla Trapanese (Sicilian Almond Pesto Pasta)

*Insalata di Rucola con Pomodori e Ricotta Salata
(Arugula Salad with Tomatoes and Ricotta Salata)*

Olive Aromatiche (Aromatic Olives)

SECOND SUMMER

Ditalini con Lenticchie (Ditalini Pasta with Lentils)

Purea de Fave con Crostini (Pureed Fava Beans with Crostini)

*Pesce Spada alla Griglia con Salsa Salmoriglio
(Grilled Swordfish with Salsa Salmoriglio)*

Caponata Classica (Classic Caponata)

Melanzane alla Parmigiana (Eggplant Parmigiana)

Sfuagghiu ("Schiavelli's Cake")

THIRD SUMMER

Salsa Pronta (Classic Tomato Sauce)

Pasta con Zucchini (Sicilian Summer Pasta)

Penne con Finocchio e Fave (Penne with Fennel and Fava Beans)

Insalata di Finocchio (Shaved Fennel and Citrus Salad)

Granita di Gelsi Neri (Mulberry Granita)

First Summer

CARCIOFI CON POMODORI E MENTA

Artichokes Braised in Tomatoes with Mint

Each spring my mother-in-law makes artichokes this way. She is kind enough to freeze them for me to enjoy when I arrive in summer. When I take my first bite, I think of them as being braised in kindness. At home in Los Angeles, Saro made this variation of her dish whenever artichokes were in season.

1 (28-ounce) can whole peeled tomatoes, preferably Italian San Marzano

1 $1/2$ cups dry white wine

$1/2$ teaspoon red pepper flakes, crushed

2 teaspoons Sicilian sea salt, plus more to taste

1 cup extra-virgin olive oil

8 garlic cloves

$1/2$ cup bread crumbs

1 cup fresh mint leaves, lightly packed

6 medium artichokes

2 lemons, halved

Place the tomatoes in a large, heavy pot and crush them with your hands or a fork. Add the wine, red pepper flakes, 2 teaspoons salt, $1/2$ cup olive oil, and 2 cups water. Set aside.

In a food processor, pulse the garlic, bread crumbs, and mint leaves until coarsely chopped. While the motor is going, stream in the remaining $1/2$ cup olive oil to make a thick paste. Set aside.

Remove several layers of dark green outer leaves from the artichoke. Keep going until you reach the tender light green leaves. Use a serrated knife to cut off the top 1 inch or more of the artichokes and trim the stem ends. Rub the cut ends with lemon halves to prevent browning. Use a paring knife or vegetable peeler to remove the tough outer green layer from the base and stem to reveal the pale green flesh underneath. Rub with lemon. Cut in half through the stem and rub the cut sides with lemon. Use a spoon to scoop out the choke and pull out the spiky inner leaves.

With a spoon, rub the pesto all over the artichoke halves. Place them into the large pot in a single layer with the tomato mixture, submerging them. Sprinkle a thin layer of bread crumbs on the surface.

Bring to a simmer over a medium-low flame and cook, covered, turning the artichokes once or twice, until they are fork tender, about 55 to 60 minutes.

Serves 6 to 8.

PESTO DI POMODORI SECCHI, OLIVA E MANDORLE

Sundried Tomatoes and Almond Tapanade

This Sicilian-inspired pesto is a staple in our home. I keep it on hand to smear on crostini, spread on sandwiches, or, most notably, use as a mouth-watering pasta sauce. The combination of almonds, sundried tomatoes, and oil-cured black olives always takes me right back to Sicily.

$^{1}/_{2}$ cup raw almonds, roughly chopped

2 tablespoons minced fresh rosemary leaves

$^{1}/_{4}$ cup chopped fresh basil leaves

2 teaspoons balsamic vinegar

2 teaspoons sugar

$^{1}/_{2}$ teaspoon smoked paprika

20 pitted oil-cured olives

10 to 15 sundried tomatoes in oil, chopped

4 cloves garlic, chopped

1 cup extra-virgin olive oil

Coarse sea salt and freshly ground black pepper to taste

Put the almonds, rosemary, basil, vinegar, sugar, paprika, olives, tomatoes, and garlic into a food processor. Blend, streaming in the olive oil as you go, until finely chopped into a thick paste. Add more olive oil if you want a smoother consistency. Season with salt and pepper to taste.

Makes about $1^{1}/_{2}$ cups.

SPAGHETTI CON PESTO ALLA TRAPANESE
Sicilian Almond Pesto Pasta

This was one of the first dishes I learned to make after that first summer in Sicily. It's simple and direct. Though it originates from the city of Trapani, it is found on menus all over the island. I have eaten it everywhere from Stromboli to Palermo to Taormina. Each time the chef adds his or her own touch, adding less tomato or more. When making it stateside, I prepare it at the height of the summer tomato season because the dish is all about the simplicity of natural flavors coming together in perfect harmony. Each ingredient is a star.

4 cloves garlic
¾ cup raw almonds
1 cup extra-virgin olive oil
5 cups basil
1 medium to large raw tomato, peeled and chopped into
   ½-inch pieces
Sea salt and freshly cracked black pepper to taste
1 (16-ounce) spaghetti
Grated pecorino or parmigiano cheese for garnishing
   (optional)

In a blender, combine the garlic and almonds. Blend, streaming in half of the olive oil until it forms a uniform, even cream.

Add the basil, the tomatoes, and the other half of the oil while blending to make it extra smooth. Add sea salt and pepper to taste. Let the sauce sit while you cook the pasta.

Drain the pasta, return it to the pot, and add the pesto, mixing gently and thoroughly. Add a touch more olive oil to help coat the pasta with the sauce. Serve immediately. I like to dust it with grated pecorino or parmigiano cheese.

Serves 4 to 6.

INSALATA DI RUCOLA CON
POMODORI E RICOTTA SALATA

Arugula Salad with Tomatoes and Ricotta Salata

I found this recipe in Saro's personal notes. He intended it as an anti-pasto in a menu he entitled "Summer Dinner on a Sicilian Terrace." When I first came across it, I felt nothing but the bittersweetness of imagining another dinner with him on some terrace in Sicily. Now I make this simple salad for my friends as part of summer in Silver Lake.

$1/2$ cup extra-virgin olive oil

2 tablespoons red wine vinegar

1 teaspoon honey

3 bunches arugula, stems discarded

$1 1/2$ pounds fresh summer tomatoes, cut into quarters

1 small red onion, thinly sliced

$1/2$ pound *ricotta salata* cheese, shaved with a peeler

Sea salt and freshly ground black pepper to taste

To make the dressing, in a small bowl, whisk together the oil, vinegar, and honey with a pinch of salt.

Make a bed of arugula on a plate. Top with tomatoes, place sliced onion throughout, and top with the *ricotta salata*. Season with salt and pepper to taste. Drizzle with the dressing. Serve immediately.

Serves 4 to 6.

OLIVE AROMATICHE

Aromatic Olives

Aromatic olives are always resting in bowls on the table during Nonna's meals. She has two varieties, black and green, picked from the family orchard. She makes a batch when we arrive, and I eat them for the duration of our stay. In Los Angeles, I make my own and serve them on my favorite Sicilian ceramic dishes at parties.

Aromatic Black Olives

1 pound oil-cured black olives
$\frac{1}{2}$ cup extra-virgin olive oil
2 tablespoons balsamic vinegar
2 cloves garlic, minced
1 teaspoon coarsely chopped rosemary leaves
$\frac{1}{2}$ teaspoon red pepper flakes
Grated zest of 1 orange and $\frac{1}{2}$ lemon
Pinch of brown sugar

In a bowl, combine the olives with the olive oil, vinegar, garlic, rosemary, red pepper flakes, orange and lemon zests, and brown sugar. Stir well and allow to marinate for an hour or so. Serve at room temperature.

Aromatic Green Olives

1 pound pitted green olives
$\frac{1}{2}$ cup extra-virgin olive oil
$\frac{1}{2}$ cup carrots, finely diced
1 celery stalk with some tender leaves, chopped
2 garlic cloves, minced
2 tablespoons dried Sicilian oregano
$\frac{1}{2}$ teaspoon red pepper flakes
1 tablespoon red wine vinegar

If you are using vinegar-cured green olives, drain them of excess liquid and pat dry. In a bowl, combine the olives with the olive oil, carrots, celery, garlic, oregano, red pepper flakes, and vinegar. Stir well and allow to marinate for an hour or so. Serve at room temperature.

Makes 2 cups.

Second Summer

DITALINI CON LENTICCHIE
Ditalini Pasta with Lentils

This is always the first dish Nonna serves us when we arrive. When I see the steaming plate hit the table, it is absolutely poetic. I know I am home. This dish tells any traveler that home is sharing a table with the people you love.

$^1/_4$ cup extra-virgin olive oil

1 red onion

$3^1/_2$ cups dry lentils, green or brown (not Le Puy)

2 small carrots, chopped

1 celery stalk or 1 small bunch celery leaves, chopped

1 clove garlic

1 tablespoon sea salt plus additional if desired

Black pepper to taste

$^1/_2$ cup fresh chard or fresh spinach, chopped (optional)

Pinch of dried oregano

1 box ditalini pasta

In a saucepan, combine the olive oil and onion and cook over a medium flame for about 5 minutes. Add the lentils and stir to coat with the oil. Add 4 cups water and the carrots and celery and bring to a boil. Add the garlic, 1 tablespoon sea salt, and black pepper to taste. Reduce the heat, cover, and simmer for about 20 minutes. Add the chard or spinach and oregano and simmer for another 20 to 25 minutes. Season with additional salt to taste.

Meanwhile, cook the pasta in a large pot of boiling well-salted water. Drain well. Transfer the pasta to the saucepan and mix well, coating all the pasta with the lentil mixture. Add an additional bit of olive oil to bring it all together. Dust with pecorino or parmigiano cheese, if desired. Serve immediately.

Serves 4 to 6.

PUREA DE FAVE CON CROSTINI

Pureed Fava Beans with Crostini

Shelling fresh fava beans is a labor of love. Removing the hull and peeling back the outer skin of each bean takes time, patience, and a soulful respect for the cultivation of this generous bean. There is a reason it has been a Mediterranean mainstay for centuries. For me, preparing fava beans is a kind of meditation. I put on some music, pour myself a glass of wine, and ready the beans. It is the way Saro taught me. Once prepared, these crostini are a sublime delicacy, earthy and inspired.

2 pounds of fresh fava beans, still in the pod
2 1/4 teaspoons sea salt
2 tablespoons extra-virgin olive oil
1/2 small white onion, finely chopped
2 tablespoons fresh mint, chopped
1/2 teaspoon lemon juice
Sea salt and freshly cracked black pepper to taste
1 baguette or loaf of artisanal bread
1 clove garlic to rub on the bread
Thinly sliced pecorino cheese for garnish (optional)

Shuck the fava beans (remove the beans from their bulky pods). Fill a large saucepan half full of water and add 2 teaspoons of salt. Bring the water to a boil. Meanwhile, put a few cups of ice in a medium mixing bowl and fill with water.

Add the beans to the boiling water and cook for 2 to 3 minutes, *no more.* Turn off the heat and strain the beans into the ice-water bath. (Be careful to save a bit of the water that the beans were boiled in.) Let the beans sit in the ice bath for 1 to 2 minutes. Drain the ice water from the pan. Remove the outer coating of each bean, pinching the end and slipping the bean out of the skin.

In a medium skillet, heat the olive oil and add the onion. Cook until translucent, about 2 minutes. Add the beans, the saved bean water, and the remaining salt. Stir and allow to simmer for 5 minutes. Remove the pan from the heat, stir in the mint, and add the lemon juice. Put the mixture into a food processor and blend until creamy smooth, streaming in a little more olive oil if necessary to make it creamier. Add salt and pepper to taste. Set aside.

Slice the bread into 1-inch-thick slices. Grill or broil until lightly golden. Remove, rub with a clove of garlic, and brush with olive oil. Top each piece of bread with a hearty heap of fava bean puree. Garnish with a slice of pecorino, if desired. Top with the remaining mint.

Makes a dozen pieces.

PESCE SPADA ALLA GRIGLIA
CON SALSA SALMORIGLIO

Grilled Swordfish with Salsa Salmoriglio

On the coast of Sicily, we eat a lot of fresh fish. In the seaside town of Cefalù, it is not uncommon to see whole or halves of freshly caught swordfish on display at the markets throughout town. On one trip, Zoela and I were seated in a restaurant when a fisherman brought his catch directly to the chef, who prepared only the freshest fish. In Sicily, grilled swordfish is served with *salmoriglio* sauce, which is both a marinade and a dressing. It is impressive, beautifully flavored, and easy to prepare.

2 tablespoons Sicilian oregano, dried or fresh (finely chopped if fresh)

2 tablespoons fresh chopped parsley

2 tablespoons fresh chopped mint (optional)

Juice of 2 to 3 lemons, strained

1 cup extra-virgin olive oil

2 cloves garlic, finely chopped

Coarse sea salt and cracked black pepper to taste

4 swordfish steaks, 5 to 6 ounces each

Rinse the fresh herbs and pat them dry. Set aside 2 teaspoons of lemon juice for later.

Pour the olive oil into a bowl and whisk, gradually adding the garlic, the remaining lemon juice, and the herbs. The marinade will be a bit dense, almost a paste. Add pepper to taste. Set aside.

Brush the swordfish with 2 teaspoons of lemon juice and the olive oil marinade. Dust with sea salt. Grill the swordfish until cooked through, about 3 minutes on each side, depending on the thickness of the steaks. Transfer to plates. Spoon the remaining sauce over each steak and serve.

Serves 4.

CAPONATA CLASSICA

Classic Caponata

For me, this classic sweet-and-sour eggplant dish is the heart of Sicily. No two caponata dishes are exactly alike, however; each is an expression of the heart and imagination of the person who made it. I have had it in Nonna's kitchen and as far away as Siracusa. Dark, savory, briny, and sweet, I call this dish heaven.

Vegetable oil, for frying
2 medium to large eggplants, cut into 1½ inch cubes
Salt to taste
½ cup extra-virgin olive oil
1 red onion, cut lengthwise and thinly sliced
3 celery stalks, blanched 1 minute in boiling water, then
   coarsely chopped
2 carrots, chopped
10 pitted green olives, cut lengthwise into thirds
¼ cup capers, rinsed and drained
1½ cups good-quality tomato sauce (see recipe for *Salsa Pronta*, page 326)
1 small bunch of fresh basil, chopped
¼ cup white or red wine vinegar
1 tablespoon honey or sugar, or to taste
½ cup raisins (optional)
½ cup fresh flat-leaf parsley, for garnish

Heat 1 inch of vegetable oil in a large, heavy skillet. Add the cubed eggplant in batches and fry until well browned all over, about 5 minutes. Drain on paper towels. Season with salt. Set aside.

In another large skillet, combine the olive oil and onion and sauté over medium-high heat until just golden, about 5 minutes. Add the celery, carrots, olives, capers, tomato sauce, basil, vinegar, and honey or sugar. Stir gently. Salt to taste.

Gently add the eggplant, being careful not to break it up into pieces. Add the raisins, if desired. Simmer for 2 to 3 minutes. Correct the salt. Then transfer to a large bowl or platter and allow to cool. Garnish the caponata with chopped parsley. Serve at room temperature.

Caponata can also be served cold on a hot summer day. For added flavor and an extra bit of texture, sprinkle toasted almonds on top.

Serves 4 to 6.

MELANZANE ALLA PARMIGIANA
Eggplant Parmigiana

Chargrilled eggplant works beautifully in this classic dish. It's actually the only way I make it in L.A. I have a weakness for the chargrilled flavor that you won't get with frying. The joy of this dish is in the layering. Two layers of eggplant will do, but three or four are divine.

4 to 5 medium to large eggplants, cut in ¹/₂-inch-thick rounds
Coarse sea salt
1 cup extra-virgin olive oil
Freshly ground black pepper
2 cloves garlic, chopped
1 teaspoon Sicilian dried oregano
6 cups quality tomato sauce (see recipe for *Salsa Pronta*, page 326)
¹/₃ cup pecorino or parmigiano cheese, finely grated
1 bunch of basil, stems removed and chopped

Preheat the oven to 375° F.

Place the eggplant rounds in a large bowl. Liberally sprinkle salt all over them and allow them to sit in the bowl to release the excess water from the eggplant. After 45 minutes to 1 hour, drain the water from the bowl. Drizzle with olive oil, coating each slice, then season with the black pepper, garlic, and oregano.

Grill each round 1 to 2 minutes on each side. Set aside.

Heat the tomato sauce on medium-high flame.

Drizzle the bottom of a large ceramic or glass baking dish with olive oil and cover it with 1 cup of tomato sauce. Line the bottom of the baking dish with a layer of eggplant. Spoon tomato sauce on top of the eggplant. Add grated cheese and basil leaves. Then repeat with another layer of eggplant. Coat with another layer of sauce, cheese, and basil. Bake until the cheese has melted and the sauce is bubbling, about 30 minutes.

Serves 4 to 6.

SFUAGGHIU

"Schiavelli's Cake"

This cake is about adventure, longing, persistence, and hope all at once. Today, when I see the photograph of Saro and Vincent Schiavelli in our L.A. apartment long ago, smiling and holding the cake, my heart soars. I like to imagine that those immigrant sons are enjoying a bite together wherever their souls may be. (*Note:* To my knowledge, Pino the baker never divulged his recipe to Schiavelli. It does not appear in Schiavelli's book, *Many Beautiful Things*. I found this recipe, a variation of the cake he discussed in his book, on the official site of the town of Polizzi Generosa.) I've included the recipe here for the truly adventurous baker.

For the filling:

1 pound fresh tuma cheese

5 egg whites, room temperature

2 cups sugar

1 tablespoon ground cinnamon

Dark chocolate, to taste

$1/3$ cup candied fruit, cut into pieces

For the cake:

4 cups flour

1 cup lard, cut into pieces, plus more for greasing the pan

6 egg yolks, beaten, room temperature

1 cup sugar

$1/4$ cup powdered sugar

Preheat the oven to 375° F.

Make the filling: Grate the cheese very fine into a bowl. Add the egg whites, beating in the sugar, cinnamon, chocolate, and candied fruit alternately. Mix well and set aside.

Make the cake: Add the flour to a bowl and make an indentation in it. Add the lard to the indentation, then fold in the flour, mixing well with your hands. Add the sugar and egg yolks. Continue to mix well with your hands. If it is dry, feel free to add a little water. Roll out half the batter into a thin layer about $1/2$-inch thick. Place on the bottom of a 9-inch round springform baking pan greased with lard and dusted with flour.

Assemble the cake: Pour the filling over the dough, being careful not to pour it too high as it will swell when baking. Cover it with another layer of dough. Pinch the sides closed along the edges. Bake for about 1 hour. Remove from the oven and dust with powdered sugar. Let the cake rest for a whole day before eating.

Serves 12 to 14.

Third Summer

SALSA PRONTA

Classic Tomato Sauce

Normally, this sauce would be made with fresh San Marzano tomatoes in a large cauldron over a wood-burning fire. This recipe is a version you can do any time of year in your home kitchen. I make large pots of it, then store it in the refrigerator or freezer. That way, I am never without "ready sauce" for pasta, lasagna, soups, or eggplant parmigiana. (*Note:* the longer you cook the sauce, the denser it will be. If desired, you can cook it into a loose paste. It is delicious as a pizza sauce.)

> 2 (28-ounce) cans San Marzano tomatoes, chopped
> 2 large red onions, coarsely chopped
> 4 cloves garlic, peeled
> $\frac{1}{2}$ cup extra-virgin olive oil
> Large bunch of basil
> 1 tablespoon sea salt, or to taste
> 1 tablespoon sugar
> Oregano and red pepper flakes (optional)

Combine the tomatoes and $\frac{1}{2}$ cup water in a large pot. Add half of the onion and half of the garlic. Bring to a boil, then reduce and simmer, covered, for about 40 minutes, stirring frequently to keep from sticking. Remove from the heat. Pass through a food mill or blend in a blender to make a puree.

In a food processor, combine the olive oil, basil, and the remaining onion and garlic. Puree until very smooth.

In a clean pot, combine the tomato puree and the basil puree. Cook over medium heat, uncovered, until it thickens, 20 to 30 minutes (longer if you are going for a paste consistency). Remove from heat. Add the salt and sugar. If you are making sauce for pizza or prefer a little spicier flavor, add a small amount of oregano and/or pinch of red pepper flakes.

This sauce can be canned in sterilized jars while still hot or stored in the refrigerator for up to 3 to 4 days or in the freezer for up to a month.

Makes about 8 cups.

PASTA CON ZUCCHINI

Sicilian Summer Pasta

There are many varieties of Sicilian zucchini; the most majestic is the long, pale green type known as *cucuzze*. Farmers all around Aliminusa grow them in abundance. Unpretentious, they are featured in soups, in pastas, and on the grill. *Cucuzze* are not found in supermarkets stateside. However, this recipe works just as well with the zucchini found in your local grocery store. This can be made as a pasta sauce or as a stand-alone side dish.

1 medium red onion, chopped

$1/2$ cup extra-virgin olive oil

1 pound fresh summer tomatoes, Roma or plum, peeled and chopped

3 medium zucchini, chopped (peeled if you prefer, but not necessary)

1 vegetable bouillon cube

$1/2$ cup torn fresh basil leaves

Sea salt and black pepper to taste

Spaghetti or your preferred long pasta

Shredded *ricotta salata* or grated pecorino for garnish

In a saucepan, sauté the onion in olive oil over medium-high heat for about 2 to 3 minutes, until golden. Add the tomatoes and cook for another two minutes. Add the zucchini and stir. Break the bouillon cube into the saucepan, then add the basil, $3/4$ cup water, and salt and pepper to taste. Cover and cook over medium heat, until the zucchini is soft, about 20 minutes. Turn off the heat and allow to sit.

Boil the pasta in well-salted water. Drain. Return to pot. Add the zucchini and tomato sauce and stir well, streaming in a bit of additional olive oil to bring together the sauce and the pasta. Plate and sprinkle with cheese as a garnish or abundantly, if you desire.

Serves 4 to 6.

PENNE CON FINOCCHIO E FAVE

Penne with Fennel and Fava Beans

If there is one dish that transports me to my first trip to Sicily with Saro, the time he unfurled the island to me in all its glory, this dish is it. It reminds me of his life force, his "spring," his ultimate evolution of spirit. Plus it is just damn good. (This recipe calls for the fennel found at your local grocer. But if you want to grow your own fennel, you will marvel at what nature can do.) Saro, I hope I make you proud with this one.

1 teaspoon coarse sea salt

2 cups fresh fava beans, shelled

2 cups chopped fennel greens (the top of the bulb)

$^3/_4$ cup extra-virgin olive oil

Coarse sea salt and freshly cracked pepper to taste

$1^1/_2$ tablespoons coarse sea salt

1 white onion, chopped

1 pound penne pasta

Freshly grated pecorino cheese

Cracked pepper for garnish (optional)

Bring 1 quart of water to a boil. Add the sea salt and stir. Add the fava beans and fennel greens. Simmer until the vegetables are very tender, about 10 minutes.

Using a strainer, remove the beans and greens. Briefly set aside the vegetable water, then transfer it into a large pot you'll use for cooking the pasta.

In a food processor, puree the beans and the greens with $^1/_2$ cup of the olive oil and add salt and pepper to taste. Set aside.

Add 3 quarts of water to the vegetable water in the pot and bring to a boil. Add $1^1/_2$ tablespoons sea salt.

Meanwhile, in a large sauté pan, heat the remaining $^1/_4$ cup of olive oil and the onion over a medium-high flame until it turns golden brown, stirring often, about 2 minutes. Reduce the heat and fold in the puree. Simmer over a very low flame for 5 minutes.

Cook the pasta in the well-salted boiling water, stirring often, until al dente. Drain the penne and return it to the pot. Add the puree of beans and greens, toss well, stream in a bit of olive oil, and simmer on low heat for 1 minute. Add a little extra pasta water if you like a thinner sauce.

Serve hot, garnished liberally with pecorino and a bit of cracked pepper if desired. Then toast to your life.

Serves 4 to 6.

INSALATA DI FINOCCHIO

Shaved Fennel and Citrus Salad

Being in Sicily has taught me the pleasure of eating raw fennel, often sprinkled with just a little salt, at the end of a meal. It is an old island custom to eat the fennel as a digestive, like a piece of fruit. At home I turn to this recipe as an alternative to a traditional lettuce salad. I adore the contrast of textures and the bright citrus flavors. In my version, I forgo including slices of orange in the salad itself. Instead, I prefer the zesty citrus essence to come through in the dressing. This salad is at once crispy, citrusy, and salty with a hint of sweetness—a refreshing Sicilian pick-me-up.

2 tablespoons fresh orange or blood orange juice

2 tablespoons white or red wine vinegar

$^{1}/_{4}$ cup extra-virgin olive oil

1 tablespoon honey

1 teaspoon fennel seeds

$^{1}/_{2}$ teaspoon salt

$^{1}/_{4}$ teaspoon freshly ground black pepper

1 fennel bulb with fronds, thinly sliced

Juice of half a lemon

$^{1}/_{2}$ large red onion, thinly sliced

$^{1}/_{4}$ cup oil-cured black olives

$^{1}/_{4}$ cup chopped fresh mint leaves

Fine sea salt and freshly ground black pepper to taste

Shaved parmigiano cheese

Combine the orange juice, vinegar, olive oil, honey, fennel seeds, salt, and pepper. Whisk vigorously until well blended. Set aside.

Cut the stems off the fennel, reserving the fronds for garnishing the salad. Cut the fennel in half, remove the core, and cut into quarters. Using a mandoline or small sharp knife, slice the fennel pieces thinly. Place them in a bowl. Sprinkle with lemon juice and dust with a pinch of salt. Add the onion and olives. Pour the vinaigrette over the salad and toss. Place in a shallow salad bowl or rimmed platter and garnish with the fennel fronds and mint. Add sliced parmigiano cheese (if desired). Dust with a few grinds of black pepper and serve immediately.

Serves 4.

GRANITA DI GELSI NERI

Mulberry Granita

The mulberry is an edible ode to summer in Sicily. I am never happier than when Zoela and I are picking them directly from the tree. They stain our hands, and they stain our clothes. Those stains tell our story of encountering the goddess of all orchard fruits. This recipe should be made anytime you come across fresh black mulberries. Stop what you are doing, marvel at the fleeting fruit, and then welcome the beautiful stains of summer by making this quick, delicious granita. When all is said and done, chill out and enjoy the Sicilian way.

2 cups fresh mulberries, washed and then allowed to dry
Juice of 2 lemons
1/3 cup sugar (honey or maple syrup is also suitable)

Wash the mulberries under gently running water and allow them to dry thoroughly. Using a food processor, puree them. Set aside.

In a saucepan, combine half of the lemon juice, 1/2 cup cold water, and sugar and warm on gentle heat until the sugar is dissolved. Add the mulberry puree to the syrup followed by the remaining lemon juice.

Mix and then place in the freezer in a metal baking dish with low sides for 30 to 40 minutes. Remove and stir with a fork. This will break it up to provide a softer texture. Put back into the freezer and repeat again in 30 minutes. Repeat these steps off and on for about 3 hours. You want the granita to be firm but not frozen.

Before serving, scrape the granita with a fork to lighten the texture. Enjoy.

Makes 2 cups.

Author's Note

To write this book, I drew from my personal journals, letters, emails, texts, and my late husband's personal writings. When I could, I consulted with several people who appear in the book. The stories told to me—often in dialect—are full of the blanks and missing portions that characterize oral storytelling. I have changed the names and certain identifying details of most individuals in the book and some individuals are composites. Occasionally, I conflated similar events into one for clarity. I also omitted people but only when that omission had no impact on the truth or the substance of the story. Otherwise, this book is a true account of experiences as I remember them.

The recipes are mostly from my late husband's personal notes; some are from my memory of what we ate. Some are from my mother-in-law. A few I researched and then modified, as I imagined he might do.

Acknowledgments

My first thanks go to Christine Pride, my insightful and gifted editor, for her belief in this book. With her, it grew by leaps and bounds, becoming far better because of her incisive questions and wise editorial guidance.

A very big thank-you to Richard Abate. My life became fuller and more creative from the moment he said, "I think there's more."

If you're going to write a book, it helps to have a sister like Attica. She'll read your 2:00 a.m. emails sent from a small town half a world away and say, "This is a book. I want to read this book!" Years later, she'll remind you that she is still waiting for your book. She has all my bottomless gratitude and love.

The other person who is good to have in your corner is Shawna Kenney. She read my manuscript ten pages at a time, week after week, for a year. She generously brainstormed, listened, gently probed. Her steady and well-placed observations guided me up the mountain. And when the air felt too thin and I thought I needed to turn back, she told me to take a breath and to climb on. Thank you, dear friend.

I am grateful to my team at Simon & Schuster for their care and enthusiasm.

A resounding thank-you to . . .

My parents. Their support for this book is only surpassed by their support of me. My mother, Sherra, has always honored my life as an artist. My father, Gene, encourages me to live big. My stepmom, Aubrey, is unwavering in her belief in my dreams and her eternal optimism.

Nonna, who, through her quiet and constant love, has taught me about motherhood, fortitude, and heart. It will take a lifetime to tell her how much I love her.

Franca, Cosimo, Giusy, Laura, and Karl for lovingly supporting the idea of this book.

Sarah Gosssage, Nicole Ribaudi, Richard Courtney, Patrick Huey, Christine Bode, Ellen Ancui, Dorrie LaMarr, Susan Barragan, and the incredible Donna Chaney, for listening, always.

Solome Williams, Amy Elliott, and Aubrey for being early, attentive, and eager readers.

Monica Freeman, Glenda Hale, and Thomas Locke for testing recipes with zeal.

Julie Ariola, Maria Bartolotta, Sally Kemp, and Lina Kaplan, my wonderful guides, teachers, and exemplars who show me what I can't always see.

Robert for being full of exquisite bravehearted love and willing to hold my hand while I looked to my past so that I could more fully step into my present.

The communities of Oak Glen, Sequoyah, and Soaring Spirits. UCLA Extension Writers Program and its many brilliant teachers, including Alison Singh Gee, Kimberlee Auerbach Berlin, and Lynn Lauber.

Ira Byock, for his work as a physician and writer and mentor.

Amy Bloom, who told me long ago, "Go to Italy."

Vincent Schiavelli, the actor, writer, cook who came to our apartment to pick up the cake. None of us knew where our stories would lead.

Catherine Winteringham, who nursed us all in our most vulnerable hour.

A forever thank-you to . . .

The people of Aliminusa for your open hearts, indomitable spirits, and rich humor that reaches back ages. I hope to have shared even a fraction of your grandness.

Zoela, the effervescent spirit and wise soul who inspires me to live bravely and fully. How blessed I am to walk through this world by your side as your *mammina. Amore, quanto ti amo.*

And Saro, his belief in me was and is my North Star.